Calling All Heroes: A Manual for Taking Power

Paco Ignacio Taibo II

ISBN: 978-1-60486-205-8
$12.00   128 pages

The euphoric idealism of grassroots reform and the tragic reality of revolutionary failure are at the center of this speculative novel that opens with a real historical event. On October 2, 1968, 10 days before the Summer Olympics in Mexico, the Mexican government responds to a student demonstration in Tlatelolco by firing into the crowd, killing more than 200 students and civilians and wounding hundreds more. The Tlatelolco massacre was erased from the official record as easily as authorities washing the blood from the streets, and no one was ever held accountable.

It is two years later and Nestor, a journalist and participant in the fateful events, lies recovering in the hospital from a knife wound. His fevered imagination leads him in the collection of facts and memories of the movement and its assassination in the company of figures from his childhood. Nestor calls on the heroes of his youth—Sherlock Holmes, Doc Holliday, Wyatt Earp, and D'Artagnan among them—to join him in launching a new reform movement conceived by his intensely active imagination.

"Taibo's writing is witty, provocative, finely nuanced and well worth the challenge."
—*Publishers Weekly*

"I am his number one fan. . . I can always lose myself in one of his novels because of their intelligence and humor. My secret wish is to become one of the characters in his fiction, all of them drawn from the wit and wisdom of popular imagination. Yet make no mistake, Paco Taibo—sociologist and historian—is recovering the political history of Mexico to offer a vital, compelling vision of our reality."
—Laura Esquivel, author of *Like Water for Chocolate*

"The real enchantment of Mr. Taibo's storytelling lies in the wild and melancholy tangle of life he sees everywhere."
—*New York Times Book Review*

Send My Love and a Molotov Cocktail: Stories of Crime, Love and Rebellion

Edited by Gary Phillips
and Andrea Gibbons

ISBN: 978-1-60486-096-2
$19.95   368 pages

An incendiary mixture of genres and voices, this
collection of short stories compiles a unique
set of work that revolves around riots, revolts, and revolution. From the
turbulent days of unionism in the streets of New York City during the Great
Depression to a group of old women who meet at their local café to plan
a radical act that will change the world forever, these original and once
out-of-print stories capture the various ways people rise up to challenge
the status quo and change up the relationships of power. Ideal for any fan
of noir, science fiction, and revolution and mayhem, this collection includes
works from Sara Paretsky, Paco Ignacio Taibo II, Cory Doctorow, Kim
Stanley Robinson, and Summer Brenner.

Full list of contributors:

Summer Brenner
Rick Dakan
Barry Graham
Penny Mickelbury
Gary Phillips
Luis Rodriguez
Benjamin Whitmer
Michael Moorcock
Larry Fondation

Cory Doctorow
Andrea Gibbons
John A. Imani
Sara Paretsky
Kim Stanley Robinson
Paco Ignacio Taibo II
Ken Wishnia
Michael Skeet
Tim Wohlforth

"The year is 1987, the traditional commodity traders have gone and the new boys with their free market doctrines of unfettered competition have taken over the commodities asylum, two of them, the profligate protagonists of the story, with a not-too-fantastic plan to develop a cocaine 'futures' market. In *Futures*, John Barker has produced a fast-paced, 'hardboiled' novel that pulls you back, effortlessly, into morally corrupt Thatcherite London in the dramatic aftermath of the 'Bosh, Bosh, Bosh' 'Big Bang'—creatively mining the rich vein of extraordinary characters, situations, dialogue, and experiences distilled during the eight years he spent banged up at Her Majesty's pleasure. Coupled with his later European journeyings and travails, Barker's crisp, laconic prose, eye-for-detail storytelling, command of the art of narrative, and his ear for fluid and convincing dialogue makes him, in my view, Hackney's worthy successor to Tom Wolfe."
—Stuart Christie, coauthor of *The Floodgates of Anarchy*

"John Barker's prose is so downbeat he leaves even the most gritty of crime novelists looking like they're aiming for the preteen market. But if you want to get beyond the fairy-tale version of the sordid underbelly of life, then you gotta check *Futures* out."
—Stewart Home, author of *The Assault on Culture* and *69 Things to Do with a Dead Princess*

"In this fast-paced, streetwise take on 1980s London, boundaries blur between the cocaine trade and newly deregulated financial markets. High and low life don't look so different, as everyone tries to make a killing. Barker's portrait of a cynical, money-hungry culture skewers a moment in history that for good or ill (and mostly for ill) made Britain what it is today."
—Hari Kunzru, author of *Gods without Men*

"It's great. Rollicking, uncompromising stuff. The prose grabs you by the throat and squeezes. The characters are by turns reckless, ambitious, vulnerable, and weak. The story is set in the past but couldn't be more relevant. *Futures* is funny, frightening, and very dark."
—Ronan Bennett, author of *The Catastrophist* and *Havoc, in Its Third Year*

FUTURES

John Barker

Futures
John Barker

© John Barker 2014
This edition© 2014 PM Press

ISBN: 978–1–60486–961–3
Library of Congress Control Number: 2013956918

Cover artwork by Ines Doujak and Markus Wörgötter.
Cover design by John Yates / www.stealworks.com
Interior design by briandesign

10 9 8 7 6 5 4 3 2 1

PM Press
PO Box 23912
Oakland, CA 94623
www.pmpress.org

Printed in the USA by the Employee Owners of Thomson-Shore
in Dexter, Michigan.
www.thomsonshore.com

To the memory of Noreen "Noni" Macdowell (1951–2011)
and for Philippe Garnier without both of whom . . .

CHAPTER ONE

I wanted to say: Look pal I read the papers, I know the flavour of the month when I see it, and I've got a body to offer. What else do you want?

That's what I wanted to tell Graham Curtis. He's the DCS who came out smelling of roses when they had the stampede out of the Robbery squad and on to the Drugs. You know, just to speed the whole thing up because I had a lot on my mind plus the Italian at six, the Iranian at eight and a social function at which nine was the latest I could show my face. What I said was, Quite Graham, quite. You've got to be reasonable, Graham's got to talk in code. Him and his dad, maybe even his grandad, they've been at it a long time and he likes a bit of respect for the form or maybe he's just forgotten how to talk any other way. But this time the thing was it was so simple, and I was busy. That's what was giving me the hump.

I waited for him to say his next bit, to put it on the line, and stared at the pastel colours on my office wall. It's a bit of a joke this particular place of mine, a wine bar top end of Commercial Road, but my property advisor tells me it's a good bet for the long run. How long's the long run I ask myself. I mean Docklands Development, millionaire's enclave and all that, all very well but the Commercial Road? The Pakis have got most of it for one thing. But when all's said and done I like having my office here. It's modest and if there's one thing I don't like it's flash.

I sat there waiting for Graham to get down to business and carried on looking at the walls that are in ochre and light olive green. They're supposed to be calming. That's what my Design

1

Advisor told me. Funny thing is while I was staring I remembered that even as a young jack-the-lad I'd known how to say, Is-there-anything-we-can-do-about-this-guv to a Curtis clone. There was as it happened. Cost me but it kept me clean and that's the way I still am. A bit of Borstal that's all, and who gives a monkey's about a youthful transgression these days. Some places it's a plus.

"You see Gordon, it's a social evil," Curtis said.

I nodded and told him how true that was. Chasing dragons on council estates, I said, they ought to put a stop to it. That and the spades, they're making themselves busy just lately.

"Which is exactly what we're trying to do Gordon, but to do that it's no good just hitting a few pathetic users. We've got to hit the suppliers and hit them hard."

I nodded again, said Quite and resigned myself to more bollox. What it is, is maybe Curtis half thinks I'm taping our little chats. Which I'm not. I've dabbled with the idea. Several times. But in the death there's something gives me the creeps. Like these mobile phones things.

I looked at those walls again. When that Design Consultant of mine said they create a relaxing ambience I wanted to say, A relaxing ambience you cunt. But I didn't. It might be true, and if so it can only benefit my brothers, Keith and Derek.

"We're looking for the public's help on this one Gordon, to combat this evil."

Now that is code for you. Now I was a member of the public, what I call an MPP, a mug of preposterous proportions. I asked him if he thought I could help while I livened up his drink and felt a sudden impulse to drag him down the gym for a work-out all scotched up. He's as sharp as a rat, Graham is, but he's overweight and not very healthy which does no one any good. I mean who wants the cardiac arrest of a guy you're paying grands to; of a guy who can ridicule the suggestion that Gordon Murray has got anything to do with anything from behind a plastic cup of scotch; of a guy who can convince any junior zealot that Gordon Murray isn't worth a moment of anyone's attention, which is what counts when manpower shortage is the name of the game. I mean who wants it? Keith maybe. Wouldn't mind Curtis stiff and purple at the bottom of the wall bars because that Five stretch did embitter him. Think of your wife and kids I keep telling him. Two he's got, Keith, a boy and a girl. Plus I drop hints to Graham, I even thrust a BMA report under his nose one time but it didn't do any good. It's like the cunt actually likes having a belly.

"That's up to you of course Gordon," he said.

And I wondered. I have to say that at that moment in time I did wonder about Graham's long-term viability. It wasn't just the health question but knowing that Her Majesty's Customs and Excise Branch have recently received a large injection of capital and Graham doesn't cut much ice with them.

I looked at his shifty eyes across the table and decided that a long-term investment couldn't be dumped, not just like that. If there's one thing my nearly ex–Investment Advisor's emphasised it's to keep your nerve with an investment you really fancy. Besides which I could expect some short-term gains from Curtis at a time when Mickey White was giving me the hump like he was. Mouthy bastard. Robs this and fences that and with enough bevies inside him calls me a no-good cunt in the Ripened Hop.

So I started to tell him how it was, being a club owner. One of my first investments in fact. At one stage I had my doubts but the last two or three years it's come up trumps.

His eyes were greedy out of his pudgy cheeks.

"With a club up West one can't help but pick up a few bits and pieces," I said.

"It's exactly the bits and pieces that can help make the whole picture, like a jigsaw," he said filling his pipe. It may be good for the image but I wanted to say, You don't have to come that pipe shit here Graham, have a Dunhill. I checked myself, at the end of the day you've got to go by the rules. If there were no rules where the fuck would we be. It's something I've been telling Keith for years. As for Derek, I've got to tell him at least twice a week.

"Well Graham, it so happens that a barmaid in my employ reported something directly to me. This very morning in fact."

"Yes," Graham said lighting his pipe in a drawn out way that would have had Derek going potty. But he's still young Derek is and in certain aspects of our business he's a good operative.

"She happened to overhear this conversation at the bar and she's a girl can put two and two together."

"Yes?" Graham said trying to make his eyes twinkle and that's not easy when you put away the scotch he does. I looked at my watch. Ten to four, just one hour and ten minutes before I had to meet Mario, which is what he calls himself. Still he's all right Mario is and if I do have to pay a bit over the odds it's worth having him there in the middle. Who wants to do business direct with Colombians. Now they are headbangers. South Americans, and you remember what old Sir Alf said about them when we won the World Cup. Animals he called them. Yes, ten to four and I suddenly realized everything was on the hurry-up.

"Tony, at least three ounces a week," I said and gave him the address.

Was this Tony mug enough to go spewing out his address as well as his business over a bar counter? Was he fuck. But it wasn't a question Curtis was going to ask because he was going to get a result. Tony was a guy who plied the upper class trade. No problem there but he was a flash little bastard and that's something I can't stand. Just as important there are a lot of Tonys around and he'd do his bird quietly. Name names? No way. Derek would have spelled out the consequences of that kind of stupidity. Crippled nothing. Derek's very good at that kind of thing, he's got this way of coming on like a psychopath from Mars who happens to speak cockney. It goes down a treat that end of the business. Sure he's got Gary and Mo behind him but mostly they're surplus.

In as far as Curtis's face showed anything at all there was a bit of a grin. A grin pal, that's a fucking luxury on top of what I'm already giving you. That's what I wanted to say but I didn't. I had Mickey White on my mind as well as my Desk Diary that was choc-a. And there was Mario at six, the Iranian, and my function. Deprived kids? Now look at me, I've got to admit I was a bit of a tearaway when I was young and you know what saved me, a boxing club. That's what I'd tell the Princess or whoever

I wound up chatting to. The fact was that Tony was replaceable and if Curtis didn't know that he was ten times the plum I took him for. But of course he plays the rules too and he gave me an eye-to-eye Good Citizen of the Month award while pocketing his monthly slice of my money and pulling on that pipe.

Which is when I livened up his scotch for the last time and started the final number of the routine which includes me asking after his yacht. I think he expects me to see him standing at the wheel, pipe in his mouth. Looking at him with his belly and his grey skin I don't think that boat of his ever leaves its mooring. In fact I bet the bar is the only thing in working order. But the rules had to be played down to the last minute so I sat there listening to him going on about tacking and mainbraces while I thought again about Mickey White. Mickey White is a loudmouthed cunt. He's an anachronism. If I'd ever thought it was worth the bother I'd say, Wise up Mickey, this is the 1980s. The truth is that Mickey White is an old-fashioned cop-hater, and mouthy with it.

"You see Gordon it gives you a sense of perspective, the sea does. Here we are, rushing about in this urban world, this . . ."

"Concrete jungle," I said.

"Exactly Gordon, rushing about with everything so important but when you're out on the boat there's just the sea and the elements. You can't play around with them."

I thought for a moment he was coming on like some old gyppo woman telling me not to take a journey across water, and then of this feller based on the Isle of Man, a feller with some very interesting financial ideas. I dismissed it as paranoia and carried on saying yes in all the right places. Finally he managed to drag himself away from my scotch and make the great effort required to storm Tony's drum mob-handed.

When he'd gone I forced myself to sit still and not think of anything at all but Mickey White's face bobbed up again. The fact is he's started to be more than an irritant. I got it off Billy Mac the other day when I looked in on the Betting Shop I've got him fronting for me. Shocked he was. You haven't got anything to do with that smack stuff or that cocaine, he says to me. What,

I said. Now like Keith says, Billy's as thick as fifteen rounds of ham sandwich but that don't stop him telling me what evil stuff it is and what he's heard. A rumour that has its origins with Mickey White and if he says it enough times some tearaway who's not under Curtis's control might start to take it seriously. And what's more Mickey's started to get mob-handed himself. He's been lording it in the Ripened Hop for years but now he fancies himself as the manor's elder statesman instead of the close to retirement fence he is.

My secretary Chloe came in and asked if there was anything else. I told her to get herself home and tried to concentrate on Mario's little tricks with the sterling-lira exchange rate but Mickey's ugly mug kept popping up. The fact is that Mickey White should not exist. He's an old-fashioned bastard with a big mouth and a lot of luck behind him. Give him half a shake or half a bitter and he'll start on about his working class roots and his working class principles. With another effort of will I got him out of my head and thought about Mario. The simple fact was I wanted a price reduction. He pays a dollar price and the dollar's getting cheaper. He'll say they've raised the dollar price to compensate but that wouldn't be good enough this time. Even from reading the fucking newspapers a member of the public would know that the American market is saturated and they've turned their sights on Europe. Which gives you two reasons they'll swallow a price fall.

It's not a business I'm going to stay in forever but I wanted a bigger slice of it.

Just then Derek rang. Got a problem. Had to have Keith there as well.

CHAPTER TWO

Phil Stone's office was marked Chief Dollar Analyst, engraved on the door. He was working on-screen, sifting the data on continued Japanese interest in U.S. Treasury bonds. He'd always believed there was an element of We're Here Because We're Here Because We're Here in the strength of the dollar but now in decline, it was the hard bones underneath mattered. Across the room Vicki was typing out the middle section of his monthly analysis which went out-house to institutional investors. He was respected. The firm was respected, strengthened by a pre–Big Bang merger with serious American money.

There was a knock at the door as it opened. Phil looked up, saw Tom Arthur Chief Currency Dealer and looked studiously back at the screen and a rundown of Nomura Securities buying habits.

"Is it serious Phil? Will it hold?"

Phil looked up.

Tom's face showed an unacceptable level of worry.

"What Tom? The dike? Western civilization?"

"Oh thanks. Bloody great. What did you get, an honours degree in being blasé?"

"Look Tom, I'm working. Right? Correction, I'm trying to work, and my job is the Fundamentals. OK, if Sir George comes in and changes my job description, that's another matter. I can resign or accept and if do accept, why then I'll be rushing down in the lift every half hour to give you the gen you've probably already got."

"Look I'm just asking Phil, all right? Just asking."

"OK you're asking, so let's see what's happened. The rest of the world, the world that counts, is saying OK, we did a good job with the Plaza deal. Got the dollar down with no dramatics, an agreement that worked with nothing formal on paper. Now it's time to hold its value for a while. Right?"

"But will it hold, that's what I'm asking."

"I'm doing my best, and take a seat for God's sake. With the Plaza deal all national interests coincided. Not quite like that this time. Strikes me the Europeans and the Japs want jam on it, stabilize the dollar but without them changing their domestic policies to help. Seen any serious moves from them to stoke up their economies? Nakasone promises this and that but has he got the clout? And as for Herr Poehl."

Tom's forehead creased.

"Boss of the Bundesbank, remember him, scarred for life by stories of his granny losing her *schloss* in the Great Inflation, thinks dropping interest rate on a par with dropping his pants at an IMF meeting."

Tom Arthur sighed. "OK Phil, down a point or two."

"Your interpretation Tom. If it's tomorrow you want, who knows, but seen any sign of a dent in the U.S. trade deficit?"

"So again you're saying, mark it down."

"Take it easy, it's not the whole story. The Japs are still in there holding their U.S. Treasury bonds for the simple reason that the return's still better than anything they'll get at home and with their holdings we're talking $150 billion. Chunky."

"You're sure? No sign of a move out?"

"Well when we've finished this little chat Tom, I'll be back at my screen checking and rechecking but generally speaking I'd say the one thing they're agreed on is not wanting the dollar in freefall. We can curse the average American for not saving enough, we can curse that bloody budget deficit but the fact is even the Yanks don't want a freefall. If it drifts too low all your Japanese dentists might just pull their funds out and then that's exactly what you will get."

"So you're saying a cushioned fall."

"Look what they've got out of the Louvre deal is a commitment from James Baker not to open his gob, no downward nudges thank you. As to Central Banks putting their money where their mouth is, what money they've got, I'd guess it's only the Japs will have a go and there'll be a drift down into late spring. Might change after that, the G7 jamboree in June, Venice this time, and they like to show the world it hasn't just been smalltalk."

Tom Arthur grinned, said when you were in the trees all day long it was good to see some shape to the woods, and how about a drink, his treat.

"Next week Tom, I'm on the wagon. Head down for now."

Tom hurried out the door.

Phil gave a shrug of his eyes.

"When's his ulcer due?" Vicky said.

"Haven't got the data yet. Do we run to in-house medical material?"

"Not mine, that's strictly between me and my GP."

"So you think," Phil said, picking up a phone and tapping out familiar numbers. "Jack, how's life in bullion . . . Sure, Futures, but give me Options anytime . . . Yes your lobby in an hour. My wheels. By the way, Comrade Brezhnev, last days of, did you get a peek at his medicals . . . cardiograph print-out great stuff . . . See you soon."

He put the phone down and turned to Vicki.

"There you are. My pal Jack Sharp over in Stammer Casey and Mangledorf, gold analyst, says he had a good look at Brezhnev's health when it mattered."

"That was him," Vicki said. "Anything else to be typed?"

"Just a few liquid uncertainties."

"Got a dictionary?"

"No but I've got a prick in good running order."

"Is that right?"

An hour later after a reassuring look at the data, a quick park on some double-yellow, a glorious burst of freedom on the Aldgate roundabout and a skidding halt halfway down the Commercial Road Phil was sitting in Bubbles wine bar with his very oldest friend. Jack Sharp was considered by some to be the best gold analyst this side of the Atlantic to which he'd said, Both sides, both sides. Though there's an old boy in Singapore I might give way to.

"Bubbles, I like it. It's always that or Champers or Bucks Fizz, you know, as if froth were the height of working class chic," he said.

"Excitement," Phil said.

"What?"

"Gas, fizz, call it what you will. Carries within it the sensation both tactile and suggestive . . . Christ you know how they talk in marketing. So kids like lemonade, big deal."

"Cocaine on the cheap."

They laughed loud. In Bubbles, heads turned. Jack saw the woman at the bar staring at them. She was arguably sexy.

"Shrewd mover though, whoever put this place together. Well ahead of the pack. Not like Whitechapel Road, that's another story. Wine bars springing up faster than new Financial Instruments."

"Junk Bond and son of Junk Bond. Like doing business in used hamburgers."

"You're getting out of touch in bullion. Vanilla these days, flavour of the month bond-wise."

One of two large men in dark suits who were the only other drinkers had got up and was making the woman behind the bar laugh. Jack decided that after all she was verging on the blowsy.

"Mind you you didn't do so badly yourself when it came to Wapping."

"I will have Jack, when I get the smell of when to sell."

"What, an inevitable burst of the property boom? 1974 all over again? You see it coming?"

The doors opened and a crowd of men in pinstripe and in donkey jackets entered the bar.

"Inevitable? Christ sake Jack this is the 1980s."

Surely Jack wasn't envious, he must have done well enough out of Esher. No, surely not.

"Tell you what though, what I am looking out for with residential property is a shake-out in our neck of the employment market. To be specific I'll be selling up no more than three months after they give the chop to some deadhead like Alan Lewis over at Schumberg, Smith and Moody."

"Alan Lewis?"

"Likes to think he knows a thing or two about the greenback but gets his knickers in a twist every time Secretary Baker opens his gob. You think the Investment Manager at the Pru wants to go on paying through the nose for Alan's Mights and Maybes."

"Wouldn't mind something through my nose."

"Great minds do think alike. Hey remember that time we both caught out old one-lung in a dodgy declension. Redder than a double-decker and a clutch at the chest for the sympathy vote. A little powder then, my place," Phil said getting up to pay.

At the bar he heard, "Your Porsche outside pal?"

He turned stuffing change in his pocket. An overalls was staring at him. "I'd garage it mate, know what I mean. A bit rapid."

Outside he held in his rage. What was the guy talking about! Trying to take him for a mug! The car had been on its own for just forty minutes. On a main road. In broad daylight.

He drove off with a roar and turned south down a cobbled street full of Bengali grocers, mashing down some empty cardboard boxes. An old man in a skullcap jumped back on to broken pavement. Approaching The Highway he saw a gap in the dual carriage way and went for it, foot down.

"Cheeky bastard," he said.

"Who?"

"An overalls in Bubbles."

"What cheeky overalls need now and then is a good oldfashioned run on the pound, then they know what's what."

It was not the right thing to say. Phil was in a mood. Said it was his dollar in the firing line. That was the thing with Phil, a bit intense. Always had been, given old one-lung a terrible time in the classroom.

CHAPTER THREE

I arrived at the All-London Boys Clubs bash remarkably relaxed considering. Just like I thought there had been Mario, back room of his Greasy Spoon wearing his camel-hair and giving me his The Colombians Do Their Sums Too patter. But I wasn't wearing it, not just like that. He began to weaken. The result, a postponement. He'd got some thinking to do and a round of consultations. Course he did. We were to meet again in four days after he'd met up with Interested Parties.

The Iranian was all right, he always is. It was just a rush getting there. I tell him the situation and he accepts it. Course he does, he knows what side his bread's buttered, what with a saturated market and his Shah long gone.

First thing at the function I was pumping hands with Steve Burke. Never rated him as a singer but I admire the way he used his wedge when he got out. Didn't piss and snort it away like some of them. Married well too. Lady Bridget. I shook hands and she said she was glad to see me again.

I've got no illusions. I wouldn't be where I am today if I'd trifled with them. A lot of people say they're pleased to see you when they're not. Half the time they don't even remember who you are but Steve and Bridget, well I don't make a habit of it but I'd laid some of the purest on them saying it had come off a mate. I bet there was a gram or two wound up on her clit never mind up her nose.

I picked up some bits and pieces off the buffet table and took a glass of chilled white wine. There was a tug on my arm. Lady Bridget. Very pally. I don't know what she expected, I wasn't going to bring a packet out, I rarely carry and never at a function. Whether she was disappointed or not, and the aristocracy's been trained to hide it, she introduced me to a special friend of hers, Lady Hoare. Late fifties, a bit plump and too much tom around her neck. She gave me one of those sharp looks that's never quite sharp enough and asked me if Boys Clubs could really play a part in the fight against hooliganism and petty crime.

"Well, I'm no expert, no sociology degrees or anything," I said. She laughed at that. It's not hard is it, even an ordinary feller like me knows sociologists aren't flavour of the month. "But to be honest I could easily have turned out a hooligan myself and I'd say that for me personally, the club was a great help in my not doing so. Brought some discipline into my life."

That's what they want to hear isn't it and when they hear it they're not going to start arguing the toss. Mind you there was another old biddy I met at a function, Lady Caroline something, now she was sharp, not a person to tangle with for any length of time. "These young criminals want their whack, as I think you put it, and they simply can't have it. End of story." That's what she said.

This Lady Hoare on the other hand, she was a doddle. "I do feel however that there ought to be the cultural dimension too, I rather fear that the schools now have simply given up." As she chattered away I had a sudden memory of that cunt Mickey White. It was some years ago when I wasn't properly organized and he was a business acquaintance. A right fucking know-all he was, even then. Says to me, Those boys clubs, boxing clubs, who set them up? The Public Schools, Oxford and Cambridge. And what for, charity? No way, they wanted to keep tabs on the working class is what. That's Mickey White for you. You can't get more working class than me but I don't go around wearing it on my sleeve. I made something of myself. The cunt probably thinks the saloon bar of the Ripened Hop is keeping his roots.

She could talk, that Lady Hoare.

"So I feel that there has to be a place for that too. So that young people, especially in the deprived inner city areas don't feel that culture, the arts, somehow belong to another world."

"To be perfectly honest Lady Hoare I think you might be being a bit idealistic. Course it would do them good, a bit of Shakespeare in the inner city but it's all that surplus energy we've got to find an outlet for first."

I kept up my end a bit longer and stayed cheerful. There might be one or two people think I'm a bit of a rogue but as long as you're cheerful it don't matter. You know why? Because a cheerful rogue winds up either doing fuck all, or getting badly nicked.

I made it home by half eleven, quietened the dogs, checked the alarms, and finally put my feet up. There've been times when I've thought about full-time staff but something's always held me back. They'd get to know too much about you.

I've lived here for ten years. Let's call it the edge of London. What I've wound up with is an old boy who does the garden and looks after the dogs when I'm not here, him and some part-time cleaning help. Marcie her name is. An unsupported mother. Even out here they've got a bit of a Council Estate, getting bought up most of it but Marcie's hanging on in. I got things straight with her right from the start. I pay her good money, but just in case I left a bundle of notes out on my desk. About six hundred it was. So I drove off with plenty of noise and parked up in the lane. I sat there for a while then walked back through the grounds. I heard the Hoover upstairs and went and counted that little bundle. It was a hundred short. I waited till I heard the Hoover stop and her coming downstairs. She was on the bottom flight when I grabbed her. She squealed like a pig. I just said, Give us the hundred Marcie and we'll be all right. And that's how it's been, we've been fine ever since. The old boy doesn't come in the house. So when you look at it, what's the point of full-time staff?

I had a full-time wife once, I'm not afraid to admit it. Tina, the slag. A cheapskate slag. So she fucked off, Canada I believe. If and when I want to know more, I will. Yes, she fucked off just like that. I can be philosophical about it except it just so happened, I was younger then and not so well organized, she happened to be holding thirty grand cash for me. Just two days I needed her to hold it and it was quite a bit of wedge for me in those days. The slag. I had to cover it myself. One day, if it still matters, I'll give her a surprise.

I got up off the sofa and poured myself a cognac. Have a drink or two when it's decent quality and there's nothing important needs doing, no harm in that. I even take a line or two of the dollop now and then. Mickey White's face bobbed up again but I slapped it down. Then Tina's. So I thought of ringing Sarah. I married Tina when I was twenty-one and she was eighteen. It's a good thing you learn as you get older except I do worry about my brothers in this respect. It's not something you can define so easily, maturity, but I know it when I see it.

I paused over the phone. No, Sarah would be too much hassle and I was tired. I've never made the mistake of marrying her and she's never made the mistake of even hinting at it. Of course I'd like to have kids. It's natural isn't it, you build something up and you want it carried on. It was me who wanted kids but Tina was always saying we should wait a bit. There are times, remembering that, when I think she had it planned for a very long time and that one is difficult. In fact I have to stop thinking about it. Because that would mean all those times I was rumping her she was only pretending. Not just faking orgasms like they can, but pretending through and through and that's a thought can make me a bit dizzy. And out of all of us who does have kids? Keith. Now there's what some clever cunts would call an irony, the same ones who'd probably say I was too doting an uncle and have an explanation for it, leastways they would if I told them my dreams. Me, I wouldn't tell any cunt my dreams let alone pay for the privilege.

What I needed was something to stop me from thinking for a while. I had a quick flick through my video library. There was one the Iranian had given me, better than average. A man gets out of a decent looking motor. He's wearing a good suit and leather gloves. Knocks on the door of a terraced house. A girl opens it in a tight dress. She's not white, but she's not black either. I've wondered now and then if she's one of his, the Iranian's, dirty bastard.

Well he don't mess about. Doesn't take his gloves off but rips her dress off there and then. Doesn't even look excited. That's the trick of it and you can see, that's what turns her on. With his other glove he grabs her right there. Her tits are bursting out.

He just gave it me one time, the Iranian. Never mentioned it since. That's why we get on whereas Mario, my opening shot with him was for a 25 percent price cut. While he's giving me his pitch about the Colombians he's looking at me like I've given him indigestion. Course I know he's not going to lay down and give it me but if he's got a head on his shoulders he knows 15 percent is minimum. Minimum.

He's got her tits in his black-gloved hands right now. Not even bothering to undress himself. Undoing his flies and no more. And doing it really smooth considering that hand's still got the glove on.

CHAPTER FOUR

To Phil's credit he had insisted on running up a couple of steaks before they got down to any serious consumption.

"There's times when I feel the whole world is passing through my hands," Jack said pushing away an empty plate. "It's like I'm a touchstone just to keep the wheels turning."

"Start thinking like that and it'll be an ulcer and then where will you be? Out with a Portfolio Manager at Le Jardin d'Or and yours will be gruel with a dry biscuit on the side. Au Loire of course."

"Thanks Phil."

Phil said he was only saying London in 1987 was a pretty good place to be. Jack didn't disagree. That wasn't his point.

"I mean there I am evaluating the Russian harvest and other reasons they might up or cut their gold sales. Weighing that against some bloody dispute on the Rand or how desperate the Iraqis are getting or whether some big punter in the Far East has got the heebie-jeebies. And that's not even mentioning Comrade Gorbachev. When it comes to gold price he's got more spin-offs than ET."

"OK, OK. Want my thoughts on that lot and it'll cost you a line. Got one?"

Phil worried for his friend. He'd seen colleagues get philosophical before. They wound up as financial journalists in the twenty grand bracket.

"Of course," Jack said pulling a small white packet from his jacket pocket. "Mind you experience tells me the cost will wind up as several lines."

"Spot on analysis Sharp. We expect nothing less. That sparkle augurs well. Very crystalline."

"All that glitters is not gold."

"What's that, a professional opinion?" Phil said. He snorted a fat line.

"The Bible."

"Jesus, I rather think we'd have been amongst the throng getting the heave-ho out of the temple."

"Result, a collapse of the Palestinian economy."

"I rather think the Israelis have already seen to that and the Israelis Jack, are just another bunch of freeloaders on the federal budget. I've got some time for James Baker's Treasury team but when it comes to that budget they've as much power as a Tanzanian shilling. You know, when they're up against Senator Sludge from the midwest, the bleeding-heart lobby, nuclear energy interests, failing banks with dodgy oil collateral and the Zionists."

"Voodoo economics, still it's kept the world moving. Mind you, as far as I'm concerned, the greenback's in the ex–hard currency bracket for the time being."

Phil was snorting his second line. He sat up piqued. "Christ Jack, who're you talking to? At least the Japs are holding their Treasury bonds and you know why, because there's too much dosh in Tokyo and fuck all to give them a decent return."

Jack said that was subversive talk. He bent over for seconds.

Phil was shocked. He demanded clarification.

"Your analysis questions automatic right of saver to his return. Can't get more subversive than that."

"Fact is Jack you've had a world awash with liquidity *and* low inflation for a long time."

"Precisely queasy situation."

"Don't say the chips are down for Christ's sake."

"Indeed yes, ten pints a night outings, too much liquidity followed by chips. Result inevitable. Much spewing."

"What is it with this 'inevitable' Jack? What are you, a closet Marxist waiting to come out with your sandwich board?"

Jack let it pass. The initial rush had tapered off and he

walked to the window. An empty black river glistened below. The up-and-down skyline of the south side was reflected in patches. The window was view and mirror, he could see Phil bent over the mirror, chopping. He turned back towards him.

"You know what Phil?"

"No rhetorical questions Jack, you know the rules."

It was true, they'd made that rule as fifteen-year-olds in a shared dorm. Only Phil could be a mite fanatical.

"All right then, a statement. Mr Jack Sharp, well-known city analyst, has it in mind to open a Cocaine Futures Market."

Phil's head stayed close to the mirror. "Tricky. American policy hard to gauge. Statistics messy," he said.

"Agreed but if you joined up, I was thinking of a modernist floor, plenty of mirrors, if you joined what position would you take?"

"It's the old story isn't it, our game, market forces overlaid by intermittent political action. Take the Americans for example, they're making a more sustained effort than usual. Aircraft gun-ships they've had in Bolivia."

"It's unsustainable."

"What?"

"Can't see how they can push it, not with the collapse of the tin price which they had a big hand in. I mean what are they going to do with all those tin miners out on their ear, bump them all off before they reach the Coca fields?"

"True, but they have an uncanny knack for getting stuck in their own rhetoric. I mean now you've got the whole of the White House trooping off to piss for the analysts and if they're prepared to look ridiculous, they must be serious," Phil said. He hunched closer to the mirror, snorted his line, and came up again. "So why is this, we ask ourselves. Worry about the rifeness of crack amongst young executives?"

"The crack is fierce," Jack said. He laughed loudly and bent for his own line.

"So they say. Supposed to be like freebasing. I've tried that a few times. Very nice but heavy on the pocket and a bit rough on the working week."

Jack asked if this wasn't a marginal issue. Surely there weren't that many executives at it.

"Marginal, what's marginal in this day and age? Another consideration is their attitude to all that Miami money."

"What do you mean, Miami money? Might just as well say New York or London, all the same stuff."

"Disagree. World of difference between massive wealth accruing to some gold-chained Colombian and a WASP in defence contracts."

"So they get it laundered, all comes out in the wash."

"Tricky business these days, laundering. Follow money catchee monkey. That's the law enforcement slogan of the month. Otherwise I'd be tempted myself. On the other hand while they're making such a fuss about it, how much dosh are we really talking about. Say in comparison to the federal budget deficit. I spend half my time wondering if they really worry about that deficit and it's the fact the Japs are financing it."

"Not a lot. Still full marks to the Japs, I was on to that Hirohito commemorative gold coin like a shot. Did my precious metal a power of good for a while."

"Hirohito? I thought he was some old fascist, Bridge Over the River Kwai."

"Rehabilitated, all water under the bridge."

"Is that right Jack, is that right. What I'm saying is that at the end of the day the American attitude is that a Colombian is a spic. Get us some water Jack, and why don't you stay the night. Don't know how you manage the travelling."

"Wouldn't mind. Will this shirt pass muster another day?"

"No problem. Water for pity's sake."

Jack went to the kitchen and filled a jug from an Evian bottle. It was the least he could do. He found a lacquered tray propped up on the kitchen unit, two tall glasses and a bowl into which he put ice cubes from the freezer. Virtuous and efficient. What a pleasant feeling.

Phil was sprawled out in the dining area. The tray went heavy.

"Fancy a Benedictine to take off the edge?"

"Where's the edge?"

"Over the top," Phil roared. "Just like that Alan Lewis I mentioned. Once had a coup with a notch up in U.S. Treasury base rate. Been living off it ever since but it's wearing a bit thin these days. Should have packed up eighteen months ago but he's an addict. Won't find me hanging on past my sell-by date."

"Old analysts never die."

"A bit on my own account maybe, just following my nose."

"If you've still got one left. Maybe you can get it insured."

"What? Oh, my nose. Don't worry about that Jack, I plan to keep it in good nick. For one thing I quite fancy being the quality arbiter when you get your coke floor set up."

"An assayer. Wonderful."

"What?"

"The guys who check the quality of my precious metal. A Jewish mafia," Jack said. There appeared to be no sign of the promised Benedictine. He got up to look for the bottle.

"Hey Jack, you think there's Japanese Jews?"

The prospect was staggering. Jack grabbed for the good-looking bottle in the drinks cabinet.

CHAPTER FIVE

The rain was working up for a proper downpour. Carol Curbishley felt it, the air colder and the drops heavy. At least she had a coat on and the red beret. She wasn't that stupid except somewhere at home there was a handy little umbrella which could have kept it right out. So it was her fault. If she got wet it was her fault.

Shitty city.

She saw a pavement puddle just in time. A case of overconfidence, thinking she didn't need to set alarm clocks anymore, which mostly she didn't. Only there were times when obviously she did, she'd been pulled out of a dream by Sheila's voice and Sheila's tugging, and woken to see her daughter anxious like she was every time there was a chance of being late for school. Then it was a rush. She hadn't put the right shoes on either.

She walked faster. Dodged the spoke of a black umbrella. The guy started to speak. She gave him the glare and hurried on.

In the flat Carol lit the gas fire, kicked off her shoes, put on woolly socks and went into the kitchen to boil water. Her face was reflected in the window. She poked a finger at its. There was no point hanging around for the kettle, it would switch itself off. That was the whole point of it.

A cupboard had been fitted into the front door passageway when the house had been converted to flats. She scrabbled in the dark and took out the wooden clothes-horse she'd bought one late Saturday afternoon off a stall in the Golbourne Road. She put it up to the side of the gas fire. It wobbled till the weight of her coat held it steady. The kettle clicked.

In front of the fire steam rose from her cup then steam from the clothes. She put the tea down and went to the sound system. João Gilberto, who'd never let her down, whose voice had never not stroked her light and warm.

Before she'd finished her next cup it was just another sound in the room. Her fault. In the first place she should have set the damn alarm: it was at least two thirty when she'd gone to bed, fed up. The night had started well enough. Marie'd been around, they had a smoke and watched a film on TV. Gangster's moll turns funny, Marie'd said when the sexy lady had said to the guy in the black suit who was always irritable, that with him it was business, business and business and she was fed up with it. "I'll bet you the Mafia run to psychologists, they'll sort her out."

If Marie was in the mood she could go on like that all night but then her feller Pat had dropped by and somehow they'd got on to talking about mortgages and she'd had nothing to say. Worse, she felt bad about it: her inability to see herself having one, her ignorance about its mechanics and the shifting flat prices of London, could only mean she had never really grown up, that she was incapable of being an adult.

The tea in her cup had gone cold. She got up to go to the kitchen and switched off the cassette-player. It was unfair to João Gilberto, unfair to herself when he could never have had such a miserable morning in mind. She waited by the kettle. What was worse was her passivity: she who'd resolved never to stay in situations that without drama, she didn't like, that were routinely boring, had done just that. When she'd finally said something it must have come out rushed, angry sounding, because Marie had given her a look while Pat made a big deal out of looking at his watch and saying he hadn't realized how late it was.

Still the kettle hadn't boiled. It was ridiculous. The whole thing was ridiculous, her standing there and waiting. She ran down the passage to the bathroom, put the plug in the bath and turned the hot tap as far as it would go.

The bathroom was full of steam when she returned in a towelling robe, with a blue and white hooped mug. She checked to see there was a bath towel on the hook behind the door, then closed it and sat on the edge of the bath. The water was hot to her fingers but ran lukewarm from the tap. She turned it off and swirled the water up and down the bath. There was enough time to take it slowly but no more than that.

She brushed the steamed-up mirror with the back of her hand and made a shiny wet, clear patch in the middle. Some drops made a path down through the mist below. Carol's face looked back at her solemn and pale. OK, she was pale. Big deal, hardly surprising was it, and the winter still not finished with.

She poured in a good splash of bath oil and tried the water. The steam had thinned out but even to her fingers the water was too hot. So what was she doing waiting when there was a cold tap? She turned it on, closed her eyes, counted to thirty and turned it off again. Her feet and shins tingled. She waited some more and let the heat travel up her legs before lowering herself in. There was a shock to her bum as it touched the surface. She crouched and counted another twenty. When she was in, her shoulders under the water, the weight fell away like she'd put down shopping bags. The light on wall tiles played waves. She took her mug off the bath's curved corner edge. Later she soaped and rinsed herself, then lay still for a final minute till the heat of the water lost its edge.

Up and about in fresh clothes she was ready for some get-up-and-move music. Toots and the Maytals. There was an hour before her rendezvous with Daniel in the pub a block away from the studio. He had something Really Special on the go, he'd said. The seven grams was all ready which made everything straightforward though she didn't like holding anything over-night. She'd just thought a quarter ounce was not so much she couldn't call it personal use in the event of the very worst happening. She waited for Funky Kingston to have a dance in the space between the eating table and sofa in front of the gas fire.

When the track finished she was sweating. All she needed to go out of the door was the little packet in the flour jar and an umbrella. She blew at the double wrap polythene. Flour grains wavered in the air.

In the bathroom the steam had cleared away but the bath was full of water. It was unclean and ridiculous. She pulled up her sleeve to pull at the bath plug chain and saw the round black rubber sitting on the bath edge.

What the hell was this?

She pulled her sleeve up till it gripped her biceps. The water was cold. Her fingers felt around the metal ribs of the plughole. There were hairs that she folded in her palm and dropped in the small red bucket below the washbasin.

The water didn't move. Another shot at the plughole. It was clear. She had twenty-five minutes. Make it forty because Steve would wait a quarter hour. She might just as well phone the Housing Association and get them to send someone round.

Some time tomorrow was the earliest possible they said, and then she'd be lucky. Could she ring back tomorrow.

It wouldn't do. It was out of the question to have it sitting there a whole day. She pictured a plunger, a weird-looking thing with a black rubber sucker with a wooden handle. It was in the cupboard under the kitchen sink. It wasn't in the cupboard under the kitchen sink.

In the pub Daniel was waiting.

"Here I am on the Never Quite Made It edges for years but this time Carol, this time," he said crossing the fingers of his left hand. With his right he slid an envelope under the table. She said Great, and handed him the parcel in an empty B&H packet over the table. Under was naff. She thought of telling him but he looked too cheerful to take it in.

"The guys would be wanting to shake you by the hand themselves Carol but I tell you they are very black Brazilians, six foot three to a man. Stand out a bit, five of them in this place. Tell you what though why not drop by the studio later?"

It was tempting. Eighty pounds she'd made on the deal but the bathwater was on her mind, greyer by the moment. There was no point in any misunderstanding like him thinking she was being graceless so she told him the score.

"Blocked pipes, Christ Carol. Urban nightmare. Call a plumber. Listen sorry, got to run."

She finished her gin slowly and made out a programme for the afternoon. A plunger. Archaic sort of thing. Not very expensive and therefore, therefuckingfore a hassle to find. She needed a crowded bits-and-pieces hardware shop smelling of paraffin. She stared at the slice of lemon and ran through film of the streets on her way home. The deli with the veg outside; The bakers; the video place; electrical appliances; car insurance office; and the corner shop that you couldn't call a deli, mini-market more like it but it wouldn't have plungers. No.

But there was a man with a bald head, a white coverall thing and a northern accent. She finished her drink trying to place the shop and came up with a memory of her old place with its garden. A Saturday afternoon and she'd wanted a trowel to turn over the border round the grass. She'd risk it, go out of her way, and then pay fifty of the profit into her Treats and Emergency PO account.

It took an hour and a half to get home. She had a carrier bag of food with plunger. The hardware man was still there, paint tins, hand tools, and hose pipe filling the place to bursting. Didn't bother with the paraffin anymore. She hadn't bothered with the Post Office. She'd passed two. Both had queues out on the pavement. Next on the timetable, the school gates by 3:30. Half an hour to deal with the bath, give it a go. She started laughing like a crazy as her arm went up and down, a sudden picture of suave Arthur. Her best customer, dead suave Arthur. Watery gurgles, watery farts sounded from down in the cold grey. Her arm was up and down faster. Plop. Bingo. She waited, gave a whoop when she saw the rim of smudge high up on the bath. It sounded greedy, a mini-whirlpool.

CHAPTER SIX

They met at the Commercial Road premises. Keith Murray ran a lightweight contraption around walls, ceiling, and floor. A bug detector. Gordon insisted. Derek stood next to the pool table which took up one wall. He moved to let Keith do his stuff. Keith moved on to the window. Derek rolled the white ball into a bunch of stripes. It span off and down a pocket.

"Check your motor this morning?" Gordon said.

"Yes. Can we get started?"

Keith switched off the detector, put it in a wall cupboard and walked over to the window behind the desk to switch on the transistor. Radio Three at low volume. Gordon said, Good, and picked up the phone.

"Don't want to be disturbed for the next half hour Chloe. Not unless we're on fire."

He put the phone down. "Got a problem have we Derek? Nothing too serious I hope. The gym OK? The Squash Club?"

Derek rolled the black ball with deliberation towards a bottom pocket. "It's competition. Three times I've heard it in the last week. Twice off Terry and Terry's not just reliable, he's a pal."

"All right, all right Del, I think Terry's great too. Ever heard me say a bad word about the geezer? So what commodity are we talking about?"

The black ball was still on the table. Derek stood up straight.

"I said Terry, the Italian's of course."

"OK Del. What's he want your pal, a testimonial, I never touched that nasty smack stuff in my life. Now my first observation is that we shouldn't get too excited at this stage. I mean it does make a bit of sense doesn't it, you know, given previous discussions about price trends. So just before you go any further Derek, I'd like to report back on yesterday's meeting with Mario. I opened by asking for 25 percent off"

Keith left off fiddling with the radio tuner.

"Yes, 25 percent, for openers. So he looks at me like I've just called his mum a whore but he doesn't blank it out of hand. What he says is he's got to think about it, and talk with other interested parties. Now what you're telling us Derek is something I can throw at him."

Keith bounced off the wall by the radio. "Here you see that the other day. A Colombian. Not Medellín Maf but close. A fortified gaff in Miami, scanners, Tremblers, Rotweillers, never mind his own torpedoes, and you know what happens? Shot to fuck. And his family. Machine gun job."

"All very interesting I'm sure Keith, but unless I've got the wrong end of the stick Derek has some important information of direct concern to us. By the way Del, I had to give Curtis what's his name, Tony. We did agree I think that he wasn't too relevant."

Derek's fists were held down tight in line with his trouser creases. "What do you mean, 'had to'?"

"Tactical Derek. If Mr Curtis is to continue to be of use to us given the rising star of Her Majesty's Customs, then he's got to have something to show hasn't he. I mean he's got to make a half decent nicking now and then."

"So what do we pay the prick for?"

"Come with that stinky pipe did he," Keith said moving to the bottom end of the pool table. "Ever thought of snapping off the bowl, you know, when it's well alight, and sending it helter-skelter down his windpipe."

"Do you mind Keith, do you fucking mind. It's me's got to wear him. Get that. Me. Me who's got to sit there listening to all his bollox. And Derek, in answer to your question, what we pay him for is to keep him off our backs. OK? And in order to make sure he is a worthwhile investment and does perform this function, we have to be sure Curtis keeps a bit of cred his end. Right? And Graham's got a way of telling me when he thinks it's slipping. Anyway we have more things to deal with. If I've understood you correctly Derek, another firm in the charlie business. Now as I've already pointed out we have to look at this in the context of current negotiations with Mario. We also have to acknowledge that we are living in a competitive world. That's a reality. The world doesn't owe us a living."

Keith was whistling with the radio and looking out the window like he was making a point of it. Gordon picked up an envelope from his desk to point at Derek.

"However that does not mean that we don't take a grave view of the matter, so here's a first question, is it the spades. And question two, how much is this cost-cutting taking place at the price of quality."

Derek too a step towards the desk. "Not spades and from what Terry's heard not so much quality wise but then you know what the cunts are like with that, poncey. Drop a flake in the Milton's Fluid and they look at it like it's going to tell them the answer to the mystery of life."

"What's that Del, death? Pussy?"

"Do you mind Keith. I mean do you fucking mind. I've got an appointment with this William the Isle of Man face later on. Preliminary discussions. Important for all of us, right. So Derek, why not get some of this other firm's dollop anyway, shove it in front of what's his name in the lab just to see."

"Stuart."

"Yes, Stuart, get him to look it over."

Derek was right up at the desk. "But you know what they're like. I mean I can tell them ours is purer . . ."

"Del, I know the patter, believe me. I've been in this business a long time and I'm a consumer myself, me and my people want only the best and our test is what it's like up the nose. All that bollox, I've heard it all."

Derek stepped back. His big brother went nowhere near retailers, a wholesaler only if something was bugging him and yet it was word for word what Max, one of Terry's people had said.

"Fucking posers. And here's another point to consider Derek, if our people have been approached with these shoddy goods, and have no doubts, they will have been severely stepped on, how did this other firm know where to go?"

"You know how it is Gordon, most of them have known."

"Yeah yeah, known each other for years, knocked about Ladbroke Grove together in the year dot, drank together in the same Crouch End boozer ditto. Yes, it's the Coke Retailers Trades and Social Club."

Gordon had got it right again, the words, but so what. So what. Derek moved forward again.

"OK, so that is how it is, so what do you expect me to do. I can give them the fucking willies about naming names but I can't run a curfew."

Gordon smiled. He leaned back in his chair.

"Fair enough Del, fair enough. Point taken. But look at it another way because you know what, however this works out, loyalty during this period should be rewarded, First choice if supplies are limited. What you've got to bear in mind is that competition and loyalty are not incompatible. I was saying it to Lady Hoare just the other evening."

"Lady Hoare, that's her name? Are you kidding."

"Thank you Keith, what a helpful contribution to the discussion. Let me translate it into language you can understand. I'm saying given the snidey aggravation Mario gives me I've half a mind to jack the whole thing in for a while. Cut off their dollop and we'd hear the pips squeak when their lifestyles feel the pinch."

Derek looked worried.

Keith laughed. "There is another way to look at it," he said.

It took a while, then Gordon laughed.

"You crafty cunt. You know. The other firm. A name."

"Scousers is what I've heard, some face called Tommy Ryan with a pub and video shops in Huyton and as likely as not a feller called Stevie Scott this end."

Derek was bursting to tell while Gordon was saying he had to hand it to Keith. He leaned back on the pool table and spoke slowly. "I've got a couple of bits and pieces to go with that."

His big brothers stopped grinning at each other and looked at him.

"A couple of retail names this end. A Geoff out in Muswell Hill and another geezer called Ray Stewart down Cricklewood way."

"Got a name to go with the Geoff has he?"

No he fucking didn't.

"Don't get me wrong Del, you've given us a lot to go on, you and Keith, it's just I think I can make a small contribution here. It rings bells, Geoff and Muswell Hill. A pal of Mickey White. Was going with Mickey's daughter for a while except he took a liberty."

CHAPTER SEVEN

Phil was working late with an in-house report on current trends. He'd been right in consistently marking the dollar high in the early eighties despite the conventional indicators showing otherwise, and then decisive in predicting its fall from those dizzy heights. He settled down to read through the latest statements of Federal Reserve Chief Paul Volcker. He knew that as a leading analyst his own words could affect market sentiment, but big Paul's could make it. He admired the man, had a well-printed original photo of his six foot six frame as a pin up in the Wapping bedroom. Gina'd said it put her right off her stroke: Here I am wanting to do the dirtiest things I can imagine and we've got God staring down at us. He'd laughed but the picture stayed.

Vicky came in with a sheaf of photocopied newspaper clippings he'd asked for before she went home.

"Crisis in the library," she said.

"Is nowhere safe or is crisis the most overused word in the language?"

"They'd lost everything from last Tuesday's FT."

"Ah, the former. So are we on for the weekend?"

"I've already got a date."

Outside it was dark. From the window he could see people of ant size hurrying in random knots and a thicker, steadier pattern around the tube entrance. A red bus was farting along the street. With his overall picture, seeing the jam ahead, he had a quick desire to shout at the driver not to bother. Pointless.

He returned to his desk and moved on to another pressing question of the short-to-medium term: what were the alternative

options for the holders and prospective holders of U.S. Treasury bonds? He was not an expert on equities but from what he could see the bull market looked unsustainable. Earnings ratios were seriously stretched. If an investment in equity stock involved plenty of wishful thinking, what else was possible?

He lost track of time as he twisted and turned through the gamut of interest rates and bond yields on offer and slowly, a picture began to emerge. Trouble was it took just one crass statement from Secretary Baker and his picture would be blown out of the water.

His bladder whinged.

Down the corridor the glare and mirrors of the washroom were a shock. He made a snap decision to swathe through the details and took a neat piece of tackle out of his pocket. It looked like a miniature stainless steel salt-cellar. The coke crystals were in the lower half of the cylinder. He ground it into consumable powder by turning it round on the axis which joined it to the upper half, then turned it upside down and snorted the equivalent of a generous line.

Out in the corridor his heart jumped, a figure looming up from the open door of his office.

"Philip, still at it? An example to us all," Sir George said, stepping back into the office.

"Stormy weather imminent."

"Really?" Bossman made an elaborate play of looking out of the window. "I know appearances can be deceptive but we do expect the Weather People to tell us in advance of any divergence between appearance and reality."

Phil must speak, he must say something; only his mouth was stuck, lips, tongue and teeth in a twist.

"Climate of the markets," he said

"Ah yes of course. I have sometimes heard your reports described as laconic. Excellent, an economy of words is an economy. But then Philip there's been stormy weather ahead for as long as I can remember. However as long as the tiller is in good order, and the pilot fully in control, I'm not apt to worry overmuch."

Paranoia came in a rush, effortless poetry. Idle talk of coke use in the city . . . wild calls . . . stories of tankers sailing empty round the world on the say-so of drug-crazed shipping managers . . . rumours of in-house urine analysis . . .

"We do our best," he said cautiously.

"And very good it is. I do hope I'm not interrupting it's just that sometimes in this computerized age I feel it's especially important to keep in touch with staff. People count. And your forecast, is it a squall or a regular tempest we're expecting?"

"Veering to the latter. If Volcker leaves the tiller."

Sir George said nothing. He wanted more? Surely not. "Leaves the Fed. that is."

"Ah Paul yes, a very sound man," Sir George said. "On the other hand age I suppose has made me wary of dramatic gloom of any sort, otherwise I'd no doubt be down there with my sandwich board," Sir George said with a wave to the window. "Not that I'm urging complacency, God knows we've had enough of that lately."

Paranoia hit the stomach in a lump.

It passed away in a silent fart. Phil girded himself for a prolonged tour de force of flim-flam.

"This insider trading business for one thing, you'd have thought the Americans could have cleaned up their act before they had sheriffs on the trading floor waving their handcuffs . . ."

He had no choice. Forty minutes of endurance with some golfing gibberish thrown in, an incomprehensible analysis which lead Sir George to conclude that the Europeans would beat the Yanks again in something called the Ryder Cup. How this could be seen as symbolic of a changing transatlantic relationship.

Phil was tempted to ask why, in that case had the firm gone for an American partner.

He did not. He restrained himself.

Finally Sir George slapped him on the back and called him a droll fellow. He apologised for the interruption.

Which, raging behind a closed door, Phil took to mean he should be grateful. As if his horizons had been broadened at a stroke.

He looked back at his notes. He cursored through the on-screen material. The pattern had gone cold, the data returned to its original state of ifs and buts. He pictured dirty goings-on with Gina, his flat or hers, and picked up the phone. It was her voice: Obviously it's because I'm having such a fun time that I can't come to the phone right now but if you'd care to leave your . . .

Back home on the right side of the Double Chubb he took a toot; turned on the TV and snorted at the president chopping logs on the ranch; touched the remote control; laughed at an advert in which two clean-looking punks were shown to have hearts of gold and an insatiable appetite for Bovril; drank two glasses of milk; felt virtuous; collapsed on his bed; and constructed a wank around a wanton Vicky.

CHAPTER EIGHT

Gordon had been busy. Preliminary discussions with William were promising; Mario had offered a 12 percent price cut, and on that basis he'd put in a thirty kilo order; plus he'd put in some work on the competition. His first thought had been to take a look at the Liverpool face through official channels. Via Curtis he had a line into a Sergeant in the Records Office. A very careful guy Curtis had said, won't be rushed and will turn down anything he doesn't like the look of. Which had suited, seven years in Records and not a smell. Expensive too, two grand for a named CRO, but Gordon hadn't argued. What he read on a CRO was not just straight from the horse's mouth, it was also up to date. His own had been a shock. Some regional mob had tailed him for a few days. Their interest was way off-beam but it had worried him that they'd even thought it might be worthwhile and done it without him twigging it.

It would be useful to see what the law had on Ryan but he finally decided against the approach. Not the expense or that it might take a while, but a gut feeling that it would be dumb to signal so clearly to Curtis that he was interested in the Huyton guy. Instead he called in Keith.

They met one early evening in the Commercial Road office. Seeing as it was him had called the meet, Gordon ran the bug-detector round the place, then placed the transistor on the window sill and turned it on.

"I came through the wine bar," Keith said. "It's not bad. Tell you the truth I never really believed in it, not this dump, but you are pulling the pinstripes."

"Not bad is it," Gordon said. He was smiling. "Got to hand it to our ex–financial advisor and his little pal in property."

Keith was at the window to re-tune the radio.

"Definitely ex is he, our Charles," he said.

Gordon swivelled his chair away from the desk. He spoke quietly. "Figures speak for themselves don't they. I mean if you look carefully at all aspects of the package our Isle of Man friend is offering, it does rather put Charles in perspective. All right in his own way but not exactly sparkling when it comes to offshore investments."

Keith had come across some passionate chamber music. He moved the dial fractionally and stopped to listen.

"Reception good enough for you?" Gordon said.

"You should rename the gaff bruv, call it Charlie's Golden Handshake."

Gordon lifted his eyes towards the ceiling. He brought them down again and gave a small smile. "Keith, do me a favour. You know, try and be serious just this once."

"But I am Gordon, I am. I mean Bubbles, it's a bit fucking naff ain't it. You know, when you really look at it."

"What do you mean naff. You come in here and tell me you're pleasantly surprised at the clientele, next minute you're slagging it off."

"OK Gordon it doesn't matter. It's not important," Keith said looking out the window.

"So what is it with this scouse prick," Gordon said.

"That's exactly the question I was asking Jackie Pitt."

"Jackie Pitt?"

"Last of the pick-axe handle and stick them up mob. Missed out on chain saws and security wagons and hasn't got the stomach for petrol dowsing. I palled up with him for a spell in the shit-hole."

Gordon waited. He was frowning.

"So I happened to bump into him the other day and he happens to mention he ran across our man on the island. Where friend Ryan got a big chunk of parole and was heard singing 'I Did It My Way' on his way to the gate."

"Did he? Someone to be reckoned with. Maybe. So what about the present business?"

Keith got up and moved to sit on the edge of the pool table.

"I had a chat with Eddie Quinn."

"Fuck me you do get about Keith. Still telling good-old-days stories is he, Eddie?"

"Yes but he's up to date as well, dabbling in parcels himself now and then. So he knows this Steve Scott from a time they were both in Wandsworth chokey though what the fuck Eddie was doing in the chokey I can't imagine. Anyway they meet up now and then and he's the guy shifting down here. No question."

"Just the charlie."

"Oh yes, He was insistent. Gave me a pal-to-pal on the evils of smack. His son's been dabbling."

"It's a lack of moral fibre."

"Too much moral fibre, no dosh," Keith said. He was laughing.

Gordon was out of his chair and fast at his brother. He waved his fingers close.

"Look Keith you're my brother. You're my partner, but right now you are really giving me the hump. You got that? You think I like being the one who has to be serious all the while? You think I fucking enjoy it or something?"

He turned back to his desk. "So is this information all definite?"

"Definite? Nothing's fucking definite till they slam the door and throw away the keys. But as it happens, as it fucking happens I've had to make myself very busy. Yes, and he may be moving towards has-been class, Eddie Quinn, but he's not a mug."

"OK Keith, OK, I'm not looking for a row. It's a luxury at a time like this and right now we need you up in Huyton, get this firmed up."

Keith was up off the pool table to the desk.

"So now I'm serious am I, when I'm needed. They're fucking headcases up there, Huyton. Nutters. Do the business for a tenner so long as there's a few kicks in it and there fucking will be when they hear my voice. Cockney cunt, that kind of caper.

So why is it I'm indispensable when it comes to tangling with mad bastards like that."

"Obviously I said something out of turn Keith, and if that's the case, I apologise. I'm sorry. It's just you're the man for the job. Fucks sake you scare me sometimes, the way you carry on. It's one of the hard things in life but we've got to get to know what we're good at."

The announcer said something. Keith crossed to the radio. He put his ear close. He said it was Brahms slush and turned the dial into some cackle and on through to some soft rock.

"OK I'll talk to Linda but I'm not having it take more than a few days."

"Of course, and you'll have some help. I'll get that Kevin moving up there, time he earned his keep. He can do the ground-work, get his ears working. But he'll need you to give him a push, keep his mind on the job in hand. I'll go down the betting shop and ring him now."

"Fucks sake Gordon why don't you get yourself a mobile. Nationwide if you want it."

"I do sometimes wonder if you ever listen to me. I don't trust the fucking things. Yeah and if you had my interests at heart like I've got yours you wouldn't either."

Keith shook his head.

Gordon shook his head.

"Let me tell you something," he said. "You get these sex-cases talking dirty to some sort they don't even know. On a normal phone. And the law don't get to nick them unless the geezer rabbits on for twenty-four hours till he creams himself. That tell you something."

"Low sperm count. No sorry bruv, only kidding. Old bill can't be bothered. Where's the cred in nicking a semi-nonce."

"Whereas with a mobile, who fucking knows. That's what I'm saying. Got to be easier to monitor."

"I think there might be a logical fallacy involved here Gordon."

"Is that right? Is that fucking right?"

"Yes, as it happens. If you're right why not just phone him from here."

"Fuck off, I'm not a complete div. Not off my own doorstep. The point is with a mobile you don't even know if you're on it."

"What?"

"Your own doorstep."

Keith shrugged. "Whatever you say," he said. "But all that running about you've got to do without one, it's no good for you."

CHAPTER NINE

As soon as I've got things sorted I'm going to have a holiday. Thailand maybe. A cruise possibly. Take Sarah with me. You can only operate full stretch for a given length of time if you want to stay at your best. It's something I've always said. I was at my best with Mario though. The only thing niggling me is he didn't argue the toss half as much as I'd have expected. So I've swallowed 12 percent for the time being but from what I can make out, his attitude, there's still got to be plenty of fat his end. For our part we're going to have to look carefully at how things are going at the retail end and where necessary be flexible with our wholesale pricing policy.

For the last few days I've been working flat out on two priorities, these scouse arseholes and our new friend on the Isle of Man. There was a moment when I was tempted to ask him, William, about this Ryan. Think about it, if you're a scouse face who's suddenly making good money, a lot more than you need for a fucking video outlet, where are you going to look. A few miles across the Irish Sea to a nice little tax haven.

I didn't. At the end of the day, when you're talking about the long term health of your money, you're talking confidentiality. In fact when we did meet we spent most of our time discussing the pros and cons of Lichtenstein, the Caymans, and Liberia. I told him I'd give my final answer when I'd considered it myself. It was a lot of money we were talking about.

I'm also glad I didn't think seriously about going through Curtis for a peek at Ryan's CRO. Graham is one greedy bastard, no two ways about it. Whereas if I just pass on to him something

I've heard there can't be any complaints can there, even if the Colombians have bought Curtis and Ryan's a pal of theirs. So instead I got Kevin who we've got on a retainer up there to get moving with the promise of a bonus. I tumbled it a long time ago but now it's generally recognized isn't it, that information is the name of the game. In fact I was at a function recently where some feller was going on about the Information Revolution. Like I told him, it's hardly something new. At this end I also got a man who knows Gordon Murray is a kosher person checking the Shipping Lists into Liverpool. Finally I sent Keith up there to oversee things.

Keith, I do worry about him. It was that five stretch he did early on, a stretch he wouldn't have done at all if he'd listened to me. It was kid gloves when I asked him to go up to Liverpool and pull his weight. Maybe I'm deceiving myself about it being the jail, maybe he's always been the same. There was this time when we were kids and we rolled this beatnik in the street, what they call mugging these days. We were only kids, twelve or thirteen, and a bit wild. We got forty quid out of it which was good money in those days. So that's it, you get your money and you scarper. Not Keith, he's only had to push the guy into the gutter with his foot and tell him we're North London's number-one rock and roll band. Only twelve he was.

Perhaps I just worry too much. It's not just Keith but the both of them. Take the rules we've got on personal motor checks. They can stick on a tail bleeper easy these days so our rule is to run a scan for them every morning before we set out. I do mine in the privacy of my garage. Every morning. Without fail. But Keith and Derek? Do they? Do they really? I ask them now and then, you know, it's in their interests as well, and they just say, Of course, of course they have. I can't go on fathering them through life. They're grown men I know that, but there's a bottom line and that's security and the important thing to remember about security is that it's interdependent.

At least Keith's been doing his job up north. He phoned in his first report to Billy Mac's just before I went to see our new financial friend. It appeared that Ryan played the jolly landlord but was never around Tuesday or Wednesday; that he was pally with a Londoner who sounded like Stevie Scott; and that he was definitely in the money. The rumour was he'd bought up three video shops in one hit, the mug. Then I got a call from Curtis and when we met I knew everything was going to fall into place.

I'd scotched him up and he'd gone through the pipe business before he got to the point which was a liberty when it was him had wanted the meet.

"One of the things I have to deal with Gordon is public perception. It can be a problem. Take cocaine for example. Now there is a popular but misguided notion that it is not as bad, not as addictive as heroin. But the lawmakers in their wisdom have also classified it as a Class A drug, rightly so in my opinion. You see Gordon, it's a social problem that's classless." The upper classes dabble do they, I wanted to say. I said yes it was a terrible thing though personally I'd also believed it wasn't as bad as the heroin, what they call smack.

"I have to take you into my confidence on this one Gordon. The thing is that there's people in important and responsible positions, you'll have heard of the fabulous salaries some very young and possibly immature men and women are getting in these days of financial revolution, for whom the stigma of cocaine abuse simply doesn't count."

For a moment I thought it was him, the slippery bastard, was recording the conversation, the thinking man's copper speaking his thoughts to a member of the public. It was only for a moment and surely everyone in this day and age is liable to a bit of the old paranoia. In fact anyone who isn't is either very, very rich or dangerously fucking innocent. Yes, only for a moment because he got started on that pipe again and I don't know why, I'd put up with it enough times, but this time it got right on my tits and as a person who's always kept themselves fit I said, "Fancy a workout in the gym Graham?"

"Love to Gordon, love to, but you know how it is, the young detectives, so much enthusiasm, so much zeal. Just doesn't give me the time. At this very moment they're probably wasting a lot of energy on some wild goose-chase or asking, Where's the Super, What's the Super think of this prospect."

The slippery bastard. What could I do except nod and then he was off again.

"Now this is really confidential Gordon but there's a potential crisis. Potential but a crisis nonetheless."

"Yes," I said.

"Look at it like this. Supposing I was to say to you as one citizen to another that there is a danger of this evil spreading so far as to make for a string of overconfident judgments in the City of London. I've talked to the Super down there, we were in B Division together years ago. Well he's in a difficult position, you can see that."

When it comes to What A Hard Time We've Got the rozzers are second to none.

I waited.

"On the one hand he understands the possible consequences of the widespread use of this seductive drug and on the other he knows he's got to step lightly, walk on eggshells. Publicized arrests could have a shattering effect on confidence. Either way the impact could be enormous. You can see that can't you. The City is not on another planet, what happens there has an effect on all of us, our assets, futures, pensions."

Yes Graham, with the wedge you've got tucked away I bet you're really worried about your pension. It'll meet the bill for the scotch maybe, a fucking bonus. I happen to know, not that I've ever tried to get myself an invite, that Mr Curtis has a very nice three-bedroomed in Esher, Surrey. In fact I wouldn't have stood his whingeing at all if it wasn't that my information from Liverpool wasn't quite hard enough so I said yes, it obviously was a serious problem and started telling him about my club. "It obviously attracts a certain kind of clientele and though the security staff have been instructed to be vigilant you know how it is. Inevitably I hear bits and pieces."

He said yes and I had to make sure he understood I was stalling but with a carrot in prospect. Told him I didn't want to fuck up any man's future and prospects on the basis of tittle tattle but that when there was anything of substance I'd be on to him straight away.

It was a few days later before I heard from Keith again. A quick call sent me down to Billy Mac's for a proper chat. Give Keith his due, he was doing it from a call box on the first half decent stop-off on the M6. Billy was full of the usual. "I know some of them really rate that Hernanadez but Bobby's got a never-say-die heart. And a punch. Backed him myself."

For old time's sake I decided then and there to lay something on the Mex.

What Keith told me was unbelievable. Our Tommy obviously thought running a serious business was like a boozer. Regular hours and the same place. Every second week some eating place on the edge of Liverpool Eight where the spades do business and they call Toxteth these days. Tuesdays afternoons regular as clockwork, the mug.

I waited till Keith was back in town before ringing Curtis. I questioned him carefully, Keith, and there was no doubt he'd got the meat of it. So the next morning I went down to Billy's to phone the Super. On the way I picked up my dough off this other bookie. Three to one I'd got the Mex at and three grand in the pocket's not to be sneezed at, don't matter how rich you are. Course after I'd made the call I had to listen to Billy telling me how the ref had let the Mex get away with some diabolical liberties. You know something, that fight was over in the third, that's a lot of liberties in a short space of time.

On an impulse I made the meet at a Brasserie in Covent Garden. Not really my cup of tea either but no way could I have looked more out of place than the Super with his suit creased in all the wrong places. It's a funny thing but you'll find that if you make a meet on neutral territory it's usually the case that you don't have to put up with so much bollox from the other party. In fact I've read it in a Yankee book. Negotiating Tactics, it's called. I'll tell you something else, if I'd been in charge of the muscle at the Brasserie I'd have given Curtis the heave-ho just on the strength of that fucking pipe.

He was sweating over a Stella when I arrived. Nasty stuff, hangovers and hooliganism. I took a Russian tea for myself and after a while I gave him what I'd already decided to give him, which was Ryan himself plus a couple at this end, Ray someone and another geezer. Muscle man in Muswell Hill I was going to keep on hold. I've a gut feeling he may come in handy. He has had a reef of Susan White's knickers, it's definite. And Mickey didn't like it. Stevie Scott? I've got my principles and Stevie was a friend of a friend so to speak, in fact I might even have a word with Keith to mark his card. Of course Curtis, the greedy bastard, he's asked for more with that quizzical look he's been working on for years. So I waited. Then I said, "Detective Chief Superintendent in the last month I reckon I've done more than most to combat certain social evils."

Couldn't do anything else but nod could he. Then I said from what I've heard the black community could bear some looking at these days.

He nodded at that too. They could as well. I've heard whispers they're branching out of the weed and into the charlie. Keith said, "Yeah, take a look at the Caribbean on the map. The Colombians have." Like I've said many times, it's an interdependent world these days but I'm not having them on my patch.

CHAPTER TEN

The squad set off seven-handed in two cars at 5:15 A.M. It was cold and dark, the dampness hanging on. DI Nye Edwards had been left in charge, DCS Curtis having gone up to Liverpool to coordinate operations there. Edwards had never been able to find fault with information originating from his hands-on superior but had, as a matter of course, ordered a watch on the earmarked North West London premises. A dull boyo, DS Jones had reported when his two car team had tailed the suspect to a car-park meet in West Hampstead. Parcels had changed hands with a thin-faced longhair. This character's car reg had been noted. DCS Curtis had said to leave him for now, a distraction. What mattered was that the raids were synchronised. 5:45 A.M. "It's not a stopwatch job Nye, but let's have it close."

"A bugger of a time I know," Edwards had said in the warmth of the canteen. "But you know the s-p, better to have boyo with his pants off."

The streets were smudgy dark, quiet like they belonged to another planet. On Kilburn High Road men in overalls and Borough-stamped donkey jackets were moving quietly. A delivery van pulled up at a lit-up corner shop, a crate of milk cartons sat outside. The lead car pulled up next to a six-year-old BMW at the lights by the railway bridge. Edwards saw a dapper young man at the wheel.

"If that black cunt's not at it, I'm on the beat," his driver said.

"Not our job you lucky bastard."

"Very lucky bastard. Chancing your arm son," DC Thomas said, noting the reg as they moved forward with the BMW which took the first available left. The police car surged up Shoot-Up Hill.

"Boyo's the right side, ground floor. We'll have two at the back and sledge the main front door."

"No problem," said DC Thomas. He had considered London Welsh but was front row for the Metropolitan Police.

They were over the crest of the hill and began to cruise down. Big detached houses and low-storey flats stuck out of the dark. At lights at the bottom of the hill a group of men stood in the courtyard of a large pub. A heavy-built lorry topped with aggregate reversed out.

"Paddy mafia, think they've got it made with the docklands," the driver said.

"Wait for the Channel Tunnel, you haven't seen anything yet," Edwards grunted as the lorry straightened up and they made a left turn towards Willesden.

"I thought security was going to be tight on that."

"Don't be kidding yourself Brian. Slippery bastards with their exemptions and subcontracts and you know where half their money goes."

"Paddies? Down the boozer."

"Don't be dull Brian. Those murdering bastards over the water, they'll be getting their whack. Take the first left thirty yards on the right hand side."

* * *

The wall was magnificent, painted light ochre, satin finish. It stretched further than the eye could see in tight, night time city. He brought out the second aerosol from a jacket pocket and began again, an E, M, E, R. He glanced up at the sound of traffic. Across the street was a row of low shops and then an unlit church-high building of grey stone and glass running far into the distance where the dark of the sky was lifting. He must hurry on this miracle of clean wall. It would be dumb to be caught. He sprayed a clumsy G. The traffic was loud. Fuck it, finish it another time and he was on a bicycle rushing down a madly corrugated road. An expanse of moorland opened out ahead. the road began to twist, hemmed in by dry stone walls. In the mid-distance a man was knocking up a rough wooden shelter. He braked, wobbled, and got off to watch. The banging was louder. One man and his hammer. One man and his lawn mower. BANG BANG. Surely not at such a distance, the man away in the field. BANGCRASH.

Ray woke instantly. Where was?

What was?

He jumped out of bed naked. His door. His door splintering.

Had to make it to the kitchen. But the lights were on. There was the kitchen, there was the flour jar. There were big men everywhere. A voice said: OK Ray.

His stomach fell into his bladder.

"What is this? What is it?"

"Fuck off Ray. You know what a search warrant is. We have reason to believe you are in possession of dangerous drugs on these premises and that means Ray we're going to take apart your horrible little drum. Brian, you and Jason take the other room. Wyn, you and Gary do the kitchen."

Shit shit shit

"Interrupted a wet dream is it Ray?"

Why hadn't he found a safe deposit box. Why? Or someone paid to stash it. He'd been going to. He was. He'd had it in mind. Would have done it next week if only.

And he was shivering.

"Put some pants on Ray, fucks sake. That shrivelled little thing's going to put me off my breakfast."

"I thought you were off bangers but."

How, the bastards. And just when he'd got the best connection ever. The connection. The bastards. Had to be.

"So how about a sweatshirt and some trousers," he said.

"Who's speaking to you Ray?" Edwards said. He waited a while then kicked a pair of cords across the floor. "Pick them up and turn out the pockets."

"Careful but," DC Thomas said as DC Phillips shook out the bedclothes. "Boyo might have had an early morning strop. Where's the bird Ray, never pulled on? Or a pouf is it. Very careful Dai."

Two twenties, a box of matches, coins, a key ring and used Kleenex fell to the ground. DI Edwards picked up the keys and dropped then in a thick plastic bag.

"Using twenties to put it up your nose Ray? Pick them up and drop them in this bag."

Bastards. Maybe they weren't that good. He'd put a pound of flour, at least that, around the bag. Just there were so many of them. And like they had all the time in the world. If only he'd been quicker getting the stash sorted. He'd been going to do it. It was on his list.

Still he was shivering. He grabbed at the sweatshirt from the floor as a slow jumble of pants, shirts and vests fell from ripped out drawers.

"All good runs come to an end Ray. DC Thomas, didn't I say those very words at the Arms Park in 1980?"

Ray sat down on a hard chair by the window. DC Thomas was over in two strides and yanking the chair away from the back. "Who told you to sit down boyo. And stay away from that window. In fact go and stand in that corner, dunce isn't it Nye."

"Looks like it," DI Edwards said, pointing raised eyebrows at the kitchen doorway where DS Jones stood with a packet covered in white dust.

"The sugar was it?"

"Bloody flour Nye."

CHAPTER ELEVEN

At the end of a week in which he'd had serious doubts as to the long term viability of First Secretary Mikhail Gorbachev, Jack was shattered. By late Friday afternoon he decided enough was enough; with a lifetime of Cold War behind him he would give Mikhail the benefit of the doubt in the short term and mark him as dodgy for the medium. Decision made he set off for the monthly meeting with his coke dealer. He'd made a confirmation call at the beginning of the week and slogged through perestroika on the strength of it.

The cab fought its way through a mish-mash of dispatch riders. Further west, a more car-orientated crowd. Arab headdresses were frequent as they moved into Kensington proper, immaculate in the diesel.

The tea room was full of greenery, double-breasted suits and silk print dresses. His man wasn't there. A small matter of waiting. Give Ray his due he was reliable and had standards when it came to product quality. True he didn't run to a suit or perhaps disliked them on principle but his tweed jacket and grey trousers did not have waiters in hysterics.

He ordered tea. The first cup was pleasant.

The second cup was less pleasant. London's traffic problems were getting out of hand it was true but Ray should have learned to take this into account when agreeing a rendezvous. His fingers drummed the table.

He stopped his fingers drumming the table.

His patience snapped over a third cucumber sandwich. He

got up, paid in sober fashion, walked into the hotel's lobby, and selected a vacant payphone.

There were some numbers one knew by heart.

"Disco Rentals please," he said.

"Just one moment sir."

Inside the folded doors his bladder whinged. He squeezed his thighs together and read the printed instructions by the phone. Handy if one should wish to ring Botswana on the off chance. There was some crackle and a Yes?

"Any message from Disco Rentals for Mr Kruger? It's urgent."

"Oh yes Mr Kruger. Message reads, Apologies for missed appointment, could you rearrange."

Delays could happen. That was a reality in an imperfect world. Ray did at least make provisions. His bladder eased a point.

"I suppose I'll have to. Let's say five thirty on Monday afternoon."

Through the folding door windows he saw a gross man in a Stetson crossing the lobby.

"And the place Mr Kruger?"

His bladder stretched to the full. He would piss himself. It would drip through the finite absorbency of his pants and pin-stripe. The answering service simply did not ask questions of this sort and the girl's voice, surely it was not the same as usual. He rallied himself as if the global bullion market depended on it.

"Oh the usual."

"The usual? There's a definite instruction here for a location."

Just who did this slimy bitch take him for. He slammed down the phone and ran for the men's room.

The release was exquisite. It was on a par with orgasm. It was better than orgasm. A guy in a Stetson was pissing two places down. He heard no piss on porcelain. What was this? He wheeled out and plunged into traffic for a cab.

Back home after standing all the way on the 6:40. he found his emergency gram not to exist. Consumed on an earlier occasion he concluded after an extensive search. Instead he enjoyed a bout of self-control, attacked a bottle of Martell, read through a quarterly breakdown of Australian mining shares and went early to bed.

His feeling virtuous continued into the morning with a brisk walk through some adjacent woodland. Hearing a whole orchestra of singing birds and seeing real buds on the trees he conceded that Phil was right after all, life was great. He wavered around lunchtime but then, with that good timing for which he was professionally famous, Phil rang and said he'd be down early evening.

They had been friends for a very long time but somehow had an unspoken agreement not to talk about their coke supplies. Some barrow-boy's been tampering with this, or blue chip, straight from a Bolivian earth-digger was as far as it went. It went against the grain telling Phil his story. Very much against the grain. But give him his due, Phil was not merely sympathetic, he'd had the foresight to motor down to Surrey with a couple of grams.

"Merely a hiccough in Mr Supply meeting Mrs Demand," he said. "Hey remember old Barley Jack. I bet he asked himself what he'd done to deserve us."

Jack had not forgotten, Phil ripping into him like there was something personal.

"You describe your Ray to me and I'll be there Monday, just in case. And if, if it's a no-no I'll work something out with my man."

He wasn't sure he liked it at all. But perhaps he was being childish. After all Phil had understood straightaway without analysis or explanation. He offered dinner in the best restaurant Surrey could offer but by then Phil was a couple of toots to the good and plumped for as many tins of tomato soup as were in the house.

"I honestly couldn't face anything that required an effort. You know, chewing, masticating. Nothing like that."

Swallowing spoonfuls of the stuff, found at the back of the larder and heated, Jack reckoned he'd been put on to a good thing, not just effortless but virtuously plain and inexpensive. He stayed in this mode, clearing the table and washing up.

"So," Phil said when they'd settled with a bottle of the lightest Vinho Verde and a fresh line waiting, "when I've had enough of reading inscrutable U.S. Fed policy papers like they're the fucking *Beijing Daily*, I've been thinking about your fantasy on and off."

"My fantasy."

"Well unless I'm dangerously out of touch it's not reality yet."

"What?"

"What are you doing to me Jack? Your idea. A charlie Futures market."

"Ah that. How about a toot in the present."

"Sure. Evidently needed," Phil said, chopping all the while.

"If it existed, this is as far as I've got, and I was a player I guess I'd be looking to buy a six-month option with a reasonable premium. Delivered in London. Then I'd take another look."

"Think it would have to be a Future. I've always thought in my heart of hearts that an option is not quite putting your money where your mouth is."

"That's verging on the irresponsible Jack. Are you sure you want another line?"

"Bloody right I do," Jack said, grabbing the note and letting rip with his favoured left nostril.

He passed on the curled-up note.

"Hey this tenner's a bit snotty Sharp."

Retorts rushed through Jack's brain. He held them in. Phil could be infantile. It was just the way he was. For himself he would speak soberly.

"Your position as I understand it relates to American attitudes."

"More or less. The gunships and the rest do matter now though in the medium term I'd predict increased production. You know, when they've no alternative to offer."

Phil was on his feet. He waved his arms. "I mean can you imagine it, there's this WASP wants to Do Good In The World. and he's explaining to the peasants how wonderful it would be to switch from Coca to Cocoa. He's into his stride. The future looks bright. When up jumps this guy Hernandez in sweat-stained overalls. He's been about a bit, Hernandez has. Been a sailor or his mum and dad swept apartments in NYC. He's a wise guy returned home, speaks good Brooklyn. But there's no dough in cocoa, he says. End of the Hearts & Minds campaign for that year."

Jack nodded. Phil sat down again like he was exhausted. He went on talking. "Anyway fuck all that. I'm still after the Quality Control job. All known Optrex, Quinine, Speed and Borax cutters to be suspended from floor trading till they've learned their lesson."

His laughter sounded crazed. Jack looked at his watch, told Phil the job was his if he kept his head clear and touched the TV remote control.

The screen cut fast from Talking Head to Talking Head. Behind them stood the White House and the Kremlin with passing quiet traffic.

—General Secretary Gorbachev does not have absolute control, one said.

—On the one hand there is his need to release resources into a civilian economy that is demanding a better standard of living and on the other Military demands which will grow more insistent if . . .

Jack flipped the sound down to zero.

"I wonder sometimes if the Americans want Mikhail to succeed or not."

"Told you before, if I knew what they wanted I wouldn't be here. Be retired. Elsewhere."

On screen the anchor man was nodding, left and right; right and left.

"But then it's always going to be hawks and doves," Phil said.

"It's two in a row they've had over isn't it?"

"What? Who?"

"The Iranians. Reagan and Carter. Reminds me of old red-nose-and-shakes. History of England. Some English queen dies with CALAIS engraved on her heart. For years I thought a heart looked like a red jam tart, you know that could be inscribed."

"Christ you should have told me."

Jack wished he'd not told him at all. Get a grip.

On screen he saw an empty field near tower blocks. He turned up the volume.

—A thorough search is being made of wasteland around Sarah's home.

—In an operation codenamed Operation Gray Fox police raided a number of addresses in London and Liverpool. Nine men and a woman are helping police with their inquiries after quantities of cocaine and two hundred thousand pounds in cash were seized by police in dawn raids led by Detective Chief Superintendent Graham Curtis.

"Oh"

"Yes."

"Should have bought up last week mate. Give your Monday afternoon a miss eh?"

"Looks like it Phil. Could be."

"Odds-on I'd say. Tell you what, I'll give my man a ring next week, double up."

Jack said nothing.

"Hey, my favourite bit," Phil shouted. "The paper shuffling at the end but you hear nothing. See what I mean, not a sound and paper's loud fucking stuff."

Jack said nothing.

Phil looked at him. Poor sod. Worrying about fallout?

"Doesn't know who you are does he, your man. Your ex-man."

Jack spoke in a rush. "No. No problem there. I always phoned him. As Mr Kruger."

"Kruger? Oh I like it Jack, like it."

CHAPTER TWELVE

Phil's man was a woman called Simone. He had known her directly for a year after a lot of hassle. It had been through Gina and Gina had been bloody expensive one way or another, old money herself but never seeming to understand there was a bill to be paid after a night of wildness. But he had found Simone. A bit of a mystery, not really part of Gina's scene at all.

He had her down as a worrier who never seemed more affluent from one month to another. They tended to meet in pubs or smarter cafes but never the same place more than three times. These were Her Rules. To make contact he would ring a number. Another woman would answer. Then he would ring at 4:30 the next afternoon and talk to Simone herself. The other woman had a London accent and sounded bored. Sometimes he could hear a TV, sometimes the voices of children.

"I'm sorry, Simone's not here right now," the other woman would say. "Can she reach you?"

"Unfortunately I'm out of town right now. It's Arthur, maybe if I tried tomorrow," he would say, and she'd say 4:30 was a good time.

It was their last meeting in the latest place, a Saloon Bar in Clerkenwell. He bought a pint for himself, her a gin and tonic.

"It's good to see you," he said, "certain recent news items did worry me slightly."

"Worried you?"

"You know, certain activities in the law enforcement field."

"As you can see Arthur, I am here. So what is it you were wanting?"

What he'd like, he said, was a price on two ounces.

"Two? Multiply by two."

"I was rather hoping for a discount. You know, given the obvious benefit to your turnover and profit."

"I don't see the benefit to me. I simply won't see you for two months instead of one. Obviously there is a gain from the point of view of convenience and safety and that's always appreciated, but I'd have thought it was a mutual gain."

"Oh lucid Simone. Very lucid. If only some of the people I have to work with could put the situation with such clarity. But no doubt because I didn't put it clearly, you've misunderstood what I was saying."

Simone laughed. It sounded good and natural. The lemon slice swirled in her glass.

"Is that what these people you work with pay for, back-handed compliments."

"Unfortunately not. Contrary to what you may believe I have to work hard for my bread and butter. No, what I meant was two ounces at the same monthly intervals."

"I see. Well let's say 2750."

"Seems a bit meagre, given the advantages mentioned earlier.

"Fifty pounds may be meagre in your world Arthur, not mine."

"Oh come on Simone, same world, buys the same quantity of goods. And, forgive me if it sounds patronizing, a bit of advice from my world. Never show you're uptight even when you are."

"Is that what they say in your world Arthur? Really? How very interesting. My offer works out at approximately a pound off each small unit and given certain publicized problems you've raised, I'd call that generous."

"OK, OK," Phil said. He was grinning. "So tomorrow night all right? Two ounces."

"The Bishop in Holland Park, I've told you where it is. Six thirty."

"Fridays are Fridays Simone, very difficult."

"Six thirty," she said, her weekends sacrosanct, part of her rules and beginning at seven on Friday evenings in her own home.

"Six forty-five and that's a rush."

He saw her hesitate. She really wanted the deal, she might need the money in a hurry. One didn't know.

"Six forty," she said.

"It'll be a rush."

At 6:42 the next evening Phil was surprised to bump into Simone in the doorway of the Bishop. She was leaving.

OK, rules were rules but this kind of inflexibility was too much. He thought instinctively of the unsustainabilty of Bretton Woods and the Fixed Exchange Rate system.

"Am I late? Bloody traffic. Surely you can give a bit of leeway."

"Arthur I'm in a terrible hurry, I'm not playing games. Can you give me a lift?"

"Sure."

The car stood out. It was gross. But she was already in it. They exchanged parcels as he pulled away.

"Just keep going straight."

"Not going to count the money? You trust me?"

"What's eating you Arthur?"

"Eating me?"

"Anyway I'm hardly going to be counting pound notes in a car like this, not here," Carol said and carried on pointing him towards the Harrow Road.

He waited till she asked him to pull up before dropping his bombshell.

"I wonder if you could get me a price on ten and also five kilos. I assume there will be a pro rata discount a little more substantial than fifty pounds."

Simone slowed right down. She closed the passenger door again and looked at him.

"If it's possible of course."

"Phone next week," she said.

"Have a good weekend."

Carol Curbishley walked away quickly. She'd been having kittens in the pub; to be stuck with two ounces for the weekend at the very least would have been all sorts of worry; to have started to break her rules could only end in disaster. She didn't turn left till she'd heard the Porsche roar away. Then she turned right and left again and stopped at Marie's. She walked up the steps to the front door and rang the bottom bell. Soul music sounded out of the ground floor. Marie opened the door. Carol slowed her down in the corridor.

"Sorry I'm late. Bloody Arthur. Is Sheila OK?"

"Course she is. They've had their tea. Arthur, you mean the posh one on the phone."

"Yes him," Carol said. She smiled, unexpected. Out of her shoulder bag she pulled some money. "He'll call early next week likely as not. Is fifty OK?"

"Sure is."

In the front room the Soul was loud. Two girls were dancing a routine.

"Hang on Mum, just watch this."

Carol smiled. They looked good, Lilly maybe better than her Sheila, stronger and more fluid. So? They looked good, both of them.

"You want a cup of tea," Marie said.

"Please."

The music stopped. Carol clapped. Sheila ran across and gave her a kiss.

"You were marvellous."

"Not bad," Lilly said. She was stood at the tape deck ejecting a cassette.

"Only not bad," Sheila said.

"We've got to work on it. Look, I'll show you some pictures of real dancers."

On TV a bearded man stood in front of a graph.

—Of the two deficits it is that on balance of trade which is showing no sign of improvement and is having the biggest impact on U.S. policymakers

Ten and Five kilos Arthur had said. Serious money. Which didn't mean he was being serious. Flash maybe because she'd shocked him, her leaving the pub. She had shocked him, shocked herself come to that.

"If you're at home here's your cup of tea."

"Thanks Marie."

"You got anything decent to smoke. It's like there's nothing about except that red seal soft black and God knows what they do to that."

"Knock it up in an Amsterdam factory."

"Is that right? Gives me a headache is all I know."

"I've got a bit of red Leb that Is red," Carol said getting out blue Rizla to put one together, half an eye on Lilly who'd dived into the box of exotic clothing that Marie was always picking up on the Golbourne Road. She came out with an embroidered gold jacket. Enormous on a nine-year-old. What could she wear underneath, baggy trousers maybe. Sheikh of Araby. Sheikhess. Even if it was just the Five, if Arthur was serious. If he was serious it had to be proper money. Sheila was tying a headscarf from some ragged pink silk. Carol lit up.

The door burst open, a boy charged towards the TV. Marie's Fred. After Engels, Marie'd said one time on account of him holding it together with the other Manchester Top Hats and all the time screwing the wild Irish girl on the floor.

"You ever going to pass that joint?"

"Sorry Marie."

"Bloody hippies," Fred said. He was channel hopping. "Where's football preview. What's this crap?"

"Have you got a calculator Marie?"

"Don't you ever stop Carol. You don't laugh as much as you used to."

There was no football on any channel. Fred looked at his watch and took the paper from his mum's lap. Lilly was helping Sheila make a twirling and tasselled skirt out of what once must have been a very expensive shawl.

"Don't I?"

"No, and I don't have a calculator. Fred."

"What?"

"You got a calculator?"

Of course he had, he said, and whipped one out.

"For Carol."

"It's solar," Fred said, bringing it to Carol. "All you've got to do is hold it under the light. See."

"Very smart."

The girls were excited, their giggles loud. Fred turned, screwed his face and turned back to Carol.

"So what you want to know. I'm so fast, I'm the fastest in the class. Just ain't the one can catch my arse."

"Can't I do it myself?"

"I told you, I'm express. Give you the answer without no mess."

"OK then, 5,000 multiplied by thirty-four and then by thirty-seven."

"Lilly says we both look sexy. Do we?"

"Terribly," Carol said. "Just a moment, let's see how fast Fred really is."

"I can do that. I know those."

"170,000 and 185,000," Fred said, tapping again. "Difference of fifeen G."

"Pretty good."

"That's nothing to what I can do," Fred said, pocketing the calculator and checking his watch. "Hey, the football—"

"Do we look really good?"

"Outrageous. What do you think Marie?"

"Nice draw," Marie said, handing back the nearly finished joint. "Going to be rock stars aren't you, The Bold Sisters, then you'll be able to look after your poor old mums in their old age.

"Could be," Lilly said.

"Of course. Of course," Sheila said.

"Goal. There's only one Clive Allen. Goal. Hey, what's this."

"I'm just going to try on another headscarf."

The TV had gone into black and white. The players wore baggy shorts. There were goals left, right and centre. "See, we were great even then, years and years ago," Fred shouted. "Up the Spurs."

"Yeah all right Fred. Ever thought you were out of date Carol."

"No, I do the samba."

"You laughed. You bloody laughed and you know how beautiful you are when you do."

"Come off it Marie, I'm an old woman of 35."

"Oh God. Bring on the violins. So where does that leave me? Well just for the record I don't feel old at all. Why not come out tonight, there's a Salsa band. You haven't been out for weeks."

"Salsa? Too much dum dum dum."

"Oh misery."

"We haven't fixed up baby-sitting and I'm tired. Maybe tomorrow night. I've kept a bit of personal, couple of lines."

"OK but let's do it Carol. Take the dance floor by storm."

* * *

Carol held off thinking of Arthur's parting shot until Sheila was asleep. Only it took a reading of *The Ugly Duckling*, *The Emperor's Suit of Clothes*, and a very moral story about a tailor making a pact with the devil to introduce the blackberry into the world before her eyes had closed. It was like there was thinking and thinking.

She put on a Nina Simone tape and lit a single-skinner. Fred's figures began to hum. Fifteen Thousand Pounds. Out loud it sounded good. And she wasn't going for the moon. Fifteen grand on the five kees and it would be that because surely Arthur would take it at 37 the gram when he'd started at seventy odd off of crazy Gina. That and Terry talking one time about Big bizz and thirty-four being on the high side his end. Her profit a modest three quid the gram, thus fifteen thousand all told and if thirty-two was nearer the mark, twenty-five. Twentyfuckingfive thousand pounds.

Pain blistered her fingers. She stubbed out the joint.

Oh yes Carol Curbishley.

Just the five kees would be One Eight Five thousand changing hands. Or it was the ten and some discount, say three fifty. Thousand. People could do nasty things that kind of money. And how not get cut out. Thanks for the Intro darling, see you. You know how it is love.

Bollox, she was just thinking tough words. She was just.

On the way to the kitchen she opened the door to Sheila's room and looked in. She could make out a shape in the bed but heard nothing. She tip-toed, heard steady breathing and knelt by the bed. Wonderful Sheila who could make her mum fell solid and steady.

Kept her on the rails.

Made her laugh.

No laughing if it did go wrong. Or it came on top. Ten kees and she'd be locked away, no messing. Fuck the sob story, unsupported mum and all that, five kees, ten kees same difference, they'd be locking her up and Sheila in care.

Madness.

The kitchen light was bright glare. She flipped the kettle's On/Off and still wasn't thinking straight. She took risks anyway didn't she. Two ounces and they might not go for the sob story. OK she had her rules and fair play to herself she'd stuck to them. They involved a lot more running about but she'd stuck to them like tonight, looking at the clock, leaving half a G&T and going to the door.

Only she couldn't enforce her rules on anyone else and people got nicked. She'd been cool with Arthur when he'd mentioned arrests because if you weren't cool with Arthur you might as well give up only she would have liked to know how it had happened, had even asked Terry.

Just a bunch of cowboys, he'd said. Only what did that mean. A bunch of cowboys, him talking tough words. Him being cool with her like she was cool with Arthur.

A trace of steam hung in the kitchen. She flipped the toggle to On. The water reboiled. She made tea, took it back to the gas fire and rolled a fresh single-skinner. There were facts had to be held on to like, she ran risks anyway and with Fifteen or Twenty-five in the one hit she could stop running risks. Just because she'd always been small time did not mean she had to think small time. Don't get nicked was all that mattered.

Small time and busy. Busybusy. Marie saying she didn't laugh anymore.

There was a small mirror face down by the armchair. She held it to her face.

Herself not so good. Not in fact so good and not the lines on the face the problem, she knew them, the bigger ones on the forehead and the wrinkles round the eyes. No there was a wooden set to her mouth, to her face, like it was stuck.

She put fingers in her mouth and pulled her face into new shapes. Then without the fingers and saw a fluid gargoyle with her own eyes steady. Onlooker's eyes. What a performance. She opened her eyes as far as they'd go. The forehead went concertina. She looked on. So what did Marie expect, that Carol Curbishley on her own could somehow be above just how mean and shitty it was these days. Drip drip, bit by bit. So she worried about money. So she looked wooden. So.

So along came Arthur with a question that might be a proposition. Behind the wheel of his Porsche. Not just the Porsche but steady business. Arthur was not a chancer. These were facts. Only there was also Arthur the whinger, professional negotiator. Fifty pounds Simone, like he was a tough nut in Monty Python. Give him a price on five kees and he'd be haggling over ounce ones. There are discounts and discounts Simone.

No, that she would not worry about. If he started that kind of haggling she'd tell him straight out he was a cheapskate and unless she'd got it seriously wrong Arthur would hate being called a cheapskate. He would hate to think even for a moment that he *was* a cheapskate.

Take it that it was real. Take it that you didn't have to be caught. Take it that you didn't have to be ripped off.

And focus.

Step by step.

Would Terry trust her enough. More to the point could *he* pull that kind of credit. Take it that he could pull that kind of credit and trusted her enough. How then not to get cut out and how to do it so she could check the stuff.

Checking the stuff was basic, dead easy for it to be a good sample plus four kilos and nine hundred and ninety-eight grams of borax when the comebacks would be directed at her. Comebacks, thinking tough words like she was in someone else's movie. Getting her head kicked in, her legs broken, something happening to Sheila. No. No hysteria. If it came to anything Sheila would be in Wales for the duration. No hysteria, step by step. She could do it. All those years with Chris and it had been her making the decisions. Him the world's number one on pro's and cons, she making the decisions that were difficult till one fell in his lap. Bollox.

She got up and took a couple of steps to the tape deck. Below it were a jumble of cassettes and cassette boxes. That was something she could do for a start, sort them out. Yes, and once she'd sorted them put them back in their boxes each time.

Step by step.

In the meanwhile here was the old Maxell 60 and sure enough Chuck Berry came bounding into the room with "Marie," the guitar loping over eggshells and a story that could wring tears out of you except she mistrusted it, the father's hard times, cut off from his daughter in the rooming house with the numbers on the wall. Then the guitar was back, lightfooted with all the beauty of the running giraffe she'd seen once in a documentary, it's feet seeming not to touch the ground and the long neck swaying back and forth. What she felt dancing when it was good. Her shoulders that were dancing here and now and why not at least ask Terry prices. Why not hat. No commitment but a maybe step one. And in the meanwhile if Arthur's two oz was regular she could relax anyway. Why not.

CHAPTER THIRTEEN

Gordon Murray was in the Merc, approaching Dalston in need of a phone box. He pulled up suddenly on double-yellow lines. A woman in the Morris Minor behind shook her fist as she passed. He gave her the finger and looked down the road for Traffic Wardens. Out into the traffic he waited for a bus and delivery van to pass before stepping out in front of a red Deux-Cheveaux. He heard brakes and opened the box door. The receiver was light in his hand. He looked anyway and saw a tangle of wires in the empty shells of mouth and earpiece.

Further up towards Stoke Newington there were two boxes together. He took the next left, parked on a single yellow and walked back to the main road. One box was empty. He had no illusions. It would be fucked. In the other was a man in tweed jacket and clean jeans. In need of a haircut. An old dear was stood outside. Gordon moved in close. He could hear the guy.

—Given that the funding ceiling is in the region of two hundred thousand . . . well yes obviously . . . but the real point is the make-up of the Management Committee . . .

Gordon pictured a Yellow Cap, unambitious himself but resentful of anyone that looked as though they'd gone out into the real world, made something of himself and got a decent motor. He pictured the Yellow Cap sticking the flimsy under the Merc's wipers.

—As I see it, it's a situation that should be treated case by case though obviously that doesn't mean we shouldn't take account of the track record of applicants.

They were important calls, the Italian and Isle of Man

William. Mobiles were tempting. They were and he didn't need Keith telling him. But what were temptations there for, they were there to resist.

And still the old dear stood there, clutching her purse, a scrap of paper and a ten pence. Just stood there without a word. It was a fucking liberty, if it had been in his power Gordon would have had her on the blower straightaway.

—Oh absolutely, there mustn't be even the slightest hint of pre-judgment. Absolutely not. On the other hand we can hardly not take into account track-records and what we know.

Gordon shifted his weight, saw a pile of ten pences on the Directory rack and yanked the door open.

"Oy, you. You know how long this poor old lady's been standing here."

"It's OK love, I mean," the old lady said.

The man in the box gave a grin. "Only a minute mate."

"Only a minute you cunt."

"I'll have to call you back Sarah, there's a bit of a queue." Gordon held the door open for the old lady. She said it was terrible, the boxes. He watched her looking carefully at the paper as she dialled. She put the phone down, picked it up and dialled again. He could see her mouth opening and closing, the receiver tight to her ear. She went quiet and looked anxious. Put the phone down. Poked about in the purse.

She came out of the box slowly.

"They told me the extension was engaged but to wait."

"Diabolical," Gordon said and stepped into the box. Dialled the Isle of Man. The receptionist started her stuff and the pips sounded his end. He put the first of his Fifty pences into the slot. It was resisted. The pips went on relentless. He pushed harder with the thumb. Nothing budged. He looked into the slot and saw a grinning curve of silver. His bladder whinged. He lifted the receiver to smash it, saw inevitable arrest and heard a Curtis tour de force: I know it can be frustrating Gordon, but really, a public phone. He breathed deeply and put the receiver down gently.

The street was a chaos. He needed a piss. A bright painted

cafe stood out. Inside he tackled a flight of stairs, followed cray-oned arrows to a toilet.

Back downstairs he ordered a tea from a woman in overalls. The place was full of chess-players. One of them stood out in smart casuals, something familiar about the shoulders. He went closer, tea in hand.

It was Eddie Quinn. Absorbed in a game with a big guy in beard, lumberjack shirt, and Parka.

Gordon shook his head, had to be what the boob did to people these days, modern rehabilitation and your con came out an intellectual, Keith with his smart comments and now Eddie Quinn, chess wizard. Eddie suddenly moved a tall piece. The guy with the beard looked shocked. Eddie sat back. He took his eyes off the board, looked up and was on the way to his feet.

"All right Eddie? I can see you're busy, maybe when you've finished."

"Great Gordon."

"They run to a phone here?"

It was in a bare wood corridor. It worked. He made his meet with Mario. William pissed him off straightaway after he'd battled his way through a posh voiced woman on the switchboard.

"I'm with a client Gordon."

"Listen pal as of last week you're holding a lot of my money."

"Gordon, if I could phone you"

"No I'm phoning you. Haven't made a mistake have I, this is a fucking phone I'm holding. Certain items I want to discuss. Early next week."

"I quite realize the substantial nature of your funds Gordon but I have got . . ."

"Monday, Tuesday, or Wednesday."

"OK, OK. Just checking my diary. Tuesday lunchtime's possible but it will have to be Manchester, Piccadilly Hotel dining room."

"Pencil it in. It's a journey for me but it so happens I might have other business up there. Yeah, pencil it in," Gordon said and put the phone down.

Eddie had very few pieces his side of the board. Looked like he was in the shit. His eyes were round and round the board. "I resign," he said.

A slim young guy in steel rimmed specs and a parka took his place.

"You busy Eddie?"

"Not now. Bishop to Queen's Rook Five, I kind of knew it was trouble."

"Back to the drawing board is it? Got a motor, mine'll have a ticket anyway."

"Early for a drink, how about a tea up the road. Saw your Keith the other day, helped me mark an old mate's card."

"Oh yes."

"Seems Keith had heard something. Amazed my pal was. Grateful."

"He gets about Keith does, has his ear to the ground."

They went in an empty gingham clothed cafe. Gordon ordered two teas and apple strudel.

"Don't see so much of Keith these days as it happens," he said.

"Is that right? So how's it going these days Gordon. I heard you was doing very well. Always knew you would."

"A club, a wine bar and some bibs and bobs, it's enough isn't it, at our age. In the end it's all down to what you want, what you really want out of life. I mean look at Mickey White, still going strong I heard. You see Mickey at all these days?"

"You know, now and then, like as often as I see you. Bit of a surprise seeing you there. I know it's not much of a place but I like to drop in for a game."

"Don't apologize Eddie, fucks sake. To be honest I don't understand chess but it looks educational. Got to be better than the boozer which is something I'd tell Mickey if I saw him.

Someone was telling me he half lives in that Ripened Hop."

"Some needle between you and Mickey?"

"Me? Christ I hope not. Fuck me you wouldn't find me tangling with Mickey even if I wanted to, which I don't. No just wanted a word in his ear."

Eddie was intent on the strudel, forking it round his plate.

"See Eddie I'm a club owner and you know the score, we get some right types, hard druggies the lot and you'd be surprised how much of it is hoi polloi."

"Is that right?"

"So there's this one face I see there who's a bit familiar, and definitely at it. I'm not going to give you any fanny about how I'm there pulling pints every night but I'm there enough to see what's what. So I see this geezer, mid-thirties, a muscle man giving it with the T-shirt and who do I see him with the other week, large as life, Susan White. You remember young Susan, a lovely girl."

"Got you, Geoff Christian. No problem there. Mickey was fucking wild when he found out, didn't want Susan in that kind of scene. Gave him a right bollocking, Mickey did, and I heard the feller had pulled some other stroke. Yes, a right bollocking."

"Love to have seen it. Good for Mickey."

"Pulled strips of him, called him a no good cunt right to his face."

"You've got to haven't you, your own daughter."

"In that Greek drinker it was. I mean he's got some arsehole, Mickey, Geoff's a big bastard."

"Yes, wouldn't fancy it myself. That time in the club you'd have thought it was Tarzan's night out. So tell me Eddie, what is it with this chess, clears the mind does it."

CHAPTER FOURTEEN

"No . . . come on . . . yeah that's it, it's just that madman again . . . A custard pie in the face if he gets any closer? I should say so."

The eager voice played havoc with Carol's extra half an hour in bed. Children's TV? Mother's little helper but not this loud on a Saturday morning.

"Nice one Cheryl, nice one girl. That'll teach him, creeping up like that. But Cheryl spotted him, didn't you and took Appropriate Action . . . Thanks Cheryl. And Brian. And Kate, even if you were asleep on the job. And after all that I could do with a rest so here's Julia with something . . . Something?"

"Thanks Simon. Something old, something new. Plasticine . . . OK I can hear you, Plasticine boring, boring but then there's plasticine and plasticine."

Carol leaped out of bed, closed the door, and stopped by the tape deck. She read off the cassette titles neatly stacked. Lee Morgan looked good. She shoved it in the deck and picked up yesterday's paper. Back in bed was warm. The Sidewinder boomed out dancey. And an unread paper in her hands. Saturday morning.

In the paper was another spy story. It turned out a dead one had been gay. Big deal. She turned on a page and got a shiver. A man, a teacher, obsessed with a teenage girl and the wife wound up strangled. There was a six-year-old daughter. Hard to credit, hard to stomach. In an ordinary street in an ordinary town. And so much for infatuation, there they were grassing each other up. What of the daughter, what of her? The paper had nothing to say. Had she been there? And even if she wasn't, what was she supposed to become, an orphan with no memory.

Carol jumped pages and landed on the Financial section. There was Soaring, Plunges, Plummets, and Surges. There was GOLD RUSH. She saw wild west desperados, an old prospector knees in the river hitting jackpot, a young guy with a grin and a gun right behind him. The paper said the price of gold had risen eighteen dollars in one day. Which could mean something or very little. It would depend on the original price. Obviously.

The door popped open and Sheila was at her side, drawing a pattern in the air.

"Look, if you draw a star like this and then five sides round it"

"A pentangle."

"You know."

"I did go to school you know. Hey, you know what, if you're careful you can draw smaller and smaller stars inside."

"Where's my paper and pencil," Sheila said running back to the door.

"Under the front room window on that shelf," Carol said, and something about a barn.

The original price was $450 the ounce. OK, a 5 percent rise in one day. What would that mean in her market? Further down the page was a table with the dollar-pound exchange rate. She did the sum. Weird. She did it again. Same result, obviously not weird. At the prices she paid it would take four ounces of gold to buy one of coke. So if it was 5 percent she'd have gone to Terry's, bought at the usual, found business was good, gone back the next morning and found his price up fifty quid. Substantial, they weren't bullshitting.

Last time she had been round to his place had been to ask those prices for Arthur and she fancied Terry'd been shocked. Or maybe not shocked, just not happy about it. Perhaps his own use had got out of hand.

No, not fair. In business he was careful and reliable. And a gent. Crude only the one time when there'd been a big bloke there. Maybe a partner. Maybe a supplier, coming on like a gangster leastways, all Cunts and Slags like he was trying to provoke her and Terry going along with it. And then the next time coming on heavy about what happened to grasses which had been all right because there and then she'd made her rules. And it had got better and better after he'd made a pass, she'd said No and he hadn't made a big deal out of it. Had been very funny in fact so she nearly did fancy him. That was how it was, never come on heavy again, good to work with only he hadn't been happy when she'd said, It's speculative for now Terry but could you give me a price on five kees.

"Mum, Mum, look at this, look how small I've made the stars."

"Infinity."

"What?"

"For ever and ever."

Sheila looked at the pentangles over her mother's shoulder. She frowned then put her arms round Carol's neck. "I'll love you for ever and ever."

"Even when I'm an old mum?"

"Of course I will."

"You want some breakfast?"

"I've had a glass of milk. I'm not hungry. You just stay in bed a bit longer, I'm going to cut out my stars. Why are you laughing?"

"Sometimes it feels as though you're my mum. Hey, now you're laughing at me."

"Course I am, there wouldn't have been room for you in my tummy would there?" Sheila lifted her sweatshirt to show. Carol gave it a gentle pinch and got a passionate embrace.

Of course there'd have been no room, feet on the ground her daughter. Where they had to be. Only she wouldn't mind flying. And why not. Round Terry's when she'd asked the question and him not pleased, it had been a bloody Monday morning hadn't it. Not going to be at his best was he, and there's small time Carol asking big time questions. The thing was, he had gone out to make the call. And she'd been spot on with the price, 34 on the Five, nearer 30 on the Ten. Never mind how he looked he'd given her a price. Then asked her if she'd had a good weekend. Bloody right I did, she'd said. Because it had been all right, surprised

Marie by fixing up baby-sitting with Gloria, Ben and Jaycinthe's mum so all the kids had stayed round there. They'd gone local but struck lucky, a rare Steel Band event and she'd danced like she hadn't for a long time. Even met, leastways danced with, the first man she'd half way fancied for even longer. He'd danced without looking at himself, lithe and happy. Bought her a couple of drinks without making a big deal out of it. Jimmy. Hadn't gone any further except him saying they would definitely meet again.

She'd said the same to Arthur, when he'd opened with small talk. Then he'd been straight into how he assumed the Five and Ten prices were negotiable. At which point she'd got the feeling it was just a try-on and said they were the prices she was giving him and was he serious. He'd leaned back in his chair and said he wouldn't be there if he wasn't, despite the attractions of her repartee. He'd said that. It was how he spoke. He was serious but it would take time, it was a lot of money, he had a partner. It didn't have to be bollox so she'd shrugged. It would happen or it wouldn't happen. It was the only way to look at it.

And it was time to get up. She took one last look at the paper. Turned out there was a real joker in the pack, new mines and mining technology that could bring the gold price tumbling down. Yes, so why had it gone up eighteen dollars in a day. Half an hour wasted. Time to get up.

CHAPTER FIFTEEN

It had been a hell of a week and triumphant Jack was exhausted—shagged out, he'd said to Alice, and she hadn't blanched.

His prediction had been a hunch. Even in the early days he'd had a nose for the impact of local demands, their relative weight and shifts, on the overall price-making of the global market. In 1978, even as a relative novice, he had known that an explosion in the gold price was on the cards. It hadn't been difficult, not with the take-off of the Great Inflation and the presence in the White House of a misplaced Thinking Man who'd never realized that an essential job requirement was to see things in Black and White when it mattered. That had been common knowledge, what had marked him, later in '79 was the way he picked up on a boost to this trend from the Far East. The de facto recognition of the Republic of China and the subsequent expulsion of Taiwan from the IMF, had lit up the green light for him. That was when he'd first made a name for himself.

This time around disparate factors had jelled that much Faster. A flurry of worry in Hong Kong over the shape of things to come in the great mass of China. That had Jack poised. A rumour that a shrewd big-time player stateside had liquidated his entire equity portfolio had lit up the GO sign, and he'd gone for it. There'd even been a note of congratulation from Sir Nick.

Less fortunately it came with an invitation to a dinner party at the great man's house, Friday evening, Hampstead. Sir Nick no doubt thought it part of his reward though he must surely know that a full course dinner was beyond the pale for a man who'd been under the strain Jack had endured.

And there was no getting out of it.

He was in the Top Ten when it came to the Head-Hunter's desirable property list, true. No question. But still one couldn't stand up the boss. Hints that even the best and the brightest had no manners would work their way around the circuit and leave a black mark.

It was a sweaty job, scrambling into his dinner jacket in the office cloakroom. He collapsed into a cab, the prospect of course after course of rich food and the inevitable saddle of lamb positively nauseating. At Kings Cross he opened the taxi window and breathed deeply. Diesel and dodgy kebab. He reacted promptly and lit a Silk Cut. By his elbow he saw a red diagonal through a black cigarette. He stubbed out the cigarette. They passed St Pancras. He closed the window.

They sat down as twelve for dinner, talking of Wimbledon tennis. Jack had a passing interest, he'd watched one or two finals of the Men's Singles. Sir Nick was saying that the rise in playing standards was matched by a decline in one's enjoyment of all other aspects of the sport.

"I'm not such an old fogey as to say that professionalisation was not inevitable, though I do worry about rugby football, but you would think they might look as though they enjoyed playing."

"Pressure ought not to preclude pleasure," said Sir John Mitchinson, a banker. "Otherwise we'd have all retired years ago."

He was one of the few people Jack recognized, along with his wife, the sharp-witted Lady Caroline. There was also Paul Swift, one of the most brilliant men of his generation and so on, now back with the BBC for the third time; his wife Veronica who wrote biographies of the nineteenth century and looked to Jack as though she belonged there; Professor Sparks, a monetarist economist with a South London accent, a zealot Jack remembered, who believed the tautological equation $MV=PT$ had been handed down to Moses on a tablet; and a man called Steve, a rock star of Jack's youth, now a producer.

He was relieved to find some kind of soufflé on his plate for starters. It went easy on his throat and the conversation went on with no effort on his part.

"It's surely the sheer repetition," Lady Caroline was saying. "They play week in week out and though I can understand the transformation of pastime into profession, it would not suit me. Even bridge would pall above two full evenings a week."

"But surely," said the Professor, for whom marketable skills were marketable skills, "a concert pianist is no different. Think of the practice they have to put in."

"An invidious comparison Professor," said Lady Hoare. "One is not just hitting the keys for desperate effect."

"The comparison would not have been so invidious in the nineteenth century," said Veronica Swift.

"Ah the nineteenth century, what a mercy we are not living then," Lady Caroline said. "A vulgar and brutish age when all is said and done."

"It did at least produce St Pancras Station," Jack said for something to say.

"Since its principle destinations are Derby and Sheffield it might do better as a museum piece," said Jack's neighbour in a bitter voice with a northern accent. She had been introduced as Geraldine someone, a brilliant barrister. Veronica Swift was no doubt a brilliant biographer. He was certainly a brilliant gold analyst but did not remember Sir Nick having said so when he'd done the introductions.

"No politics till after dinner Geraldine," said Sir Nick.

It was roast saddle of lamb.

Jack took an uninhibited swig of claret.

"And no politics in sport, people are heartily sick of it." It was Steve. Jack had a sudden memory of the school TV, a Friday evening treat and this guy smashing his guitar.

"Hear hear," said the ancient lady who'd been introduced as the widow of a Conservative minister back in the pre-history of the 1950s. "I do remember my husband saying that it served Herr Hitler right when that black man won all those races back in '36."

"Ah yes, Jesse Owens. Now there was an athlete, the epitome of a sportsman."

"Unlike the soccer stars of today," said Lady Caroline. "Why is it they all seem to have perms. How I long to see a centre-forward with a mohican. Is the perm working class macho these days?"

"As working class myself and a football director who does not have a perm, in fact all too little on top, I'd say it's the foot-work really counts.

"Even so surely since the abolition of the maximum wage the game does seem to have been strangled by defensive tactics and bad behaviour," said Sir Nick.

"And some awfully bad judgment. There we were in the early '70s finding out what we'd always known, that Spend, Spend Spend was just a passing hocus pocus . . ."

"As indeed some of us have been saying for forty years, the sheer flippancy of Keynes . . ."

Sir Jack ignored the Professor.

". . . On you went regardless in the football world. Inflated wage bills, inflated transfer prices on some frankly untested players as if the real world were a pinball machine on the never never."

Jack picked at his lamb and concentrated on the potatoes. He saw them forming a soft, absorbent ballast in his stomach.

"But surely we are missing the sheer aesthetic pleasure that the modern game can afford," Paul Swift said. "I'm not saying it always does but the development of tactics is a challenge to the truly great player whose off-the-cuff brilliance within the confines of those tactics in turn forces their development to the level of a chess game in which individual brilliance is possible. One only has to look at Kasparov. At the same time football retains its physical immediacy, its pace and passion. Like it or not, it is a theatre in which one always hopes for the victory of individual genius against the machine while knowing that such a victory is uncertain. Indeed the odds are stacked against it. But speaking professionally, and remember it is a mass media, I'd like to see something pretty damn good to compete against a football match because there's always the on-the-day chance . . ."

"Lamb not to your taste Mr Sharp," Jack heard close by from the lady barrister. Her accusing voice suggested waste was a sin.

He turned to her and said that although not a fully-fledged vegetarian, he was not a keen carnivore. He saw with wary pleasure
that this was not what she had expected. She carried on regardless.

"I understood from the Introductions that you are in the
futures market. What I want to know is when you are going
to turn your eyes, and no doubt talent, to the regeneration of
British industry."

The few small bits of lamb he had eaten felt like lead pellets
that released a steady flow of acid into his stomach. He found
this hard to reconcile with fluffy little white things frisking
about in a meadow. Instead he had a vivid picture of the internal
workings of a car battery.

"Is this a party political?" he said.

"It's a question on behalf of millions of ordinary, decent
British people."

From across the table he could hear Steve.

"Yes he's been really great, our manager. We're not one of
the big fashionable clubs but he has instilled in the players some
good, old-fashioned values, loyalty, dignity and team spirit."

"Two things," Jack said. "First it depends on which industries you're talking about and secondly it always comes down to
relative costs of production. Ask the British public as consumers
if they prefer to buy British or Japanese or Taiwanese. You don't
hear anyone saying Jap crap, not these days."

"If, and it is an if, they decided against buying British that's
because of decades of under-investment while capital is being
exported by the bucketful."

". . . far better that the working classes beat each other up."

"But what of the ordinary, decent people who have the mis-
fortune to live close to football grounds."

"Then you should be talking of expropriating capital and
imposing investment decisions."

"But we don't want to impose."

"Ah, 'we' is it, so it is a Party Political."

"You're being flippant and that in itself is half the problem
with the City. Look, we're not stupid, we understand that imposition is not an answer in the modern world, we just want you to

see that the decline of our manufacturing base undermines the whole country, at the end of the day, even the City."

Dessert arrived in the shape of a sorbet. A sorbet was feasible.

Paul Swift was still going strong, Jack could hear it.

"Perhaps we do show too much snooker but the punters like it. Or do you want to return to some elitist Reithian policy. It simply wouldn't wash. What we can do is at least try and do intelligent current affairs but that doesn't affect the snooker. Anyway it's not us who are responsible for three million unemployed. And finally . . ."

Finally? The man jested.

"The same drama which is surely the central drama of our times, the very possibility that the maverick could beat the machine, be it Steve Davis or Ivan Lendl."

When the ladies had retired upstairs, Sir Nick believing that old-fashioned customs had their own virtue in a fast-changing world, a bottle of old port was brought out. This was heavy drinking. Jack was going to drink a lot of water before sleeping. Except sleep was a prospect that seemed far off. And the Professor was in his stride.

A long, long way off.

". . . the results. The groundwork has been laid and there have never, and I repeat never, been any promises that they would come overnight and now the results are coming. The British economy hasn't been as healthy for years."

Paul Swift had recently heard a colleague say that for a lot of people there was a difference between Not Overnight and Seven Years. Now he said it himself.

The sparks flew.

Two hours later Jack was in Geraldine's car, a lift towards the City, Sir Nick's arrangement. It had always been a risk making the last train but he'd wishfully thought Sir Nick might offer him a bed for the night. As it turned out his boss was an absolute fucker, knew where he lived, how much he'd had to drink to play his part, how late when they were finally allowed to leave. And to complete the punishment had fixed him up with this

Brilliant Barrister. She said she lived in the Barbican, he would find cabs there.

"Oh deep in the heart of the proletariat," he said.

"What a rude young man you are, is that a professional requirement?"

Jack didn't like the Young Man, said she was confusing rudeness with honesty.

"I've a good mind to throw you out of my car."

"That's the trouble with your Labour party. You're always threatening to do nasty things to people like me but never do."

"And you're drunk."

He got out promptly at the next bank of telephones. The first box didn't run to a dialling tone. He slapped it about. Perhaps he was a bit drunk. The adjoining box was phone cards only. The gods shone down, gave him a break, a forgotten green card in his jacket, a single unit left.

Phil was sympathetic, free and invited him over. Jack snapped the card in two, threw it in the gutter and set off in search of a cab.

"I despair sometimes," Phil said, "bloody spot dealers having kittens on my lap. What do they get paid for?"

Jack grunted.

Phil was in his stride. "This week, for the very first time, I've begun to take your view of things, that we are some of the very few steadying forces in the world. Anyway never mind, let's give this a whirl. A humble representative of the two ounces I've purchased at 1375 the ounce."

He had it out of the paper to make two wavy lines.

Jack came to life. "A bit pricey. Ray's was 1350."

"Why didn't you tell me you dog. But then according to all known data, friend Ray is nicked."

Jack said he wasn't complaining.

After a line he went further, said it was good stuff, that he wished he'd had a line at Sir Nick's.

"Yes yes yes, I sympathize. However, while you've been theorizing and doing your guts in your pal Phil has been researching in the real world. Current unit price on two ounce purchase is 49 quid. OK, you say it should have been 48 but get this. If we move up to five kilos we're talking 185 grand. Got that, 37 a gram. On ten kees, 33. Both of these are opening shots of course. Room for negotiation. Add to this my forecast that prices will rise in the short term and that current selling price in Kensington et al. is high sixties. What do you think?"

"Interesting if resellable in similar bulk otherwise return on outlay dependent on turnover time. Marketing."

"What are you, a telegram? Compare rate of return to base interest rate."

"Pass. Must have rest. Fancy a game?" Jack said, scrabbling for the backgammon board.

"At your present speed I'm not at all sure I would," Phil said.

"Present speed purely illusory. Thinking more of a complete medical check-up."

"Illusory depression. Bad was it your dinner party, a mixed crowd."

"Every arsehole under the sun, a cross-section of the cream, and you know what they talked about all night, sport. All night, except for an interlude of how-do-you-see-the-future. I'd a good mind to tell them I get paid for that kind of thing. Just held myself back. Finally they got round to cricket. Went bananas. Cricket of all games, drugs and decadent living scandals."

"That's the West Indians Jack, smoke the ganja and then it's holy war. Smack the colonialists in the gob at a hundred miles an hour. And our silly batsmen wear white helmets like they are colonialists. Red rag to a bull isn't it."

"Pity you couldn't have come on at Sir Nick's as a substitute."

"Twelfth man Jack."

"For God's sake lay out a line. Yes, it must have been the ganja, I've never seen Sir Nick so outraged."

"That's the West Indies for you. OK for retirement. OK when they bang their beer cans calypso style on the Intro to the Highlights but otherwise unsound. Which I put down to the weed man. I tried it a few times, didn't go for it. Clouds the judgement. In fact, positively dreamy."

CHAPTER SIXTEEN

I thought the train would be a good idea. If there's one thing I've learned it's that when you've got an important meeting on, it's as well to be well-briefed *and* fresh. Mind you, I had my doubts at Euston. I mean what is it, a railway station or a fucking doss-house? I'll tell you one of the advantages of First Class and that's before you get on the train, there's no queue for a ticket like there is for the second. Two queues there were, going twice round the Booking Hall. It still didn't stop some wino trying it on, Hey Jimmy, right in my earhole. For one thing my name is Gordon and I happen to like it and for another I turn round and see it's a young feller. Young, with the whole of his life in front of him and there he is, mumbling about a cup of tea and a smoke and giving me a noseful of spirit in the process. So what is it about me, I don't go around coming on heavy, I just said, You talking to me pal, and he backs off cringing like I'd given him a slap.

It looked like all hell had broke loose in most of the car-riages but when I got to my section I found an empty compart-ment, opened my attaché case and started on the first of my folders. I wasn't sure just how much I wanted to tell this new feller, William, but I did know that I needed an overall picture of our liquid and physical assets to weigh up the tax implications. So I got started on the gymnasium file and I find I'm think-ing about Eddie Quinn. He's some fucking case, Eddie. Now when I was a youngster he was quite tasty, at least that's the way he seemed, maybe it's just because I was young. I mean a man goes through that period of life when he hasn't seen too much of the world and ten to one, he's looking at life through rose-tinted specs. As it happens Keith's wearing them tinted these days, grey they are. They change shade depending on how much light there is. It's automatic: the sun gets brighter, the specs get darker. Now that is something, meet the guy who thought that up and you are meeting someone.

So you know how it is, when you're young you tend to see everything in terms of black and white. So you reckon, least you do where I come from, that a geezer is not just a bit tasty but a fucking hero just because he's knocked over a bank or two and give him his due, Eddie did have a few over. Mind you, if you look at it now, if you look at it objectively, it was a bit of a doddle in those days, a bank. I mean since the banks wised up you don't see many people at that game, not these days.

Maybe it isn't just me and the way I saw things but Eddie himself. It's like he's never grown up, still thinks the world is made up of heroes and villains with him as a hero. I ran into him the other day down in Dalston. Some fucking place that is. You wouldn't credit it but property prices are going through the roof and the place is full of spades. I don't mind the Asians because you've got to hand it to them, they are grafters, but the fucking spades. You know who they remind me of, all those Catholics who used to have the old man hopping mad, noisy flash, and thinking life was just there for having a good time. Yes, I wound up in some weird fucking place for a cup of tea and there was Eddie playing chess. Anyway I get him out of there to a cafe that was trying to be halfway decent and you know what he says to me, What's it all about Gordon, what's it all for, what do we want out of life.

OK, to be fair Eddie's not still trying it out with the old sawn-off and pick-axe handle which don't cut much ice with those security screens they've got these days, but what a fucking question when it's me whose just bought him a tea and strudel. I told him, What you get out of life Eddie is what you put in, and I was surprised after all these years that it was me having to tell him who's older and was a half-tasty feller when I was a kid. So what is it with him? I told him, What you get out of life is what you put in, and what does he say? You'll have to define your terms Gordon.

Define my fucking terms! Him and Keith, the kind of crap they come out with. Like you do a stretch and that makes you a philosopher. Still, over time Keith has become a fully-integrated member of the team, pulling his weight, playing his role, and of course he's got older. Mind you, if he was out there on his own, I don't know. It's not that he hasn't got a good head on him but he's always got to be making some flash remark. It's like he's an addict. Take that time he was up in Liverpool, did a good job in fact, but when he phones in his last report on Ryan he says something like Shovel his carcass through the close-circuit and sink it in cement. Take it easy Keith, I said, just the facts. But he wouldn't leave it alone, said the facts of course Gordon but pure Webster. OK, the line wasn't too good and maybe I'd misheard or it was some code. Webster, he said again so there was no mistaking it, Jacobean, blood, envy, and reality. I remember it word for word because I had to take a deep breath and wait for him to come to the point.

It's a funny old thing, the mind. All that going through it with the folder still open on my knees. Then some BR flunkey stuck his head in and I took a coffee. Not bad as it happens and despite what you might think British Rail is getting its act together. It was quite a while since I was on a train and I can say it had got a whole lot better, the service as a whole. I looked out the window for a bit. Big green fields and plenty of trees. Sometimes it's easy to forget England's a green and pleasant land, that's what I realized even though I live on the edge of the country myself. I also realized I'd spent too much time thinking about Eddie Quinn. I was only in Dalston at all to find a working phone box.

And what happened with Eddie? Apart from his meaning-of-life patter he then starts going on about Mickey White. Mickey White for fucks sake. You'd think half the world had nothing better to do with its time than talk about an old has-been like Mickey White. Several things he'd done had wound me up but there's a lot more important things in life. A transition to a new financial advisor for one thing, a major event in anyone's life. He's someone you've got to get to know. You've got to listen to what he says and at the same time make him understand the score, that he's working for you.

I got back to the gym file. I'd opened the first one a few years back and I hadn't needed Charles to tell me that Keeping Fit is a growth area. What's more, I'm all for it. The figures spoke for themselves. Membership Fees are a very sound starting point, with them you'll find a good chunk of your investment comes back straight away. As it happens it was his investment policy that first alerted me to Tommy Ryan being a mug. Video outlets! In 1987! I was in and out of video by the mid eighties, never touched it since except for a little wholesale business for what they call the Third World.

Operationally the gym was doing fine. West London of course, Fulham in fact. There was however the question of its place in the company structure as a whole. It was nominally in Keith's name but I'd been thinking of lumping it together as in independent company along with the new one that's just about to open in Clerkenwell. Credit where credit's due, that was Keith's idea. Like I said, when he can be bothered to use it, he has got a head on him. Anyway about nine months ago he tells me that's where it's all happening. Blink your eyes and there's a new design studio, he said. And if you're in design you're sitting down a lot but equally, if you're in that game, who wants you if you've got a pudge. I listened to him of course but did my own checks because I happened to know Keith has a long term bit on the side in that neck of the woods. A designer herself. Maybe they talk about all that stuff he read in the jail. So I checked because he could be prejudiced. What I did was make myself early for a meet with Mario in that caff he likes down there, a pal of his. Gianni's. And Gianni was dead chuffed. Told me he'd been worried when The Times and whatnot moved down to Wapping but then he starts getting this new crowd. He's worried about them at first as well, all T-shirts and jeans he said, but when it came to it, nothing wrong with their credit cards.

Something had happened to the train as well. There I was thinking about Clerkenwell and suddenly I realized there was no chug chug. I got up, looked out the window and didn't see a station. What I saw was a wasteland, smoking chimneys and ratty looking grass. Everything had just been going too well and that's exactly the moment in any situation when you've got to be on your guard. I looked at my watch and was glad I'd allowed myself an hour's grace. I told myself not to get wound up.

The thing was that if the structure I had in mind came to fruition, an anonymous company—Liberia or somewhere in the Caribbean being favourite—Keith and Derek would have to be its employees. That also meant, and there was no way around it, that all the tangible English assets would have to be in my name, It would cost a bit on the tax side but there's a commercial logic to it.

There was more scratching on the tannoy and then it died out. I looked out the window again, even the fields looked dirty. The tannoy crackled: Owing to a signals failure the train has now stopped three minutes from Stoke-on-Trent but don't worry, sunny Manchester won't disappear. A fucking joker but he must have soon wised up or there was an old head in the Guard's van because the next thing was BR was apologizing for any delays, you know, just in case his humour wasn't to everyone's taste.

These things happen, even in the most efficient of organizations so I wasn't going to start throwing a wobbler. Instead I picked up the folder and thought of the concept of a Leisure Grouping. OK, three snooker clubs, two gyms, two music clubs, and a wine bar might be modest, though snooker is a lot more than it used to be, modest but not laughable. Billy Mac and the bookies were definitely out. If only he could accumulate a few bob I'd have sold out a long time ago. I couldn't give it away, start giving things away and you get taken for a cunt, but I resolved to look seriously for someone to buy out my stake, someone who'd be chuffed by a photo of him and Billy. One of those rock stars who fancies looking half dodgy. I made a note to ask Steve Burke if he knew a face and that did the trick, made me decisive about everything. I knew exactly what I was going to tell William.

I looked out the window again. What a place. A depressed area and proud of it. If I was really in the boxing game, which I'm not, it's exactly the kind of place I'd be looking for talent. Living there, you'd have to be mean and hungry which is what it's all about in that game. I mean why do you think the Colombians and the Mex's have got to the top in the lower weights. As it happens it was a Colombian finished off Billy Mac. It went four rounds so we all said Billy was game but when it comes down to it you've got to have that hunger.

Then I'd had enough of that window. I'd paid a lot of money for my ticket. First thing I'd be saying to William was, any future meets and they'd be in London.

* * *

Sometimes you have to compromise. It's one of the things you learn when you have grown up. In fact we settled on quarterly meetings alternate, London and Manchester. I like getting my own way as much as the next man, of course I do, but what's the point of getting steamed up over a trip to Manchester twice a year. Not a bad city from what I saw. Definitely perking up. I've half an idea to keep poor old Charles's property feller on the books and get him to give the city a looking over.

If you've got to travel you can't lose out by keeping your eyes open while you're doing it. The fact is, and it was one of the reasons I'd agreed to meeting our man up there, I had another acquaintance I quite wanted to see. A jock. He lives there now, got a four-bedroomed semi-detached, in the city but a nice enough area with plenty of trees, and what did he pay for it? Nineteen grand. Yes, Nineteen, I could hardly credit it.

I caught the 6:50 back to London. That was a tip from him, Willie he calls himself. You know how they talk even if he hasn't been near Glasgow for ten years minimum. "All those wee commuters before, then all those wee City-savers afterwards." Still that shows you doesn't it. Even with the small things and Willie's got his eyes open. That's what marks him out as one of the best if not The. I didn't need to see him, it wasn't like that but what I say is, it's no bad thing to keep up personal contacts. Anyway when it came to this train he'd been spot on. I'd got a compartment to myself. I'd given Sarah a bell too. She's going to pick me up at Euston. You can't be on the go all the time. So I'd treated myself to a pair of new black leather gloves and told her what to wear. I figured she and me could start off in the study. The preliminaries over the desk. I don't know how that came to me, something new like that. I mean normally my study is the one place I don't like anyone to come, and I mean anyone. It's just I'd got this picture of her, the desk and most of all the desk light. Made of brass. The idea just came to me out of nowhere. We'd just finished our hors d'oeuvres, me and our new financial advisor, and he's started going on about interest rate spreads. He'd lost me there for a moment and then that picture just popped up. A simple dress with just a belt, one that undid easily without any fucking about.

So what with that he'd really lost me. No one likes to look slow on the uptake do they, but better that than missing a point which may just turn out to be vital, so I asked him to go over it again. His spread across the spectrum of international equities looked more interesting to me. A nice mixed balance of flexibility, one or two hunches with a breadth of portfolio and some blue chip as a solid safety net, he said, tossing his side salad.

One of the impressive things about the International Equity market is that the Japanese have moved into it in a big way recently. Our man said that was good for share values. No doubt, but it's much simpler than that to my way of thinking. If the Japs have moved in it's got to be all right because, whether you like them or not, they're shrewd and they're successful. Mind you, you know what someone was telling me about the big firms who are at it there. It would have been Keith, he'd read it somewhere. You know what their business is? Amphetamine. What they call speed. One cheap, nasty, synthetic product that is. Maybe it did help with their economic miracle but you'd have thought with the wedge they've got now, they'd have moved on to something a bit classier.

If there's been one grit in the works it was that the Liberian company structure is going to take longer to put in place than I'd expected. I always like to have a definite date but the fact is I don't have one. But then as our man said, "We want this to be really watertight don't we." I don't what the feller who put me on to William said, but he obviously understands a bit. One thing he'll definitely have appreciated is that I'm not a man to get the wrong side of.

Let's hope that at the end of the day, Mickey White understands that too. Apart from the fact he's past it, Mickey White takes liberties because once, just once when I was starting out in business and didn't know any better, the cunt had me over. It was some not very wonderful slush he was punting, you know, long before all those dotted silver lines and the rest. It so happened that it was only after we'd done the business that I tumbled I'd paid way over the odds. The next time I saw him I could see that he knew I knew. Of course Mickey was a lot better organized than I was in those days and there was no way I was actually going to show him I'd lost out. So we were sitting there, a boozer in the Cally Road it was, a right shithole, and that one bit of business is the one thing we're not talking about. That's the way it's got to be. I mean I don't mind admitting I've had one or two people over in my time but you don't crow over them afterwards. But this time, when we'd finished and got up to go, I'd have been around 24 then and him 34, you know what the cunt does? Gives me a pat on the shoulder, says, "that's the way it goes son," and to top it off, gives me a wink.

That's what he remembers, Mickey does. That he once had me over and got away with it because I wasn't in a position to take him on. So he thinks nothing's changed. But the world's moved on and time waits for no man does it.

You'd have thought the train stopped on purpose, just when we were only a few minutes out of London. It was as if the cunts thought that after a problem-free couple of hundred miles, no journey was complete without a stoppage. And after looking out into murky nowhere for a couple of minutes I was sure in the mood for Sarah. I even took the gloves out of my attaché case and tried them on. They were good, thin leather that felt like an extra skin when I flexed my fingers inside of them. And the thing about Sarah is she'd be there at the station. That was one of the certainties in life that everyone needs. And she'd be wearing what I'd said, an old dress. It'll be tighter that way because she's got bigger in all the right places. And what's more she's not like Tina at all. For one thing Tina is a 22-carat slag and Keith of all people should know that. He was around when she upped and away with my fucking money. But what do I hear him saying one time after I'd introduced him to Sarah. He's saying to Derek, who can hardly remember Tina, he's saying something like, it's funny how Gordon's new sort looks a dead ringer for Tina. He couldn't see me of course. It was in our old office behind the Fulham gym. I was fucking mad with him but didn't let on I'd twigged. Just let him rattle on like people do when they think they might have been caught out. No, I never let on. There's some things you've got to keep to yourself. And it's not true, Sarah and Tina, what you see on the outside, that's nothing. It's the character counts and there, there's no comparison.

Just as I could almost feel that material ripping under my fingers, the train decides that after all, it can lurch into Euston. Terrific.

But all things considered I could see a thoroughness to our man's approach to the Liberian structure as a definite plus which made it a very successful day. Our first quarterly dividend was due in a few weeks and it looked handsome even under the temporary structure. I reckoned with figures like that, just another two or three years in the business. I'd worked hard to build it up and the next few years looked like being the best ever but after that, fuck it, why not farm it out, lock, stock, and barrel. No more headaches, enjoy life to the full.

CHAPTER SEVENTEEN

"Trying not to make a habit out of it," DCS Curtis said.

He was sat in the booth of a pub halfway between the Yard and Victoria Station. A late Saturday afternoon, and still it was crowded, baggage and drinkers. He stubbed out one of DCS Bob Lumley's Dunhills halfway down. Either Bob was going to have something to say or was content with his overwork-ulcer-diabolical-duty-rota routine. Bob was a mate from way back with a handy niche in the Serious Crime Squad but they did have fortnightly official liaison meetings for this kind of thing and were surely getting a bit old for socialising. So if he did have something to say why not get to the point. One thing he was sure of, Glenfiddich out of a plastic cup was a lot preferable to a blended something in a pub tumbler.

"Though it may prove inconvenient you will find it a fact of life that chummy, if and when he works at all, does not observe the normal conventions of a five day week," Lumley said, his imitation of old Brewer, an old-school intake of the pre-war. As an imitation it was spot on and Curtis had heard it many times. He laughed slightly.

"Coming out on top Graham?"

"A holding operation Bob, I wouldn't put it higher than that."

"Exactly what I tell the AC who then says, Follow the money, follow the money and Bob's your uncle. It's his joke of the year."

"The cunt," Curtis said. He felt the true strength of the blended testing his stomach lining. What was Bob getting at.

"Accountants Graham. The time's coming when the good old-fashioned copper won't exist."

"That's how Her Majesty's fucking Customs see it as it happens Bob and they're the one's with the Minister's ear. And money come to that."

Looking at Bob's face wily under a sunlamped glow, DCS Curtis thought he might have sounded bitter. Bad tactics. He took out his pipe and rephrased.

"Not that they're not good, I'm not saying that. Shit hot at PR for one thing and with the money they've got they ought to be good. Trouble is, what they don't see is a trail's got two ends to it."

"Yes?"

What? Had he not made himself clear? What was this Yes? He didn't fall over himself to work Saturdays but to have this as well when he had faith in Gordon Murray's confidence in his accountancy advisors. A fast cartoon of paranoia rolled out: sharp, pinstriped accountants working for the Rubber-Heels flipping confidently through files and print-outs; asking for old-time expertise to follow it up; and recruiting Bob Lumley.

"You know what I mean Bob. OK the Colombians are sophisticated but they've got to have partners this end and where are they going to look? At the kind of people we know about."

"Colombians Graham?" Bob Lumley was frowning.

What was this, what was happening to Bob? If this was the Serious Crime Squad no wonder Her Majesty's Customs were taking over, their empire growing by the day.

"I think we can assume they're getting active in the European direction. I have to skim through page after page of fucking photocopy from the Minister's Drugs Intelligence Unit . . ."

"Me too," Bob said. He was grinning.

"Well that's the message isn't it, the Colombians are coming. They might as well write that a thousand times and have done with it."

"I wouldn't put it quite like that Graham. For one thing, and it's something a lot of people forget, we're an island."

Paranoia flowed into bewilderment. Where was Bob at? He'd be on about Spitfires and Hitler given half the chance.

"You've got a point there Bob," he said.

"Of course Europeanisation is becoming a reality but even

then Graham, I'd say the Colombians are only a part of, how can I put it, the whole jigsaw. But I interrupted you, the Colombians and leading chummies, you were saying. Leading chummies?"

Graham lurched back into paranoia. Bob had just been playing dumb, the copper's old standby. In the process of calling him out for an unnecessary pal-to-pal drink. Gordon. The possibility.

"Them," he said.

"But our big boys of today, they've got first rate financial advice and what with the way money can be shifted around the world these days . . ."

"It's called progress," Graham said.

"Liquidity."

"What, fancy another Bob? Liquid progress, I'm all for it," Graham said. He was laughing loud and on his feet. He elbowed through two Australians and came back with doubles. If Bob was right he said, why didn't they get seconded good accountants, temporary contracts.

"Can't see the financial rewards would be attractive. No, what'll happen is they'll do in-house training. Like the Army does. Get your degree or Charter while you're a serving copper. What I'm saying is when that happens they should service us detectives. What I can see though is them taking us over with all their fucking cost-benefit analysis."

Graham couldn't credit it, all this aggravation just for Bob's analysis of the future face of the Force. The cunt hadn't long till retirement.

"Bunch of prats," he said. "Cost benefit! What do they know about what it's like on the ground."

"There's another way of course," Lumley said, sucking scotch out of his moustache. "Here we are, trying to fight the villain with his expensive advice, while we've got one arm tied behind our backs."

"When haven't we?"

"A general round-up of leading faces. Use holding charges. Give us time. Then access to all the books, squeeze hard enough and the pips will jump out however clever the cash-flow."

"The public won't stomach that, not with the Civil Liberties mob."

"Don't think they pull much weight these days. As long as we don't start doing something daft like clubbing nurses, the public will stomach anything."

"All right, I take your point Bob but it's a bit hypothetical, let's get down to brass tacks, leading faces, who are we talking about, and how many."

"You know who I'm talking about Graham.

Never had Scotch tasted so bitter in his guts.

"Fucks sake Bob, let's not play round and round the roses."

"OK, take an old cunt like Mickey White."

"What, is he still at it?"

"Cunts like Mr White will always be at it, except now he's got his accounts. All very tidy. I know there's a tie-up with Jersey and one way or another I will have that bastard."

"Mouthy as I remember," Graham said. He felt cheerful. Life was good.

He would walk back to the Yard in the sunshine. Why not?

To find a cocksure DCI Edwards with the name Anthony Charles Tolliver sweated out of a Peckham street dealer by DS Jones with the assistance of DC Thomas. He'd once told Bob Lumley it was like trying to do a job of work in the midst of a Welsh Male Voice choir in full voice. He suspected Bob hadn't got it but with Bob, he'd been playing dumb for so long, you just never knew.

And of course efficient Edwards had already CRO'd friend Tolliver who'd shown up ten years previously with a hundred grams of black hash and got away with a bender, possession only.

"Not a whisper since?"

"Smart boyo I'd say, till he started the smack."

"Nice work Nye. Worth a look after ten years. Can we cobble together surveillance. Got to be worth thirty-six hours for starters."

"Photographer might be a problem."

"If we were Customs we'd have a full-time video crew on tap. Still, I thought Brian did a course."

"So he did but. Just a couple of days."

"Can't be that hard to teach, how about a spot of on-the-job-training. It's not a fucking computer is it, a camera. We're not aiming at *Paris Match* standards."

"Never read it myself Graham. *Swansea Evening Post* was my limit."

"They won't hold it against you, I've never seen a Newspapers Read on a CV yet. Thank Christ. So can do?"

"Problem but no problem," Edwards said.

"Anything else?"

"For you, through the Governor of Walton, one Ryan T. 134737, wants a personal word with the officer in charge."

"Bit late isn't he, Ryan?"

"Dull as he is, still fancies himself."

"Do we though Nye, do we? You take care of Tolliver. I'll be here Monday morning, eight sharp. Not a move till then, definitely a prospect. As to Ryan, let him wait a while then maybe you'd fancy him yourself."

He'd grab at that, Nye would. Wishful thinking but all power to his elbow.

DCS Curtis walked back to Victoria for his train home. Fifteen minutes to wait. He strolled over to a row of phones in the station. The only vacant hood had no receiver at all. He closed in on a sideways Japanese man and made his call.

This is Gordon Murray. I'm not available at present but if you leave your name and number I'll get back to you.

"It's a very old friend Gordon," Graham shouted.

It took a minute then Gordon said, I'm here.

"One Tolliver, Tony probably, Islington. He's a name I'm visibly interested in."

CHAPTER EIGHTEEN

Phil was stateside for a week. Jack opted for a Saturday stint in the Stammer, Case and Mangledorf building. Out of the sporting nonsense at Sir Nick's one thought had stood out, Steve Burke saying how it was just after a team had scored they had to be most careful defensively. One of a hundred clichés from the evening but with his recent coup still fresh it prompted him to take undisturbed time to see if the price rise had been just a local flash in the pan or something more. His focus would be Hong Kong.

On his desk was a neat pile of translated abstracts from the Beijing Daily and a recent analytical article by a specialist at the School of African and Oriental Studies. He binned it after a glance, the guy making a comparison between the future for Mikhail and that for shrewd old Mr Deng. What a bozo. For one thing Mr Deng was surely close to death whereas Mikhail, though as yet he had no confidential medical analysis, appeared to have years to go. And if both men could be defined as reacting against what had gone before there was surely a world of difference between complacent Mr Brezhnev and manic Mao.

Wading through the abstracts he took out his gizmo, ground some flake and took a snort. The rush got him to his feet and across to the window. The street below was small and fluid. A red double-decker swung into view. Lucky bugger, the driver, no responsibility at all beyond turning up for work and driving his picturesque anachronism. There he was, gone already, exit stage right with the street to himself and not even the bother of stopping at the Request Stop. Not on a Saturday.

A matte-black reflecting window in a chamfered highrise

opposite caught his eye. Some little fucker behind it might be staring at him. It was possible, like some South American dictator with the mirror shades. Didn't they know that polychromatic tinting was now available, made in Hong Kong. Manufactured by Li Chu Boyo in the thousands with the advantage of a fall in the dollar-linked currency and an absence of labour troubles.

Pacing up and down his own window Jack put himself in the shoes of his competitive Boyo. If he was as sharp as Jack took him to be he'd know exports were always politically vulnerable; that if the American trade deficit didn't get dented soon the Administration might get tired of leaning on the Japs and Germans and turn the spotlight on people like himself. And of course he'd be well aware of the medium-term political reality of absorption into mainline China. At one time the prospect would have been a nightmare but then resilient Mr Deng had bounced back from roadsweeper to power behind the Politburo and swept the Gang of Four into the dustbin of history along with their inevitably unpopular mix of righteous zeal and corruption.

In Jack's business the shifts that mattered were not absolute, his Boyo would not suddenly decide to switch all his liquid assets into gold. It was rather a question of whether he, his friends, and assorted Pension Fund managers and corporate finance directors would be thinking of bringing bullion into their portfolio spread or increasing an existing holding from say, five to 10 percent.

Boyo would be well aware that although his cheap domestic currency was helping export sales of his shades, any cash held in same currency was losing its value. If he was a gambling man he might plump for Japanese yen but some genetic instinct, telling him that these too were just bits of paper, might hold him back. And on top of that it did seem that political worries had resurfaced.

He was back at his desk, feet drumming the spongey carpet. But why now? Surely those fears had already surfaced and had their impact back in January when Hu Yao Bang had been given the heave-ho after those ubiquitous students had taken liberties and given the old Long Marchers something to gripe about.

He read on in search of clues.

The brown tinted outside light was darkening. He opened the window. A pink streak behind St Pauls caught his eye. St Pauls, that splendid dome that had somehow survived the blitz. A miracle. He felt a surge in his chest and looked down. A group of midgets holding midget banners was making its way along the street. He could see the words SOUTH AFRICA and SANCTIONS NOW. Not many of them, he'd been right to suspend work on his Bleeding Hearts file though he'd asked Phil for some on-the-ground assessment of the Rev Jackson's likely showing in the Democratic primaries when they finally got underway.

He went back to his desk refreshed. A broader picture of Chinese stop-go re-formed. The Long Marchers for whom hardship was a virtue, for the masses at any rate, had a more dramatic stick with which to beat those like Deng whose only crime was to try and bring China into the second half of the twentieth century: the old hardliners had become the party of Law'n Order. Crime, that's where all your reforms lead, they said like a chorus of old crows.

Having got the picture Jack felt entitled to another modest snort, calculating his gizmo would still be holding another three. He could picture them, the geriatric militants with their bureaucratic perks wagging their fingers, We told you so.

A personal letter to Mr Deng started to take shape after a disciplined snort through Phil's handy gift.

He switched software mode and began.

—Dear Mr Deng, I don't know you and you don't know me but as a distant well-wisher who has at least experienced the same niggling criticisms as your esteemed self

He stopped. Perhaps it was to the Japs one wrote Esteemed. He deleted.

—As someone constantly trying to evaluate and re-evaluate what pass for eternal truths I humbly suggest

He deleted, substituted Fraternally and slowed his typing.

—I would fraternally suggest a ruthless example be made of those anti-social elements trying to take criminal advantage of an unquestionably beneficial process of modernisation and liberalisation. To be truly exemplary I suggest beheading and a subsequent public display of all relevant severed skulls. Yours etc.

A pithy letter, yes indeed. But not the time to be complacent. Crime was not the only problem, this time in the Stop-Go cycle the modernisers were faced with nitty gritty choices, ones that would be visible even to Li Chu Muckraker on his acre by the Mongolian border. As things were Deng's PR boys had dressed up a formula which differentiated between ownership, national; and management, a specialized national task. No problem there, the Technocrats or whoever they were managed things on behalf of the overalls. Nothing wrong with the formula, the formulation of words, only the fucking thing didn't work. It was ridiculous, the Bull had to be taken by the Horn. What did faint heart ever win? Where would Jack Sharp be if he hadn't the stomach for tough decision making? Selling insurance on the phone for a meagre commission is where. It was obvious where the problem lay, the refusal to tackle price reform was matched by a lack of real penalties for managers who made wrong decisions.

He snorted a line and lit a fresh cigarette. Send some budding Chinese managers to the City of London and they'd see what penalties meant. Start with a look at Sims, chief dollar analyst at Taylor, Zoot and MacArthur who'd taken Donald Regan's What's Good For Merrill Lynch Is Good For America at face value, marked the dollar strong for far too long. And what had happened to Sims? Out on his ear with a low-carat handshake. If such penalties did not exist for Liu-Chi Technocrat how could anything develop in China.

Oh yes indeed. He strode to the window. It was dark. Fact registered. He took a new cigarette packet from his pocket, ripped at the cellophane wrapping, rolled it between thumb and forefinger, crushed the crinkle, thrust a cigarette in his mouth, screwed the final spring from the cellophane, took out his Zippo, lit his cigarette, got a mouthful of acrid, pulled a face, and looked down at the cigarette.

He gripped the smouldering filter to extinguish. He walked back to his desk with deliberation.

The letter on screen started at him. Christ, close to the manic bracket. He had overheated and must pay the penalty. The letter was deleted at a stroke and he resolved on a conscientious step-by-step approach. He selected another cigarette and checked the difference between the mottled brown of the tip and the white cylinder of the cigarette proper, lit up and pushed his papers into three piles.

What was this now.

"We can no longer regard Egalitarianism—which is in fact equal pay for unequal work—as an Ethical Principle."

Indeed not. Jack was impressed with this clarity when ethics seemed such an elastic business. He had not used public transport for some time so that the question of whether one should give up one's seat to a pregnant woman or someone with a grotesque limp had not arisen, but where would it stop? Why not someone with a grotesque lisp.

A new slogan emerged from the text, "Some of the People become Rich First" Christ, it was like cajoling children but if that's how they had to do it, so be it.

Oh.

Oh. Came the compromise. Came the qualifications. No sooner had the buggers said what was what than they condemned, "The pursuit of personal interest at the expense of others."

They were joking. Surely. Fudging of the worst sort. Enterprise was enterprise. If Liu-Chi Boyo was having to think all the time about whether his personal advancement was at the expense of others he'd have no time to manage. Without management, disaster for all. Why, he'd be spending 90 percent of his time listening to every sob story going: Liu-Chi Overalls with his backache and widowed mother; Liu-Chi Apprentice asking for a postponement of objectively necessary redundancies on account of his two illegal sisters. Where would that get anyone. If either supplicant had medium-term aspirations of a family TV, nowhere at all.

His reading material was down to cigarette pack thickness, a piece on Shanghai and the country's Enterprise Zones and another on the political realities of Hong Kong. They could wait. His own exemplary diligence rubbed up against a desire for some short-term reward. He rang Alice, endured flat-mate Lisa, and got a date.

At which point he came face to face with the logistics. What lay in the lower chamber of the gizmo didn't amount to much, a decent line at most. He supposed that if he was to stomach the proposed dinner this was probably to the good. He had his car and could therefore drive her to his place where he was well stocked after eating had been completed. Tomorrow they could walk in the woods, healthy certainly, possibly romantic. In the meanwhile as many toots as she could manage.

He stepped out into the corridor and summoned the elevator. Down in the foyer was only whatsisname, the old one of the Security team, wishing him goodnight sir.

He turned left to the Company Car Park undid the chain across its entrance and walked towards the Volvo stood on its own in the corner. His foot scrunched some brittle as he unlocked the door. A shower of rubbery shards dropped down on his trousers in slow motion. The side window was a feeble cobweb. An outrage. It was outrageous, a company car park, in the City, on a Saturday. Inside was a tangle of wires of many colours. The tape deck was still there, buckled, a heap of scrap. The stupid incompetent bastards. Hadn't even managed to steal it. Hadn't even brought any tools, a screwdriver evidently a bit too sophisticated. Whatsisname was going to get a piece of his mind. Security was meant to mean security. Why the hell did the company bother adding to its overheads if the sanctity of a senior employee's motor wasn't inviolate. If he was not working his arse off generating income for the company how would old sods like him in the foyer have a job. Outrageous.

However.

If he went and told the guy just what he thought of him . . . No, besides he would be late for Alice. Fuck it, there was glass crumble clinging to his seat but the window hadn't caved in as such. He brushed the seat with the back of his hand and sat down. If the window held there's only be the slightest of draughts and the heater was good. He would raise the matter in the strongest terms. No question, Monday morning and he'd tell them what's what. Hassle, more hassle just because some envious, resentful little bastard had seen a decent motor.

Perhaps after all there should be no coke for Alice. Reaction unpredictable. Even a whisper of his name as a user, not to be contemplated. Not at all.

CHAPTER NINETEEN

"Come on," Sheila shouted. She was running full speed towards the flat's front steps. Lilly could see Carol and some friend of hers called Dave were at least a hundred yards behind and it was Carol had the keys. She was way too old to be playing I'm The Queen Of The Castle on the steps: The Dirty Rascal, no way.

"Come on Lilly, come on."

Lilly didn't shout back. Her voice was gone, it was a croak like a frogs. It sounded silly because she wasn't a frog but a human being. She'd shouted all the way to Trafalgar Square not sure exactly who Nelson Mandela was except he looked a kind man, handsome too like Jaycinthe's dad with the same moustache only older. That and he'd been locked up for years and years in South Africa even though he wasn't a killer or a thief.

Inside the flat Carol turned on the TV and said they might be on it but Dave said no, not these days, and started looking at Carol's single shelf of books. He turned away when Carol shouted there'd be salad, fish fingers, and did they want chips. Of course they wanted chips and the man Dave started on about what could he do to help till Carol said the best thing he could do was stay where he was.

She'd known Dave years before, a friend of Chris who'd stayed in touch when Chris had fucked off. Now he lived south of the river. When he'd rung about the demonstration she'd said she'd think about it and ring him back. She wasn't sure. Then she'd been round at Marie's, happened to mention it, and Pat had gone about how demonstrations were just a self-indulgence to assuage guilt feelings. She'd got angry then, wound up calling the him faster rationaliser in West London, and phoned Dave to say yes.

The chip fat was bubbling. She put in the cut-up potatoes, washed lettuce and quartered tomatoes.

In the front room Dave and the girls were sat round one end of the table.

"But you can't put your card down now, it's not your turn," he said.

"But it is," said stubborn Sheila.

"Snap," said hoarse Lilly slapping her card down.

"But we weren't ready."

"OK, OK, that was just a try-out. You won that one Lilly. Now let's try it again now we're used to it."

The girls looked at him. The phone rang. It was Marie, would it be all right if Lilly stayed the night. Fred was at a friend's, it was an opportunity for her to have a night with Pat alone.

It was OK, didn't need spelling out. "But you'd better ask Lilly."

Lilly took the phone. Dave said the rules were only there to make the game more interesting. Sheila said she wasn't a cheat.

The girls finished their tea first. Carol told Dave not to hurry. There was still half the flagon of Strongbow she'd found in the fridge. She lit a cigarette and told him what Pat had said.

"Pat Johnson. Oh yes, saw what way the early eighties were going and shifted fast. When the going gets tough the children of the rich see what side their bread's buttered."

Carol said she wasn't his number One fan either but he did have a point.

"What do you want Carol, we're not kids anymore. We know it's not going to change overnight but if we ended doing up nothing, nothing would happen."

The girls were whispering on top of the bunk bed.

"I'm not stupid," Carol said.

"Who said you were stupid? Christ Carol no need to be so prickly."

One of the girls did a loud fart and they were rolling about on the bed. Carol would not get angry. She would not. If she did? It would confirm the Prickly label is what it would do.

"When you've finished whispering you two, how about clearing the table."

Dave said he'd do it, *and* the washing up.

She told the girls they should be thinking of bed and did they want half an hour's TV. They didn't. They were mega-tired they said, had walked Miles and Miles. The TV was on a plastic gilt trolley that Marie'd said even kitsch fans would give it a miss. She said it did the job, just a gentle push and it wheeled into her room. She turned it on with the Volume down and went back to the girls.

You want a story?"

"No we're going to read this one to each other aren't we Lilly."

Dave came into her room when she was rolling a joint, half an eye on the screen. It was ballet, a lovely looking feller crumpled up, not bothering to hide his pain after the rejection.

"So where did you cross swords with Pat Johnson?"

"Pat? At Marie's, that's Lilly's mum. You remember her."

"Of course, Lilly. She must have been three or four, a bit bossy even then. So how is Marie?"

Carol lit the joint, said Marie was fine and glanced back at the TV. The dancer was dead on stage, surrounded by sly, guilty faces.

"I ought to give Pat a ring, remind him of a few home truths," Dave said.

There didn't seem like anything to say to that so she took another toke on the joint and passed it to him. Just about the last of the Leb, it had lasted well.

"So what is going to get those South African bastards to give it up Dave, sitting on everyone, squashing the life out of everyone and everything just to hold on to what they've got. I mean what is?"

"Technically . . ."

"Technically?"

"I mean if there weren't interests tied up, if the west was serious, a simple declaration that their gold reserves were up for sale on the open market would do it. The price would drop through the floor and they're so dependent on the stuff."

"But they're not going to do that are they. Hey, you know what I worked out the other week, it takes four ounces of gold to buy one of coke."

"Still bloody dealing are you Carol?"

What!

He was smoking her spliff as he spoke. What!

"Still at it with the scales and the ten pound notes?"

"You shit, you prissy little shit."

"What? Look I only said . . ."

She was up out of the cushions.

"Get out."

He wasn't moving.

"What are you on now Dave? Sixteen grand, or is it a bit more with London weighting? Got a fucking mortgage yet because if you haven't you're behind the times. Still teaching apprentice boys how society Really works. Ever wondered why Maggie T hasn't given you the chop? Cuts here, cuts there, meanness everywhere but you're all right."

He was up, hurt but fighting.

"Hysteria Carol, save the performance for someone else. I'm Dave, remember, I've seen it all before."

"Seen it? Seen what you prick. Smoked my joint which by the way is getting very pricey and then started moralizing."

"Moralizing!" he shouted, lunging.

"Just get out. Please. Or is it a scene you want, got to have a scene to get your money's worth?"

"Me? I'm making a scene? You should see yourself, hear yourself. Really you should Carol."

"And you've still got my spliff."

He stuck it out towards her. "Take your bloody joint. 'My joint'."

"All I'm asking is that you leave now Dave."

"OK, OK, I am. Bloody right I am."

The door slammed. Carol shook in the doorway of her own room. Warm, salty liquid in the corners of her eyes.

An oblong of paint was coming away from the corridor wall.

She opened the door of the front room carefully. They were asleep on the bunk bed, Sheila on the bottom bed, the side of her face in the pillow. That was her style, her breathing light and steady. Lily was on her back, open and confident. She wished Sheila might just wake up for a moment and give her a hug.

No. Stupid. Selfish.

"Still bloody dealing Carol?" Like she was an anachronism and immoral with it. It had been a good day. It had. Out with people, doing something. Only he'd had to spoil it. Like it was some compulsion. Always judging. She went to turn on the gas fire, stopped and took a thick woolly jacket out of the chest of drawers.

"Still dealing Carol?"

No, not that again.

Arthur stepped briskly into the picture. His pinstripe was immaculate but the shirt collar undone, the tie loose. Probably spent all his time negotiating with tough cookies and getting his own way. Creepy bastard. All that soul-searching she'd done and what was it, just one more move in the price-haggling he'd do as a point of honour, chipping away for an advantage.

And there she'd been actually getting a price, puzzling out the logistics and getting the odd funny look off of Terry. What a mug.

The TV was in one of it's moods. Two green and purple heads bobbed up and down. Her, Mrs Thatcher, live in Moscow with Mr Gorbachev. Weird shakes! On about how charming he was like that was enough to put her right on her guard. Like she was a wallflower and he was creepy Arthur.

And here was Carol Curbishley on her own again. With a telly showing a green yacht on a purple sea. She got up and gave the set a smack. The sea went red. She counted Five. And switched it off.

It wasn't as if she fancied Dave, she never had fancied him. It was just to have an evening with an adult friend who lived somewhere else, saw different things she'd looked forward to but it turned out no, she couldn't have it. And that Jimmy, they'd danced half the night hadn't they. What, was it down to her to say she fancied him, was that how it was these days, she having to make the move just not to be on her own another night.

This was pointless. If she stayed wound up it would mean Dave had had his little victory. No, tomorrow would come around and all that mattered was to put one foot in front of the other. All that mattered was not ending up in the loony bin. Screw the lot of them, she would go to bed with a book, then she'd fall asleep, and then she'd wake up and Lilly and Sheila would be bouncing around. Maybe she'd get breakfast in bed. Maybe the sun would be shining.

CHAPTER TWENTY

Back from the States Phil was at full stretch. No time to register jet-lag. What he'd seen and heard was fresh, he wanted it in his data base immediately. The Japanese Central Bank was leery of buying more dollars on account of its impact on Japanese inflation. An old Tokyo hand he'd taken for a Manhattan lunch told him, They've seen a lot of froth in the Share and Property market and they don't like what they see. Neither did big Paul. Doesn't want to bow out of the Fed knee deep in froth, his friend Harry'd said. It all confirmed the gut feeling Phil had had from the moment the Louvre deal was stitched up, Exchange Rate instability had shifted to interest rate instability.

Mostly, his trip had fine-tuned the vibes. A few times he'd got lost in the face of Harry's reel of football statistics, passes, averages, touchdowns and strikes, but had realized it was only in this ambience one could give due weight to American political realities. For one thing his arithmetic of protectionist sentiment in Congress was on sounder footing. For another he'd got a clearer picture of the Fed-after-big Paul, an inside tip that veteran board member Henry Wallich would not be replaced by a market-knows-best fanatic, a Mr Sprinkel, as had been expected.

Hour after hour he'd sifted and distilled the data, nuances and talk he'd accumulated on the visit. Finally, after sixty hours non-stop and repeated use of his gizmo, he'd re-jigged his programme model, left his personal report to Sir George to be typed, drank ten consecutive cups of Horlicks, shown himself as a normal human being in the lobby, called a taxi and slept for sixteen hours. When he woke he switched on the radio. It said

Stockport County had drawn nil-nil with Swansea City. From this he deduced that the world of a sort was ticking over and that it was a Saturday afternoon at the end of a very long football season. He tried phoning Vicki. At some point in the marathon stint he'd suggested a quick tumble in the office, it would add a bit of spice. She'd said maybe, but she didn't think the main course would be up to much which put her straight into the Definitely Desirable Division. He tried her several times. She moved further up the league till he said reality was reality and scored with Zena, friend of Gina: not as unshockable he knew, but with proportionately less expensive tastes.

Only then did he ring Jack and fix Sunday lunch in Surrey.

Driving Zena home along the Embankment in the morning he sensed some dissatisfaction and gave her a full glance as he slowed down for lights opposite the Battersea Power Station. Her hair was black. Natural? Permed? What the fuck, it was curly. In the night he'd felt it caressing his balls, now it looked like a forlorn helmet in need of a wash. So what the hell was it with her?

"OK Zena? Can be really something, springtime in London."

"What."

"Not bad the spring in London, you can almost feel it."

"Phil . . ."

He said Yes in a hurry, pulling up at an unambiguous red. Zena was going to Say Something. He looked out of the window in readiness. Studiously. Some kind of hippy woman was bobbing up and down on the pavement with two young girls. Dancing maybe. He must tell Jack, there really were still hippies around.

"I've got a window, right. I've got a pair of eyes. Don't tell me what I can see," Zena said.

The hippy woman with the kids crossed the road cautiously. She wore weird trousers and a coat of many colours. It was Simone. It was. He felt like hooting his horn; restrained himself; saw the lights go orange; took another look at Simone's back; understood that Zena was a NoNo even in the short term; and drove off soberly in first.

Jack's suggestion was a walk in the woods followed by lunch at his local. During their walk he talked only of those aspects of nature on display among the trees. He was enthusiastic about bluebells and what he claimed was a squirrel. For some moments Phil was convinced he was on the end of an elaborate joke.

Sat down with the roast beef Jack asked how it had been.

"Full of crack, NYC leastways."

"They do say the East Coast has really perked up in the eighties."

"What? This woolly-head to wiseguy, over. What the fuck are you talking about?"

Jack glanced round. There were families eating, the pub was mega-local and he had a loud, finger-jabbing Phil the other side of the table. He spoke quietly.

"East Coast Phil. Oil crisis. 1970s basket case. Right back in the game now was my understanding. With hi-tech."

"Christ's sake Jack, slow down. Wait till I've had a couple of lines to catch up."

Jack leaned across the table. He was outraged, whispering.

"I haven't had a toot for a week."

"Well you're doing a bloody good imitation."

His laugh was loud. Heads from two family groups turned warily. He was giving a good imitation! This was beyond a joke.

"Give the dessert a miss, eh," he said.

"No way, I want your money's worth."

More heads turned. Jack put it down as a no-win situation and gave the nice young waitress a tentative smile. He admired her cool as she took in her stride Phil's demand for both Creme Caramels. She smiled and said she'd bring the coffee at the same time if that was all right.

Of course it was all right, of course, he said but Phil was off again an absolute classic he'd heard, a classic, from his friend Harry.

Jack tried to slow things down. Who was Harry?

"Oh a sympatico in the Wall Street office."

"What's he like?"

"Very good for an unambiguously American viewpoint," Phil said.

"Which is?"

"What is this Jack, the third degree? If you really want to know, the price-elasticity of blue-chip exports and getting their table confirmed for lunch. Hey, where are those Creme Caramels?"

Two blonde haired kids were staring at them, fascinated. When the nice waitress put the two puddings on Phil's side of the table Jack said, That's wonderful, thank you so much, wonderful.

When she put the coffee down straight after, he said it again.

"An absolute classic Jack. Tall Paul at his best. The Emminger funeral, all Bonn and black hats."

Jack had tasted the coffee. There was always going to be Cona and Cona but this was disgusting. Under no circumstances must Phil taste it. Anything might happen.

"Emminger?" he said and caught the nice waitress's eye. "Two brandies love."

Phil was giving him a sharp look over the table.

"What is it with you Jack, you don't have to come on ESN just to prove how abstemious you've been. I'm your friend, I believe you. Emminger, Kurt, Karl-Heinz, what the hell."

Jack felt weary.

"Who was he?" he said.

"Oh, you really don't know. My apologies. Top man at the Bank of International Settlements. Bundesbank in its heyday, done the lot. Sound man, greatly missed etc. etc."

"I see. His funeral I think you said. By the way, don't drink the coffee, it's terrible."

"Thanks for the tip pal. So of course tall Paul's there, pay his respects and whatnot. And Poehl's there naturally, representing the Bundesbank. They're standing together as the coffin's getting lowered into the ground and just at that very moment, when it comes to timing there's no one to match Paul, he says to Poehl. Are you going to lower your interest rates or are you going to lower your interest rates you tight-arsed little kraut."

In other circumstances it might have been funny, only Phil's laugh was loud. It was crazy.

Outside they stood at the edge of the copse. Jack was not going to say anything. He would not do it. For a moment he'd thought it might have been some kind of protest on Phil's part at it being an eight-quid lunch, but had dismissed it as farfetched. For himself, he would simply not use the Inn for any reason at all for a period of six months.

But what was it with Phil? Had his initial slowness in getting some straightforward point that he, Jack, had made about the East Coast made him competitive in noisy fashion. If so, bloody childish. Which he could be. Hard to say about a friend but he could be.

Or had the crafty bugger had a couple of lines beforehand? No, not the way he'd tucked away his roast beef.

He tamped down a nostril and breathed deeply; held it; then let the air out of the other in a misty line. The sun glowed, two thirds of a circle on the horizon. He would be generous, his friend's behaviour merely showed what two weeks in the United States could do to a person. Equally he would be very sharp if there was any repetition. Just then Phil asked for a toot on the gizmo.

"There's a time and place," he said. "Besides there's nothing quite like deferred gratification."

"What's that out of, *Beginner's Guide to the Protestant Work Ethic*?" Phil said with a stare.

"An Asiatic sex manual."

"Oh sharp. Sharp."

"Don't go infantile Phil."

That stung. He could tell. It showed when, back at home, Phil demanded a couple of lines and taken it meekly when told to do it himself. Just made a meal out of the meekness, how he didn't mind doing the donkey work if he must.

Jack wasn't having it.

"Better a donkey than a mule. Sex at least possible and no sweaty moments at Customs."

Phil surrendered and snorted.

Then, "Woolly head to sharp brain. Me no understand."

Jack grabbed at the rolled note and took a line. "Mule. Figurative sense, *i.e.* he or she who transports cocaine from one sovereign territory to another. Even best laid plans must involve sweat at moment of truth."

Phil shook his head, admitted he was slow and put it down to delayed jet lag. Jack said not to worry.

Phil livened up with a second line. Not only had he sorted out a transatlantic corporate research and analysis structure; not only had he been up to his neck in international currency phenomena; he had also researched more personal areas of interest. His pal Harry had been helpful.

"Into the crack is he?"

"Absolutely not, lines yes, crack no. The latter considered to be nasty, dangerous and vulgar. Good news for you however. What does your average crack trader spend his dough on?"

"Jaguar saloon cars."

"Not bad, but no. Gold chains, gold bracelets, gold watches. You should see them, warm your heart. They know solid worth when they see it, greenbacks, no way. My loss, your gain."

Jack registered it as a new, minor factor in the global demand picture and asked if his friend had learned anything of more practical interest. Phil pulled a face. He said the crucial thing was what appeared to be a decisive change to the good from the consumer's point of view around the end of '82 and into 1983. He'd thought this must be due to the strength of the dollar at the time but Harry'd said no, its cheapness survived its subsequent fall in value. Sure Harry'd said, the tin price collapse had helped but mostly he reckoned they managed the business, processing and transportation and marketing, far more efficiently.

"Who is They?" Jack asked.

"The Colombians Jack, the entrepreneurs of our times who, it seems, are facing a saturated market stateside. Are they whingeing? No, they're facing facts, forming a global strategy, and targeting Europe."

"So a price decrease our neck of the woods."

"That's a bit A to B Jack. I mean there's planning and there's execution."

What was this, Phil teaching his granny to suck eggs, two-weeks-in-the-states-Phil cocky again.

"Don't look like that Jack."

What! What was he looking like. This was intolerable. Was it after all due to him being dependent for supplies since the demise of Ray? If so, doubly intolerable.

"Here this is a great one I heard," Phil started, sensing something not quite right. Jack stayed silent and walked over to the leaded diamond windows. The sun was streaming through, making patterns.

"In-house drug testing, some arseholes in arbitrage over there, McDermott, Schniff and Howard. Big thing the test looks for is quinine, standard cut internationally, shows up as clear as old Stinks' litmus paper."

"This does run to a punchline I take it."

"Tonic Jack, as in G&T, full of quinine. Picture it, Sir George strides forward for the test, a tedious formality but got to show a lead. Red light. Security man doesn't know what to do. End of civilization as we know it."

Jack smiled in spite of himself.

Phil sensed a thaw and got back to the point.

"It's like this sharpie in pork bellies was saying, there's millions of spics in the States and the Colombians don't stand out. They know the scene, close links, same continent. Europe's a different story and as for here, like this guy said, You limies gotta helluva coastguard."

Backgammon went to the third. Jack saw it as a simple case of impossible dice, four consecutive double fives just when he didn't want them. Phil said one made one's own luck and baulked at the rolled-up twenty in his winnings.

"Cash is cash," Jack said.

"Not that again, A heretical sentiment in your market I'd have thought."

"I'll tell you if and when Sir Nick introduces thumbscrews into management structures."

"Sleep deprivation these days."

"That's already in place, we can ride that one."

How right he was, Phil said. "Sixty hours consec I did when I got back."

They laughed together and Jack understood how it had been, a session like that could leave anyone on edge. They settled on joint research into the domestic cocaine market, shook on it.

CHAPTER TWENTY-ONE

"Steve, you're a diamond," Gordon said.

"A real pal."

They were bunched up high in an aisle of the main stand, Wembley Cup Final day. Steve Burke had a guy with them they didn't know only smart Keith thought he might. From somewhere.

"Nothing Gordon. One of the perks. What a harassed Club Chairman needs, something to make up for the worries. Anyway as soon as I knew the Spurs had made sure . . ."

The sun was bright. On the turf an army band was walking patterns, its brass instruments glinting.

"Wembley, there's something special isn't there, the atmosphere, electric."

"And Derek here, have you met my brother, he's chuffed," Gordon said, draping an arm.

"Pleased to meet you, and this is a friend of mine Gordon," Steve Burke said. "Paul Swift, he's always trying to inject some intelligence into TV."

"An uphill task, what," Keith said. "Got you. A few years back, on the box, your own programme. Sunday lunchtime, just when you're thinking about getting up."

Paul Swift grinned. He shook hands, the two big guys and the slim one in tinted glasses who'd recognised him.

"Gordon Murray, Paul." Steve said. "Gordon put a bit of class into music clubs before it got fashionable."

"So who do you fancy Steve?"

They moved down a couple of tiers, the five of them, as

a rush made for the seats. Gordon pulled out a hip flask and offered it to the guy he didn't know. Malt, he said. Keith winced.

"Got to be neutral Gordon. Strictly. When you're a one team man," Steve said. "We were pleased to have made the fourth round."

"You know us Steve, Spurs through and through. Of course I don't have as much time as I'd like but Derek here, never misses a game at the Lane."

"We'll eat them," Derek said.

Steve laughed. The band turned for the last time. Steve waved at someone down the row. Gordon asked the other one, Paul, who he fancied.

"I feel a bit torn. Here's Spurs playing the most exciting football we've seen in this country for a long time, the room given to the blossoming of individual genius, Hoddle, Waddle, always liable to do the unexpected and turn a game. And yet, Coventry, first time in the final. Wonderful for the town too, it's been through a rough patch. Always got to be something in one's heart for the underdog."

Derek tried to say something.

Gordon turned to Steve.

"So what's an underdog," Keith said. Dead and buried. Ever seen a canine funeral parlour."

Gordon was in like a shot. "Yes, me and Keith when we were nippers. Danny Blanchflower, John White. Rarely had a ticket but we never missed a game."

He draped an arm round the guy Paul, and gave him a wink.

They started for their seats, tucked up tight, looking straight down on the centre circle.

"Got to be a few butterflies Steve."

"Any manager worth his salt, he'll sort that out."

"Correct me if I'm wrong Mr Swift but I don't believe I've seen you recently, you know, fronting a programme. Taking a back seat these days."

"Back room, Keith. Yes, trying to provide a perspective, a framework."

"Ever worry about getting out of touch though, that up-front feel, the challenge of the moment."

There was a roar round the stadium. Derek was on his feet. Paul Swift apologized with a frown.

"Sorry. What?"

"The challenge Mr Swift. Comes a point and you've had enough of it."

"Oh I wouldn't say that. I mean in your terms I'd say it was more a change of challenge. It's surely not something we can live without.

A tall man in a double-breasted grey suit was shaking hands along a row of players. He paused with one. The player laughed.

"A great moment for any player Gordon, they'll all tell you that, even the really experienced ones who've seen it all."

"Got to be Steve, got to be."

The tall man in the grey suit was animated with the referee. Whatever he said had the ref showing who was in charge right from the off. It was the way he put the ball on the spot, looked at his watch. The way he looked at the linesmen.

"A game for gentlemen played by hooligans," Paul Swift said. "But like most aphorisms . . ."

The referee blew his whistle.

The opener was a stunner. The equalizer another.

The Spurs second, just on half time looked a killer.

"A key psychological moment but like they say, it's never over till the final whistle."

"Did you see that, Clive Allen."

"I haven't had my eyes shut Derek. You got the rest of the malt."

"More than that, the sheer synthesis of idea and execution, the second Spurs goal."

"All manner of things can happen 'twixt cup and lip," Keith said. "I mean you must have seen that Mr Swift. You think you've got it taped and Wham Bang there's the Hezbollah. Thought they were finished. Definitely. Then one day, BangBangBang."

"I'd be the first to admit I'm partisan Steve but I'd still like to see the Sky Blues make a fight of it. For the sake of the game as a spectacle."

Derek was half listening. The bollox the brothers could talk. If it wasn't Keith winding up this other geezer, it was Gordon sounding like a ponce. Where was his loyalty. Not even out of their seats for the second goal.

The second half didn't look so good but what the hell, until the jammy bastards tucked away an equalizer.

"Sheer grit and teamwork and though I'm loath to see the defeat of skill, I do rather sense some shift in the balance. Confidence? Stamina? I'm not sure, one of those mysteries of cause and effect, but it's almost palpable isn't it."

"That's what Extra Time's all about Gordon, sorts out the men from the boys."

"What Del?" Keith turned in his seat and back again. "My brother says we're just toying with them, winding them up."

"Ah."

"It's all a question of motivation Gordon."

"I think you'll find experience is going to have quite a say in it Steve, motivation, that's just your pride isn't it."

The referee blew his whistle. The teams kicked off. Derek was up shouting.

Soon Paul Swift said, "It does rather look like one-way traffic doesn't it?"

When it was all over they waited in the seats for the Presentation. Derek was sick. He was gutted. Sky Blue scarves rippled everywhere, one end of the stadium cocky. What was the point of it all when so much jam could decide the outcome. And his brothers? A pair of cunts. It was like nothing had happened. He should have got Terrace tickets for him and Terry. That's what he'd been going to do. But oh no, Gordon had insisted. His mate Steve and in the grandstand.

He could hear them now, still poncing on. Words, words, and more words.

"The very shape of Tragedy, the purity of its structure. That oh so confident beginning and then, that it should be Gary, one of those whose heart was really in it, all the way."

"In the end Gordon you can't beat the sheer will to win. Spurs who've won so much in their time."

And they sat there listening to it, lapping it up, just waiting to get their end in to this fucking nonsense.

"I've always said it myself Steve, you know, where we were brought up, it's something you either learn quickly, or you don't learn it at all."

It was too fucking much. Talking bollox. Derek was off. He'd ring Terry and they'd have a proper piss-up. Standing up and moving he could feel Gordon's eyes into his neck, wanting to know, wanting to say something.

"You off Del? Come on, you win some, you lose some. That's the way it goes."

He turned in the aisle. Gordon was half up out of his seat. "It's only a game. Don't take it to heart."

Derek grunted and set off up towards the exit.

* * *

"Wizz? You're joking."

"Old time's sake Tel. As it happens I like it now and then, got an edge to it."

"I can't take the come-downs Derek."

"Suit yourself. Here, what is this stuff, the brewers piss it out do they?"

The bar was full of mirrors, painted pink with twirly stucco in gilt. Derek took a lick of some yellow-white sulphate out of silver paper.

"Go on then Derek, I'll have a lick, just for the memory. Keep my end up.

Terry put his hand over his lower face, licked, pulled a face and took a swig of Keg.

"You've got a point."

"What Tel?"

"Secret plan for the unemployment problem. Have them down the brewery every morning eight o'clock sharp. A couple of free mugs of tea and barrel up the results."

"Tell you what, let's make a move. The Ripened Hop, it's not the Ritz but the pint's drinkable.

Out in the motor they were immediately into a blur of corrugated iron. Terry tried to focus on page 46 that might be running into page 47 of the A-to-Z. It was a jumble of black and white scrawl. Could be anywhere, likely as not the streets didn't run to names.

Derek pulled up at red lights. Reassuring, and A Decent Pint, he'd said.

"Moving north," Derek said, nodding at the globular compass on the dash. "Fancy some music?"

Terry leant back in his seat. Guitar with soft percussion attacked from the left. Then it was everywhere, I WAS BORN AN OUTLAW TOO.

Eagles' shit but it was Derek's motor, if the man wanted to listen to shit he was entitled to listen to shit.

"Good speakers," he said. Good? The fucking bodywork was shaking.

"Club standard," Derek said.

They were back among the corrugated. Terry felt the start of a buzz. In the corrugated in a grey BM. Grey on grey. Alias camouflage. City butterflies went grey. Bats, butterflies, they were all at it cos that's all what alki Mr Smith Biology teacher knew. So they all had to be at it whether they wanted or not. Adaptation in the natural world. Grey charlie, why not? No way, the punters wouldn't wear it. But it's natural. Bollox.

"Bollox," Derek said.

"What?"

"The lot of it."

The Ripened Hop was bright lights stood on its own. Oasis. Maybe camels made themselves look like sand, So what. Some scorpion wouldn't give a fuck, the camel's hoof coming down on its little world. Not going to bother about the colour of what it couldn't even see. Bite the fucker's ankle.

"See how the other half drink," Derek said.

The bar was mahogany. Real stuff Derek said. "Have a chaser with it Tel, my treat. The whizz'll keep you going."

He had a point. Derek had a point. Drink and drink with the wizz and not get legless. No hangover either. The lights must all point outwards. The bar was big, that was all could be told. He couldn't put a face to the voice.

"A Murray," it said.

Derek had brought him, Derek had to know the score.

The scotch was a double with the pint. Voices everywhere, and nook benches.

"A junior but a Murray all the same."

"Get a table eh," Terry said, making the move to the emptiest corner. By the table silent speakers stood either side a pair of record decks. Faces were staring at them? No, just the old speed paranoia.

"It's not just a defeat for eleven players Derek, nor even for their thousands of supporters. That's the pity of it, a defeat for skill in the game."

"Yeah."

"A defeat for skill, for how the game should be played. They may have called Ozzie an Argie one time but he's provided the missing link, made the team purr. I mean you've just got to watch the guy."

"Yeah right Tel."

"You were right, not a bad pint, not bad at all."

"Fuck me you're right, a junior Murray it is."

"A Murray clone."

"What they're that advanced, genetic engineering? I thought smack was about their limit."

He could have said, Sorry Derek I'm busy tonight. A doddle, telephone to telephone. Sorry Del, love to but I'm a bit tied up.

"This one's just second eleven."

"But in the end Derek, you know, if we're ever to be a force in Europe, in the world, that's the way it's got to be. Of course it's never easy to say but they're a team ahead of their time." Christ he was trying. Derek was fucking mad and he was trying.

"That's the sign of a great team Derek, taking defeat in its stride. Not changing, not becoming another bunch of work-horses just because of one defeat. Sticking to its principles."

"Course if you're just a junior you like to think you're still in touch with your roots. Gordon a cut above us is he?" Derek was crazy. He was crazy. Sorry Del I'm a bit tied up tonight.

Derek was up on his feet. "You talking to me cunt!"

Terry was half up. Not with broken glasses. Fucks sake. Leave it out.

CHAPTER TWENTY-TWO

As far as she could see the road ahead was desolate. The fields on either side, treeless and scrubby. She walked on feeling no thirst, knowing it was not possible to feel no thirst.

Ahead was pink flashing in the blank sky. She screwed up her eyes. TEA and BREAKFAST, the neon said. I don't believe you, she said out loud, hearing her own voice and the distant sound of a vehicle. She turned slowly and picked out a flash of headlights in the grey light.

They disappeared and she turned forwards again. The pink had gone and the definition of the road's edges with it. They returned with the headlights showing up strong and tall. She would not be fooled but turned once more and caught the glare glancing sideways into the flat nowhere on the right side of the road before it disappeared. She felt stupid and obstinate. Never again. She would never ever get herself in such a situation again.

Never.

She walked on, watching her feet kick up an explosion of powdery dust with each step. The vehicle engine was louder. TEA TEA TEA flashed up in the old pink. She would put her thumb out, there was nothing to lose, but never again. A window flashed past. The window of a landrover. Arthur was at the wheel. In the passenger seat Dave was sat with a bottle of whiskey on his lap. They were grinning. The sound receded.

TEA TEA.

"You took so long Mum." Sheila was grinning. The room was all shapes and shadows. "Mum."

"Tea. Where's Lilly?"

"Lilly?"

"Yes Lilly and breakfast."

Sheila disappeared. There'd been a dream and she must hold on to it. A road and stars. A road and stars. Stars? In a grey-blue sky. And the promise of tea. She felt the weight of the mug in her hand and Sheila's breathe on her neck.

"And breakfast?" Sheila was holding a tray, steam arose from thick slabs of butter on toast."

"Angels. Is Lilly in hiding, gone shy has she?"

"Mum?"

"Yes?"

"You crazy?"

"Me?" Carol was up, putting her cup down on the tray. "No I'm not. A lot of times I think I should be, but I'm not."

"So you love Lilly more than me?"

There was worry in Sheila's eyes, a frown in the forehead that shouldn't be there and some crazy question. She pulled at Sheila.

"Are you crazy too?"

"Of course not."

"Sorry I just got mixed up. She's not here is she."

"Lilly, of course not," Sheila said

"Last weekend maybe?"

"Yes."

"I've just woken up."

"So you should eat some toast."

The butter was dripping through. Carol placed her fingers right, took a bit, and sucked.

"Great," she said, her mouth a mass of slippery, crisp mush.

She got up as soon as she'd finished the toast and made another cup of tea in the kitchen pleased to be at home and not in that empty place she'd been in her dream.

They went for a swim, came home for lunch and settled down to a Fred Astaire–Ginger Rogers film on TV, Sheila's head on her mum's shoulders. It was halfway through when Ginger'd seen this sailor boy is a dancer and a half, that the phone rang.

"It's Sunday afternoon Daniel."

"I'll never get this mix in the studio again. Jose's between flights. Phil's on call but it's not just Jose, you know who I've got here?"

"Don't tell me, Fred Astaire."

"Don't be sarky darling, he's dead.

"OK, it's Frank Sinatra and don't tell me he's dead."

"If only you could see me Carol, I'm down on my knees honest, and on the other side of the doors I've got Carlos. Incredible. I keep having to headbutt the wall to know it's real. This guy makes seven-eight and nine-eight rhythms look as easy as . . ."

"One, two, three."

"Come on love, a one-off. If you can."

"Maybe Daniel and I'm not playing hard to get, if I can."

"Got you Carol. I mean stretch it a bit and I'll . . ." She put the phone down, something naff about to be said. Fred in the sailor gear was back on board holding off questions from pokey crew members. Sheila's forehead was corrugated. Carol didn't know. Daniel was an old customer, local. It would be, could be a nice quick turnover but it was Sunday afternoon and here was Fred again transformed into a diffident guy dancing on air. Sheila was impressed, it was that obvious. It wouldn't be tap-dancing, but if Daniel wasn't bullshitting it sounded like it might be some session and she could take Sheila and she'd love that too. OK, she'd phone Terry and if it could be done without drama or running about she'd do it when the film ended.

He sounded funny when she rang, like he had a bad cold and was speaking slowly. Laconic with it. Said he wasn't in the best of shape but if she fancied it, come over anyway. He'd be making money out of it: she'd be making money out of it, not to be sneezed at. She said forty minutes. It was too good not to see the end. Fred and Ginger were eyeing each other up. Neither was going to be bowled over till the final number.

"Are they really old now?"

"The film must be fifty years old."

"Fifty years. Fifty. That's 1937. Isn't it, 1937. When were you born Mum?"

"Oh just around then it would have been. Had good dancers in those days."

"Not bad. No you weren't. You weren't." Carol said maybe it had been a bit later, a little bit but Sheila put a stop to it, told her straight she was thirty-five and had therefore been born. Had therefore been born, eyes closed and counting her fingers, been born in 1952.

She liked the idea of a walk. Out in the sun there were people sat on house steps and the sound of Freddie McGregor.

Terry's street was quieter. Four-storey houses in yellow-black brick. Sheila was telling her about the Sahara. She had Geography in the morning. "You can go for miles and miles and miles, well a camel is best."

Carol listened and checked for occupied cars and vans with reflector glass windows. Nothing. She rang the third floor bell and said camels were wonderful. "It's like they've got mini-fridges in their humps."

It was a long climb and she didn't see him properly in the doorway but in the room, what a mess. What a mess he was and she was angry with herself, then angry with him. He could have said. He should have said. Sheila was staring at him.

"Poor Terry had a terrible smash on his bike," Carol said.

Terry tried a grin out of a swollen multi-coloured face.

"There I was, cycling along, not a care in the world, minding my own business and out of nowhere. Bam."

"Oh I see, it was a stupid driver."

Terry made his way to the big green armchair. He walked like an old man.

"Stupid? I should say so, needs a pair of glasses, a strong pair. Sorry, it'll have to be self-service today but if you fancy tea."

"Where's your bike?" Sheila asked. She was frowning.

"My bike? Never see that again. In a scrap yard. I've heard they'll give me fifty pence for it. Fifty pence, I ask you. A racer it was."

Carol's anger eased, he was doing his best and it had to be very painful. But he'd been beaten up. That was the reality, some people had beaten him up.

"You put the kettle on Sheila," she said, pointing to the kitchen door.

"We even run to a chocolate cake in the cake tin, or are you off chocolate these days."

"And then we'll have to be nurses, real nurses."

Sheila turned in the doorway. "I'll put lots of sugar in your tea, that's what you need after an accident."

Carol heard clattering and a tap running.

"What the hell happened?"

Terry gave her a small packet in an envelope.

"Sort out the money next week. Stop worrying, it wasn't bizz."

He couldn't see too well but tried to look at her closely.

"It wasn't I tell you. This is what comes of socializing with old mates in their grass roots."

"You do need a nurse. My God, what did they do to you?"

"It's what they call a leisure activity down there."

Sheila's face came round the doorway. "How are you going to eat any cake?"

"Me? I'm sticking to a cup of tea, doctor's orders."

Carol went into the kitchen. The cake was on a plate. "Maniac drivers, that's why you've got to be so careful crossing the road Sheila. Now what nurses need in this situation are some ice cubes."

There were some in the fridge. She took out the tray and a carton of milk and then poured cold water on the back of the tray of cubes and pushed them out into a bowl.

Sheila ate little cake. The ice cubes on the man's face were more interesting. His eyes especially. They were in many colours, black, blue, green, and yellow. He begged for a cup of tea. His mouth was a big blister and it was hard for him, getting it round the rim of the cup. She'd had a blister once but it had only been on her arm and smaller. He must be brave though because he kept making jokes: it was psychedelic face he had; he was thinking of getting a tricycle; it only hurt when he laughed; life was not so sweet when he was a bicycle seat.

A buzzer sounded in the room. Terry lifted the cubes off his face and put them back in the bowl. He got up slowly and spoke slowly to a sort of telephone on the wall.

He undid the door latch. He was frowning. "Friends and relations of old friends," he said.

"We'll be off in a minute Terry. I'll come back tomorrow morning Sheila when you're in school. The ice has to be applied regularly."

The man who came in was big. No fat. He looked irritated. Carol saw Terry nervous and fragile. The man tried to soften his face.

"You've got company Terry. Sorry to disturb. Well, well."

"Yes, an old friend who very kindly dropped in when she heard about my bicycle accident."

The man frowned.

"We're just off," Carol said. She hoped it wasn't more trouble for Terry but she just wanted out. Out before the uptight man put his foot right through the bicycle story.

"I'll drop by tomorrow then, see how you are."

"Yeah right. That's great. Yeah, thanks."

"So tell me what happened Tel. Take your time but let's get it right," she heard as she hurried Sheila out of the door.

"An uncle," she said to her on the stairs. "There'll be things like insurance to talk about."

On the street she was angry only with herself. She was crazy, completely mad to have anything to do with all this. To be there with Sheila and that man coming in who'd give anyone the shivers. Terry was all right but what kind of a world was he in; yes and here and now, she was out on the street, with a parcel.

"Do you think your friend likes his uncle?"

Oh God. It would have to be good, the music in the studio. If Daniel had been bullshitting she would never, ever talk to him again.

CHAPTER TWENTY-THREE

What's the point? What's the fucking point? I've told Del enough times, Why not come and have a Perrier Water with me and then maybe after we can go and live it up a bit. How many times? But does he listen. And Keith's not much better. Maybe the geezer was a berk I don't know, but what was Keith's game, riling him just for the sake of it. I could have got tickets myself and maybe that's what I should have done only Steve rang first. Del, he'd been going on about Terrace tickets like that's where his horizons are, like that's as far as he'll ever aspire. It should have warned me, and then of all the places on this fucking earth it has to be the Ripened Hop. And does he take Billy or Mo with. No, naked into the lion's den with that Terry. I said to him in the stand, I'm as upset as you are Derek. And I fucking was too. During that Extra Time I could see them wilting like Extra Time was a hassle. Now when we had a team, and I mean A Team, you think a player like Bobby Smith would have given up the ghost? He'd sooner have died Bobby would than not have fought for every ball. It did upset me but the way Derek was performing you'd think it was only him had any feelings.

I blame myself. I should have spoke to him there and then, seen he was in the mood to do something stupid. What I should have said is we'd made a date for Cup Final night weeks ago.

But he's a grown man for fucks sake. That's what I was telling myself when he just upped and left with a cob on.

I'm talking bollox, I know that, just sometimes you've got to get it off your chest. You'd just blow up inside otherwise. But the fact is, and this is a time to stick to the facts, that Mr Mickey

White has overstepped the mark just once too often. It was friends of his. No doubt about it. And the thing is, I'd put him right out of my mind. Despite all the liberties he's taken over the years I'd just stopped thinking about him. There's a lot more important things on my plate than an old tosser like Mickey White. But there comes a point, even when you're talking about a museum piece, that enough is enough. When you've got to act decisively, stand up for yourself and make an example. Because if you don't, well the word gets around slowly but surely that you can be taken for a cunt. And he was having a pop at me, Mickey was. No question.

Now I am Not flash. I detest it. I don't flaunt what I've got but he knows, Mickey does, and whatever else I think about him he's still as sharp as a rat, that I've done a lot better than him. A lot better, and that really gives him the hump. Plain, old-fashioned envy. Except of course he's got to dress it up. Can't stand looking at it straight in the face. So he makes out his dough's cleaner than mine. Can you credit it. He's up to all sorts and then comes on like he's Mr Clean.

I've called Keith in though he was well out of order the other day. I know because Steve Burke was giving me funny looks every time Keith was coming it. Fuck knows what the other face thought about it. I mean what's the point of needling someone when there's no need for it. I don't do it. No, not even when I've every reason to. Take yesterday. A Sunday. And I've got a nice day worked out with Sarah. A drive in the country, a good lunch and then a proper session when we get back. So what happens? I get Derek phoning me in the morning. Perhaps I should have phoned her there and then, postponed, but you can't let people down can you, I knew she was looking forward to it. So I picked her up and then had to drive to his; he's got his own drum, Baker Street, says it's central and handy. I left her in the motor. She didn't whinge did she, not like some people would. I left with a few hundred pages of Sunday paper and that was that, she didn't create.

I have to say that when I saw him I did get a bit emotional. Fucks sake, he's my brother. There was a moment, just a moment, seeing him like that, I said to myself, OK Mickey you cunt, we can come in mob-handed as well. But it was only for a moment. I mean he'd have loved that wouldn't he, me coming down to his level and on his manor. But I got a grip of myself and when I spoke to Derek it was more in sorrow than anger. I told him to use ice and whatnot, and not to show himself till he was decent. I said I'd make sure he got some supplies, videos, food and whatever else he needed. I also said that however much it stretched us, we'd take over his appointments. Derek has a few people working for him, doing the running around with the dollop, Billy and Mo minding, but they all need managing which takes time. And that's another thing. If Derek's got to be stupid enough to go to the Ripened Hop of all fucking places why doesn't he take Billy and Mo with instead of this fucking Terry.

So we did make it to the country, me and Sarah. East of where I live. At least we got a feel, a smell of the place that I've loved since I was a nipper. Some people call it flat, boring, and muddy but I say you can't beat it. That special salty smell. And it gives you an appetite. We had a late lunch but Derek must have been at the back of my mind because Sarah noticed it. I clocked her noticing it. She didn't start asking questions mind. That's the kind of girl she is. But she noticed. Some remark she made while I was toying with a brûlée dessert.

And that wasn't even the end of it. I knew I had a duty. I dropped Sarah at my place and excused myself for a couple of hours knowing I'm definitely going to be in the mood, those black gloves are a treat, but also knowing that she might not be after I got back from all that running around. So I have to admit I wasn't exactly cheerful when I got to this Terry's gaff which is over West.

But then, did I blow my top at the guy? Did I? Christ knows I had enough reasons. OK I've got nothing against the feller. No complaints there. It's always possible that Del has covered for him when he's been short. It would be mistaken on Del's part and it's possible but as far as I know, the guy has been a perfect business representative. But what the fuck is he doing on a mad jaunt, aiding and abetting my young brother.

And what's the scene when I get into his drum, this fucking lunatic who's gone along with the maddest pub crawl in history? There's a woman there, a woman with a kid. I could hardly credit it. Of course he wasn't as badly marked as Del but no sight for a kid, a young girl. So what's she playing at, the mother? A bit of business I shouldn't wonder. A Sunday. God give me strength. And then to cap it all, she'd scarpered by then a bit sharpish, just as I'm ready to leave after I've tried to get some solid facts off of him, he says to me that though he knows it isn't the time or place, he really needs to have a discussion about prices.

It all fell into place then but I still didn't lose my rag. He's giving it like he didn't really want to go out that night but Del's phoned after the Final and how he's always believed friendship is an important part of a business relationship. Real friendship he said. How he tried to dissuade Derek but when it came to it . . .

So why's he gone along with it if that's how it was. Because he's such a weak character. Or is he doing it so he can start hustling Derek over prices when he knows that Del is in a bit of a state. Yes, he came right out with it. But did I throw a wobbler? That's the point I'm making, I was well entitled but I didn't. All I said was I'd come back to him. That's the point, I didn't aggravate the guy though I had plenty of reason whereas Keith, he had no reason at all, just did it for the sake of it. Nevertheless I've called him in on this one. I can't handle everything on my own and Keith, maybe it's because he's got kids now, Keith, if you ignore all his wisecracks, can be spot-on when there's a project that requires planning, especially if it appeals to his bloody mad sense of humour.

* * *

"Sounds like leading with the chin Billy Mac style but at least Billy had the punters paying for the entertainment," Keith said.

"He's your kid brother Keith."

"OK. I'm just saying I could think of better places for Cup Final blues. Sky blues. When you wind up seeing stars."

Gordon took it. He had to take it *and* stick to the point.

"I couldn't agree more," he said. "And I made the point in no uncertain terms. I did. But the fact remains that it happened."

"Mickey was there was he? Personally ? Old villains never die but they could at least fade away gracefully."

Gordon chuckled. He liked it.

"Mickey was in his nook. With George Limanski, that's what it sounds like."

"Didn't play a kicking, punching, no-holes barred role himself?"

"It's hardly the point. It was the Ripened Hop and Mickey was there."

"Call it a conspiracy rap."

"What," Gordon said. He was frowning.

"Definition of. A nod and a wink. OK I take your point."

"I'm glad about that Keith, very glad. Because it's obvious isn't it. He was having a pop at us, you and me, via a Derek who showed a terrible lack of judgement that night."

Keith came off the wall by the pool table. He thought he would ask again. Fuck the striped balls, fuck the spots, he wanted it as it was.

"But was he there? At the relevant moment?"

Gordon was up out of his chair. "You want a fucking photo or something. Is that it?"

Keith grinned and stepped back. "Yes so one battered brother and one Mickey White, a prick well past his time. So?"

"So? So help me God."

Keith moved fast round the pool table seeing his brother upset beyond his years. Shouting in fact.

"He was having a pop at us, you get it. That includes you Keith."

"You want to turn that transistor up a bit?"

That stopped him. Gordon even said sorry as he turned to the radio.

"Radio Three please."

Gordon turned the dial with exaggerated care. The music was sedate.

"All right now? Happy are you?"

"You could do worse Gordon. So some drinkers, and you know how that stuff can addle the brain, attacked for whatever reason . . ."

"Keith, you're not fucking listening are you."

"You're whingeing, I'm listening."

"Are we doing all right Keith, or are we doing all right? I take it you did take a look at the projection of our first quarterly dividend off the new face."

"OK, what's it to be, a full-frontal assault," Keith said moving back towards the desk.

"They'll get you in trouble one day Keith."

"What?" said Keith. He looked innocent. He looked pleased.

"The wisecracks. You could have left off that geezer even if he was a wollie."

"What geezer?" Keith's innocence was confident. He sat down right next to his brother.

"The geezer who for some reason of your own you were winding up at the match. Steve noticed."

It took a while for Keith to understand.

"Fucks sake Gordon, he loved it. Can't you see that, they love it."

"It was your own brother got it. You haven't seen him, I have."

Keith retreated to the pool table. He rolled a spot down the middle hole off the cush. It clattered away.

"And I take a very dim view of it because it wasn't an isolated event. Mickey mouthing off about us. He has been you know, it can't continue."

"So we go in mob-handed."

"Fuck off. Mob-handed? No, I was thinking of the jock plus. I saw him the other week you know, when I was up north."

"Yes, he's tasty, I'll give him that. Expensive though."

"Expensive? Do me a favour Keith, take a look at that quarterly dividend projection, maybe you missed a nought or two."

"No I had a good look, very impressive. But you know what it made me think, what the fuck are we playing around with smack for. I mean do we need it?"

"Keith there's a time and a place. You've just raised a very

large strategic question there but right now we have an immediate situation to be dealt with."

"You'll have to give the jock something to work on."

"I had Geoff Christian in mind. Remember him, the one we
saved for a rainy day."

"I do believe the penny's dropped bruv. Tricky mind."

"That's what we pay the jock for."

"All right is he, in good shape?"

"That was my impression and he'd take it I reckon. He's
settled up there but he wouldn't mind a long holiday in the sun.
And he's got his old age to think of, same as the rest of us."

"So the angle is Mickey's daughter."

"Why not."

"Sure, why not, it's just not enough."

"So?"

"What's the budget?"

"Unlimited. Up to a hundred G say. What do you think
Mickey's worth?"

"Not a lot," Keith said fetching a few balls out of the slot. He
let them go down the table. "Tell you the truth I don't think the
old tosser's worth a carrot but if it's a job, let's do it right."

"Yeah?"

"What do you mean, Yeah? The jock sure, plus beefing up
the angle. The daughter OK but let's have this Christian owing
Mickey a good lump."

"What's Let's Have Him Owing supposed to mean?"

"Start a rumour for one. Then there's the old boy. Reilly. Get
him a sample of Christian's handwriting, if he's up to writing,
and the old boy can ramp up an account book. Not obvious but
clear enough."

"Yeah, we could manage that."

"Plus access to some premises Mickey can be tied to. The old
cunt's probably still got lock-ups."

"Yeah. I like it."

"Course you could have a witness. Mickey on the yard in
Brixton, Mr White Told Me In Confidence. Always messy though
and we'd have to have something to offer."

"OK, leave that bit to me."

"That bit? What about the rest?"

"It's a job Keith, affects all our futures."

Keith went to the cupboard and poured a small scotch.

"Make it a bit dramatic too I would Gordon, for the judge and jury."

"That's not the jock's style."

"His style? Just tell him what you want and he'll say, A bit dramatic and that. Aye no bother, five grand on top but no bother. That's what he'll say."

CHAPTER TWENTY-FOUR

And still no holiday. June had come and gone with a chunk of July.

"Can't flog a dead analyst," Jack had said to Hudson, a nickel specialist, and got a speech on stamina delivered with a wolfish grin.

As it was he'd tried to keep a tighter grip on volume of consumption and started haggling over holidays with Sanders, the one with the sinecure in Personnel. It didn't help when he found out why Hudson had been so cocky: two separate whispers of a short to mid-term bottleneck on the supply side of his metal. Then that was what his followers, his readers, wanted from him. The same bastards who'd be demanding his head if he called it wrong, wanted him bullish on bullion. They waved random indices of inflationary tendencies; made references to the Gulf War; a potential overspill into oil supplies; and surely he'd heard the rumblings of labour discontent on the Rand.

Stranded indefinitely in London he had tried to put his ear to the ground on matters of more personal interest after his most recent ounce from Phil had shown a twenty-pound discount. But they had cost him, his market investigations. Several phone calls to Julia for a start. Interminable they'd been and involved some elliptical abuse aimed in his direction before he even got a date. She liked him, she said finally even though this liking was in spite of her better judgement and his many faults and false gods. He'd said that personally he was a committed agnostic, but it still took another twenty minutes for the date to be firmed up.

If it hadn't been his idea in the first place; if Phil hadn't been so enthusiastic; and if, most of all, there had been anyone else to turn to, he wouldn't have endured it. It hadn't ended with the phone calls either. On the two dates that followed the criticism of his lifestyle encompassed the practical, Watch out for the coronary; the psychological, Aren't you just playing boys' games; the metaphysical, What will you be able to say you've achieved on your deathbed; and the ethical, Aren't you some kind of parasite.

They hadn't come cheap either. One had believed that the main expense when it came to eating was meat, that somehow one had to pay more for what was arguably unsound, ecologically speaking. Or if not that, because at least one could eat the stuff safe in the knowledge that the cows or sheep had done the farting for one, in advance. Not a bit of it, it turned out when the bills dropped on his side of the table at Julia's favourite vegetarian restaurants.

It also transpired that personally, she didn't even touch the stuff, called it a steel drug, but after several of these outings he'd made it to a party given by friends of hers and seen a different crowd. He'd laid out several lines on a small mirror in a bedroom. A tall man with a lopsided grin and smart casuals approached him as they left the bedroom. The tall man made a meal of it but got round to asking prices. Jack said he'd just laid out some lines, was glad they'd gone down well.

"Up," the tall man said. "So come on, what's the big deal."

"No way me."

"A gram?"

"What do you pay?"

Seventy-five quid it transpired. Not surprising the guy was asking around. Jack took his phone number.

Later, when he'd left with Julia he'd agreed that there were times when his view of things was a bit short term after she'd made some remark about rainforests and spaceship earth. Later still, after they'd made it, he'd made a crack about wealth creation, something about how little seeds could grow.

"Not me darling, I use the cap," she'd said laughing.

Then it was back to the grindstone. A fax from a pal in Johannesburg gave him what he'd expected. "Strike looms. But durable?" it said. Even less of a scratch on over-supply than it might have been. The sheer volume of recent Russian sales in lieu of a falling oil price and the rapid growth of mining outside the Russian–South African axis, had pegged his course. He might allow for one or two little surges given the Gulf and the obvious overpricing of equities but was sure that, as in May, they would not last.

He also wondered what the tall man's interest might be worth. It was good he had the guy's number on an I'll-call-you basis, but what did an ounce count for even if the charlie price was holding up well at the retail end?

* * *

It was Phil's car but the cobbles looked seriously greasy. In a roundabout way Jack tried to make the point. Phil mercifully slowed down at a vicious kink in the road and was positively careful driving into his own garage. In the flat he produced a couple of cans of lager covered in heavy German lettering.

"A line too please Phil. You don't know just how abstemious I've been."

"Oh yes I do."

"Sobering."

"Not half as much as a portfolio manager taking a close look at the price-earnings ratio of just about any bit of equity stock you'd care to mention and wondering what the hell happened to that Japanese wall of money that was supposed to pour in after Mrs T's return to Number Ten," Phil said.

He was dissatisfied with the composition of the lines he'd made. He pushed the powder back into a small pyramid.

"Rather. And the word is one or two big players stateside have pulled right out of equities. And I mean right out, not even a minimal stake in blue chip."

"Blue chip? What's blue chip these days when you've got Browning our electronics specialist telling me IBM's stuck up a mainframe cul-de-sac. Got to be something frothy when you get a billion odd wiped out on the strength of one bloody opinion poll. Still at work?"

"Too bloody true," Jack said. He thought Phil's thoroughness overdone and got up. A fat newspaper sat in the armchair by the window. From deep inside he pulled out a section with a cover that showed palefaces on camels. Could that rate as a holiday? He had something to say on the subject. No he didn't; any diversion and that line might never get up his nose. The supplement was titled travel. Was there a difference? Did a person have to travel in order to have a holiday? He looked carefully at the faces for signs of batteries being recharged. Bland faces, hard to say. Below the foot of newsprint was a boxed inset, the price list. Three grand. He reached for his lager. It wasn't there. He stood up. From behind Phil looked like an anteater, the tube from his nose roving the mirror surface. He sat down on the other side of the table. He touched his can. There was a sparkle in Phil's eyes. He reached over and grabbed the rolled note.

"So Jack, we left you in the middle of a vegetable ragout while on duty."

"An aubergine and okhra sog. With brown rice."

"All in a good cause," Phil said. "Results?"

Jack was not going to be rushed.

Phil drummed the table.

"Wanted an ounce even at Two Seven Zero above your price," Jack said, gripping his can tighter. Phil bent forward resting his fingertips on the bridge of his nose.

"Did he indeed. A bit sordid perhaps but from small beginnings. You want to go through with it?"

"Is it a problem?"

"Not from my point of view. Unless you've been exceptionally abstemious I was reckoning on seeing my man in the very near future," Phil said. "Anyway you think you've had a hard time. Gina doesn't like a bit of rough, she is one. And all I got out of it was to meet Max, and Max was just my man's old, pre-discount prices. Wouldn't budge. Would not fucking budge despite some powder room repartee on Colombian strategy and a stern lecture on the realities of competition."

"We live on an island, freight and insurance costs so to speak, they're bound to be high."

"As I believe I've pointed out once or twice. Hey Jack, news time." He waved the remote control in the direction of the TV. "And still two lines remaining. Full marks for self-control, what."

—The body was found in a lock up garage in this quiet North London street.

On screen policemen and dogs shuffled around parked Transit vans. Then a long lumpy plastic sack was carried out of the garage.

—Police efforts to identify the victim have been hampered by the fact that the hands had been severed at the wrists and have not yet been found. Detective Chief Superintendent Bob Lumley of the Serious Crime Squad called it an especially brutal murder that showed all the hallmarks of a gangland killing.

"Bit crude."

"Caught with his hands in the till."

"North London's what I thought I heard Jack. I think you're talking Riyadh South."

—This is the fourth day of clashes between police and students.

Crew-cut oriental faces wobbled over the screen.

—A change of mood with bystanders cheering, and in some cases joining the students

"Time for the Koreans to let go a bit. The economy's strong enough. Always got to know when to let go a bit."

"Still value for money though, the Koreans. A 250 percent rise in foreign investment this year they've had," Jack said. He saw no reason to be fanatical about self control and snorted his waiting line.

—Five men were sentenced for their part in what the prosecution called a large and ruthless network of cocaine smugglers and dealers

Phil sniffed. Jack said Oh.

—Aged 47 from Liverpool to Twelve years. Brian Vaughan, also of Liverpool to Nine years, Ray Stewart of Cricklewood North West London to six years.

"Your man, ex-man rather."

"Christ, six years."

"Of eating porridge. Good for the ulcer."

"Thought it was a bit more sophisticated these days, Video and ping-pong."

"Tea and Valium I heard," Phil said.

CHAPTER TWENTY-FIVE

Carol stood on the pavement by the school playground her eyes on Sheila in a red top and Lilly in white. There was a sudden move into the building and they were gone, not a kid left on the yard. She thought about buying a newspaper. A girl sprinted across the yard, a schoolbag up and down on her shoulders.

Carol turned away. She couldn't be bothered with a paper. There was a pile of ironing in the house. She turned the corner for home and gave way across the pavement. The man said Hiya. He was carrying a bulky canvas bag. A chippie he'd said during numbers on the dance floor. The blood rose in her face but she never did blush.

"Jimmy."

"The very same man." Five years younger he looked, on the spot.

"I knew we'd meet see. I just knew it or is that romantic? Childish? But I did know. I'm working just down there."

"Boyish."

"What?"

"Not childish, boyish."

He laughed and put his bag down on the low brick wall. "Must be your effect on me."

She wanted more. "What?"

"Well you are pretty stunning. On the dance floor. Off the dance floor. But you know that." A rush of pleasure went off in her stomach and her head felt light. "So you're free with the compliments," she said.

He said No, he wasn't, still boyish but something else.

Solemn. He'd gone silent. Too solemn, his hand still gripping the handle of his bag. It couldn't go on like this so she said she lived just up the road at number Thirty-One. He was smiling again, on his toes in trainers.

"It was odds-on you were local though you never said. Yes and you are stunning see, Carol Paranoid."

"I am not paranoid."

"My mistake. I'm good at those. Except when I'm working."

"I'm glad to hear it, if there's one thing I hate . . ."

"It's a window that doesn't shut properly."

"It was doors I had in mind."

"If that wasn't a joke which passed me by, I'll fix it."

"The problem of a previous flat," she said. It was getting ridiculous, still out on the corner like they were. "Tell you what I'll make you lunch, say half one. You do have lunch do you?"

"Fucking right."

"This street, Thirty-One, Ground Floor."

Back home she was glowing inside. So it was her who'd had to take the initiative but he wasn't a creep. She felt sure of that, no uptight or conniving. She put an old favourite into the tape deck, Eric Dolphy and Booker Little playing live someplace. She sorted the clean, wrinkled clothes in to two piles, the smaller things, Sheila's stuff and her own knickers in one and the other her own clothes.

And he was coming round to eat. No plan of action but she'd know and at the very least unless it was really shitty, he'd know too. One way or the other. And if it didn't work out it wouldn't be because she was paranoid because she wasn't and unless he was stupid he'd see that. Just as long as he wasn't. She dampened Sheila's best ordinary dress with her flower-watering spray. The white cotton and its two black vees went smooth under the iron. She folded it and picked up the dark green school skirt that was nothing but tricky pleats.

The first pile was still bulky, the clothes Sheila got through in a week. Sod Arthur too. Some weird message Marie'd passed on when they'd picked up Lilly for school, how he'd love to take her to a recital of chamber music, a wonderful trio. She folded the dress of many pleats and laid out a pair of jeans. No way she was going to get three off Terry with all the worry, not on the strength of some improvised code that Marie could have got wrong. There was some low-key clapping. The tape ended with a loud click.

When she'd finished both piles of clothes she felt a moment's satisfaction. The fridge was empty. Lunch wasn't going to make itself. OK, she was going to have to shop anyway, Jimmy or no Jimmy.

Passing the row of phone boxes on the way to the shops she thought to phone Terry. Even if it wasn't three it would be something, she should make a date for the next day. A drag having to meet Arthur twice but the new meeting-place was local, Queensway. She had a phone card but there was a queue at the green-striped box too.

On the way back there was someone else inside. Outside, an Italian-looking guy in a suit. Muttering. Not a nutter from the look of him, seriously impatient. It was a woman inside, she was talking and laughing.

The man gave her a mean look and turned to try it on the woman. He caught her eye. Fatal to the woman.

Carol edged her shopping bag forward. His unit display was in the Nineties. Worth waiting? Not worth waiting?

The guy was tap-dancing. He was shaking his head. Then started to talk. She shuddered and turned her head at the squeal of brakes. Between the bonnet of the red car and the rear-bumper of the white was a matter of inches. The guy in the red car had his head out of the window shouting, giving the finger.

She turned her head back. Fifty-six units showed.

Fifty-five.

Fifty-four. Had to be abroad. Had to be. The guy was speaking fast, finger-jabbing the air. Till he shook the phone. Shook his head.

Carol was thinking, Please don't smash the phone. However pissed off. On the pavement he broke the brittle plastic in half and tossed the pieces towards the gutter. She made a date with Terry and with fifteen units left phoned Pauline in Wales and talked about how it would be, having a holiday there.

When she got home it was twenty to two and Jimmy was sat out on the stairs.

He was a good-looking feller all right but there were plenty of those. Pat, he was, but she never fancied him even before he'd been going steady with Marie. With Jimmy, he was so relaxed, that's what made her heart stand on end, just sitting there with a roll-up and a newspaper.

"Confidence has its own rewards," he said. "Or maybe it's self-confidence which could, so Mr Hurst said, easily become cockiness."

All that said before he'd even stood up and offered to take the carrier bags.

"Cocky were you?"

"Not enough, obviously."

She opened the front door. He picked up the bags and followed her through the plain red door to her own flat.

"Housing Association style the door, 1976 to '82 period," he said, putting the bags down in the kitchen.

"So who was Mr Hurst?"

"English teacher, my last year in school."

"I can see how he reached his conclusion," she said. She was sorting out what was for lunch, what the fridge and what the cupboards. "It would have to be English. Mavericks. Or was he an alki?"

He gave her his solemn look. "No, don't be cynical. You need a hand."

She thought of saying something to this Cynical but said No, she didn't need a hand and what job was he doing.

"Fitted bookshelves for some cunt of a TV producer. Whoops. Sorry."

"Sorry!" she said, poking his ribs. "I've got cheese, a couple of roll-mops, tomato and lettuce." And he was still dancing. In and out, round and about on his trainers. "Don't you ever stop. Want some music to go with it?"

"The chippie's shuffle. How about an onion on the side."

How about you on the side she'd wanted to say then, thinking of being fucked or fucking him there and then. Instead they swapped phone numbers. He made some remark about how that made it a whirlwind romance. When he left, they kissed in the doorway.

Which made the equations of the next few weeks more complicated. To go on holiday to Pauline's and just leave it as it was? They seemed both to have decided to take it slowly which might mean they both felt it was going to be serious, or at least that they were old enough to know that making love could really change things if it was good. But going on holiday now? That might be pushing the slowness too far into a coolness that could go cold. Perhaps he could come too, for a bit of the time at least, assuming he could take the time off, assuming he wanted to.

And the very idea of a holiday would be helped if Arthur really did mean three. Smooth as ever he'd pushed her down twenty pounds the last time but that was because with very little resistance, she'd pushed Terry down fifty. She would not wear anything like that this time, not even if it was three. For one thing he'd had no more to say about the big deal he'd mentioned except was it negotiable. He said that every time but she had no intention of hustling Terry till it got more serious. No way. Just the three would be very nice thank you. For now. It would see to the holiday. Maybe Jimmy would come for a week, would be the best in fact. Neutral ground. A bit of time. Meeting Sheila and seeing if it was nice in bed.

She picked up the paper he'd left. A handless corpse had been identified. Someone called Geoffrey Michael Christian. Aged thirty-five. A smudgy photo of a guy with bulging muscles. What the hell kind of picture was it. He looked manly and uneasy. A mug shot maybe. It turned out he had done time, it was possible. But what the hell, there you were, alive, not without a care in the world because that was wishful thinking, but alive, with possibilities, when along came some other real bastard with their own mad interests, and snuffed you out.

The paper speculated as to why the hands had been cut off. One explanation was that it was to delay identification because the poor guy had been in prison and fingerprints would make it easy.

Stupid stuff, but the speculations sucked her in. What was the point in delaying identification? Prevention yes, but that's not what had happened. The corpse did have a name and surely delay only helped the killer to run when a killer wouldn't want having to run. It became more ridiculous when she read that three men were helping police with their inquiries followed by a rundown on the exact punishments of Islamic Law. She looked at the paper again. The muscles were enormous. Poor bastard. A gun, the paper said. A lot of good your muscles would have been then Geoffrey Christian. And your hands cut off afterwards. Surely to God afterwards.

On that the paper said nothing. A hacksaw? A really sharp knife? A chopper like the old boy in the butcher's shop? She pictured the hacksaw and felt the rhythm of the sawing arm. She felt sick and looked at her watch.

3:15.

Shit. Just in time and a mercy at that, wishing she'd never looked at the paper at all. Not just Sheila but Lilly too, they'd be standing there not sure what to do if she didn't get her skates on.

Three hours later she'd picked up the girls, been in the park, dropped them off at Marie's, and was stood on a tube platform. It was OK, relaxed, a low-density scattering of tired-looking people. She looked at an advertisement for the Blood Transfusion Service. A shortage of donors.

She heard footsteps on the platform, clear and getting louder. She turned. A man stopped close by. He was carrying a bag like Jimmy's, floppy canvas with something heavy inside. His was blue. She saw it flop down by the ochre-tiled wall and got a picture of Jimmy sharp and clear, bopping up and down in her narrow kitchen and making her laugh. His TV producer agonizing over whether the shelves should be angular or rounded. "In fact he wants a decent bookcase but after a good look at Camden Town prices he's gone for me. Hendon born and bred he told me and his salary is not what the public thinks. Aesthetically he's all for the angular but is scared his balls will come a cropper." She'd asked him if he rehearsed his lines and didn't give a damn whether he did or not: he'd made her laugh.

Tube air gusted with a rumble in the tunnel. Everyone's head turned except him with the bag. He was reading the paper.

She'd told him about Sheila and it was no problem. OK they both had pasts, and pasts could be full of icebergs but not if they got talked out nice and easy, not if they were out in the open without it being a big deal. The rumble took on momentum. The man folded his paper. There was an explosion from the mouth of the tunnel with a rushing wind. Silver carriages clattered along the platform. Carol took a step backwards.

CHAPTER TWENTY-SIX

It had been a chore, travelling twice for Phil to get what he wanted when he'd surely made himself clear enough. He'd wanted to tell Jack but hadn't because in the telling it might have slipped out that his man was a woman and he'd never been sure just how his friend might take that. And then, when he had said to Simone, lightly enough, that his message had been, if anything, somewhat on the transparent side she'd made some bloody inscrutable remark about the thinness of the line between the over-subtle and the bloody obvious. No, not inscrutable, cheeky coming from Simone the hippy. And she hadn't as much as mentioned the very substantial deal he had mooted. If only Max had been prepared to give a little ground.

Instead there she'd been in jeans and T-shirt and very cool. Said she would be away on holiday for around three weeks and mentioned it Just In Case It Might Be Relevant To His Own Plans. He didn't like it, had sat back, taken a long sip of his beer and said he envied her.

"Envy me?" she'd said with a straight face, the minx, like she was the most downtrodden overalls in the world. He'd kept his reply light. "The way my boss replies to my delicate inquiries about holiday time can make one feel big-headed and still very much in need of a break. Therefore, envy." And she'd just sat there working that inscrutable look for all it was worth. "So how would you feel if he said, your boss, Yes Arthur my boy, take a holiday any time you want, you're not essential."

He'd kept his grin going and decided four ounces might be wiser in the circumstances. The money was no problem, he'd been shifting money into a safe deposit box on a regular basis. The extra ounce could stay there too.

"Phil! Phil!"

Christ, Vicky flashing her pink nails across his line of vision.

"OK Vicky I give in."

"No need for that. Listen to the Ayatollah. No surrender."

God preserve him from women who read a bit, worked regular hours and had no hassle when it came to their holiday dates. She dropped a bundle of photocopy and fax on his desk and stood there. The latest developments on the Iran-Iraq war and its spillage into the Gulf shipping lanes. He looked up again. She was still there, her tits cocky. He rallied round.

"But did we win the war Vicky, did we win?"

"My gran says yes but my grandad says when it comes to it the Japs and the Krauts, that's what he calls them, they won hands down."

She was relentless.

To break up the rhythm of Simone's cheek he'd flicked *The Standard* towards her and made a light remark about the head-lined story. Something about Christians into the Lion's Den, he'd said. At first he thought she just hadn't understood. "With one Michael Edward White in the role of Roman Emperor." And then he'd seen she was wincing. Perhaps she was simply humourless or maybe just couldn't take it when it came to the real rough and tumble. Probably both.

He picked up some photocopy. When the very first tanker to have a full U.S. Navy escort, *The Bridgetown*, had been mined it had looked like another case of the Angels not knowing where they should fear to tread. He remembered the fiasco in Beirut and mentioned it to Liam Yeats in sober Deutschmarks. But in his innermost heart he'd known it was different. The Lebanon was feudal, uncontrollable and, in the final analysis, irrelevant. The Gulf War which had become a constant in one's life, the balance of obsolete armaments almost too good to be true, hadn't been pressing either but the Gulf itself, that was another story.

So he'd put it to Simone as a quarter of a pound weight,

a different level of transaction, and waited for her to respond. She'd deliberately missed the point, the hippie minx. "Well it's a bit short notice Arthur but I'll see what I can do."

He'd just nodded.

There was nothing else for it.

But had made a bit of a comeback on the Big One even if it was him who'd had to mention it. Asked her if she'd made any headway on those prices as his interest Was serious, given a bit of flexibility on her part.

"You know how headway is, it only gets made if some serious money is visible."

He'd had to change the picture and dress her in the hippy clothes to keep going.

"I'm not going to flash a wad," he'd said. "I know I'm serious but I figure you're stalling."

"Stalling?" she'd said, with that same damn innocence plastered over her face.

"Put some steel in your backbone Phil."

He looked up. Vicky was grappling with the second sleeve of a lime-coloured lightweight jacket.

"What?"

"The Ayatollah," she said.

"Not him again. If you don't mind me saying so love, never overdo a joke."

Which stopped her in her tracks.

"Thanks for the tip Phil. I'm off."

Phil counted to five.

He refocused.

The Louvre deal had after all worked remarkably well. A now steady greenback. But this Gulf business could jump it up fast. It was an old argument with Jack but the evidence showed that the dollar benefitted most from symptoms of International Insecurity; far more than his pal's bullion. A paradox however, stared him in the face. As paradoxes did. If he was right and the Americans really had to tough this one out and they succeeded, then the greenback would fall back down again. What's more falls could develop their own momentum.

He would mark it up for two weeks but advise caution thereafter. A decision made.

He phoned Jack. "Shoulder still to the wheel?"

"Every gold freak in the world seems to have access to my phone."

"Well I'm not one and don't take it all to heart, all work and no play. How about half an hour. My wheels, my treat. Remembering your social acquaintance."

"What?"

"A tall man. Vegetarian jet set. Remember?"

Phil opted for the Commercial Road, Bubbles, and the lightest Vinho Verde on offer.

"OK worrier, so what is it? The Gulf and interest rate sums clogging up the Fed's computers," Jack said.

"Information overload. And I am not worrying, just we did I believe have some business of our own to discuss."

"Ah. Business."

Phil frowned. He looked stern. "A line or two in the gents was it?"

Jack jabbed his finger back across the table. "You my friend have never had the Gold Nut on your case. The Gulf's good for a week or two. We know that. The NUM are looking for a fight on the Veldt. Ditto. Try telling them Natal's a no-no with Buthulezi and there's a hell of a lot of unemployed miners. Never mind Anglo-American's stockpiles. Try telling them when they've got that gleam in their eyes."

"Submission. I submit. No I haven't. Can't your firm filter calls? Anyway it's your tall man I'm interested in. Since I've got the wherewithal I think you should give him a ring."

A gang of young pinstripes surged through the door. They were everywhere. Shouting. Jack grabbed his glass.

"Where's the leverage," roared the first to the bar.

"UNDER THE TITS." In loud chorus.

"Market-makers in underwear," Jack said. "Frothy. No, frilly."

Phil waved a hand across his face. "Focus. Our own business."

A cork popped.

Jack ducked.

Phil was relentless. "Let's see how we're going to do it. My suggestion is you go to his place but I'm outside with the powder until you're satisfied. I mean we do have to take into account that your tall pal who likes to party might not be all he seems to be."

Jack frowned. The youth were sprawled around Bubbles's biggest table. Their leader vaulted up on it.

"You take my point," Phil said.

"We are the bulls," the guy up on the table shouted.

"WE'LL RUN AND RUN."

"I look around my man's flat, make sure there's no hanky panky then come and get it."

Phil nodded. The chanting trailed away to a solo voice. He looked up, saw the blush of the one who would always be left behind, and grinned.

The phone call was made, the ounce collected. Sloane Square the tall man lived, just off.

They took the Embankment route.

"Must keep a decent wad of readies, your man," Phil said. "At the ready." They were in the City stretch of underpass. He glanced in the mirror and moved out into the fast lane.

"As would any sensible person these days. Must have been a good boy and liquidated some Equity."

They passed the Temple and drove under bridges.

"You can't beat the Thames at dusk," Jack said. "Got your tackle with you, wouldn't mind a line."

"Are you sure?"

"Bloody right I am."

It was 1920s, the tall man's block. No skimping on the brickwork. The street was full of trees. Phil found a space between a Volvo and a Morris Minor.

They walked down the street together. No sign of stern-faced men in moustaches in any of the parked cars. The tall man however Might Not Be All He Appears To Be. Jack stopped. Looked in the back window of the Volvo. At the seat. At the floor under the seat.

"OK Jack, let's go for it. Anything you don't like and we'll just drive away, OK."

Like he was a mindreader. OK? what was that. A rhetorical question first class was what it was. He had a mind to say so. He had a mind to.

He crossed the road and scanned the bank of Ansafones. He Was Not Carrying Anything Illegal. It was OK. He heard a bird in the trees, then some crackle and the tall man's voice.

Across the marble floor of the lobby was a lift, its gate surrounded with Art Deco twirls. He jabbed at the chest high button. Nothing happened. OK, no problem. The elevator was there already. He pulled at the wooden door, dragged the inner gate open and saw himself in an upper-half mirror.

Sweaty Sharp. He was not carrying anything illegal.

He pulled off his jacket and draped it over his shoulder.

It was OK.

He pulled at his collar and tie.

The lift stopped abruptly. Across a stretch of soft blue carpeting a door opened.

"Good to see you," the tall man said. Fucker. Perfect casuals, tailored poplin shirt and pure-cotton slacks. "Come in. My place."

It was too ready a smile. Smarmy. A double-agent would be smarmy. He was not carrying anything illegal.

There was a height to the ceiling, good parquet on the floor. Jack eyed cupboards. He looked at a sofa in maroon.

"A gin and tonic? It is summer after all even if in England it likes to kid us a bit."

Jack looked at the door. He eyed a slice of cool dark corridor leading off the far side of the room.

The tall man had evidently taken his silence as an answer, and walked off into the same corridor. And if there was some zealot with a moustache in there, whispering over the kitchen fridge. If there was, so what. He was not carrying anything illegal.

"Nice place you've got here," he shouted as he opened a cupboard at random. Full of porcelain. He peeped over the back of the sofa. He saw carpet. He saw carpet but they would not be so crude. They would be cunning and sly, parked down that corridor.

The tall man reappeared in the room with chinking glasses.

"You think so? Old history now but I simply beat the mad price rise. You remember, the one Mr Heath thought so immoral."

Jack felt on surer footing. "The unacceptable face of capitalism," he said.

The tall man laughed. Jack sipped at his gin, a proper slice of lemon floated on its surface.

"It was good to see you the other evening," the tall man said. "It had been a mite boring. But then I believe I said my thankyous there and then. This is rather more for my partner."

What partner? Where was he? What was a partner? You had a girlfriend these days, she was a partner; you had a nightstick and patrolled the streets, you had a partner to go with.

"Partner?"

"Let's say we're in show business. The critics think it's tacky but the punters love it so what can we do. Anyway he has the habit of being invariably right. This is the least I can do for him."

The invisible partner, a paragon. Of what?

"Must be handy, being invariably right."

The tall man laughed. He laughed too much. Jack wanted a trip down that dim corridor. Inspired, he demanded a leak.

"Second on the right or fourth on the left."

Jack tried both. A poky affair with books and a poster for *Some Like It Hot*. The second, a proper bathroom, lights bright on the tiles. A wardrobe size wall cupboard caught his eyes. Inside stacks of sheets. It was quiet. The tall man might be crafty, Jack was craftier still. He tried two other doors in quick succession, nipped back into the bathroom and pulled the chain.

"Drinking water," he shouted.

"Kitchen's on the left.

It was lit up. It was smart. He looked behind the fridge. He looked behind the freezer. He opened a pantry door.

"Feeling peckish," the tall man said from the doorway.

Jack turned, ready to blush.

"Rather," he said. "It came on suddenly."

CHAPTER TWENTY-SEVEN

"Ali the Paki, Mr Curtis." It was DS Jones. DCI Edwards had somehow got himself the best part of the summer for his holidays.

"So what's he want, diplomatic status is it?," Curtis said.

"Bit lightweight for that sir," DS Jones said. He was laughing.

"Habeas Corpus?"

"Not that dull guv. A name he said."

"It'll be some cunt has got diplomatic status. Or is safely back in Lahore. Is that why you're asking me Dai?"

"No sir, said he wanted to speak to most esteemed senior officer."

"Did he Dai, is that what he said? What the fuck did you do to him, tell him his circumcision wasn't up to scratch?"

"Me Mr Curtis? Obviously I reminded him of the serious-ness of the offence involved and at the very most I might have reminded him that his mammie was far far away."

"Anything else Dai?"

"Well there's our boyo Steve Scott."

"Ah, Mr Scott. Ryan's rather belated contribution to the fight against organised crime." There'd been a moment when Curtis had half regretted giving DCI Edwards his head with the Ryan interview; a look through CRO and the name he'd come back with looked tasty. Mr Scott had been something of a heavy in his time. Come out well from his last caper with a twelve stretch. Released twenty months previously.

"So, Mr Scott?" he said.

DS Jones looked unhappy.

"We've had one or two interesting photos and IDs but I don't think we're going to get any more in the near future. Nothing that will stick. I'd say let's target him again for a week in a couple of months time rather than this on-off stuff we're doing now."

"Did you discuss this with Nye before he took his leave?" he said. DS Jones squirmed. "In general terms of course sir. DCI Edwards realized himself that we were a bit late for any direct results but that it was a good time for us to see who he might know."

"Of course. Makes sense as I told Nye but now, with the manpower shortages we've got, reckon you've squeezed it dry for now do you?"

DS Jones nodded, looked happy. A not guilty verdict, no disloyalty shown to a pal from the valleys and senior officer.

"OK Dai I take your point. It's Nye's business of course but feeling as you do I'll just throw the name out, a propos of nothing of course, to my one real long-term snout. Long term, you wouldn't believe it. I've told him if he lasts another couple of years I'll have him a medallion minted. Motif of some long grass in the breeze with a bit of Latin round the edges. Know any Latin Dai?"

"I had other interests at the time sir, DS Jones said with a grin."

All too many. Pakistan was Pakistan. Ali was Iranian, caught bang to rights in possession of several ounces of the nasty. Had the name of a compatriot domiciled in South Kensington.

"I can't make any promises at this stage," he'd said, "but if anything does come of it I'll do my best to have the Judge take it into consideration."

Upstairs he gave Dai the address. "Surveillance only. I don't want diplomatic incidents and I don't want this party scared off. It's a priority. I'll be back at six thirty. Brief me then. By radio if necessary."

It took two public box calls to get hold of Gordon Murray. They made a meet for late afternoon, Gordon's office, his new gymnasium complex in Clerkenwell. The cab fare was on him, Gordon said.

That fixed he returned to his own office and a piece of work. Bob Lumley had got him thinking. There would be no resentful references to the resources available to HM Customs and Excise but he would argue the case for an officer with Accountancy training to be seconded to the squad. Either they'd get one or they wouldn't, what mattered was that he wrote the memo well.

The squad really did need such a person and another of Bob's phrases came to mind. He would use it. Bob wouldn't give a monkey's, not when one of the nickings of the decade had fallen in his lap, Mickey White on a murder charge, the mug. What the squad needed was an accountant who would service it, pointed in the right direction by its detectives. Directed. To show what this meant he would need an example of such a person following up something off his own bat, one that turned out to be a wild goose chase and would make the AC laugh. It hadn't needed some cunt at a Communication Skills seminar for Senior Officers to tell him that a laugh made an example more telling.

There was a knock at the door. DC Thomson fresh on the squad and starting with a spell on Filing and Communications. Message personal from an AG in HMP Wakefield. One Ryan T. 134737 requests a personal interview with the above mentioned officer DCS G. Curtis.

"Ryan T, DC Thomson, a classic case."

"Classic sir?"

"The informant who always speaks too late." DC Thomson laughed.

"In the wild old days DC Thomson, when men went into banks with the express intent of letting of shotguns or going berserk with pick-axe handles, we had the Super Grass. Know what we used to say about them?"

"No sir."

"He was the villain got nicked first. Got his informing in straightaway. Like a headbutt." The DC frowned. He laughed. Curtis waved him away.

So what was it with Ryan, he'd been weighed off. Very quickly. So cut and dried his mouthpiece had kept his gob shut till the end when he'd done a deprived childhood number.

Which can't have counted for much, not with Ryan at his age. But then he hadn't needed it, had pulled a do-gooder of a judge. Had praised the detectives concerned but gone soft when it came to sentence. Now here he was again, slow off the mark with the Scott info and surely a backwater now.

Or maybe not.

Ryan was a chancer on the job but a bit shrewd after a nicking the record showed. He'd know Appeal against Conviction was out of the question and Sentence unlikely unless he came up with something tasty. Seriously. It was possible there was some mug in Walton opening his heart to the wrong man. It was possible.

More likely stale stuff from his own dildo operation. Still it only involved a return rail journey and Closer Liason with Prison Intelligence on his timesheet. Nothing to lose, just possibly something to gain.

He looked up at the wall clock. 3:00. Time to go.

"Clerkenwell? You don't look like graphics or design," the cabbie said.

Curtis scowled.

Gordon's place was the ground floor of a warehouse conversion job with a rubbery-lettered signboard. STAMINA STUDIO. Curtis walked right round the building. Two guys in moustaches and immaculate tracksuits came out of the main entrance. He walked on and turned left past a multiple Company Car Park towards the Grays Inn Road. He turned into it and proceeded northwards towards Kings Cross. A newsagents with a sideline in attaché cases, a second-hand office furniture frontage, metal filing cabinets out on the pavement, a sandwich bar with exotic fillings. He paused at an office building. There were three separate plaques: brass, Mount Insurance Services; one in dark wood and gold lettering, Mind & Body (Holistic Services); and an aluminium frame with polythene covering printed cardboard, Tristar Travel (incorporating Acropolis Air). He scowled and turned right. There was a specialist shop, weighing machines of all sorts, scales of every dimension and design. There were old-fashioned balances and there was electronic stuff.

Nice one.

Oh yes. Very nice one.

He would put it down on paper first so there was no mistaking it was his idea. Random periods of sustained surveillance. It might only be the dealer starting out on his career, but everyone needed his scales. He looked to the opposite side of the road and saw further down, Bob Lumley. Looking wary. Bob whose idea he'd been knocking into shape. Bob who'd just come out of somewhere and was giving the street an up and down.

Curtis got the angle right to use the shop window as a mirror. Bob was still hovering. The door he'd come out of was restaurant, an upmarket greasy spoon. He was moving in his direction. Curtis stepped inside the shop. The restaurant called itself Gianni's. Bob stopped at the Grays Inn Road junction. He was carrying an attaché case and looked back the way he had come.

"Can I help you sir?"

Curtis turned. A tall thin guy in his fifties, wearing a white overall coat.

I'm interested in something that's accurate in the one to five hundred gram range," he said. Bob finally turned the corner. The relic had started his patter. Curtis turned so that Gianni's was in his line of sight.

"But perhaps this would give you the best of both worlds. As I said it does depend on the exact tolerance you're working to but it is a robust, all-round piece of equipment."

Two big guys in suits were stood in Gianni's doorway. They looked foreign.

"I'll have to consult a colleague on that, then I'll get back to you," Curtis said. He was at the door. It tinkled as he opened it. The two men were chatting. And there was a third. Another foreigner in jeans and T-shirt. He was clocking the road, then nodded at the good-suits. They shook hands as Curtis walked towards them. The shorter suit walked off with T-shirt. The other guy nearly bumped into him. Grey flannel, double-breasted. They did a misunderstanding two-step. Grey suit laughed, stopped where he was and let Curtis forward. He saw the other two getting into an Audi. He clocked the number, stopped at a shop, checked his tobacco tin, bought a Standard and wrote the Audi number on the Stop Press. He walked back to Gianni's with the paper under his arm. Mickey White was on the front page, an old photo to go with his first remand appearance.

"A cappuccino love," he said to a bronze-haired woman. "And a toilet?"

It was downstairs. He couldn't piss but made noise at the wash basin. There was a door at the back and a nervy looking guy stood next to gas stoves. There was another closed door and a smell of cigarettes. Back at his table he looked at his watch and picked up the *Standard*. Mickey White looked tougher than he remembered but it was the same Mickey who'd got up Bob's nose and fallen into Bob's lap. Very nice for Bob but then what? Celebrating his coup over a grappa in a greasy spoon? No fucking way.

CHAPTER TWENTY-EIGHT

"Yes I was shocked. I can't say as I know him well but I have known him and I can imagine he's a bit of a villain, Mickey White, but I wouldn't have thought that sort of thing was his style."

That's what I said to the old Super who'd started off with a bit of gossip. Had his pipe out for five minutes by then and still hadn't got it lit. I'd got him over to Clerkenwell this time where I've a bit of an office rigged up. A change isn't a bad thing now and then and Chloe doesn't mind. She was typing letters to a soft drinks distributor who thinks he can take me for a cunt.

There's a lot more space than in the other place, no pool table but plenty of houseplants. Graham looked just the same: meet him in a brieze-block bunker and he would be no different.

"There's colleagues of mine in the Force who take a much less charitable view of Mr White. Yes indeed."

I didn't say anything but you'd have thought he could have fucking told me before. It's turned out to be an expensive business and there's till a loose end or two. Mind you when our first Quarterly dividend came, down in black and white, Keith could see my point of view. But what I say is, never spend a pound where fifty pence will do and if Graham had spoken earlier there might have been other and cheaper avenues to explore. Still, there's no point crying over spilled milk and if I didn't hurry him Graham just might come up with something to help tidy up those loose ends.

"Yes, they'd argue, some colleagues of mine, that Mr White's public persona was very different to the real man underneath."

"Like I said I didn't know him very well and it's true, appearances can be deceptive."

"A very good thing that you didn't know him well Gordon if you don't mind me saying," Curtis said. He pulled a stern face. So what the fuck is he getting at with a remark like that.

"A fine place you've got here Gordon, I couldn't help but notice."

I smiled.

"Yes I like to think so too. Of course it's always a question of giving the public what it wants. but it's nice when it's something that's doing them a bit of good. And I'll tell you something else Graham, it's something I've been saying for years, you can do it with a bit of style. Keeping fit, it doesn't have to be all pain and sweaty armpits.

The Super grinned and said I'd got a point. I asked him if he fancied a look around the place or a drink. That's what they call a rhetorical question. I poured him a scotch and came on with the soda siphon. That's what Keith calls a rhetorical gesture. The Super shook his head like he was some Scottish peasant living on oats and a dram.

"I take your point Gordon but me, I think I'm a bit old for what do you call it, circuits. The old boat's about enough for me. By the way, ever come across a Stevie Scott on your travels?"

That pulled me up, the way he just stuck that name in his usual bollox.

"Steve Scott? Should I?"

"Just a possible Gordon."

"Works out does he? Clubs it?"

"It's possible."

"So I could ask around."

"It might be a help Gordon if you could. I've probably said it before but it's amazing, it still amazes me after all these years, how even the smallest detail, just one fact to go with a name can make a sense out of what was just a mess . . ."

"Of jigsaw pieces," I said. Tommy Ryan, it had to be. As thick as pigshit but dead slippery once nicked.

"Exactly Gordon," Curtis said and at last got his pipe going, sending spirals of nasty smoke into my clean office.

"What did you say his name was again Mr Curtis?"

"Scott, Steven, aged thirty-seven. Out of Lewisham."

I wrote the name down on a notepad with my fountain pen. He didn't say anything for a while so I livened up his scotch. I said I'd join him in a tipple now seeing as it was evening and I'd completed my circuit in the morning.

Curtis didn't rise to that. Not a word. So what was it with him. Normally he'd still be gabbing away. In fact if he'd been different I might have got worried about the way he'd dropped two names that were a bit close to home, but you know what it was like, it was like he didn't care too much, like his mind was somewhere else. I coughed in the smoke and took a sip of my scotch.

"How's it going Chief Superintendent?" I asked to keep things moving.

"Up and down Gordon, up and down. A breakthrough now and then though we often have to be pointed in the right direction."

He laughed then, the Super. I said it was the way things went. To which he said you never could tell, that you had to follow things up even if they lead nowhere.

"Take today, there's a fellow, we'll call him Ali, on a possession charge. Over an ounce of heroin which means Gordon, he's a supplier."

"I see."

"So after a while he asks to see the officer in charge who happens to be me. So he gives me another name, a certain Akbar Hajani, another Iranian, a cousin so he said."

I gave the office walls a careful looking over.

"You take my point Gordon. Only a name but if we're to get anywhere near the big boys we've got to go for it, even if in the result there's a lot of wasted manpower to be accounted for. So in this case I'm arranging full time surveillance on the name and address supplied though it could so easily come to nothing."

If. If.

If the Iranian had anything to do with this bunch of clowns. Christ.

"And to let you in on a bit of a trade secret Gordon, South

Ken is not the easiest place in the world when it comes to the watertight discretion that effective surveillance requires."

You've got to hand it to him, Mr Curtis, he's got a lovely way of putting things. Just now and then I've known him to be a bit crude, like when he's phoned me up about people I've never heard of, but by and large you've got to hand it to him.

I was just about to give him his envelope even though it was before it was due, when he was off on another tack.

"A very good location this Gordon, from what I can see. Changed a lot since I knew it well. A period of transition I suppose you'd call it."

I nodded.

"Nice to see though that the old Italian community's still going strong. The cafes, the restaurants, a sense of continuity which, speaking as a copper and an ordinary citizen, I think is vital. It's especially in such times of rapid change that we need to keep a sense of continuity."

Surely they didn't send old tossers like Curtis on sociology courses so what was he on about, except it was the third time he'd rung a bell. And little bells are there to be listened to. I was going to be straight on to the Iranian but I was also going to tell Mario I wanted a new place for our meets. A new area in fact. And still Curtis hadn't finished.

"Perhaps it's more Mediterranean but the Italians somehow have this knack of making cafes where anyone from any walk of life can feel comfortable."

"You've got a point there Graham though of course we do our own catering here, not full meals but tasty snacks."

Finally we got round to the boat and I slipped him his envelope. Told him it was a small token of appreciation for the work he's doing.

When he'd gone I didn't move for a while. I let what he'd said trickle through and the first thing I realized was that I needed a holiday because I wasn't reading him loud and clear. Fatigue. Obviously if I'd got any of it right, there were a few things to sort out first because I wanted a really relaxing holiday which you can't do if there's still loose ends. Now Keith, he's had a couple of weeks in a beachside property we've got in Spain. Not fucking Torremolinos either, proper Spain. He's come back relaxed. Not a bad tan either.

I had a quick look through what Chloe had done then sent her home. Then I went out to a PhoneCard box I'd earmarked round the corner. I got the Iranian's answerphone. No way I was going to leave a message so it stayed an unanswered query and a unit down the drain. While I was there I phoned Keith for a morning meet and then Sarah. She wasn't in, the slag. I didn't ask much from her so you could at least expect she'd be in once in a while. By the time I did get hold of the Iranian he started poncing on about engagements.

"Fucking right, with me, forty minutes from now," I said.

I got a cab. It was a fight all the way to Knightsbridge and the cabby was gabby. I told him it had been a hard day pal, and he shut up. And then the Iranian was five minutes late but I didn't blow my top. In fact I gave him the blank for a while just to see if his magnetic personality had brought anyone with it. When I did greet him he came on all sulky. Can you fucking credit it. I had to tamp myself right down because I needed to have a clean head when it came to reading his response to the remark I was going to drop.

You know one of the problems in business. In fact it's probably the biggest of the lot. You have a colleague, partner or associate. This person makes a rick. This rick may well have consequences for you personally but your associate doesn't tell you about it. Doesn't want to lose face.

"Beautiful isn't it, London in summer," I said.

The Iranian was in a cream-coloured lightweight suit. He grunted.

"It's the long evenings and the summer of course. Makes you feel good to be alive and free, an evening stroll along the Embankment or down by Greenwich. And the sky, always changing. Akbar Hajani, South Kensington, a pal of yours is he?"

It wasn't much and it didn't last long, but it happened. His brown eyes trying to add up the whole sum on the instant.

"You prick. You long streak of stinky piss. Tell me."

CHAPTER TWENTY-NINE

"I was that riled, just wanted to get hold of the little bastard. And the worst of it was I couldn't, couldn't even shout, not there. You know the place, it's all light rendezvous and deals in the relaxed stage of completion, just the i's to be dotted"

"And the t's to be crossed," Keith said. "You should have had him in the motor."

"Thank you Keith. As it happens I took a cab."

Derek yawned. His feet tapped out no-rhythm on the office carpet.

"But I kept a grip and said to him, Has our business relationship been unfruitful, has it? That knocked the haughty look off his face."

"Like a camel was it?"

"What?"

"His face, haughty."

"Leave it out Keith," Derek said. His voice was flat.

Keith turned. He smiled. "Sure bruv," he said. "My apologies. A flight of fancy."

"When you two have finished. Yeah. I haven't exactly heard any complaints from your side, I said to him. I could see that got to him, the way he started sipping at his orange pressé."

Derek scratched the back of his neck. He stood up. He sat down again.

"And didn't it strike you that a long-term partner might just have the right to be consulted, I said."

Keith nodded.

"So what does the cunt say? Says I don't understand the demands of family loyalty. To me he's said it."

Keith mimed Ouch.

"That's when I nearly threw a wobbler. Very close. But you can't afford a fracas in Knightsbridge can you. Anyway he must have seen the look on my face. Not of course that he'd expected such a bad thing to happen, he says."

Derek brought his hands together, rested his face on the knuckles.

"Well they did happen didn't they, bad things, I said. They did fucking happen. And some family, first sign of bother and you're grassing each other up. You know who's next in line don't you."

Derek lifted his head up.

"So what's he say to that?" Keith asked.

"What's he say, he starts giving me a load of fanny. Not to worry. No problem. I don't know this Akbar like he does. Yes, and I don't fucking want to know him I said. And as it happens I don't want to know you till this thing's cleared up and I'm 100 percent sure there's no smell around you."

"Hang on a minute Gordon, he's got a big one in the pipeline. In our hands next week. It was promised. My people are waiting on it."

"So they're going to have to fucking wait aren't they. Like I told him, sample Jersey for a month, have some green and pleasant land for a while, it'll do you good."

Derek was up on his feet. "This is bollox."

Keith turned up the radio volume.

"OK it's you started the business Gordon but who's built it up, kept it running smooth."

"You Derek, no question. And you've done it well."

"So what do you think's going to happen. The punters want satisfaction today not next year. Yes, and what do you think my people are in it for, they're in it for the wedge."

"Yes, thank Christ for that. So?"

"So they're all ready for next week. I can tell them this and

I can tell them that but if we've none of the tackle they'll go elsewhere."

"I wonder about that Derek."

"Oh do you, you don't know the bizz like I do. Lost your bottle have you? For starters Akbar's only a name and who's to say he's holding any dollop."

"Who's to say he isn't," Gordon said. "And can't you stop pacing about."

"No I fucking can't. Our man'll have marked his card."

"If he has done that he'll have showed his face too."

"The only half decent radio station and it's bloody Dvorak, the late nineteenth century at its slushiest."

"You fucking what. Sitting in your chairs making poncey remarks, that's all you can do. Anyway just what the fuck is Curtis for? You know, if you don't mind telling me, very junior partner."

Gordon leaned right across the desk. "I'll tell you what he's for Derek, he's for telling us things like this Akbar caper. Telling us in his own way. And I'll tell you what he's not for, which is knowing that we're interested in anyone in particular or stopping this investigation or that unless it's very close to home. OK, because he ain't going to be able to do that too often."

Keith weighed in. "Curtis is about us, any of us not going into the slammer Del. Don't go on to me about bottle and poncey remarks, the nick's just a story to you. Personally speaking avoiding it is a number one priority."

Derek had sat down. It was coming in stereo. He was going to be cool.

"So what you're saying is I've got nothing to work with till you're satisfied our man is 100 percent clean."

Gordon smiled. He nodded.

"And when's that."

"When Akbar's on a fucking plane out of here and I know from Curtis nothing came of it."

"That old tosser, we'll be dead and buried by then."

The brothers said nothing. Keith turned down the radio volume.

"All right then but I want another meet Monday, review the situation. Before it's too late."

Keith nodded. Gordon said Sure.

Derek closed the door quietly on his way out.

"Have you got to rile him Keith?"

"He wasn't thinking straight."

"All right, but you can try and make the point with a bit of tact. He has matured you know since that stunt in the Ripened Hop. Definitely. Head down on the job, not a peep out of him about revenge. It can take something like that to mature a man."

"What, a beating? Not us bruv. Got anything else to say for himself has he, our friendly neighbourhood rozzer."

"Amongst other things Keith he showed a distinct interest in your pal Stevie Scott."

"My pal? That's stronging it. Anyway he's a bit greedy ain't he, Curtis."

"I'm just saying he showed an interest in the very same conversation he came across with the Iranian nicking."

"Yes. So. I haven't heard anything of the guy since and no way am I going around asking after him then find him nicked next week," Keith said. He lit a cigarette and crossed to the largest of the houseplants.

"You asked me what else Curtis had to say and I'm telling you."

"The absolute sophistication and perfection of pattern in the natural world," Keith said stroking a shiny green leaf as he looked it over. "What's human design ever going to be but second best. Must have been friend Ryan whispering in our Super's ear. Very Shakespearian."

"What?"

"A vulnerable aperture the ear, an entry point for poison. Claudius does it straight and Iago with a whisper. Maybe the Stratford bully used to stick twigs in his."

Gordon waited till he was sure the brother had definitely finished.

"All right say it was Ryan, what difference does that make."

Keith gave a last look at the leaf and turned away from

the plant. "Come on Gordon, liven up. It means our unhealthy Superintendent was just fishing. No consequences. Anything else?"

"Yeah, he was very late in the day telling me there was a very large black mark against Mickey in the Met."

"What, bigger than might have been expected."

"He'd got seriously up someone's nose."

"Had he? Fucks sake he might have told us."

"Quite."

"He's getting old our Graham. Did a lovely job though, the jock, and the paperwork looks good. Still want a con for the icing?"

"Funny you should say that, it's been going through my mind. If the Met have got the needle with him they'll be going flat out to stitch it up tight. But then take the hypothetical situation that Mickey somehow wriggles out of it. It's down for the Bailey where there's always going to be a chance, the hooligans they get on juries these days. If that hypothetical situation were to happen then Mickey out and about's going to start lashing out who knows where. I'd like to think we'd at least done our very best."

"So that means yes."

"Fancy a scotch."

"Bit early for you."

"Can't be in a rush all the time," Gordon said getting up to open the wall cupboard.

Keith laughed.

Gordon frowned. He put the Chivas and two cut-glass tumblers on the desk.

"I've been telling you that for years bruv. That's why I say get yourself a mobile. All that phone box stuff, rushing about. It'll be the death of you."

"How many times have I got to tell you, I don't trust the fucking things. Don't tell me calls aren't getting logged. Anyway let's not have a row," Gordon said. They touched glasses. "A con for the icing you said. Yeah. You remember Mum used to say, Never go for a wasp unless you're sure of killing it."

Keith frowned. He pictured his mother.

He pictured a wasp. He remembered the sting on his tongue as he took a first lick of the choc ice he'd had away from old Mr Darling's shop. He couldn't remember his mother saying any such thing. Maybe she had. Maybe she hadn't.

"Yes," he said. "So?"

"A little run down of the Brixton Security Wing says they're all young with the exception of Mickey himself and one Anthony Simpson. Heard of him?"

Keith lit a cigarette but no he hadn't.

"Worth tracing friends and family. He'll have one. Could probably do with some dosh."

"A friend of mine tells me even though I've got the wise-cracks I'm not Private Eye material."

"You are you know Keith, don't sell yourself short."

"Not sure I run to a heart of gold and a big dick. What's he nicked for?"

"Puff. Two tons. Maybe three."

"Got you, tidy little operation, south coast but then his right hand buys a new Porsche with readies."

"See, you're a step ahead of me already."

"Yeah but Mickey's brief could really lay into him."

"We don't know all the facts yet."

CHAPTER THIRTY

"You bolloxed?" Jimmy asked looking at Carol sat down under another low tree. The kids were nowhere in sight: her Sheila; Sheila's friend Lilly; and Pauline's two, Wat and Gwynedd. He'd only arrived the night before and this was Carol's surprise, a mossy wood, a marvel of rocky greenness and sculpted trees low to the ground.

"Just waiting for you. Stunning first time isn't it. And I'm not so unfit that I can't walk half a mile uphill. Even if I don't work like you."

He put his arms up in surrender. "Green all around me, green above and green below. And inside it beautiful Carol." He let his arms fall, gave her a hand and helped her up.

"Am I? Really?" Now it was her looked girlish. He'd never seen it before.

"Haven't you been told often enough?" He put his arm round her. Their lips touched. She was soft. He felt soft.

"Mum. Mum." They pulled apart laughing.

"The sex police," Carol said looking up the slope.

"There's a cave, a secret one," Sheila shouted.

"We're coming," Jimmy shouted back. He grabbed Carol's hand and set off in a run towards a Sheila he couldn't see. The slopes to left and right had a different gradient. He went for the steeper one shouting, Scrub oaks. They found Sheila with her arms waving on a broad ledge. Wat stood behind her, dark, quiet, a year older.

"It's a secret cave and a man lived there for years and they never found him did they?" Sheila said turning to him, handsome, solemn Wat. "It was in the war, he didn't want to fight. His sister brought him food."

Carol could picture her, giving him the chance and not making a big deal of it. She would have made some visible routine that gave her the space to pop into the wood and its cave. Every day. A lot of work.

"Let's go then, take us to your cave," Jimmy shouted grabbing Sheila by the hand till she was moving fast and he let go. Wat raced ahead. From a ledge by the cave he looked down and saw the heads of the two London grownups. They were kissing again, thinking they were hidden behind a tree. Gwynedd and the other girl from London were probably in the cave already. If he could get Sheila to be quieter on her feet he'd give them a fright from above.

Jimmy pulled away first. "See, it is a whirlwind romance."

"A gentle breeze I'd call it."

So cheeky she looked, saying it. He felt his cock pushing at the denim.

"What, even for the over-thirties," he said.

"Is it that obvious, me."

He touched her lightly on the shoulder and tried a serious eye to eye. "I thought you were the one couldn't take a compliment. You know, Give Me The Truth Whatever It Costs."

"You talk too much? You worry me to death/You talk too much," Carol sang.

There was a scream, loud, bouncing round the rocks and trees. Carol was off in a sprint. He caught up at a break in the greenness, a flat place with the rock steep behind it naked of lichen. There were three of them, her Sheila and the two Welsh kids.

"Where's Lilly?" Carol shouted.

Sheila was laughing. "Wat showed me how to be quiet and we crept up and Lilly and Gwynedd didn't know . . ."

Lilly was out of the cave and pissed off.

". . . and she thought we were a spirit and . . ."

"Well if you'd been in the cave and someone had frightened you, you'd have screamed twice as loud," Carol said.

Wat looked disgusted.

Jimmy asked Lilly to show him the famous cave, he was sure he would never have found it on his own. She said it wasn't that much really. It wasn't either but it had housed a man for years.

"Can't have been much of a life can it."

"Maybe he read a lot."

"But when? Could he have risked a candle?" Jimmy asked.

Lilly hurried out of the darkness. Sheila and Wat were quiet, they were looking at things she couldn't see.

"Did he have a candle?" she said towards the Welsh boy.

He turned. "It's possible but it would have been dangerous for him. It was very serious if you wouldn't fight."

"If they'd caught him they'd have locked him in a very hard prison."

Carol saw her daughter's head turning to each speaker. Then Jimmy, rubbing his head as he came out of the cave.

"After a more careful look, I reckon a person could be very comfortable in there, even in winter," he said.

Carol asked Sheila to show it her.

It was certainly well hidden and though it tapered inside she thought it could hold two people if they didn't move. But for years? The man must have been very frightened. Or disciplined.

"With that bracken we saw further down you could make a really comfortable bed," she said.

"But it would have been so cold in winter and he must have been so lonely," Sheila said.

"He did have his sister, she was very good to him."

But Sheila was gone, out into the sunshine. Carol went out. There was no sign of the other children, just Jimmy with his eyes closed and counting, Twenty-one, twenty-two . . .

Sheila was away at a run.

In the evening the temperature dropped quickly and it started to rain. Pauline's kids read their own stories but Carol went up to Sheila and Lilly. Sat at one end of the worn sofa in front of the fireplace, Jimmy asked if he could light a fire, it had been a long time, an open fire. Pauline waved him on like it was a daft question and pointed to the box of kindling by the small stack of logs.

She said it was fine that he'd come. No problem. That she felt sorry for anyone who lived in London. His back was to her, bent over the knit of kindling he'd made in the grate. He pulled a face. All right for her, most people had no choice.

"With your kind of skills you could get a lot of work here, there's a lot of people coming in and buying old places, wanting to convert them without changing their character."

Conversion jobs. He grinned as the fire caught.

"Of course the irony is that while we incomers want the stone cottages, the Welsh farmer wants his Dallas bungalow."

Just then the main door opened and Pauline was away with an English guy wearing high boots and an old tweed jacket. Jimmy went to the kitchen for two glasses and a bottle of Bushmills. On the way back he switched off the electric light then settled on the sofa to roll a spliff.

"What's this, a stage set?" It was Carol, from behind the sofa.

"What?"

"The seduction scene."

"Oy Carol Paranoid," he said, grabbing her under the armpits, over the top and on to the sofa. "It's called a holiday. You know, you work day in day out and then you have a holiday now and then. You treat yourself. To a spliff of Sensi, which is not so easy to find these days and which I have kept for you to light up."

"OK Jimmy prickley. I was going to say, it is seductive."

She lit up. "And it is good weed."

"You an expert?"

"I've got good taste."

"It's tempting isn't it, this," he said, waving towards the fire. "But I reckon you'd have to have a few bob. If it's not nosey . . ."

"Which means you are going to be," she said, handing him the spliff.

"Ouch ouch, Carol sharp."

"What is this, Carol this and Carol that. You want Carol bold. Got a cock?"

"What, here and now?" His heart was thumping inside. He undid his zip, taking an interested look at his half-erect penis. "What about here and soon?"

There was a hand under his shirt, two fingers on his cock and Carol on top.

"Whatever else Jim, don't panic."

Her laughing whisper tickled his ear. He found the base of her spine and caressed it with strength.

She came like a cat and he lay quiet, still big inside her.

"You didn't come?" she said.

"Does it matter? It felt good. Another time. Later. Tomorrow."

Later, when he'd slipped out, Carol asked if he would come to her bed and was it all right if he didn't come in her again till the next day, it had been a long time so she was a bit sore.

Up in the big bed he said he would have got to Wales earlier but he's had a fitted wardrobe, drawers and shelves to finish for a Mrs Swift. "Kept telling me to call her Veronica while she hustled me to get it finished. I called her Vron for the crack."

She laughed and gave him a cuddle.

"I like you Jim, I really do. You mind if I roll another one. One for the road. Local was she, your Vron?"

"No, out in the wilds of Hampstead."

"So you're high class."

"It has been said. Started as a cowboy, became a craftsman and lived off the conversion boom ever since."

"And you like it?"

He put his chin on her shoulder, his face half in her hair.

"I like the money. Sometimes there's some satisfaction but mostly it feels like being a lackey. What else can you do. You working?"

The surprisingly bold high she'd felt faltered. She said no.

"Am I allowed to be nosy," he said.

She turned and put the spliff in his mouth. "We're in bed together aren't we, how much nosier do you want to get."

She could feel his cock on her skin, asked him if he'd like her to suck him off.

"Let's leave it till tomorrow. I want the full lash."

The next night they came together, his passion unlocked by hers.

The day before they were due to set off home the rain of

the night continued into morning. The sky was low, the yard full of dirty puddles. Wat was out in his wellies seeing to the chickens. In the kitchen Jimmy brewed another pot of tea and nudged Carol and Pauline into another round of toast. It was a holiday fucks sake; the last full day; the kitchen was warm from the stove; the girls were busy with something; a slow breakfast was the height of luxury.

"That's the joke Carol, the countryside is supposed to be the clean place but you look at Dai Bevan's farmyard, crap everywhere. Plastic bags, plastic drums, broken plastic buckets and bits of machinery that don't work," Pauline said.

"Mum, Mum."

"Yes?"

"Is it really our last day?" Lilly and Gwynedd stood in the doorway.

"You know it is Sheila and I know it's raining and miserable"

"The rain's nothing new is it, they've been lucky haven't they Mum," Gwynedd said coming in and half on to Pauline's lap.

"You got that Sheila and you, Lilly in the alley, you've been lucky."

"I'm not in an alley. This is a doorway in case you didn't know."

"You learn something every day Lil."

She jumped into the kitchen in a whirl, fists out. "And I'm not Lil either."

"OK, OK, I surrender, a slip of the tongue."

Wat had taken her place in the doorway. He saw a madhouse: his sister whispering to their mum; Sheila open-mouthed; and the other London girl giving hell to Jimmy who wasn't a bad bloke.

"I've done the chickens," he said. They stopped where they were to turn towards him.

In the afternoon after a few clear spells the rain settled in for the day. Pauline said she knew just how it would be and drove off to see someone about animal feed. Jimmy tried but his style didn't suit indoors, not on this day at least. There were quarrels and then Gwynedd scraped her leg on the fireplace.

Carol fixed that and found a slow blues on the cassette player. The London girls started dancing. Jimmy joined in and pulled Gwynedd into the circle but he looked silly, too big, and trying too hard. To Carol it was no wonder that Gwynedd looked so wooden. He could dance loose and easy, Jimmy, that's how she'd met him, but now it was like the kids were his responsibility and it made him clumsy.

"We can do better than this," Carol said. "Why don't you use this scarf Lilly and make an entrance like this."

She did a demo from the kitchen door, sideways, deliberate, in time. The track ran out just as she twirled to face the girls. She turned the tape back to the start of the slow track and asked Jimmy if he'd roll a spliff. Wat was just behind him, Carol said he was needed too. "You know a man dancer has to be just about the strongest and fittest man you could imagine and he's got to work hard to do anything worthwhile."

It was hesitant, but Wat moved in front of Jim who looked peeved. If that's what it was Carol just didn't have the time. There was a storyline in her head and she had to keep things moving if Gwyneedd and Wat were not to lose interest.

When Jimmy came back holding a joint and his jacket, he saw two pairs of mirror dancers moving to the same blues track as before.

"No Sheila, it's the arm out as if to shake hands and then out, noses nearly touching."

"But that's what I did."

Wat and Gwynedd had the giggles, off balance and rubbing noses. Carol pressed Rewind.

"OK, that was really good," she said. "Let's just go back to the beginning and get the whole sequence. I really liked that left eye wink, right eye wink Gwynedd. Oh thanks Jim."

What was he giving her, some hurt, left-out look? And putting his jacket on. She asked if he was OK. He said he was fine and was going out for some air but stood irresolute midway between the dancers and the door.

"Some rain you mean," she said and pressed Play. The beat was too fast. Had to be the previous track, hopefully near its end.

"Would have been easier if ours had been at the beginning of the tape wouldn't it," she said to the children.

"I like the rain," Jimmy said. He was closer to the door. Wat was looking at him. Carol turned to him, said what. Then, "OK you pervert. Right kids here it is, ready. Come on, concentrate Wat this is it, first entrance."

She saw Jimmy turn and move slowly to the front door then turned back to the rehearsal, excited.

CHAPTER THIRTY-ONE

Phil opened the window. He'd taken off his tie and the shirt-sleeves were rolled up.

"The eighteenth isn't it?" Vicki said from across the office. She was fresh back from a holiday in Paros, Poros, Paxos, or Naxos. Had a beautiful tan lucky girl.

"Yep. All day so they say, a Tuesday with it. Lose track of time on a Greek island do you?"

"That's why you have a holiday. The only day you've got to remember's the plane back."

He turned to face her. She did look good. "You're right. If you feel like it you might make the point to that little sod in Personnel. You know, on my behalf."

"I've never known you not be able to speak up for yourself Phil."

Yeah yeah yeah. If he could just get through these days surely they couldn't refuse. The slide of the dollar had begun on Monday morning after three months of a continued though bumpy rise, just as he'd predicted. The State Department and Defence were putting a brave face on it and holding in. The smooth flow of oil was the bottom line. Question now was whether the fall would develop its own dynamic.

It was sometime in the afternoon when Vicky shouted across that Tom Arthur was on his way up. "Five to ten minutes" he said. Phil pulled a face, looked at his watch and saw lunch had passed him by. He felt too weak for the bout of wheedling and whingeing he was in for.

"Just off to the powder room for a moment Vicky," he said.

A bit risqué but it was all right, she wouldn't get it. He looked in the long mirror above the handbasins. Surely Sir George could see it did nothing for the name of the firm to have senior staff looking like forced labour in a Stalinist deep mine complex. And it wasn't the powder, he'd been consciously abstemious of late but if ever an occasion justified its use, it was a little chat with Tom Arthur. The gizmo was quick and efficient. Afterwards he pulled the chain and heard its rumble crashing round the tiles. He wondered if Tom resorted to a gizmo. He'd seen no signs but how the hell else did he control the hooligans and barrow boys of the Dealing Department, routinely smashing phones when they called it wrong. It was a mystery.

Tom started off in pally mode. He too had had his holiday but was soon chivvying away for short-term predictions. Geared up Phil said he didn't want to blow his own trumpet but he had got the post-Louvre ups and downs consistently right. And what had happened, Tom Arthur who'd come to have his nose pointed in the right direction had come on like a smartarse saying it was true, but it was the past; today was today.

"That's what they call a truism," Phil said and ran through some fundamentals. Had Tom noticed that June had seen record levels of Japanese buying of U.S. Treasury bonds, their yield up to a record 6 percent higher than that of Japanese ones. Did he also realize that this same volume of buying had then reduced the yield differential.

Tom said yes, he took the point and then waited like he was some unworldly don in a tutorial with Phil the sweaty student. It was insufferable. Phil changed tack.

"As we both know Tom there's a helluva lot of liquid money swilling round the globe. Dwarfs what Central Banks hold for a rainy day. But till now their interventions have worked. Bloody expensive mind, $80 billion plus they've laid out since Louvre."

Tom nodded again.

Phil hurtled on.

"But then in all that time there's been nothing for that liquidity to latch on to. Bit different now with this bout of Gulf 'n' Oil nerves and that fracas at Mecca. Always makes the yen look pasty and good for the old greenback but now folks are starting to see that the oil's going to flow come what may the bandwagon's going to swing into reverse and where's it going to stop once it's rolling and the punters have another look at the trade deficit."

Tom nodded again and held cup and saucer in his hands like he was a senior Treasury official circa 1920 with a coal fire of his own.

Doubly insufferable

Phil changed tack again.

"And they might start looking at interest rates. Paul's inching them up right now which is fine. Like I've said before he doesn't want to bow out knee deep in froth but how much further will he push them because he also doesn't want to go down in East Coast history as the guy who put the spoilers on the greatest bull market in history."

"A forceful argument Phil, but where's it going to lead in the short-term?"

"You do want blood out of a stone. Of the Philip variety. Let's say you can count the dollar down 10 percent from the bust-up in Mecca until the big boys get together for the IMF meeting. Then it'll rally a bit."

Only with dates and figures was Tom Arthur finally satisfied. When he'd gone Phil did a wicked mime in Vicki's direction but she just gave him a funny look. He shrugged his shoulders.

And shrugged again the following Sunday, on the phone to Jack.

"Christ's sake partner, it's me who's had to listen to Mr Tall Person rather losing his cool and full of sob stories."

"I sympathise but my man's due back tomorrow or the day after at the latest. Nothing I can do right now. People take holidays, that's reality. We're not Safeways."

"No, we just have them."

"What. Ah, right. Got you. Brilliant Jack. Just a bit elaborate for a Sunday morning, remember what him above said of the Sabbath? Take it easy as I understand it. Anyway, fancy lunch?"

"I certainly don't fancy going without it."

Phil sighed. "Right, my treat. Your tall man's just whingeing."

"It's a Force Ten whinge."

Phil sighed some more. "Yes? Well I'm going to tell you a real sob story that'll give you some sense of perspective. And Jack, today's whinge is tomorrow's business."

"Said a city analyst. OK then, I'll wait for you."

"I was rather thinking of this end, fish on the river."

"I'm not travelling for a sob story. No way."

"OK Jack you dog, I'm on my way."

Phil put the phone down. He cursed Simone and her holiday. He double-cursed Sir George and doubled it again for cheeky Tom Arthur. Then he thought about Jack, why had he given in so easily over lunch. He would surely be too late for the South coast traffic but driving through South London was never going to be a bundle of laughs and he could well meet the day-trip jam on the way back.

So why had he given in so easily when an afternoon on the river would have been as perfect as the South East could manage. Come to that what was it with Jack? Jack his faithful friend now so very cocky. Why? Why because Jack had found his man at the marketing end of the business. Exactly that. Bloody childish, they were partners. Yes cocky ever since he'd come out of the Sloane Square place the second time. With the money. Strange. Completely different from the first time when he was out for the powder. Phil had had his doubts. Jack sweaty, eyes everywhere and gabbling about sofas. He'd said, You OK partner? And Jack had just managed a nod. Weird. Like the time old blue nose had shouted, You funked the tackle Sharp and there'd been only him to commiserate. Just like that. Only ten minutes there the second time and he was out again unbearably cheerful.

And what did Jack say when he did finally arrive after jams on Brixton Hill, his oldest and best friend? That he, that he wasn't at all sure he could unleash Phil on his local for a second time. It was outrageous. What was he, mad dog Stone? Phil the Killer?

"Those are 100 percent rhetorical questions Phil!

"And here's a 100 percent statement pal, you're pushing it."

Maybe there'd been a glint in his eye but whatever way his

friend, fellow analyst, and now partner had laughed, thrown an arm round his shoulders and told him not to take everything so seriously, that he was only kidding.

There was kidding and kidding.

The walk in the woods helped. It was warm but a breeze rustled in the trees. When they came to toy with their fruit salads his equilibrium was restored.

"You know Jack I've been smitten by the thought that maybe I was never sympathetic enough when your Sir Nick favoured you with a dinner party."

"Probably not."

"Having just endured Sir George's."

"What, a dinner party in August? Still, a sorrow shared is a burden lightened."

Phil put down his spoon decisively. "You can carry public-image building a mite too far."

"What?"

"Don't give me What. Your little homily, fresh from this morning's sermon."

"What. No. Definitely no. Way off-beam, no church for me. Of course I show my face and scrape the knee at Christmas, that's normal. Any more than that and you get logged by Special Branch." Phil softened, he laughed. He laughed too much.

"Give the coffee a miss eh, Phil. So your man's back tomorrow."

"Yep, today or tomorrow," Phil said.

"About time. Yes, two cognacs please."

"He who waits appreciates Jack. Not a bad thing for your man to understand it doesn't grow on trees."

"Bushes was my understanding. Bloody phenomenal ones at that, four crops per annum if it's the right bit of the Andes. Ah thank you, and the bill is for this gentleman here." Was there no end to cocky Jack? It was remorseless. Out in the woods he suggested they stop for a while. "If your green-belt's an endangered species, let's make the most of it."

Jack said that was a fatalistic viewpoint. Phil was glad to hear it. "Because I've an idea I may not be a stranger to it much longer."

"You?"

"Yep. Even the worst of ordeals can come up with something. One of Sir George's dinner guests just happened to be one of the shrewdest barrow boys in Property."

"Who, not Reg? Left his plate clean did he?" There were moments when one realized exactly why one's best friend was one's best friend.

"Hole in one. Came of a deprived childhood graphically described. Being the well brought up boy I am I heard it out and introduced myself. To which he says, Wapping, a bit overvalued ain't it. East end charm and the river all very nice, but you're going to get a serious oversupply of square footage. He's right. It's like living on a building site."

"You'll be an asset to any neighbourhood."

"I'll take that as a compliment, provisionally. How's your week been?"

"Not bad. When I told them the South African strike didn't matter a jot the keen punters called me a spoilsport. Now I'm reinstated as superboy."

"So it didn't do your price any good."

Like I've said for weeks, it was never going to make much of a dent. Still with all that over I'm going to grab some holiday time."

"Holiday, now you're talking business. When?"

"Next Friday week, thinking of Italy or Turkey."

"Jack, wonderful. You've put the steel back in me, I'm giving them an ultimatum. You'd think they were trying to abolish holidays. Supposed to be a quiet month August but Terry Field in Equities tells me it's been a record month for Rights Issues."

"Did your Terry also tell you no one's exactly fighting to take any of it."

"Jack it's me, your pal, course I noticed. If the market doesn't take a nasty tumble before the year's out you can put me on a prolonged diet of humble pie."

"What's that taste like?"

"Bland."

Jack brought deckchairs out into the garden. Phil fell asleep.

He was woken by sounds of monotonous aggression. Jack was coming out the house with what looked like gin and tonic.

"Some chainsaw Charlie," he said.

"Bastard. Have they no respect. It's a fucking Sunday. I was having a good dream."

"What about?"

"I'd taken up squash again, giving Tom Arthur a real run-around on court. This is terrible, like being in the fucking dentist."

"Tell you what Phil, with a holiday on the horizon, fancy making it six ounces when you see your man. Keep my man happy. Need a hand with some cash?"

"No, cash isn't a problem"

"Only for the ordinary folk of Beiruit apparently. Their government of sorts is talking of selling 20 percent of the Central Bank's gold reserves to try and put a bit of purchasing power into the Lebanese pound."

"Didn't know there were any ordinary people in Beirut."

"Oh I think you'll find they're an international class."

CHAPTER THIRTY-TWO

"Not bad looking your feller. In the daylight. All right is he?"

"He's not my feller Marie."

"All right, he's not. Your holiday partner, how's that? Didn't he want to stay to tea?"

"He's got to go and look at a job, give an estimate, that's why we only stopped once on the way back. The girls were great, we had a mattress in the back of his van and they kept up I Spy for three hours out of the back window."

They were sitting on Marie's front stairs. The smell of exhaust fumes that started the moment they were off the M4 stank in Carol's nose.

"Don't worry, give it a couple of hours and you'll get your tolerance back," Marie said. Carol screwed her nose.

"You all look great. Knowing Lilly I won't hear a thing till she gets the hump about something and then it'll be, I wish I was back in Wales. Then I'll get the lot."

"Tempting, the country life"

"For a while," Marie said. "What was that crack Lilly made? Something about if it was a lady he was going to see he should try and be polite."

"Did she? Wind-up experts Jim and Lilly. Situation comedy, we should put them on TV."

"Supposed to be a sign of affection. One day she'll say, Who? Oh Jimmy, a bit of a nutter but he's all right. Sheila like him?"

"Yes. Yes, I think so."

"Cagey Carol. Lucky you."

"Maybe. What are the girls up to?"

"Lilly was putting her shells and stones in order. Where Fred can't find them. He's away with his dad. The girls'll be watching telly now. Three weeks of starvation, withdrawal symptoms. By the way your pal Arthur, very anxious to see you. He's rung a few times. In fact he'll probably ring again soon."

In the passageway they could hear the TV. The two girls were in front of it flat on their stomachs.

When the kettle boiled Carol made tea while Marie knocked up some food. There was a black-eyed bean salad and a cut up cucumber.

"Fish fingers as well?" Marie said from the fridge door.

"Eclectic."

"What?"

"An interesting or weird mixture. Maybe I got the wrong word, Pauline uses it."

"That's because she's a weird mixture. How did they make out with her two, haven't seen them for years."

"OK. In fact they were a bit sad this morning. It started with these two coming shocked that Gwynedd didn't know who Madonna was, then she laughed at them when they got freaked out over a dead rabbit but they sorted it out."

"Aren't they a bit precious, hers? Cut off. Ah there you are, smelled it did you?"

"Mum, what's been happening? Three whole weeks in nowhere we've been."

"Well as I remember it Lilly I had a rest and missed you."

"No with Rachel and the Gorgeous Robot. The last one I saw she was trapped by the Deadly Borings and they'd fixed the robot so it could only use its arms and couldn't say anything but now this week he's hiding out in this empty skyscraper looking for her."

"To be honest I've given afternoon TV a miss. I even read three books, not bad eh?"

"You could have video'd it, now I'll have to ring Kerry." The phone rang. Lilly ran for it like it was sure to be Kerry.

"Next time she's away she'll have to write a detailed list of instructions," Marie said. She was laughing.

"No she didn't mean that, she only" Sheila started.

"It's for someone called Simone, I said there wasn't one but this man said yes there was."

Marie pulled a face.

"My fault Lilly," Carol said. "She's a friend of mine, I said I'd take a message."

She went into the front room.

"Arthur, nice to hear you . . . What . . . Oh a friend of my friend's daughter . . . Anyway how are you . . . what, no rest for the virtuous . . . That's why I haven't been in touch, I hope you're not going to make me feel guilty about having a holiday . . . That sounds wonderful, a sextet. Great but I've only just got back, haven't even unpacked perhaps you could ring tomorrow . . . OK, bye now."

From the way Lilly said it Kerry's account of the missing episodes was hopeless.

"But if he could move his arms he could have fixed his wires by himself," Sheila said.

"He hasn't got wires, circuit boards."

"Well his circuit boards then."

"What are his fingers like?" Carol asked.

"Well they're like plastic but he's got nails and they're varnished all different colours."

"Oh the one Fred was rude about," Marie said.

"Fred, what's he know. But even then the Deadly Borings would have heard him and then they'd have got really boring and put him to sleep for ever."

Back home Sheila found the book she'd somehow forgotten when they'd set off for Wales and got up on her bed. Carol got down to unpacking and opening the windows. Later she sorted out the washing and decided that when she'd done the business with Arthur, six in one hit, she would get a decent washing machine. It seemed like he hadn't been bullshitting when he said it would be regular.

"Mum, who's Simone?"

She stayed bent over the olive green washing basket. "Oh she's this daft friend of mine."

"Have I ever met her?"

It's what came of relaxing. Worse, Marie'd warned her he might call. She straightened up from the basket.

"Simone? No I don't think you have. Maybe when you were very young."

"When I was a baby?"

"Yes it would have been then."

"Mum, are you all right?"

"I'm fine, just a bit whacked and her, my friend Simone, she's not happy.

"Oh."

Oh. This was awful. What the hell was she doing, lies making more lies.

It was Sheila came to the rescue.

"Knock knock."

"Who's there?" Carol had never felt so happy answering the question.

"Wat."

"What who?"

Sheila laughed so much it was a wrestling match pulling a sheet over her head.

"Wat hoo hoo," she got out before the laughing took over, louder still.

"A ghost, a ghost in the house," Carol shouted out and leapt to pull the sheet off so she could hug her little phenomena. Sheila got her head out. "What goes yellow'n black, yellow'n black?" Carol tried and got stuck on a hooped rugby shirt Chris had worn around the house.

"A drunk bumblebee," Sheila said, put her head on the pillow and closed her eyes. Carol stayed sat on the bed wanting big breaths out. She held them in. Till Sheila's breathing was even. She went into her own room, sat on the bed and let her head drop. Helter skelter went the lies. Breathe out. Get rid of it. Breathe out. Yes, and phone Terry. Yes phone him or it would all have been for nothing and her guilt another fucking luxury.

Not engaged. She could picture his phone on the low table under the doorphone, startling the der der ring. Then steady. Der Der So what did she expect? That he never went out. That he didn't have his own life. It could be anything, a drink, a movie, a girlfriend. First thing you learn is you've always got to wait. Bravo the Velvet Underground only that was years ago and smack. And what about her, worrying about bizz when just a minute before it was her stupid lies to Sheila. Like she liked worrying. Like she fucking liked it.

She looked at the cold TV in the half light.

She rang Jimmy. It was great to hear her voice he said and yes, the job looked OK, good money. What about him coming round, he said.

"I'm a bit tired Jim, a bit out of sorts. Back to reality."

"Sure."

"I'll ring you."

Next morning the old washing machine went haywire. Sheila, happy with a bowl of coco-pops after three straight weeks of muesli was keen to help mop up. By the time the kitchen was halfway dry it was half ten. Carol tried Terry's. There was no reply. The puddle on the floor had gone but Sheila had dirty wet patches on her dress. Carol stopped herself thinking out loud whether help with mopping was worth it. Terry just happened not have been in.

He wasn't in at a quarter to eleven, eleven o'clock, eleven fifteen, twelve o'clock. By then all the washing was done.

She was just inside the wire-and-glass door of the launderette when the old bag who had some number there like Manageress told her Preference on the Dryers Is Given To Those Who've Used The Washers. At the back of the place where the dryers were either side of a tight aisle a woman was pulling out her bits and pieces. Carol moved fast. The woman had half her stuff folded away in a Council-stamped black rubbish bag. She folded the remaining clothes slowly. Pillow cases. Sheets. She checked in the dryer for the sock that might have got away. The manageress was close by.

"Didn't you hear me dearie?"

Carol knew the score, had her first coin in with one hand while shoving in the mix of damp clothes: once you'd paid, that was that.

"Well don't think you're coming in here again."

The woman made her money on the Service laundry. Carol saw bags and baskets all around but if she weakened she'd be finished. Besides the woman had said exactly the same thing a couple of months back. Marie'd split herself, said it would be a first, barred out of a launderette.

She shoved in three more coins and turned away. The manageress had tired eyes and sausage legs with a tangle of blue veins. Carol faltered. She looked away. Sheila was doing a wary number with a boy by the door. By it was a scratched wallphone. It had a dialling tone.

In the afternoon they took a bus down to the river for a walk. Carol took in three working phone boxes on the way. At least Marie was in and Carol was sat over her phone when Arthur came through bang on time. She told him such things did happen and he said, So it appears. Like she was a complete arsehole. It was her fault, sure: to have thought she could go on holiday and forget everything; to have not bothered ringing Terry all that time; not to have told Pauline one night she was going out for a while and walked a mile to the phone box she'd noticed, looking like a Tardis in the year dot AD.

It was her fault. No question. But she wasn't going through this every night.

"So as things are Arthur it would be better if I could phone you except I seem to have lost your number." She spoke coolly, felt the flutters inside. He'd never given her a number, it was the way things had been and if he now turned her down flat, what then?

"I was thinking I could call you again tomorrow," he said.

But she'd committed herself.

"I'm afraid that's not possible." She waited.

It came out in a rush, a 981 number. Triumph out of adversity.

Her victory wound up bruised. For two days the sky was low and grey, everything wet. The girls spent the first day at Marie's. The second they were at hers with Ben and Jaycinthe too. She did her best. Sheila's bunk bed was many things with a bit of help: a cafe; a desert tent in which Ben said Harem over and over; a clothes shop run by Lilly; and a pirate ship where Ben was Captain, then Cabin boy, walked the plank and wound up as Captain again. It was the third day at twelve calls per day she got through. Terry answered at the second ring and she was so surprised she was incoherent.

"OK Carol slow down, take it easy and start again. You're trying to say, How's it going Tel, did you have a good holiday." Wow, it was good to hear his voice. She laughed.

"Doesn't leave me much to say though I'd been hoping to say such things personally, tomorrow. I've half a dozen things to tell you."

"A heavy load. Not sure I could handle all that tomorrow."

Shit. Shit. Shit.

Nothing for it, best foot forward. Like how about the day after tomorrow. Which was possible, he said and would throw in afternoon tea, around four.

OK it was a drag but it was something fixed. The world hadn't stopped. She phoned Arthur. Reassured him. Seven o'clock the day after tomorrow, definitely.

She switched on the TV. A man with a moustache stood in a slice of beautifully furnished drawing room. Carol thought 1920s. He took a cigarette from a silver box on a bit of table. There was his hand with long fingers. There was the whole room with a woman sat down in a sumptuous frock. Back to his face. Carol saw CRISIS OF CONSCIENCE in silent movie scroll. The man said, "Beatrice, my wife, just because she is . . ."

"Mad Philip, mad. Can't you bring yourself to say it."

Carol switched channels. A black and white furry thing with a miserable face stared at her.

"The panda too has its own natural habitat."

She switched on the main light to find her tobacco. The panda and its greenery were pale. She switched channel. A friendly cartoon bear was telling a young person that The Bank took a personal interest. She tried again. Mr Gorbachev in head-phones. And again. The man in the drawing room had his head in his hands. A butler stood immobile in the doorway. He held a sliver tray on which lay a white card.

Carol switched off the TV and the main light. All she had to do was let the furry darkness have its way. Her head sank with its weight into the pillow but Marie's voice stepped in. You poor Cancerians, sensitive, absorbent, insomniac crabs. Then Pat said, crabs should steer clear of the Sellafield coastline, Sellafield was Windscale. She shoved Pat's voice away but Chris popped up to tell her that the whole concept of a perfectly positioned resting neck was just an illusion. You want me to spell it out, he said. No she did not.

She reached for the phone and rang Jim.

"Hi, it's Carol. I know it's late, just wanted to hear your voice."

"Good to hear yours. You OK, what you up to?"

"I tried the TV. Gave up."

"Snap. Hey I know it's late but you mind if I come over?"

"Mind? No, now I can hear your voice it's exactly what I want."

CHAPTER THIRTY-THREE

A right shithole, Malaga airport. Still it hasn't dented how good I feel. It's recharged my batteries this holiday and I'll be the first to admit I needed it. At one time I had Thailand in mind but figured that would be more an adventure than a rest. Sarah's out like a light next to me but I'm going to have another half bottle of their white wine. It's on the firm and looking at what you pay for a scheduled flight you're well entitled to as much value for money as you can handle. Let's hope it's done her a bit of good too. I've done my best, tried to keep her a bit straight and she's got a bit of a tan. Normally she's very pale Sarah is so we had to go a bit easy on the old sun but we got it about right because she's got a bit of colour without getting burnt. Yes, all in all it's been well worth it. I've been able to think through a few things and there's a spring back in the step.

Course it took a lot of fixing, I couldn't just take off. It's a joke really, all the hassle you've got to go through just for a holiday but that's reality, I had a lot on my plate. Curtis for one thing. Turned out he was due for a spot of leave too but I managed to fit him in before we both left. Funnily enough it was him, Graham, who suggested a walk in the park. Maybe he really does think I'm taping him. Personally I think you can take paranoia too far. After sailing there's no better exercise than a walk in the sunshine he said. Bollox.

"Limbering up for your holiday Graham?" I said. "Off with the boat is it?"

Turned out that no, he wasn't. Just this once it was a villa in Spain. I said that was a coincidence which was a bit of a rick. For one thing it's not his business and for another he didn't like the sound of it till he worked out he was a couple of hundred miles to the north. Personally speaking I think the Rubber Heels have got about as much bite as Mickey White has these days but in the death I prefer Graham careful, even when it's treble careful. In fact it's been one of the things going through my mind while I've been away.

Here's the stewardess, not exactly a stunner but efficient which is what you want when you're a few thousand feet up in the air. She's got my half bottle and a fresh glass. It's those little touches that count so I say thanks and yes, I will fly with her again. Doesn't cost you does it, raising a smile.

Yes, it's strange what can set off things in your mind. I was having breakfast on the terrace one morning, you can't beat it can you, reading the old paper out in the sun with just your shorts on and a decent cup of coffee. It's not normally something I'd have time for but I was reading this in-depth piece on Liverpool football club. They're a success story you can't argue with, the consistency with which they've been at the top. And the secret of their success? There is no secret. What they do is stand by their quality players but as they move into their thirties they'll buy young quality players in whatever position the veteran plays. Makes sense but there's a bit more to it, there's the timing. See they don't just dump the veteran. No, what they do is keep the new one in the Reserves for a while, get him used to the club style and groom him slowly slowly. Of course that's not an absolute rule. Like I've said many times you've got to have rules but also you've got to have flexibility. If the new boy's really special he'll be in the first team a bit smart. On the other hand they're not wishful thinkers because if they've discover they've made a rick with the new signing, that he's not as good as they thought he was, they're liable to sell him. But what I'm talking about here is the norm, the talent doing his apprenticeship and in the process learning off of the veteran, the experienced player.

There I was, reading this piece, and it hit me. That's exactly what Graham is, experienced. On the other hand he's also getting on and at the end of the day, wants his retirement same as the rest of us. He's not going to be there for ever, no one is. I'm not going to just dump him, Graham's a man who's going to be on the books till he decides to call it a day, but I decided there and then that we should also start looking for someone else. Start him off with little things and impress on him we want him to be careful even with those and give him the confidence to say no to things he reckons can't be done.

Not bad for an airline, it's a Bordeaux. I'm not a serious drinker but when I do have one I want it to be something halfway decent which is something I had to impress on Miguel at that restaurant where we ate. It's a pity Graham's boy's not on the Force, he's an engineer. Very proud of him his dad is. In fact he was telling me that day in the park he's just got a senior post with the Channel Tunnel. Graham was in a very good mood altogether. Course he had his holiday coming up which helps, but I had a feeling it was more than that. I'd made the time to see him to get more on that fucking Akbar and knew I was going to have to take my time over it.

"You know I've often said Gordon that it's the little things, the details or individuals that can come together to make the whole picture," he says. If he's told me once he's told me a thousand fucking times so I nodded.

"Take an example, I go to see someone on a completely unrelated case and quite out the blue get the key that gives the whole picture to the Mickey White case."

I was all ears then and took a serious look at a gang of birds up in a tall tree.

"Not strictly my case but certain of my own suspicions about Mr White have been confirmed and as it turns out I can make my own contribution to putting a very dangerous man behind bars for a very long time."

There's two of them working their way backwards now, chocolates this time, on the house. Don't exactly go with Bordeaux. No I bided my time and after saying a bit about the birds and the trees and how there was nothing to beat London on a proper summer's day I said I hoped his jigsaw was taking shape with some Iranian he'd mentioned. As it happens I will take a couple of them chocolates, Sarah's got a sweet tooth though I've been trying to get her diet better balanced and eating more regular. It was Curtis's turn to look at the birds while he tells me he don't expect any immediate results. But it wasn't 100 percent all clear. He said some cases were slow-burners but that it was hard for him to justify man-hours spent in a climate where there's pressure for immediate results. I knew I'd have to take my time digesting that one so we stopped to look at some ducks in a pond.

No grief but don't take liberties was my interpretation and I switched the subject, said looking at the ducks, tame animals made me think of prison and mightn't prisons be a good source of those little connections he was talking about. Speaking as a layman, I said, it looked logical to me. His eyes fairly twinkled, told me it was something he couldn't emphasise strongly enough to his squad.

You know what, the feller opposite is up for a piss again. What's that, the second or third time. It's always possible he put away too much of that rubbish beer at the airport but you know what I reckon, he could be one of those mules runs the charlie out of Spain. He don't look the type but then that's what you'd be looking for in a mule. He's left his book on the seat. *Yesterday's Spy* it's called. What's one of them, a public school type pissing about with false moustaches behind enemy lines? I feel like asking the geezer when he gets back, you know, just so as to know whether he's reading it. I won't because if you want to get on in life you've got to have self-discipline. Doesn't matter how much talent you've got, without that you won't get anywhere. And one thing self-discipline means is not saying most of the things that just pop into your head. Like I was tempted to say to Curtis after he'd said his bit about prison intelligence, What does a fucking chancer like Ryan hope to get out of it. There's no parole in drug cases.

I was tempted, but I didn't say it, It would have been pure self-indulgence on my part. It wasn't just Curtis either, all that running around I had to do just to get a holiday in peace. It was worth it though, it meant I could I have a nice dip in the warm sea without worries running round my head. Like there were certain arrangements to be made for Sarah with the Iranian out the game. They cost a bit, a friend of a friend of one of Derek's outlets in fact.

And then there was Mario, had to see him to make sure everything was going to run smoothly in that direction. If there was one thing would keep Derek on the rail after he'd got a cob on about the Iranian, it was being busy with the charlie. Everyone wants to think they're being useful don't they. I didn't push Mario on price, that's what I call a slow-burner, but I did put my foot down over Clerkenwell. No way, I said. So Mario starts whingeing like the rest of London was some fucking jungle he's likely to get lost in. I had to spell it out: repetition means pattern, and pattern is just about all the Law have got to work on other than grasses.

He's back, yesterday's spy, the piss artist, and he is picking up his book. A decent tan he's got and a sober tracksuit but how do you know whether someone's really reading a book. Yes, tracksuits, we're putting some out with the club logo on. Keith's idea. Just before I left he was saying we should be looking for another site, a bigger one with floor space for badminton as well as the squash. Battersea, Stoke Newington, or Rotherhithe he reckons. It riled me when he said we were a bit late for Docklands, the north side, given how snotty he was when I just followed my nose and opened the wine bar. Anyway, I told him to do his research and present it to me and Derek when he was ready.

Sarah's still out for the count but what's nice is she looks really peaceful. You know what the joke is, that could have been Tina, the slag. Tina could have had it all: the house by the sea, out to the best flamenco joint and not worrying about the bill so long as they don't take you for a cunt, a beach that isn't full of hooligans or brummies. And that's just holidays I'm talking. She could have had it all but as it turned she was just a rip-off artist and what happens to them is, they always stay smalltime. OK, they have their little coup but what they don't understand is a rip-off is a one-off. More than that, they don't understand that the creation of real, secure wealth takes a lot of hard work, dedication and discipline. Take her now, Tina. She's got to be what, forty-six, forty-seven, which is a bit old for being on the game so you know what I reckon, right this moment she's probably sunk in front of a TV with a dodgy picture and a bottle of cheap sherry on the wrong side of Winnipeg.

The pilot's speaking. Now there's a thing, we're over Bordeaux. Several thousand fucking feet over as it happens. It's dead easy really, you just hold the empty bottle in your hand, catch the hostess's eye and you're going to get another one. Might as well enjoy your holiday right up to the last minute because once it's finished there's going to be a whole pile of things in the in-tray. For a start there's ringing the Iranian which isn't just a matter of picking up the phone. Now in life there's strategy and there's tactics. There's a lot of people think they're the same thing. Not true. Tactics with the Iranian? No problem, stall the cunt. Strategy however, that's what's been going through my head the last couple of weeks. At the end of the day it's a question of our whole future development. See Keith isn't just on about developing the gym side of the business, he wants out of the Iranians altogether so of course he's jumped on this Akbar cock-up. I'm going to have a problem there. What it amounts to is me having to steer a course that will hold the firm together. There's been plenty of instances where I've had to spend valuable time keeping the peace between Keith and Derek, times I've had to knock their heads together. With this business I can see it winding up as a full time occupation if I don't play my cards right. My own approach to the Iranian is more pragmatic. We've got to look at the case on its merits, as it develops, which is another job for me, making a meet with Curtis to see if limited manpower hours has won the day.

Still asleep Sarah is. Sure she's had her problems but there's times like this I envy her. Still I'm pencilled in for a good kip myself tonight. If there's one surefire way to lose the boost a holiday's given you, it's to try and do too much too soon. I did think of leaving the motor at the airport but it costs you an arm and a leg when a cab's just as good. Better when you think about it. Yes, then a good sleep and I'll be as fresh as a daisy come the morning. I'll have to be with what's on my plate and that's not even including William our finance man. My turn for Manchester. I don't mind, the quarterly dividend will be in by then and we'll have real figures to deal with. That Liberian structure's still not in place, shouldn't be down to me to hurry it up, but then there's a lot of things in this world shouldn't be. It's no good just saying it, you've got to get out there and do something about it. One bonus is Curtis finally managed to stumble on the relevant bit in Geoff Christian's past. He was quite funny, Keith. Said if you put an elephant right in front of Curtis's face, he'll see it. Something like that.

We must be nearly there. Better get a leak before we're all strapped in. Now there's a thing, who's this coming out of the khasi so I can get in, it's yesterday's spy. You know what, I think the cunt is carrying.

CHAPTER THIRTY-FOUR

"There was a time before you went away I thought you were slipping," Vicky said.

"Only clutch problems, nothing serious."

"Oh yeah."

The sexy disbelief she crammed into a couple of words. Natural talent.

"But we don't want to get too perky do we?"

What was this now, a reference to powder abuse in the preholiday period? OK, he had looked haggard but who wouldn't.

"Who's we Vicky, the family, the firm, the people of the world?"

That had her smiling.

"Yeah yeah you're all right Phil, I'm convinced. No need to prove it over and over."

"Wish that was true but my job description says otherwise," he said.

She was right without knowing the half of it. He was sharp on the job, dynamic on his account, hardly back from holiday when he heard there was a buyer for the flat. At his price.

They'd caught a last-minute vacancy, an upmarket complex on a beach near Rethymnon. One time after a morning's scuba diving and a lunch of fresh fish Jack had asked if he wasn't being premature, putting it on the market.

"Once your nose has spoken, can't piss about."

"There's the decisive Phil and there's the rash."

He'd had to glare. Thanks for the tip, he'd said.

Fortunately for the holiday mood it was the only time he'd

had to be firm with Sharp the whole fortnight. They'd swum a lot, been abstemious with the powder and eaten well; even had some good times with two fun designer ladies from Copenhagen who had an aversion to condoms. All in all a great time which was all to the good after the hassle with the last six ounces. Jack had given him a hard time, he'd tried passing it on to Simone. And failed. Wound up giving her his number. Not good at all.

"Anyway Vicki you seemed to have survived well without me and my chat," he said.

"Rather I hadn't would you?"

"There may be times when I sound like a yob but I'm a gent underneath."

"Does that mean no?"

"It's certainly what I meant. Tell you what, give me a couple of hours on this and I'll stand you lunch."

He got down to work. Had he really been away? Come to that had a year really passed between September last year and Now now? What was he, a peasant farmer for whom early Autumn would always mean the same thing, sowing this or harvesting that, yet the warm-up period to the annual IMF/World Bank jamboree seemed to be uncannily like that of '86. A prolonged bout of Euro-whingeing; International Equity markets hardly believing their luck; and Mr Baker caught in the same fix, hoping to reduce the trade deficit with a cheap dollar and running slap bang into big Paul seeing Inflation as the only consequence of such a thing. If the bastards would only save. And if they wouldn't, why, at least tax American citizens For Their Own Good?

Lunch went leisurely when Vicky turned out to be someone who could hold her drink and hold her own. Sharkey, the rising Yen star in Zwimmer, Monk and Gradey had passed their booth and made a comment. She'd heard him out then said, Always a tricky thing, the turn-up. I know it's hard but yours are half an inch on the short side. Just hadn't been able to stop himself, Sharkey who was said to have the best flies on the walls of the Bank of Japan and the Finance Ministry, his head went down to look and it was all over. Never had she appeared more desirable.

Back in the office they'd shown maturity, she down to the Compaq, him to his calculations. It didn't last. The phone rang, his presence required in Sir George's office. Half an hour.

He was given a sherry and told how well he looked; what a wonderful thing holidays were; and how clear his reports.

"In such an interdependent world that quality is especially impressive to an old codger like me, brought up when things were simpler."

As Phil saw it Uncanny Predictive Accuracy might have been added to the Clarity but he said nothing.

"And your Mr Volcker Philip, taking his bow. Let us hope the myth of Atlas has given way to the modern realization that no one is indispensable. Ah Tom, come in."

"Sir George. Phil."

What the hell was this, Tom Arthur looking like he'd just licked a plateful of cream.

"I'm glad I could get you both together, knowing how busy you must be. At any one time the market may be quiet but it never seems to do anything for our workload does it? Which in a way is why I've asked you both to come. As you'll know, yes of course you do I'm sounding like a headmaster, as you'll know we're living through a period of rapid transformation both technologically and in the necessary scale of our operations. In addition, as you also know, to meet this challenge we've also had to give ourselves some global muscle and taken the logical decision to go in with our American friends. The global market is a reality whether we like it or not."

Tom Arthur was nodding regularly, like this was very wise stuff.

"Now our American partners have their own ways of running things which might appear to be a tad inflexible. All it really does however is to emphasise those values we ourselves have always held dear, co-operation and teamwork. In one area of our management structure they do find a fault, one which is perhaps embedded in our national culture. We see it for example in the world of British science and technology, that entrenched, rigid and disastrous division between the theoretical and the applied."

The bastard! The whingeing fucking creep! Tom Arthur wheedling away behind his back. You went on holiday, and what happened, you not shafted.

"And with that in mind, Sir George said, they're looking for, and it's hard to argue with them on this score, a greater meshing of Analysis and the Dealing we do on our own account, while of course both will remain as departmentally independent. Now let's look at how this can be achieved."

He'd managed to stay impassive throughout. An hour of bullshit with organisational structure diagrams thrown in and he hadn't looked at Tom Arthur once but afterwards could not face returning to his own office. Try as he might there'd be a scowl on his face and he didn't want Vicky seeing it.

He did not.

He rang her from a pay phone in the lobby, told her he wouldn't be back and put the phone down before she got started. After some farting about on the Stammer, Casey and Mangledorf switchboard he got through to a relaxed Jack. Lucky guy. No pressure. Was treating himself to a look at developments in Electronics, he said. Their impact on demand for his precious metal.

Phil handled it, spoke in a normal voice and fixed a rendez-vous in St Katherine's Dock.

Outside he stopped to stare at the Bank of England, its solid structure, something sound in a floating, flexible and fucking treacherous world.

A pinstripe gave him a funny look. Christ, he must look like some absolute hick, up to the City for the first time. He turned away quickly into Lombard Street and carried on down Fenchurch Street before turning right towards the Tower. Tea merchant territory. He didn't know anyone in Tea personally but it had to be an easy number. Whereas what was he in for, twice weekly Get-Togethers and Closer Co-Ordination with Tom Arthur. Which meant being at Tom's beck and call because there was nothing he wanted off that slimeball.

It was monstrous.

It was insufferable.

Gangs of pinstripes were on the move. There you were in Tea and your working day was finished by Four. Four thirty at the latest.

The street opened up ahead by Tower Hill Tube to reveal the river and the Tower itself. A few hundred years ago and an earlier generation of men whose only crime was to be good at their job had got their heads sliced off in there. He sympathised, all the things Sir Walter had done, spuds, tobacco, and lost his head as reward.

He found a bench on a small slice of green in front of the tube station and sat down. This wasn't the Americans, surely not. He'd done well there, fixed up a system of non-duplication and Co-ordination as he understood the word. No, this was Tom and his windbag of a boss. Hadn't it been Sir George himself who said the firm would keep its autonomy within the partnership. All the old fucker had offered as a carrot was an upward revision of the bonus system. Big deal.

All he'd let himself say as the meeting broke up was that he'd be interested to see how it worked out in practice.

He got up again and hesitated. How the hell was he supposed to get into East Smithfield on foot. One zebra, cautiously: another and he was stuck on a scrap of paving, a monstrous Tanker lorry ahead, a wild paper van behind.

He shivered.

"What can I say, outrageous," Jack said. It was warm enough to sit out on one of the bench 'n tables on the cobbles in front of the bulk of the Dickens Inn.

"Outrageous."

Phil didn't seem to hear, just stared out at the back and forth of a smartish crowd.

"There's always the headhunters, you'd be snapped up."

Phil said nothing.

Jack tried the Light Hearted. "Did you see that Phil, Goldman Sachs directors locked themselves in a Manhattan hotel to sort out their re-structuring. Three weeks they've been at it, doors locked. Still even that lot can't keep it up 24 hours a day. What do you reckon they run to for relaxation? Monopoly? *Mary Poppins* on video?"

Phil grunted.

Jack heard a hello directed his way.

"Sorry I'm not the world's number one when it comes to remembering names. Jack isn't it?"

A couple in their forties were stood there. Them.

"Steve and Lady Bridget. Yes of course. Sir Nick's dinner party. Wonderful. Phil Stone, a good friend. We used to be great fans of yours didn't we Phil, when we were at school."

"When you smashed your guitars," Phil said. It was a sour voice.

Steve sort of grinned. "We've just been looking at a bit of property we've an interest in," he said.

Jack thought he should stand up and offer a drink. Steve turned to his wife.

"Recent?" Phil said.

"Sorry, what?"

"Your interest?"

"Ah that. Yes I wouldn't mind a pint as it happens. Not a bad spot on a summer's evening. Out of the traffic. A bit of character. Bridget?"

"A Perrier."

Jack hurried off determined to be quick. Phil on his own with them in his present mood, it didn't bear thinking about. He saw magnesium hitting water in the school lab. Mr Rye had been very jolly about it.

The bar inside was huge. Too big. A production line of Japanese, a camera each, and the entire bar staff busy turning out half pints. He waved a twenty towards the bar over the heads of a couple who smiled and kept a tight grip on their cameras. He got a sliver of eye contact with the fuzzy haired barmaid. She crashed a pair of half pints on the bar.

Bloody yen. Surely there had to be a better way of straightening out balance of payment imbalances. Bloody Phil. He might be running amok at this very moment. When it was him who'd suggested this old world shithole in the first place.

Bloody Steve. He'd never dreamed the guy would accept his offer. Why, he hardly knew the man.

He shoved through the cheerful cordon waving his Twenty and fixed on fuzzy-hair. He gabbled his order. She brought up a final half pint and shrugged her shoulders. She said something. What beer? Fucks sake, this was no time for choice.

"Best bitter," he said. "Regardless."

Phil could be saying almost anything, something absolutely ghastly. And how was he going to carry this lot?

"A tray?" the girl repeated like he was a nutter and gave him soggy change.

There was nothing else for it. He stuck the Perrier bottle in one jacket pocket, its glass in the other, then gripped three pint glasses tight between his hands. Tension held them up? Friction held them up? One of the two. Mr Rye knew. Mr Rye had known. He should have demanded mugs with handles.

Beer slopped out on a camera case.

On suede shoes.

Too bad mate.

His wrists hurt. He hurried forward.

They were still there. Steve was saying Everyone was entitled to their own Opinion. Jack didn't like the sound of it. Not at all. He provided instant comic relief, pulling glass and bottle out of his pockets in the manner of a magician and poured the Perrier with a flourish.

"Unconventional but effective," Lady Bridget said with a smile.

What a lady!

He smiled back. Steve was off again. "Whether it was the band, the team, a cast, a business, everyone's entitled to their own opinion. It's how you get real teamwork and if you've got that, you're in business"

Jack turned. Phil was scowling. If it came to it he'd have a coughing fit. He would have an urgent appointment. He would spill his pint down Phil's trousers. Anything.

They were in the Marina car park standing by the Volvo.

"Don't get so excited Jack, there's no harm done."

"How do you know? How do you *know*?"

"All I did was give him the heebie-jeebies on East London property prices. Doing him a favour in fact. OK maybe I did say I'd got it off our in-house astrologist but he didn't find it outlandish."

Jack said nothing. He got in the car. Thought about it and opened the passenger door. Phil got in. Jack drove off, stopped at the lowered boom and paid the parking ticket. At the Marina exit he turned right along The Highway. He turned right again at the barbed wire fortress of Murdoch.

Newspapers.

The road became cobbles.

He slowed down.

"Jack I'm really grateful for this. In fact you've been a good friend altogether. Listening to my whingeing self-pity the way you did. And that's finished with now, I've sobered up. I appreciate the way you've put up with me, listening, trying to snap me out of it."

Jack pulled off the cobbles, half way on the pavement just before a pontoon bridge, and stopped the car. Phil was looking out of the passenger window.

"Yes, I was a good friend. At your suggestion I come to this place, went through murders to buy a round, and that's not even counting exorbitant parking charges. I come to this watering hole of yours and it so happened that two social acquaintances passed by and you know what Phil, the guy knew you were winding him up. He's not an idiot. I could see it on his face. And people don't like that, they don't like thinking for even a moment that someone's taking them for Bambi."

Phil still stared out of the window, towards a man-made tributary of the Thames.

That was Phil, prickly. Very sensitive when it came to criticism.

"You see what I'm saying," Jack said to the windscreen. "People don't like it. OK, in this case it's probably not done any harm but that's not the point because it might. It just fucking might you irresponsible arsehole."

Phil spun round under the seat belt. He smiled. "Jack, I honestly don't think he realized but I'm sorry, really and truly sorry. Mind you when he gave that speech about teamwork I was a good boy then, wasn't I?"

Jack softened.

Phil turned further in his seat. "Look just so as you know I'm sincere I'm going to take you out to the best of dinners, a chastened and somewhat thoughtful Stone. Let's call it an apology, a wake, a moment of decision. Whatever. But it's an opportunity to talk seriously about the future."

To be fair, the guitar-smasher of yesteryear could get up any-one's nose, and his friend had had a terrible shock. Nevertheless he wasn't going to be a pushover, not easily-mollified Jack. He looked out of his half the windscreen. Daylight was running its course. Some overalls were packing up their brushes, paint, and whatnot. Clowning about, lucky buggers. Leisurely tarting up the bridge girders in maroon. They laughed as they slammed the tailboard shut.

"The Best of dinners?"

"Jack," the arms outstretched, "what do you take me for? If I can get a table at La Rive Gauche, La Rive Gauche it is, and if not La Republique for sure."

Work before pleasure however. Two phone calls were made. The tall person was pleased, keen for another six. Phil's stateside call was more sober, Harry too was getting earfuls of Closer Co-ordination.

"Tom Arthur just saw the drift, jumped on it with his own portfolio of inadequacies," Phil said.

His sober mood was impressive. It carried on through to a dessert of subtly charred cherry tart. Even La Rive Gauche couldn't match it, he said.

"Got to hand it to them when it comes to hors d'oeuvres though," Jack said. He wasn't going to be bullshitted where failure to get a table was involved. On the other hand he admired his friend's insistence that one bottle of a modest St Emilion was quite enough. Phil raised a half full glass.

"So Jack, the future and fuck them all," he said quietly across the candlelight. To all intents and purposes Jack's glass was empty. He raised it anyway. Nearby a crusty voice said, "The stock exchange Jeremiahs have been saying the same thing for years."

"So where is the future, not in Equities," Jack said.

"With your tall friend. In the meanwhile I can handle Tom Arthur. Go somewhere else and it might be worse, could be collective morning prayers for senior staff."

"I believe the Japs get more broad-minded when they come West. Anyway, what was your point?"

But Phil had got tied up with a waiter in black. Just the coffee it was going to be. Straightforward enough. But no, there was wrangling over Espresso.

Close by a woman said, "I see it so many times in my job, credit's so easy but then the repayments get out of hand and become tomorrow and tomorrow and tomorrow."

"Ah, Macbeth, one of his lines, a prototype dictator," a male voice said.

"No expresso Jack, machine's broken. I ask you. What I was saying was I can handle it, Tom Arthur sitting in my lap, but I'm not going to like it. To make it tolerable and at least see the possibility of real independence I want something on my own account, which leads me back to your Tall Man."

The waiter put down two cups, a jug of coffee, cream and sugar.

"Bulk-buying is not only financially advantageous, it means not having nerve-racking situations like the last one, waiting, having to sweet talk your Tall Man."

"I'm glad you appreciated what a strain it was."

"And then there's Comrade Gorbachev, what about him? A serious thawing of the Cold War. Right. So think about it, what's going to happen to all that self-righteousness? There's got to be nasties to point a finger if after all, the Russians are jolly nice. And who's going to be first in line? Those Colombian entrepreneurs. And then Mr Supply unable to easily satisfy Miss Demand."

Jack's nod was cautious but it constituted a nod.

"Even as things stand," Phil continued, "we're talking about a 100 percent mark-up untaxed. If I'm right and there's an international crusade against the Medellín it could be a lot bigger."

"All very attractive, but what of turnover time?"

"So far your Tall Man has been steadily increasing his. That's without even looking elsewhere. Even with just him I reckon we could shift ten kilos in eighteen months. Non-perishable goods. And if we did look elsewhere, quicker."

"Ten, it's a big cash lay out."

"My flat sale's going through. If you could chip in a bit, great, but I don't mind sticking up the lot. What I could do with is making the flat sale liquid without leaving any bad smell."

"Shouldn't be difficult. I've a friend in an innovative bank."

Phil grinned. He liked it, he said, then that the Cona was seriously nasty.

He repeated the point to the waiter.

Jack said, "Just pay the bill, it's all you're required to do."

"Thanks Jack. Of course. From now on, best behaviour."

He looked down at the print-out paper. "Mind you the St Emilion's a bit over the top. Oh what the hell, a hundred and thirty quid, can't complain."

CHAPTER THIRTY-FIVE

"You know what you need after a swim Lilly the pink?"

"A towel, Jiminy Cricket."

"Ouch Ouch!" Jim clutched his heart in the High Street.

"Diamond Lil, fastest shot in the West."

"Jimmy the Jack-in-the-box," Sheila said.

"Hey what is this, a two man gang."

"Two women actually," Lilly said.

"Three," said Carol up behind him as the girls made finger guns and let rip. He put his hands up, surrendered, said it was daylight robbery. Carol tickled him under the armpits. His arms fell.

"So what *do* we need after a swim?" she said.

"The full lash. What else. And it just so happens we're approaching a cafe that still does it." He made a dash for the open doorway. It smelled good. "The great escape," he shouted.

They got a table by the window.

"All right Jim," a man said.

"Doing my best."

Carol picked up *The Daily Mirror*.

"All right then, so what is the full lash?" Lilly asked.

"You'll only know when you've had it. With a breakfast it's not fixed, some things are optional."

"What's that mean Mum?"

"You can take it or leave it."

"Very clearly put and in the case of a breakfast we're talking of baked beans, chips, and even the sausage though there's some say there's got to be sausage. Personally I can do without. What's not optional is bacon, eggs, tomato, and mushroom. And toast. Got to be toast." Carol said that was for her. The girls took longer. Lilly wanted sausage, no mushrooms and she didn't care what he said it was only his rules, Sheila baked beans whatever happened.

When they'd finished Jimmy rolled an Old H. Carol was back on tailor-mades but she liked the smell and picked up Jimmy's tin.

"So what's next on the programme?"

"Next? Sleeping it off," Carol said. She tapped her stomach. The girls started tapping theirs, pullovers up. A man wearing an old tweed jacket came in the door.

"All right Jim?"

"I'm trying Frank."

"As the last horse in the race said to the jockey when he saw the whip coming."

"A talking horse I suppose," Lilly said.

"I should have warned you Frank, this is Diamond Lil, not to be messed with. Or her partner, six-shot Sheila."

"No way," Frank said. "Got a lot of work on?"

"Bits and pieces."

"I've got this job coming up, whole house in Fulham, a conversion. You fancy it?"

"Fulham, I thought they'd all been done."

"It's the one that got away. I'll have it ripped out the end of next week."

They took Lilly back to her house. Marie and Pat were in the kitchen.

"So what's the programme?"

"I don't think we've got one of those Pat, not yet."

"Long live the spontaneous eh Jim. Oh by the way Arthur rang Carol."

"Oh I've got plans," Jim said. He was frowning.

"All power to your elbow mate."

Carol went into the front room. She could feel Jim watching her. Fred was quiet in front of TV sport. The girls had out their Shells From Wales tin. She dialled the 981 number. How the man whinged.

"Yes Arthur I do understand . . . of course I liked them, the rhythm section were ace but a Sunday is a Sunday . . . A truism, is that right . . . Don't you work a five day week . . . OK I'll ring you tomorrow . . . Yes definitely."

The girls were trying to put shells in their belly buttons. Carol phoned Terry, made a date for Monday lunchtime and heard out a joke about Six of the Best.

She felt good.

What was she talking about? A nice, regular, secure six ounces.

She felt very good.

Sheila pushed her tummy out. A small crenellated shell jumped on to the carpet.

"A baby one," she shouted.

"Ee-Zee."

"Oh yes? You just wait," Carol said.

"Wait?"

"Yes, wait. I'll be round this time tomorrow to pick you up," Carol said.

"No she meant having a baby didn't you," Lilly said sticking her stomach out.

"OK then, so I did Diamond Lil but I will be here tomorrow lunchtime. Are you OK Sheila?"

"Course I am. Is Jimmy taking you out?"

"We're going dancing but, and this is a secret, I'm taking him out."

Only what a fuss he made when they reached the club. Just because it was her treat, him standing on the pavement and saying it wasn't right. She wound up having to say something stupid about him having paid for the breakfasts. "Anyway that's not the point. I just wanted to take you out tonight. It's not such a big deal is it?"

It was ridiculous standing there with the bouncer grinning in the doorway. She moved fast and paid at the door.

The live band wasn't due on till midnight but the place was packed. The Toaster had a name for rocksteady and dancey jazz. Jimmy started it again at the bar and she had to spell it out.

"It's not often I have the money in my pocket. You understand, hardly ever, but tonight I do. Don't spoil it."

"It's just I've had a good week and I'm not used to it like this," he said.

"See, I'm a force for change in your life," she said staying light.

Thank Christ he laughed. "That you are Carol so let me be reckless and male and put your jacket in the cloakroom. Is that allowed?" She told him not to be sarky, hoped he wasn't, handed him her jacket and waved a tenner at the bar. Jimmy was still stood there.

"You're stunning," he said.

"I know," she said and got her order in.

Coming back from the cloakroom Jimmy took a good look round the bar area. There were blondes to the left of him, brunettes to the right. Their skirts were short, their tops were low but none was a patch on Carol and she wasn't there. He took another look in the furthest corners of the bar. He walked through an arch that lead to the main club area, a dance floor surrounded by alcoves. The music was loud but he couldn't hear the beat. Maybe it had got her moving straight away. He looked carefully. The shifting shafts of light played tricks. There was a woman in a black dress with shoulder straps. He moved on to the floor. She turned her head. He stepped off the floor feeling clumsy. The scent of weed and perfume came in a rush. He walked clockwise skirting the dance floor peering into alcoves.

"Jim!"

He turned and saw her sat at an alcove table. Sat next to a slim, good-looking guy with long hair. He told himself he was being ridiculous. At his age he was being ridiculous but the chest was tight, a shiver licked his legs.

"Terry this is a good friend, Jim. And Terry's an old friend of mine." The guy called Terry smiled. Jim said hello, his blood on edge, and took a big mouthful of the full pint of Guinness sat on the table.

"Got to know you from somewhere Jim. Portobello Road, that possible."

Jim felt his smile wooden. He said yes, he'd drunk in Finch's for a while.

"That's got to be it. Not what it was. Looking great isn't she, Carol."

Carol said, "Not quite your style is it Terry, rock 'n' roll and the Rolling Stones, I thought that was you."

"Never to late to broaden your mind is it, though I still reckon Keith takes some beating. How's Sheila? Great kid isn't she. You got baby-sitting?"

Jim felt the sweat out from his face. He took a big swig of the Guinness.

"She's staying with friends. You going to come and dance with me Jim?"

What? She was up on her feet.

Was he? She was moving towards the dance floor.

Bloody right he was.

"Definitely six Carol, right? Monday lunchtime," Terry called out. Carol turned back. She nodded.

"Perhaps not as soft as yours, my skin, but not a fucking hot water bottle," Jim said.

She was laughing, him in speech-making pose his balls hanging loose, his cock slack out of curly hair.

"Hot rubber, man."

"Feel Jim's thermal skin. No contest," he shouted and dived at the bed. He wriggled close. Her skin was electric.

"Not bad," she said. "Could I patent you?"

He pulled away like he was thinking about it as an option.

"Tricky things patents. Anyway I'm a one-off."

"You are that Jim," she said idly stroking a nipple.

"Really? Really really truly?"

She sat up. "Tell you what, forget the patent I'll write you a reference. Being intimate with Jim, it's OK. Besides we've been very patient."

"Have we?"

"I don't know about you but I've been waiting for this ever since that slow soul number."

His cock jumped half an inch. She stretched her hand down his chest and belly and casually took it in her hand.

"Does that mean we've been very good?" he said. He was massaging her shoulders then stroking.

"We are good, period," she said putting one of his hands on her clit.

Later she said he looked so young when he came, had a foxy smell. He said she made it easy and did she fancy a cup of tea.

"Now you're talking business."

From the doorway he said, "You too, you and your mate Terry."

He was in the kitchen, waiting for the kettle to boil. A watched kettle did boil, it just took a while. Back in her room she let him pour her a cup. "What was that supposed to mean," she said.

"What?"

"Come on Jim, me and Terry since you mentioned it."

"OK take it easy, just sounded a bit obvious to me. And after he remembered me, I remembered him."

"So if you've got questions ask them, let's get it over with." He was still out of the bed, crouched. "Look it's got fuck all to do with me as long as it's not smack which I don't figure you for."

"Thanks for the vote of confidence and you're right, it's not."

"So can I get back in now, it's bloody freezing."

"Just watch where you're putting your feet then."

He eased his way back into the warmth, bent his knees so the feet were away from her body and held her close. "Just be careful Carol, please. You're very precious to me. You are."

"OK Dad."

He jerked away. "Fucks sake can't I say that, that I really care about you?"

She grabbed his head and pulled it close to hers. "I'm sorry, let's just take it slow Jim. I'm damaged goods, better you should know that now. It's made me cautious."

He looked her back straight in the eyes. "No bad thing in your line of work. Trouble is in the end you're always depending on other people to be as careful as you."

"Is that professional opinion?"

"Fucks sake I've only sold little bits of draw but it's bloody obvious."

"Semi-professional then."

"You really are prickly. All I'm saying is I really care about you and I haven't said that to anyone for a long while."

She looked hard at his face like it was something new.

"Thanks Jim. Really. Except for Marie, and she's got a funny way of saying it, no one's said that to me for a long while either. No adult."

"Maybe they have but you wouldn't let yourself hear. One last thing Carol and I'll shut up. Like I said I was just small time but what got on my wick in the end is it was such a little world. It's all we ever talked about, was it Red Leb, is this really Durban poison."

"Well personally I like to know what I'm paying for," she said. "So don't be judgmental yeah, and how about another cup." He poured the tea carefully, felt tight in the chest. Please Don't Let Me Be Misunderstood popped in his head and sounded back as self-pity in stereo.

And anyway she was stroking new patterns on his shoulders. "Sorry Jim, I didn't mean that. I appreciate it you've never asked about Sheila's dad, stuff like that. I don't want to now but when we're ready. No rushing."

CHAPTER THIRTY-SIX

It was a new place, a pub at the top end of Tottenham Court Road she knew from when Chris had been a student. Arthur said doing business with her was educational, London-wise. Then he said, No problem with the six?

"No."

"Wonderful. However I'd like to do it differently from now on. You'll remember that a while ago I asked you about bulk-buying. I mentioned a quantity, you mentioned a price."

"Yes."

He leant across the table. "You implied that I wasn't serious, a mistake on your part. I was and that's why it's taken a while because it is a lot of money. Now I'm ready to go, ten kilos."

"I see," she said. The darkness round his eyes was still there under the sun tan.

"But I'm looking for a better price given one, the size of the purchase, and two, a situation of potential if not already realized over-supply."

"What situation?"

"What Situation, she says. Take for example the evidence of the most recent aerial photographs, coca cultivation more extensive than ever, a 10 percent increase of acreage in Peru and Bolivia. And that's despite official eradication attempts. Plus the overwhelming evidence of market saturation and a significant price drop stateside."

She was frowning.

"A bit bloody abstract Arthur, we're talking about the streets of London."

"Abstract? Bullshit, we're talking market fundamentals."

She smiled. "Come off it Arthur, we're not talking about gold."

"Funny you should mention gold because in fact the same reality prevails, oversupply and more oversupply."

"Arthur you're missing the fucking point, we're talking about something that's illegal. Ill-eagle."

"Got you Simone. Sick predator's against the law. Got you, message received. Still doesn't alter fundamentals. I want it at thirty-two."

Carol leant back. She sighed. For a moment she'd thought he was on another planet. Now he'd named a price, the rest was flim-flam. Only the price put her cut out the window.

"I said 34."

"I've done my sums, at least two too much."

She asked him if he had his car and stood up. "Let's do the business in hand," she said.

Out in the street a paper-seller was packing up.

Whatever happened, whether she could push Terry or not, she would not come back with 32. Not if she could help it. She asked if he wouldn't mind driving towards Baker Street. He said sure, but it had to be 32. "To be frank it doesn't make commercial sense otherwise. The money for the six is in the case, can you organise that?"

She opened it on her knees and took out a chubby envelope. She put it in her shoulder bag. Arthur pulled up at red lights. A red bus towered above them. When they drove off she put a sellotaped chocolate box into the case.

"I'll come back to you on the other business," she said.

"When?"

"When I've got something to say."

"Do that Simone. The tube station do you?"

Carol bought a ticket and got on a steep escalator holding the strap of her bag tight to her shoulder. At the bottom a young woman was playing a classical piece on the flute. Carol bent with a pound coin.

Ten kilos.

She walked the length of the platform. Yellow brick road. The Tunnel Club, smart for a tube station.

Ten kilos.

She walked back again. The lit-up signboard said HAMMERSMITH. The silver train burst out of the tunnel. She stood on her own in the space by the doors. A battered-looking guy was crashing about at the other end. He was singing. A woman sat down spoke seriously to her shopping bag.

Carol focused on a man opposite in paint-stained overalls and a donkey jacket.

Not Jimmy, Jimmy went everywhere in the van.

Not Jimmy but solid.

Ten kees in one hit.

The train was in daylight, went into a squeal. Edgware Road. The painter got off.

Just swing it with Terry. Be persuasive and there'd be grands in her pocket. For her alone, many grands.

The train pulled away. She heard a blast of wind, felt it, and turned her head. The nearest connecting door was open, three young guys in T-shirts came through into the carriage. Her hair blew up. A smudged sheet of newsprint swirled round her feet. The door slammed behind them. What was that fucking noise. Just what the fuck was it, the lead one wanted to know, was shouting like it was a personal affront. His T-shirt was marked CHAMPION. Classified as fucking torture the second one said. The singer went quiet. They were coming her way doing random pull-ups on the hand straps. She gripped her shoulder strap tight. Seven grand's worth of bag. Most of it not hers. She looked with concentration at the strip of Circle and Metropolitan line map. Whitechapel Aldgate East Liverpool Street Moorgate

"All right lady, it must be your lucky day." Knees in denim in her face. Then he was stood down on his feet. She could see his waistband. No eye contact. That was the rule. She must not make eye contact. His trainers had. red piping on immaculate white.

"So come on then, give us a smile"

Immaculate white. Feet pumped up for gymnastics.

"Here catch a whiff of that." It was one of the others further down the carriage. She could hear him and the other one. There's bye laws old man. No fucking unwashed in this train.

The T-shirt was arched over her. Seven grand. She needed her head examining. She would have it examined. It was a promise only . . .

"Here Chris, problem down this end. Personal hygiene."

"What?" It had to be they were on the singer's case. Slag, the one called Chris called her as he turned away to join his pals. She looked straight ahead at the tartan of the seat opposite, her teeth locked together.

"You sack of shit. Shouldn't be allowed. Should not be fucking allowed."

She did not dare to look. She was mad. She was a bloody mad cheapskate. In the meanwhile, please let them not do anything to the singer who wasn't singing anymore. Just don't do it.

"I do believe some air freshener is needed. What say you?"

Please, just leave him alone.

Oh fuck him, she heard, and then a woosh. She would not look. They were coming out into daylight, the train was slowing down. The door at the far end slammed.

She was shaking. She was bloody shaking. The gymnasts had moved on. The train came to a stop. Then she looked down the carriage. He was OK, he looked to be OK the singer. She breathed out a big breath. Never again. Never ever ever again. What was she thinking of, what the bloody hell were cabs for if they weren't for women on their own carrying large amounts of money? What was it with her? Like she only knew how to live poor. No never ever again.

The next day, midday, she was at Terry's with his money.

"We can't go on meeting like this," he said pulling down the blinds. "Three days out of the last four and what do I get. Lucky sod that Jimmy."

She smiled and went into her pitch, spoke without interruption for several minutes.

"Interesting," he said when she'd finished. "Some interesting points you've made." He went to stub out his cigarette. He changed his mind.

"Thing is Carol we're talking about goods in the hand, get me. Big difference between this and stuff on the bushes, unprocessed stuff on another continent. You fancy a line," he said dropping envelope-folded paper on the table. She shook her head. Couldn't argue, Arthur's arguments had been academic, she'd said it herself.

Terry chopped fast on a hand mirror, made a snake of powder and straightened it up.

"You're saying you can't budge on that price Terry?" He sat up out of his crouch. Sniffed. "No I'm not saying that necessarily, just that right this minute I'm not leaping out to make meets to negotiate what you're saying. You got a fag?" She got out her pack, gave him one and lit up herself.

"See I did save you leaping out for a pack of fags." He gave her such a grin she wondered if his teeth were for real.

"You stay late the other night?" he said.

"Half one, two, something like that."

"Seemed like a nice feller, I seemed to remember he was. What's he think about all this." What was this, some conspiracy, the Portobello Road Old Boys Social Club?

"He is a nice feller Terry but he's not my husband, this is my business."

"Sure. Yes but see Carol there's another angle to this. We're talking a lot of dosh. Credit dosh. Don't think I don't appreciate it, every time you've upped your order, you've upped the deposit but even with that and every penny I've got, well it don't add up to much when we're talking three hundred grand plus."

"I can see that Terry, obviously I can see that. What can I say except I've worked with this guy quite a while. He's straight but he's not straight, know what I mean? A business guy who's got a taste for it but reckons he can make a few quid out of it."

"Let me tell you a story. I'm down the market, see some kiwi fruit, put a few in a bag and ask if I'm going to get any change out of three quid."

Carol had time, she watched Terry push the mirror aside and pictured the market, fruits and colours.

"So there's this girl about eighteen, looks at me like I'm a Martian and this bloke pops up behind her shoulder, got to be her dad, gives me the wink and tells me the younger generation don't know what a quid is. Like I'm a fucking OAP. So what's that tell you?"

"That I'm not as old as I look," Carol said. "And I'd better watch my language."

Terry liked it, it was so funny he gave the table a drubbing, had to clamp down the mirror before the powder bounced off.

"Course there's another angle to your biz Carol, the set-up. Thought about that?" he said, suddenly jabbing across the table. Carol laughed out loud and offered him a fag. She felt confident, tough words ready. "The guy's a straight right," Terry said. "So maybe he's got a little rap and he says to the cops give me a break and I'll give you someone serious."

She laughed again, on sure ground. Arthur might be a creep but he wasn't a cop. No way. So why not take a line. She pointed at the mirror. He said sure and sorted her a line.

She tasted the rush sweet.

"Nice?"

She gave a thumbs up. Waited for the rush to level out.

"One I met the guy too accidentally. Two, met him amongst the rich, the kind who wouldn't want to know a cop unless they'd been burgled and had to for the insurance. Three, I've been doing business with him a long while."

Terry shook his head and went to the window. Carol couldn't see how the room could be darker but he gave a tug at the cords. He sat down and lit a fresh cigarette.

Carol said, "Look Terry I know my limits, what I can handle and what I can't. You know, if it's not offensive, there's been a couple of friends of yours, big blokes in suits, that I'd never like to be in a hundred miles of tangling with."

"Big blokes in suits, I like it Carol, big blokes in suits," he said laughing till he dived in for the last line on the mirror.

"Known you a long time too Carol, only it don't necessarily signify," he said. "Where you from?"

"Greenford."

"Where the fucks that?"

"You get to West London then you just keep going till you're out in the middle of nowhere except they call it Middlesex."

"You don't rate it. Sure. West Midlands me. That's what they call it. Led Zeppelin, remember them? Robert Plant. Our claim to fame."

"You haven't got an accent. You could come from anywhere."

"Is that right? Good, got be good hasn't it. If I did have I'd still be grafting for fuck all in a carpet factory in Kiddie. Kidderminster. You know it?"

She shook her head.

"You in a hurry?" he said..

She checked her watch. Allowing for the walk, an hour before school was out. She nodded.

He was bent down flicking through video cassettes under the monitor. She heard his breathing heavy as he pushed one in.

"Maybe a bit macho but great for clearing the brain," he said.

She wanted the favour, whatever was good for the brain was good. There was a mad roar, motorbikes flashed by in a tangle, the track red, the background a brilliant green. Macho? It was bloody weird. Terry'd pulled a hard-backed chair close to the screen. She heard a mass of gear change as the bikes slithered round the curve.

"Can't beat back-wheel slide, not these days. The old classic British style just not in it anymore," Terry said. The screen was there and there was nothing else to look at. Carol kept her focus but still saw the pattern changing, the bikes spreading out, then all the attention on the first three. Then the first alone.

"Came the time I knew I'd never be good enough," Terry said, "so I gave up, that and the last spill. Spent all my time and money on it, it's how I got into this game, needed the money. But there it was, my knee fucked and knowing, yeah that's why I had the spill, I was going faster than I could control. You know, trying to stay up with the best. Always conning myself, more practice, a better bike and it'd be OK and then that last spill and my knee never going to be right again, couldn't do it anymore, con myself. Hard isn't it, when you know you're not good enough. Out of your depth. Out of your league. Yeah, it hurts. After a while it doesn't hurt as much. Not so much."

What was this, some message directed at her, all dressed up, philosophical. The lead bike roared on. She wasn't going to lose her focus. If it was a sermon it was off-beam, she hadn't tried yet. No reason to think she wasn't good enough.

Terry stopped the video. The room took time to go quiet. He went into the kitchen, took a carton of milk out of the fridge and drank it straight off. Carol put the kettle back on and sat at the kitchen table.

"You really want to do this number?"

"Sure," she said. "Wouldn't you? And what, am I being naïve, I imagine you'd get a very nice whack out of it."

"Yeah I'll get my whack. And very nice too, if it goes like you say. Thing is Carol I'd have thought you were doing very nicely thank you, you know, how it is, how it's been lately."

"Sure, it's been going well. Hard to believe sometimes. So many years I've spent half my time worrying about money. You know, down to thinking if buying a new pair of jeans wasn't reckless."

She wanted a cigarette but the packet was empty. "You know what I mean, even if it's better you're standing in M&S and you see a decent pair and they're eighteen quid and you think you're rich just cos there's four fivers in your purse."

"Fuck off Carol, what do you want, violins? Don't tell me you think twice about buying clothes these days. What are you doing, giving the stuff away?"

"It is nice money Terry, for me, the last couple of times. It's true, just I ask myself if it's going to go on and on forever. And even if it does, fucks sake Terry don't you ever get fed up with it, the phone calls, the meets, the carries. You know, the whole thing." The kettle turned itself off.

"As it happens Carol, I like this business. It's what I'm good at and I'll tell you what, you see some poor bleeders out on the street and I tell myself, Mustn't Grumble, even if my mum drove me up the wall when she said it. But then she had plenty to grumble about."

"I know that. I do know. There's this old dear runs my local launderette. So bloody worn out it scares me. Selfish, yes, maybe I've just learned to be selfish but I don't want it happening to me. I don't want to end up like her."

Terry leant forward and poked in the cigarette packet, came out with a crumpled white half tube with spotted-tan filter attached.

"Veins like Clapham Junction eh?"

"What?"

"Her in the launderette."

"Yes."

"You do want violins don't you, you're not working in a launderette."

"All right, all right but what is this. You're in business, I'm in business, it's a deal we're talking about."

"Bad was it, that place, Greenford. Yeah Greenford, got it, it's on the Central Line map, the underground."

"What's that got to do with it. Yes, as it happens. First time I was ever out of it I knew that. And since you keep asking it's not violins I want. This scene where I first met the guy I want to do this deal with. Those people. Loaded and most of them no taste at all but there was one or two, you know, they knew what they were doing with it. Why not me too? I've got a feel for quality, most of them haven't. Never will."

"Sure. Personally I think they're all wankers but at least you're speaking sense to me now, real stuff, you know, that even I can understand. I am listening to you. Yeah, because you're right, I would make a nice few bob out of this deal of yours. Mega bucks. Only I don't want to tangle with big blokes in suits either, you know what I mean."

Of course she did. Wasn't stupid. Known it was those guys she'd seen that Terry went to. Course she'd known, just the way they were, the way Terry was with them.

So.

She wasn't going to fuck up.

"Four hours Terry, that's what we're talking about. At the most."

"How you going to do it?"

"What?"

"Come on I've got to know. How are going to do the biz?"

"A hotel, Lancaster Gate area," she said.

He didn't laugh, didn't say Fucks sake like she was a complete div. He was taking her cigarette packet apart.

"It's smart but not full this place. I've agreed a time with my man but not a place. I book in then give him an hour's notice where, to book a room himself and be there. I give him the name I'm using not the room number. Tell him to ring me via Reception when he's arrived."

"No, you wait in the lobby. Either you hear his room number or you follow him."

"With a sample."

"Yeah, with a sample."

"OK, I go to his room with the sample. Count the money."

"You count and when you're counting you check a note per couple of thou. If it goes through, if, I'll have some real and some slush for you to look at. Tenners, twenties and fifties. So you can study them beforehand, so you know."

Oh.

Slush was therefore forged stuff. Forged money.

Oh.

He was looking at her, waiting, the fag packet in shreds. It would be OK. He was going to show her. So she'd know. Like he said.

"And when I'm satisfied we go to my room only I've got his key. As soon as he's satisfied I go back to his and ring you."

"You're going to have to hear his number or see it when he books in."

"What?"

"Stay in the lobby say ten minutes, make sure he's on his own. Another thing, what you going to do if he don't go along with all this. If he won't give you his key?"

"Call the deal off."

"I'm glad you said that Carol. Tell you what, give us a couple of days, I'll see what I can do. One other thing, it's heavy ten kees. If it happens I'll drive you to Paddington, get a cab from there to the hotel."

She got to the school by twenty past three. It had started to rain, soft and damp. She walked along the playground fence. Drops of rain hung on the square-patterned wire. No sign of Marie or any other mothers she knew. She crossed the road to stand under the canvas awning of a grocery shop. If it came off, if Terry could swing it with those guys, the credit, she would buy a car. She'd buy a car and then take lessons and pass the test. Buy the car first. One that wouldn't break down. Get Jim's advice.

A young guy in a track-suit bounded in under the awning and on into the shop. She heard an outbreak of shouting and stepped out from the awning. Sheila's duffel coat stood out from the rush, hood up.

"But you haven't got a proper coat on Mum."

"A coat? I'm supermum."

"If not a coat, at least an umbrella."

"I was sort of hoping for one of those for Christmas." Sheila stopped. Carol stopped. Sheila looked at her seriously.

"You might Mum, if you really wish it hard enough, you might."

"Well that's what I'll have to do then, so there's no mistake. Tell you what, race you home."

"Are you sure?"

"Sure I'm sure," Carol said and set off at a trot.

She kept it up all the way to the flat. Her chest was churning. It was burning. Inside she put her jacket and the duffel coat on the clothes-horse and lit the gas fire. Sheila had been doing geography. Maps and compasses. Carol asked where North was and got made to feel stupid.

"All right then what about Siberia and Alaska, very close right?"

"Siberia and Alaska. Yes. Very cold, very close. Just a little sea in between."

"OK then, if you're standing on the very edge of Siberia

looking towards Alaska, over the sea, which way are you looking, East or West?"

Sheila gave her mum a look. She stretched. It just had to be a trick question like the ton of iron and a ton of feathers that had caught her out the first time. She took her Atlas book out and turned the pages from Equator to Arctic. Over her shoulder Carol saw Russia and America almost touching.

"So what is the answer Mum?"

"I don't know," Carol said. She was laughing.

"Mum. Are you all right."

"Course I am, never better. Why?"

"You're in a crazy mood."

CHAPTER THIRTY-SEVEN

"It's for members only," the receptionist said. "Unless you've been invited by a member, you know, who is in the club at present."

Keith Murray's casuals were smart, his point reasonable. No he wasn't a member. No he didn't have a friend who was a member, not as far as he knew, he just wanted to try the place before taking out membership.

The receptionist called on a tannoy mike for a Mr Harris. Would he come to reception please.

Keith thought of things to say. If the situation arose he might say them to Mr Harris.

Who was taking his time.

In the reception area there was nowhere to sit down, not a single seat. It was a moot point whether it was worth seeing anymore except he'd gone to the trouble of getting to the place and If A Job's Worth Doing . . .

Yes Gordon, It's Worth Doing Properly.

The receptionist gave him a smile.

A guy in a tracksuit came through swing doors.

Keith made his point.

Mr Harris took his point. In this case an individual session ticket could be issued. He was sure Mr . . .

"White," Keith said.

He was sure Mr White would be impressed with the facilities and then, why a whole range of membership options was available.

Heavy disco bass filtered through to the changing room. From the signs on doors leading off it seemed like it served both the gym, squash and badminton courts. For all that, too cramped. Ditto the shower and sauna area.

Keith changed into shorts and a sweatshirt. In the gym the music was all beat. Everywhere. Punching the air. Adrenalin pump-up. Amphetamine pump-up. Only the place was empty bar four fellers. One doing serious bench-press on a multi-gym machine; two with moustaches and insignia'd tracksuit tops on rowing machines; the other in shorts and vest was walking the length of a full-height mirror that ran the length of the far wall behind sit-up benches and a pull-up bar.

The floor was decent wood and clean enough only it was bruised and marked around the multi-gym machines. Not enough of those either. He took the spare bench and did a set of behind the neck push-ups. Ten at twenty kilos. The oarsmen were stood around. Keith added another five kees and did another ten. The burn felt good in his shoulders. He got up and counted out thirty seconds till the next set.

One of the oarsmen was speaking to him.

"What?" he said.

"Always harder on your tod," the guy said. He was shouting.

"Except wanking," Keith said and sat back on the bench for another set.

Get the place half-full and it would be chaos round the multi-gym, fucking chaos.

Out of the shower and rubbing down he saw the one other man in the changing room was clocking him.

He edged over to the wall with his towel. Kept his back to it. A middle-aged guy putting his socks on, still giving him the eye. A pal of Mickey's? Old Bill? An iron?

"You looking for someone?" Keith said.

"Excuse me. Sorry. I just thought, you know, somewhere in the visual data bank. I mean"

Him. Right.

And they got there in the end while Keith dressed: the Spurs throwing it away; him once On but now With TV. Paul Swift laughed, said he hadn't realized Keith was a member.

Keith said he wasn't but believed in trying a thing out

before he committed himself. "Call it a Pilot Show in your game don't they?"

"Ah, the Pilot Show, a mongrel of our times. Democratic process or Market research I've often wondered before finally plumping for the view that it's a failure of nerve on the part of scheduling execs. Perhaps I can buy you a drink."

Keith looked at his watch, said Yes, why not.

The bar was towards the entrance, a box of a room with Dire Straits out of small speakers and a fruit machine in the corner. Paul rang a bell on the counter.

"What can I get you?" It was the girl out of reception.

They settled for double Britvic orange. The mini-fridge was low on ice, a cube each in pint glasses. Sat down Paul agreed, No he wouldn't say the club was especially lively, not socially speaking. "But personally speaking that's not what I'm looking for."

"Is that right," Keith said. "So how do you see the stock market these days?"

"What?" said Paul. He was frowning. "Not really my field but interesting times."

"Oh yes," Keith said. "What about equities?"

"Who can say for sure but the word on the street is they're going to come a cropper."

"Is that right."

"Price/Earnings ratios stretched beyond their limit, cause; general realisation of this fact, fulcrum; big fall in share prices, effect. If that isn't a bit too A-to-B."

"Realisation of this fact. He who realizes last being major cropper, got you," Keith said. "Didn't see you in the gym Paul, Squash is it?"

No, he was a bit old for that. Badminton in fact.

Yes, just the one court the club had.

No, if you booked for a morning session the court was usually available.

No, unfortunately it wasn't a game that lent itself to the small screen. Unlike snooker, that was a scheduling fact of life.

Yes, the area was on the up and up though he personally had bought in years earlier.

"A successful hunch eh Paul, no Pilot Show required."

Paul laughed and looked at his watch. "The pioneer spirit," he said. "Sorry, got to rush, a showing."

* * *

"I can handle it Del but if you want to come with, terrific. You're the guvnor," Mo said.

Derek grunted from the back seat. A Sierra in sober maroon.

"It's a piss-off all round but that's the way it goes. That's what I'll tell him. Stuff don't grow on trees."

"Poppies," Derek said.

"What? Oh, got you," Mo said. He laughed. "Poppies, right. I always used to think they was red. My grandad with one in his buttonhole, with a black blob in the middle. With his medal."

He pushed out into the Old Street roundabout, cut across traffic to the Shoreditch exit.

"He shot a few. Wouldn't believe it if you saw him. And got shot at."

Past the Town Hall he got into lane for the Bethnal Green Road.

"Hard to credit," Mo said.

An Express parcels van was pushing out from a side street. Mo gave him the horn.

He fancied turning on the radio.

At the junction he turned right down Cambridge Heath Road.

"What's he got out on strap, Nicky?"

"Forty G. You did say up to Fifty with him."

"I know what I said Mo, I was just asking how much it is now. And you've told me."

Mo could see him in the mirror. Del the thinking man. Hard to credit, silly sod gets himself in a scrap where even he's going to get a hammering, and what happens, he's a changed man, dead serious, uptight, none of the old chat.

"I'll take the Rotherhithe, OK?"

"You're driving Mo."

Off Jubilee Street he turned left down Commercial Road.

"He's not going to be happy is he?" Derek said.

"Who?"

"Nicky, that's who we're going to see Mo, Nicky."

Past Watney Market by the bridge, the yellow-brick bridge Mo called it, he took a right. Happy? That was pushing it, Nicky or any other cunt. In this particular case, had Nicky ever been happy? Not so long as he'd known him.

So?

No tackle but give us the money. Look at it this way Nicky, a good time to do your accounts, how much you got here and now.

He'd driven the tunnel a thousand times and it was still narrow. Tight white tiles.

A builders lorry oncoming, no room to spare. Tight white tiles.

"I'm going to be tied up all afternoon, can you manage the charlie. Eight for Marvin and four for the other face"

"Alex."

"Yes, Alex. It's all ready, separately wrapped up in Archway, you've got keys."

"Sure"

They burst out into sunlight on a roundabout. The phone rang. Derek's mobile. It rang again. And again.

"Who's that . . . How you going Terry . . ."

Derek was laughing out loud, the feller he always dealt with personally, the other one to get a pasting at Custer's last stand.

"Nice one Tel, four, five hours, yeah I don't see why not. I'll bell you later. And I'm pleased for you mate."

They drove on southwards through the backdoubles: slowing down, speeding up.

"Must be breeding them," Mo said.

"What?"

"Sleeping policemen. Like there's a few more every fucking day."

Derek was frowning.

"You know, these humps in the road, sleeping policemen they call them, like you get your jollies running them over."

Was he smiling? It was hard to say from the mirror. Mo

pulled into the Safeway carpark. They were five minutes early he said, parked up next to the entrance.

"Give it the once over eh Mo," Derek said.

From the back seat he watched his right arm walk round the car park. Only he shouldn't have had to tell him. A young couple were pushing a stuffed trolley up a line of cars. He clocked Nicky in a two-year-old Audi driving in. The entry was clearly visible in the rear mirror, he kept his eye on it. Was still watching when Mo opened the driver's door and stuck his head in.

It was sweet, he said.

Derek grunted.

Nicky was out the Audi carrying a Safeway bag. Clocked Mo like it was the surprise of the week.

Derek kept an eye on the mirror and heard them at it. Well, well, well what you doing here, the old woman got you doing the shopping. A drink? Why not. Yeah I've got an hour.

In the back Nicky said it was a surprise. "Long time no see Del, how's it going?"

"All right, thought I'd give Mo a bit of company. Drive around for ten minutes OK."

They drove out the car park and took a right. Derek said driving in London was no joke these days, the stress and that. Not just the traffic but potholes, roadworks, and obstructions in general.

Nicky nodded.

"Not so bad if you can have a bit of a natter. Know what I mean. You all right yourself Nicky, you're looking well."

"Not bad."

"Not bad you prick, you must be coining it."

"Like I said, mustn't grumble."

"Well that's a relief."

"A round trip of Greenwich do you?" Mo asked.

"Why not. Not so far, shouldn't take long, Nicky's got money for us, we've got a parcel for him. Forty G ain't it?"

Nicky nodded, said it was great doing biz with him, no pissing about.

"That's us. And here's a bit of good news, treat yourself to a holiday. We're giving the nasty a rest for a couple of weeks, a bit of re-organisation, streamlining. For everyone's good." Mo could see it in the mirror. The shock. Nicky white in the face. Then making a laugh.

"You're having me on," he said.

Derek was shaking his head like he was baffled.

"I wouldn't kid you my old mate. Maybe tell you your flies was undone at a party but not business."

"Fucks sake Del, what do you think I come to you for, cos you're reliable."

"That's right and you know why I'm reliable? Cos if I think we need to re-organise, I'll do it. For everyone's sake. You understand, for everyone's sake. And let's get it right Nicky, you come to me cos it's a good price, you get strap and you know it's been stepped on less than any other cunt's."

"But Del you don't know what it's like, the grief I'm going to get off"

"Don't give me the bollox, if you couldn't handle a few whingeing smackheads you wouldn't be sitting in my fucking motor. Or driving an Audi. I'll have Mo bell you when we're ready."

"So why's he belled me now, what are we doing here."

"Why he asks me Mo, is this real?"

Mo shook his head.

"Because Nicky, we all want to keep our accounts tidy. You do. I do. It's like my accountant says, all that cash flow you don't know where you are half the time. Have a break and you can see it, what's all yours. A nice feeling. When you've given me the forty you'll know every other penny's your own, you know what I mean. A good feeling."

Even in the mirror you could see it, sick as a parrot Nick with a calculator flat out in the forehead. And trying to nod like he believed every word. Mo took a left to start working his way back towards New Cross.

"What I've got Del, you know, like on me, is eighteen and a half. It's no problem. Just a couple of my people a day late."

"Is that right. No sense of punctuality half of them. Ever been short before has he Mo?"

"Just the once, two G held over."

Derek took the envelope. "Scratch," he said. Mo nodded.

Nicky said, What.

"Ten, eleven, twelve. Yeah, eighteen and a half. Like you said," Derek said.

If nowhere handy came up on the way the railway yard would do. Fuck it, make it the yard. Mo put his foot down.

"OK Nicky, so Mo'll bell you tomorrow, pick up the rest, and then again when I've completed my review of our operation. You can see what I'm saying, tell your people the same. For a better service in the long run, everyone's interest. Right Mo?"

"That's it Nicky, think of the long run," Mo said and pulled off the road across asphalt. Grass out of its cracks brushed the car. He stopped the car and jumped out. Nicky was half out of his door. Derek grabbed a leg and sent him on his way head first. Mo kicked his face on the volley. Derek tipped his legs out. Mo pulled him up against the car boot. Derek hit him once, twice in the belly. Nicky doubled over and went for a blade out of his sock. Slowly. Derek kicked the eyebrows on the half volley. Trod on the hand.

"All the pockets Mo."

He went straight for the trousers. Stuck a hand in the pants. Pulled out a tight polythened wad.

Nicky retched. Maybe he was speaking.

Derek counted twenty-three G.

He bent over. Stuck a grand back in a jacket pocket.

"You hearing me you cheapskate cunt, I'm taking five hundred for the dry cleaning. Sort your life out. Then we'll bell you."

"You should have been there," Gordon said. Keith was at the radio, Derek stood by the door.

"Billy Mac going on nineteen to the dozen, what a terrific geezer this Johnny is. Never met him in his fucking life before. Will do now. And him, the other face, Johnny the rock star, he's lapping it up. A sheaf of photos, him in his trilby and his arm round Billy Mac."

"An advert for matchmaking," Keith said, landing on a Beethoven late quartet and satisfied. Gordon laughed. Give him his due, Keith could be funny.

"That's right and even if it's only a dinner I reckon we owe Steve one. Maybe a few grams. Mentioned it to him just before my vacation, papers signed today, can't be bad can it. Only wants me in the photos Billy does. I told him, I'm not photogenic myself Bill, know what I mean. He doesn't as it happens but the other face did. You should have seen it."

"Terrific Gordon, I'm chuffed for you," Derek said. "As it happens I couldn't make it, a lot of work on and as it further happens my day's been a heap of shit. All I see is me out there on my own trying to hold a good business together and nothing to work with. Because that's where we're at."

"Where are we at Del?" Keith said, moving away from the radio to stand among house-plant greenery.

"Have we done badly out of the Iranian's biz? Have we?"

"No we haven't Derek, we've done very well and it's financed other things. No question. But it's not the point is it? You're talking past tense. Present perfect in fact. Same difference. We have done well, does that mean we will for ever and ever?"

At it again, the brothers. At each other's throats. Gordon sat up straight and tall.

"Fucks sake let's try and look at this objectively. Without emotion."

"Yeah, let's do just that. The Iranian's sitting on a lot of dollop, meanwhile there's a lot of people out there want it. Paying people. So what the fuck is it, Curtis don't say this and he don't say that and somehow that means we can do fuck all."

"If you want the facts, if you really want to hear them," Gordon said, "I'll give you what Curtis was saying as of yesterday. And don't let me forget I've got a report to give you, my meeting with William. Not a bad place Manchester as it goes."

"So what is the cunt saying?"

"Translated it means our Iranian friend has got to get some responsible, non-family person between him, the dollop and us."

"Well get him fucking sorting it out then."

"What is it, am I dumb? Are you deaf? Let's learn to lip read," Keith said striding out of the fat green leaves. "Do we need it? That's the question isn't it? To smack or not to smack as the child psychologist might have said to the old man. If there'd been any at the time."

"Lip-reading? Need a fucking translator with you. It's like listening to Curtis. So you've read some books. Big deal. In the meanwhile I've been out there maintaining and building up a good business."

"You can leave the old man out of it Keith, I'm not having it. And the two of you, rowing like kids. Fucks sake just look at the dividend William's come up with, there's no need for it."

"Yes, exactly," Keith said. "What do we need the Iranian's work for if we're doing so well elsewhere, though as it happens there's a couple of questions I want to ask about our William. But right now I want to talk about alternatives to more of the Iranian's tackle cos it so happens Del that I wear out some shoe leather too, out there in the real world. Yeah, and I've found *the* site for expanding the gym biz."

"Keith. Oy, Keith, do you think you could stop pacing about. We do run to chairs. At least you've moved the discussion on to a less emotional basis. Got to be a step forward. See Del what we've got here is context, and that means looking at the wonderful job you've done with the tackle in relation to our other interests."

"Hang on a minute, let's get this right. We start off with some problem the Iranian might have, or rather that friends and relations Might have. Maybe. Except you don't know cos Curtis ain't saying. So let's have it out in the open, it's an excuse you want to finish the business. As it is you don't know the aggravation I've had to put up with."

Keith had sat down. He was back up on his feet. "Derek, speaking sincerely now, as your brother, that's the whole point, I don't want for you to be having to put up with anything. Big needle, mummy, big needle, where are you? Yeah, I can imagine it."

"Great, you imagined it, I built it up. So what am I supposed to do, let some other cunt get all the benefit?"

"There's an option you're missing there."

"What Gordon, what option?"

"We could sell the business."

"Lock, stock, and syringe?"

"Keith, shut it. And don't drop your fucking fag ash in that plant. We've got ashtrays as well. OK, I haven't thought it out and I'm as keen as you Del, believe me, that no other bastard gets all the benefit. So let's say there may will be certain pavement artists out there in the big bad world who've had a coup. People we might happen to know who are looking for long term investments."

"Sounds like bollox to me, what are we going to sell?"

"Not the Iranian. Give me a bit of credit Del. No, the package would be that we keep him and sell, cash up front, all his loads, as they come with a mark up for us. OK, it's not going to be as big as now, no way, but think of all the aggravation we'd save."

Derek was listening. Gordon could see it, he'd got his attention.

"What we would be giving away is our clients at the consumer end. That way we'd know they could shift it and be back for more."

Derek said nothing. Keith said nothing.

Gordon waited.

He took a pen off the desk and put it in his top pocket.

The violins were still playing. Keith's kind of music.

Gordon took the pen out of his top pocket and put it on the desk.

Derek shook his head. He said, No.

"No what?"

"If this firm's got all our selling connections they can go where they like for the tackle."

"Bollox, no one's got a better connection than our Iranian, bless his soul."

"All right then why not knock the charlie on the head while you're at it, sorting out the future," Derek said. Next thing he was hearing it in stereo. If anything, Keith the palliest: what a wonderful job he'd done with Mario's gear; wonderful. How it was a different, classier commodity altogether. Therefore less aggravation.

"That's right isn't it Del."

"There was that Frank, remember him, freebased our money away."

"All right, there was Frank. A one-off dickhead. There's always one. The other thing is," Keith said, "you've told us your-self, it's the charlie's the real expanding market."

It was grudging but it was a Yes, Derek's reply. Then he said, "By coincidence Terry's got a ten kee deal lined up. One hit, with some straight businessman."

Gordon frowned.

"There you go," Keith said. I'm pleased for you, pleased for Terry. He's your man but never failed to impress. Right Gordon."

"It's a lot of money."

"It's a cash deal, all Terry needs is six hours strap off us."

"Yeah and where would we be if we weren't doing credit," Keith said. "There'd be no business."

Gordon looked at his pen. He frowned.

"Credit's money Keith, serious stuff and when you're give it you're saying, I believe in you son, there you go, here's the money. That's what you're saying. So there's got to be rules, limits. Not just how long but how much. This is a jump for the lad isn't it."

This was too much. This was a fucking joke, a lecture on credit after a morning of grief with tricky Nicky. Like the brother was a schoolteacher, all out of books.

"He's had four at a time," Derek said. "Never fucked up, not like some of the arseholes I have to deal with, you know, in real fucking life."

"There you go then," Keith said.

"All right then, if it keeps you happy. Now then Keith, you had something to say, a plot of land, another gym I believe you said."

CHAPTER THIRTY-EIGHT

In her kitchen Marie saw Carol looking abstracted, like she wasn't there. Nothing new, not with Carol Businesswoman though she wasn't complaining, business was good, business wasn't so good but always she paid up, a phone call here or a bit of storage there. The men were talking away.

"Maybe I have but horizons any bigger, any further away, they're likely to be a wind-up aren't they," Jim said. Not a bad feller, he'd done her mate a power of good even if she was in one of her moods.

"The poor man at his gate eh Jim? For ever and ever Amen." OK, Pat could be aggressive but he'd got a point. And it was him had cooked the couscous.

She tried a wink at Carol but her friend was far, far away. Jim sighed and poked at the Creme Caramel which had been her contribution. Then he laughed, Carol's feller.

"Come on Pat, you know that's what I'm saying. It's now, 1987 I'm talking about and we find ourselves working for people we don't want to work for but with the hope that from how we do it . . ."

"From little seeds mighty flowers grow," Marie said, standing to take the plates off.

"I had the building boom in mind. If it keeps up steam I'm in with a chance. Here let me do that."

"OK then, if you want to. Is he always like this Carol?"

"Don't make a big deal out of it Marie," her friend said like she was the Sleeping Princess.

"It's the self-categorisation, the acceptance of a limited

range of possibilities that gets me down," Pat said. "What we call internalization in the trade."

Jimmy was scraping the leftovers on to one plate. Marie saw Carol frowning. She really thought her mate had packed that in since she'd met this Jimmy but here she was, at it again like everything was a problem. He was laughing.

"I'm not too keen on that myself, and it's not what I was saying."

"All I know is there's nothing like a class of sixteen-year-olds to keep your feet on the ground."

"A son of twelve does it quicker. Then cements them," Marie said. "Your feet. In concrete."

Jimmy asked if there was a separate bucket for compost.

"A profound eco-question there Marie," Pat said. "So have you?"

"Another day Jim, just put it all in the same bin. Does he ask you Carol?"

"What?"

"If there's a . . . Shit, sorry, silly me," Marie said tapping the side of her head.

Carol said, What.

"You haven't got a garden and here's me who has and doesn't get out of it what a concerned world citizen should."

Carol had started rolling a joint. "You like feeling guilty?" she said.

"Oh vicious Carol, vicious," Pat said.

"Mea culpa, mea culpa."

"An eco-sin child? And what is that?" Jim said from the sink.

"Oh Marie admitted to a liking for her finger on her clit at an early age didn't you? They know more than they let on, those old boys in black."

"No dirty talk now Pat, not over dinner."

"I thought we'd finished."

"It's just dirty talk. All right is it voyeurism, when it's clever voyeurism?" Carol said and lit the joint. Jim saw Pat furious, he asked if there was a drying up cloth.

"Holy Mary who is this feller Carol?"

"You're just thorough aren't you Jim," Carol said.

"Just leave them in the rack. My horizon's don't stretch to drying up."

Pat poured out the last of the white wine, made a joke about a blank blanc and mocked himself for it. Jim had got on to the cooking pots. Marie got up and stuck the spliff in his mouth. He inhaled, rubbed his hands down his trousers and took it out. Outside the wind was strong, trees shaken up and shaking. Jim took another draw and passed it back.

"Just put the kettle on for coffee and leave the pans," Marie said. "Ever heard about soaking."

He shrugged and filled the kettle.

At the table Carol was rolling another joint. Pat said, "But seriously, doesn't it depress you, this internalization of limited horizons."

"Sure but for now most people don't see anything else. Be kidding themselves otherwise but it's not for ever and ever. You hear people and the joke is you'd think Mrs Thatcher's got a Thousand Year Reich all sewn up."

"That's not really what I was getting at," Pat said.

"So what is it you're getting at," Carol said, lighting a fresh spliff and seeming wide awake.

"That if you Carol, or anyone else rules out the possibility of success then it will be self-fulfilling. You won't have a chance of it."

"Well given the way things are that's reality isn't it," Jimmy said. He was gripping his empty wine glass. "And it's not even new. This brickie I worked with one time, he said supposing all the kids wanted to be lawyers, doctors or architects. Really wanted and studied for it. It just wouldn't be on would it, even if they had the talent and application."

"A Marxist structuralist obviously, your friend."

"Is that right Pat," Carol said, passing the joint to Marie.

"Certainly sounds like it Carol."

"Oh sorry, I thought you said Obviously."

"Carol, Carol, what is this? Poor Pat for the firing squad tomorrow morning is it. Tell you what, let me see the sunrise one more time."

"That's your paranoia."

"Paranoia, that's a word from the good old days," Marie said quickly. "Joe, my nephew, it was the first word he spoke. You know, before Mum or Dad."

The kettle whistled. Carol got up to take it off. The trees outside were loud, whooshing and scraping. Jim said it was a serious wind.

"They said it on the weather forecast, strongish winds tonight."

"Do you really listen to what they say Marie?" Pat asked. "Really, like you were a sailor or a farmer's wife."

"I don't listen, I just happen to remember it."

"When I'm in front of the firing squad I'll plead irresponsibility. Me, I just look to see how ghastly their clothes are and which of the buggers smiles when they give the bad news."

Carol poured the coffee. She said she must be straight off, wanted Sheila in her own bed before it started getting late. She would just look in and tell her to get ready.

In the front room the children were quiet in front of the TV.

"Mum, it's nearly finished. Honestly. Just let's see the end."

Fred said Shush and Carol laughed out loud.

"OK when it's finished, just get your coat and it's home."

She sipped her coffee and saw a rickety old plane make a landing in open country

"I told you he'd make it didn't I," Fred said. "I told you." Carol turned away and went back to the kitchen. Jimmy smiled at her, a big smile.

"OK are they?" Marie said.

"Fred's telling them the score. The hero is the hero." Pat laughed. Jim said it was only natural.

Outside there were rattles and clacks.

"Some guttering's getting tested out there," Jim said. Sheila and Lilly burst in with a story to tell.

Out on the pavement the wind ducked and dived, blew out, sucked in. It whistled. It whined. Carol was glad of the van. Outside her place the tree branches bowed and rose like they were elephant trunks. Jim had to hold on to the front door. As she turned the key it had wanted to slam into the opposite wall of the passageway. The noise outside didn't bother Sheila, she was straight asleep; didn't want a story just a hug from her mum and a kiss from Jim. He was made up and felt bold.

"A cup of tea and a joint is it Carol?"

"Am I that predictable? You know me too well"

"Me? I don't know you at all, you'd be a great spy." She turned sharply. Face to face she held it in and counted three.

"Could you put a tape on quietly and put one together Jim, I'll do the tea."

From her room she heard piano, McCoy Tyner.

"McCoy Tyner," Jim said when she went in with the tea. He gave her the unlit joint and made room on the cushions.

She lit up.

He clasped his hands and looked round the room, glanced at Carol and then back at the heavily curtained window. Now and then it rattled. The piano inside, the wind out, they sounded like they were volume-balanced.

"You're quite a minder," he said with a laugh. "I felt well-protected round at Marie's."

"So now I'm a minder and a spy. So what's that make you, a spycatcher?"

"Ouch ouch, Carol sharp."

"What is this Jim, all this sharp business? You call me this and that but the moment I call you something it's like I hit you." His eyes look hurt, like she had just hit him. He shrugged his shoulders, said he'd meant it as a joke, a light remark.

In her experience there were light remarks and light remarks.

"I'm sorry Jim, I guess I'm just tired and when I'm tired I'm not good company. I'm not always good company, better you should know that."

He nodded. She said maybe another night would be better. He nodded again but didn't move. After a while he turned and asked if she was all right.

She told him that yes, she was all right but like she'd said she was tired.

It was stupid, wrong but he couldn't help but plunge on.

"I don't want to be nosey Carol, honest. It's just you've

seemed so far away all evening, like you had something really heavy on your mind."

"OK Jim if you really want to know and it seems that you do, I'm just about to do one big deal. I'm sorry, we just shouldn't have met up tonight because yes, I suppose it is on my mind." The music sounded with a click. Jim said, Oh I see. But what was it in his voice? Like in fact he didn't see at all. She pushed her back hard into the cushions.

"It's a coke deal, that's what I deal in, to the rich. Any moral objections?"

He wanted to laugh she'd got him so wrong but his No came out wooden in his own ears.

"It's a deal that'll get me out of that boring drug world you're so good at describing."

He laughed and said she'd a hell of a memory.

She laughed back, happy to be laughing.

"Very true, Miss Curbishley, whatever else may be said about you, you have a good memory. That's what my Mr Hurst said. I'd recited some Shakespeare without a book, got it word perfect. Titania in *A Midsummer Night's Dream*, when she tells Oberon it's his jealousy's turned the season's out of joint. Hear that wind? Very relevant. The earth's poor relevant atmosphere."

"Mr Hurst! Christ you have got a good memory." He was amazed, delighted she'd remembered.

"I can see I'll have to be very careful. But don't your friends in the business get nervous of it?"

What a real smile he had now and she felt good from his touch on her shoulders. She wasn't sure about this In The Business but he did seem properly light-hearted now.

"That's their problem," she said and got up to change the tape. "That wind really is crazy."

It came, it went, it didn't stop. She saw big waves churning the shingle at Folkstone.

"Do you need a hand Carol, you know, with this big deal?" he said.

She was drenched with icy cold. The Big Deal voice was unmistakeable, regrettable but unmistakeably sarcastic.

"No thanks Jim," she said, dropping the John Coltrane cassette box. "I can handle it myself."

She heard him say Sure but what a big deal he was making out of looking at the ceiling. Outside trees were swooping and slushing. Carol stayed where she was.

Jimmy shifted on the cushions to face her.

"I just meant, you know, as long as you know what you're doing, I just thought . . ."

"Yes, I do know what I'm doing," she said, turning away from the tapes. She sat down on the edge of the cushions leaving a space.

He hadn't given up, was smiling with his mouth.

"I'm not coming the big protective man."

"But?"

"Is it a lot of money?"

She did feel tired, there was a crustiness to her eyes and something in her stomach but his eyes were still on her.

"If you really want to know, yes, it is a lot of money. Does that freak you out?"

He kept looking at her about to say something.

"I mean do you mind Jim? That it's me, a poor, helpless woman and yes, I do like it in bed with you. If you really want to know you're the best for a very, very long time."

Maybe that made him really happy, leastways his mouth was smiling again.

"I'm not sitting here needing compliments." He was up and wandering around the room, then making something of standing at the curtained window. She wanted to jump up, hold him tight but, no escaping it, she had seen his sullenness before.

"I'm saying that Jim just so there's no misunderstanding," she said stretching out on the cushions.

"There's no misunderstanding Carol, it's all very clear," he said round to face her. The trees sounded angry, she heard the word Birching inside. She wanted to go on hearing the voice because otherwise she could only see him looking hurt again and that was making her crazy.

"So maybe Pat was right and maybe I was protective as you said."

He took his place on the cushions away from her. He said, "What?"

"Horizons Jim. What is it, the poor woman to her gate."

His arms were round her. "It's just because I care about you. Something else I've said before but I really do care."

She didn't know. She did not know. His fingers were strong on her shoulders but they felt different. Desperate. She pulled away, said she wasn't elastic. "A hug doesn't solve everything Jim. I like your hug, I've enjoyed it, but now . . ."

"What?"

"It's like you think that all big horizons are bullshit, that I can't have any."

"I'm sorry."

Her fingers stroked his hair without thinking. "Don't be sorry Jim. Please."

He pulled away. "All right, not sorry. Fucks sake I'd just like to think I could help because you're such a wonderful person."

There was no way out. "So now I'm sorry too," she said. "Sorry that you feel sorry but what am I supposed to do? Have I got to feel sorry and guilty because I say to a lover, a best of lovers, that No, I don't need any help."

That got him on his feet and speaking sensibly, no mouth smile. "Fine, that's fine. Message understood. I just want you to know that I really do care about what happens to you."

Carol's smile felt tight but she could say Thanks, and that really she was just out of sorts. But he didn't get the message and she felt a chill when he asked could he see her, when the Big Deal was done. She would not cry. No she bloody would not.

"Leave it Jim, please, just leave it."

And still he was hovering when all he had to do was pick up his jacket and everything would be all right. Instead he was mumbling close by which left her having to be clear.

"It does happen Jim, it does. Accept it, Carol Curbishley is not so perfect but if you can accept that . . . Please go."

Still he made no move. His jacket was there so he could just pick it up and she was not going to move from her cushions.

"Don't let's have a scene Jim, not that."

He said No in a hurry, picked up his jacket and left quietly.

Carol went to her bed and pulled off her jeans, sitting on its edge. She swivelled up on to the cold bed in knickers and top, hunched up her knees, pushed her feet under the sheet and stretched out her legs.

It shouldn't be like this. It was ridiculous. It was ridiculous and it was a shame. Jimmy was part of her life, was going to be part of her life. She wasn't going to cut him out just because she had x number of grand in her pocket. So why all his paranoid bullshit? She liked being fucked by him, she liked fucking him. That's how it was with him, not afraid of intimacy, and that a luxury, but when she'd even mentioned something else, her work, her job, he'd come on frantic and desperate just because he wasn't part of her deal.

She'd done the work to make it happens. She on her own had finally persuaded Terry to listen, to take her seriously. Only Jimmy seemed to think it was only possible with Mr Jimmy. Arrogant bastard, as if his love was purer than hers. And he could have helped perhaps, someone for emergencies, an extra set of eyes in the lobby. Watch for any kind of tail, a face Arthur didn't know.

As it was, anything funny from Arthur and she'd just get out and leave, him and his money. So why couldn't Jim have kept his voice light, Need a hand with anything mate. Why not that? Instead . . .

No, it would be OK, one step at a time. Her rules all the way. Anything wrong and cut off. Sorry for the inconvenience she'd say and Terry would say, No problem, if you had doubts, better this way.

She heard the crazy trees outside. This time a rocky moorland. She breathed in deeply. Trees were bent on the horizon. InOut InOut InOut InOut

A Carol lookalike looked through some old papers, parchment coloured, curled at the edges. She was sat at a table, the papers under a close-to burnt out candle twined by smokey, snakey wax. An old crone entered the limitless grey room weighed down and out of shape with black plastic bags full of more parchment. Carol inched forward to look over Carol looka-like's shoulder. Two Carols bent over together. On the top sheet was written in scroll The Secret Of The Curbishleys.

Carol Lookalike looked up.

Carole froze.

"It's all right mother," Carol lookalike said. "We will get what is ours from the estate. So long as there is breath in my body, we will get what is rightly ours. No more and no less. Not a penny less."

Carol heard mad wind clattering deep windows. The candle flame shuddered. The scrape of the old crone's plastic bag was harsh across the uneven flagstones.

A scream cut through the scraping.

The old crone was a heap on the floor. A big guy in a suit stood grim faced over the bag. Mine you fucking slag, he said.

Carol sat up in her bed wide awake in the dark. She looked across at the shape of her window. Something crashed heavy. There was a scream close by. Carol jumped out of bed. Sheila was trembling in the passage. She held her tight. The house was shaking. It was fucking shaking.

"It's all right darling, it's all right, Mum's here." They pulled each other into Sheila's room, edged towards the bunk bed. The window sounded like it was ready to jump out.

"It's all right, it's all right darling," she was saying like it was a mantra. She was bloody mad, three hundred and fifty grand tripping off her tongue like it was twenty quid. Bloody mad. Grimface having her followed from Terry's. Grimface in his suit capable of anything.

Groan Snap Crash. Sheila screamed and wriggled. The whole house was under siege. She pulled Sheila down to the lower bunk bed. "It's all right, Mum's here, Mum's here. Just hang on a second."

It was OK, it was London town. She crossed the room to press the light switch. The room stayed dark. She could see the pale shape of Sheila and her pyjamas and ran back across the room. Shake, Rattle and Roll, she said in a calm voice. Oh yeah? Oh yeah? OH YEAH? the wind said and gave the window a slap.

"Let me in little pig, let me in. No? Well I'll blow and I'll blow and I'll blow your house down," Carol said holding Sheila tight.

Grim face stood over a beat-up Terry. Sly, greedy grimface taking the coke, taking the money and she'd say Oh. And Arthur'd say Excuse me, there's some mistake, that's mine. No son, you've made a fucking mistake.

The glass rattled in its frame. So fragile the transparent stuff.

Terry was good. Good at his job but nervous as hell when the wolf came in. Tell us about it son, he'd said. Grim. No, nothing to do with business Terry'd said and known about forged money that she'd never even thought of. Knew his onions. Listen out for his room number or follow him he'd said like he did it every day. Only then following Arthur to his room was suddenly not on because Terry'd thought of something else. Like he'd never done it before. He hadn't. Not ten off the Grims. Not ten at all.

"You're hurting me Mum."

What was she doing? A bear hug. She loosened her arms. She spoke.

"Well I'll tell you what happened. The wolf did get his way with the house made of reeds and the house made of wood but what's this house made of?"

"Bricks," shouted Sheila.

CHAPTER THIRTY-NINE

He's a good lad that Terry, credit where credit's due. I'll admit there's been times I've had my doubts like when Derek's been going on about what a terrific feller he is. Angels ain't going to be much cop as drug dealers are they, stands to reason. And of course this Terry was involved in that caper in the Ripened Hop which wound up causing a lot of grief all round. And a few bob. Still, what I like about him is he knows his limits. It can take a lot of courage that can, to say yes, I'm good at my job but this one's a bit beyond me. And that's exactly what Terry's done and I respect him for it.

And as it happens, taken in context, may be the Ripened Hop incident wasn't such a bad thing. There was a boil waiting to burst. It brought things to a head. Mickey White is tied up tighter than a virgin's. Curtis's words, which shows you how made-up he is, him speaking like that. Just the other day in fact. A park again. And some fucking park. Out Willesden way, North West Ten. I had to look at the old A-to-Z three times. And there he was, the rozzer, stood next to this tatty old bridge. I'd have driven past him if I hadn't caught a whiff of that stinky pipe. And by the time I'd parked up and covered the stereo he wasn't there. I found him just inside the park entrance under some tree with branches all over the place. A few whole trees blown over. Curtis says you never can tell with the elements. He's right, it was some fucking hurricane. Like I told him, I lost a few trees myself.

What is it with him and parks all of a sudden. I said to Keith I hope he ain't got problems with the Rubber Heels. Now there's times Keith can get right on my wick with his flash comments but once in a while he can be really sharp and if you can't have a laugh now and again what's the fucking point. Rubber Heels he says, the cunts gave themselves the name, loud trumpets and heavy boots from afar more like it. He's right too. Still, better safe than sorry and that's what I've always liked about Graham despite the aggravation. Gladstone, the park's called. Mr Gladstone used to stay there at weekends he tells me as we're tramping about. That's before he tells me they've got Mickey White like a kipper with a bit of help from a remand prisoner.

I shouldn't have done but I asked him, Who's that then. And of course he comes on all solemn, he can't tell me that, it's confidential. Keith creased up when I told him. Which he was entitled to because we did a good job there though I say it myself. Simpson, his evidence, it's just the icing on the cake. Keith kept saying it, Confidential, and splitting himself every time. Only what's he do then, comes on like he's a Rothschild or a Hambro, like he's now a financial expert as well. Asking me about how things were with William all on the strength of a couple of minutes chat with that friend of my pal Steve in some cheapskate gym. Which were Keith's own words. Cheapskate. If that's the only competition we're fucking made, he says. Battersea, same place as he's seen this plot of land we can build our own.

I've no complaints there. Very thorough his research and I'm convinced. A fucking fruit machine in the bar for opposition! When the clientele you're after's advertising execs and financial analysts! With a fruit machine you're talking the Old Duck and Dick, Shitown, East Six.

No, no complaints at all. And in some respects his attitude's matured. After he's pumped this pal of Steve's about this gym they're in, and I take his point about making the move to badminton at forty, yes, after that Keith said he was tempted to give him a STAMINA STUDIO card but he's resisted the temptation, hasn't mugged the feller off. I look forward to the day when Keith's not even tempted but you've got to see it as a step forward. Still didn't stop him coming on like he's a finance guru. "In banking is he, that pal of Steve's," I said. "I thought it was TV."

Of course the stock market crash has been a bit of a shock

especially when we'd just had that hurricane and lost a few trees but the way Keith's been going on about it you'd think he was the only thinking man in the world. I told you, I told you he's been saying ever since.

As it happens I could well fancy a film. You know I wouldn't be surprised if Mickey and this Simpson hadn't been on dirty-mag swapping terms in the slammer. Can you imagine it, magazines in this day and age. Pages of gloss stuck tight with old spunk. My library's grown and grown, three shelves of video. And the funny thing is I've half a mind to turf out the most of them, find someone to do a trade with. You've seen some of them and where do they leave you, hard pushed to get a hard-on. Look, here's two the Iranian gave me. One of them I half fancied, but the other one, do me favour, bird in a bikini doing poses on the seafront.

They can go.

Out.

Mind you the feller himself, been as good as gold. I spoke to him on the phone just the other day, and he says he's getting to like Jersey, got his eyes on a property there he says. Not far off exchanging contracts. Also told me that cousin of his Is on a plane to somewhere in two days. About time, I said. Not Iran, Zurich. Turns out Akbar and the Ayatollah ain't the best of friends. As if I didn't know. I asked him for the flight number and to give him a gee told him we'd not only resume business but have additional partners. He's chuffed. And Akbar was on that flight. A little bird confirmed it. Which has given Keith the green light to find someone to take over the retail side of that particular business. And he's been busy, reckons he's got a prospect already, a reliable firm out of South East London he says. Very busy, and that's because it's a priority for him. That's a thing you learn in life, it's the man who really wants something who'll go out and get it done even when the whole company or firm is supposed to be on the job. There's got to be that motivation, it's human nature. Derek on the other hand, well he's been coming round to my idea but his heart's not in it.

What's this one? Maybe came from Billy Mac. There's two

tarts touching each other up, one's blonde and the other's some kind of Malay. Thai maybe. Got to be the wrong side of thirty the both of them. The blonde, she's staring at the coloured one's tits like they're the best thing since sliced bread. More like a brown bread roll as it happens, a current bun with the current sticking out the top.

I don't know where Keith gets the time. All that running about he's been doing and it still don't stop him getting on my back. I told him straight, he's not the only one takes an interest in the stock markets of the world. Why only the last time I talked with William face to face we were saying diversity. And more diversity. The more spread our funds the better. He said it. I said it. International equity markets of course but not just that, some gilts too for ballast. It's the age old rule, Don't put all your eggs in one basket.

No this one can't be off Billy Mac. He'd be worrying about what his mum might think if she copped hold of it. I must have missed something. There they were doing their stuff in a motel and now some Latin-looking geezer's in on it. Must have had a fast motor. Or a horsebox. They're in a barn in suspenders, What's it going to be, a billy goat?

By yesterday I'd had enough of it, fronted Keith up and said I'd ring William there and then and what did he want, to listen in on the extension, or the call taped. All he could say was, Just phone him. Which I did. We'd taken a couple of losses William said, he wasn't going to deny that but they'd be self-correcting in the medium term. Mind you Gordon, he says, there's a few people who should know better, counting their pennies.

I told Keith, explained what a diversification of assets means. Don't Put All Your Eggs In The One Basket. The other face I asked about the next quarter's dividend. To be honest, he says, it won't be as spectacular as the last but not that far off.

I respect that in a man. He's straight with you. Circumstances aren't the easiest but he's done his best and gives it you straight, no false hopes. Another thing he told me was how there's Leverage merchants in plenty of schtuck. Some Aussie dickhead he mentioned, got some cash-flow problem.

No, this has got to be one of Mario's. The latin feller is sat on a bale of straw with a white shirt and a black waistcoat while the coloured bird's giving the donkey a strop. She's kneeling down with the blonde behind her, hands on her tits. She does like them. Wap, the fucking donkey's come in a great arc of gob.

It's a funny thing how Keith suddenly so pally with Derek over Terry's big deal. I could see how it was lined up, two to one against. So even though I thought the credit level was a bit over the top I went along with it becuase it was good seeing them being realistic, and ready for compromise on the other business. And now this Terry's turned out to be a realist himself.

You know what he's saying, the feller in the black waist-coat? He's speaking to the coloured one from his spot on the straw. "This donkey is my friend. You understand what that means. My best friend in the whole world. He gets up with plenty of bulge in his trousers. The two of them, the blonde well, they nod. And he's got a whip in his hand. So, he says. So, she says back, the blonde one, a cocky sort but you can see the fear in her face.

So milk maid, he says, pulling her towards him. Your hands are rough but your mouth, he says, kissing her, that is soft. Then he pushes her away.

She's doing it too, the blonde, while her pal's behind her with a finger up her cunt. Or maybe it's her arsehole. Hard to tell. Anyway I'm all eyes on the donkey, I tell you it's got a way of looking that you don't know if it's enjoying it or not.

So I wound up meeting this feller Arthur. More work for me because when it came to it, it was, Gordon, Gordon, you're the one for this kind of thing. Both the brothers. And here's the joke, the feller only wants the meet in Bubbles. For a moment, when I heard that, I wanted to call the whole thing off. But Terry says it's Arthur's local.

Turned out he was telling the truth when we did get to meet at the Hilton. Terry made the intro and kept his end up for ten minutes. We were talking about the hurricane, the damage it's done. This Arthur made some flash remark, how did the Acts of God smallprint read on your Insurance Policy, which is when

Terry took himself off. He wasn't complaining, a grand or two for half an hour's work.

Mid-thirties, Arthur. Sat there in his pinstripe with the collar and tie undone. I said I didn't know the Insurance business personally but the Act of God bit just meant they knew their limits. That tickled him. "Oh very nice Mr . . ." he said.

"Scott," I said. "Stevie Scott."

Then we got down to business. Thirty-two I said. Done, he said and what a pleasure it was doing business so decisively, the mug. Very different to working with my underlings, he said. Underlings! Some bird called Simone he said. He's some lad that Terry I bet she's the sort was up there that time with a kid.

He's not doing badly for himself, the tosser in the black waistcoat. The Malay sort's giving him a blow-job on a four-poster while the blonde one . . . What is it with the coloured bird's nipples, magnetic or something are they.

So when we've fixed the price this Arthur's only raised his glass. To a future working relationship, he says and then comes on like a know-all about the stock market. Diversification, I said and he comes on some bollox about it depending where you diversified. Natural resources and blue-chip, the cunt says like there's nothing else in the world. I liked the way he didn't piss about with the biz but I'd had enough chat so I moved it on to the Hows and Wheres of the trade. He's only given me his address, the mug, which is when I realized he could well be a patron of Bubbles. Personally I think he's a bit of a nutter. Harmless, but a nutter. Tells me that in due course we could trade Options in Mario's gear.

He's got some energy the latin feller. He's fucking the blonde from what I can see, what with her skewered up against one of the front posts. Of course the other one don't want to be left out, she's got those magic tits of hers rubbing up and down his back while she's playing with the blonde's with her fingers.

CHAPTER FORTY

"You speak to Interpol Nye?"

"Yes, we'll get the word if and when he re-enters the country. Not enough to go on in the immediate."

"Some you win, some you lose. In the short term. Got to smell a bit, Zurich. Yes, so if and when friend Akbar should return, immediate top level surveillance. I'm giving the OK on that now. We have got his pal Ali coming up."

"DS Jones's case Graham."

DCS Curtis put his coffee down.

"A word there Nye, probably better coming from you. An excellent officer DS Jones, loyal, Thorough and above all realistic, but you know what some of these defence counsel are like."

"Clever bastards with the words guv." DCS Curtis lifted his cup. Didn't like what he saw.

"Exactly Nye. Think a copper's got nothing better to do than produce immaculate prose. They can afford to, the cunts. They're not living in places where your junky's got his eyes on every drum in sight. What do they do to coffee in the canteen?"

"Warm piss with liver trouble. As DC Thomas put it."

"Did he?"

"It was an early morning meet in the canteen sir."

"At his most pungent then is he?" DCI Edwards grinned. He nodded.

"Jones's oppo with the Ali business isn't he?"

"That's right. I was on holiday myself."

"Not to put too fine a point on it Nye make sure their notebooks aren't word for word, know what I mean?" DCI Edwards grinned. He nodded.

"Point taken guv."

"How about the photos Nye? The AC approved but I know it must have looked like it was my personal whim. I'd like the whole squad to take a gander."

"There's still a place for trawls guv, when the fields well chosen. If I can speak for the squad, very impressed that you took a couple of shifts yourself."

What was he supposed to say to that?

Some bollox.

"Who can say Nye?" he said. "You follow a hunch and you hope for the best."

"Yes guv."

"You know what happens when you follow a hunch and get nothing Nye?"

"A nil-all draw when you've had all the possession guv."

What was all this Guv shit. Just what the hell was it. Didn't they have their own way of talking in those valleys. If his DCI couldn't come up with anything on top of what he'd got himself out of the photos that was his fucking problem. And what was this nil-nil bollox, rugby scores ran into double figures didn't they?

"The point about nil-nil is it's temporary," he said. "If you reckon a face like friend Akbar or even your Stevie Scott, if you really fancy him then stay with him. Still in the frame is he, Mr Scott? When things are a bit slack give him another look."

"He's one man I do fancy sir."

"That's what I'm saying, you got a hunch then, manhours permitting, go for it. So you picked up the shop receipts, feller all right about it was he?"

"Did it personally guv. Had to keep reassuring him. You know it had never occurred to the old boy." Graham Curtis grinned. He sighed.

"You know there's times I wonder if innocence just isn't on anymore."

DCI Edwards frowned.

"Don't get me wrong Nye, it ought to be, ought to be. It's the right of the civilians who pay us etc etc, leastways some of them do. But in this day and age I wonder if isn't a luxury we just can't afford. I mean it's no good being out on the old boat, a storm comes up and you ain't got a clue what to do. You take my point?"

Edwards grunted.

"The old super losing his marbles, getting a bit philosophical in his old age? Maybe. But the point is Nye it's no good being out there while the fucking boat's sinking and saying, But I didn't know it could be like this. Because you should have done, you know, before you'd even contemplated taking it out to sea." DCI Edwards grinned. He nodded.

"Point taken guv. I told him that of course we appreciated that accurate weighing tackle was crucial to productive industry but that there'd always be a boyo or two trying to take advantage of what was otherwise beneficial technology."

"I like it. You get anything out of the pics?"

DCI Edwards gave him two sheets of photocopy and explained how he'd done the breakdown.

"For one thing guv there's the type of Scales. Look at this one for example. Specifications on this sheet."

"What every wholesale Jack-the-lad would fancy for his Christmas stocking eh Nye?"

"We haven't cross-checked them against the photos yet but I'm thinking we'll follow two lines, the photos themselves, right across the squad as you suggested, and the names and addresses. The ones we're interested in are going to be moody but because everything's dated, each moody name's going to have a face to go with it."

"Sure. I mean just at a glance, who's this cunt with the Christmas gift? Kruger he calls himself. Now that has got to be one cheeky bastard."

DCI Edwards grinned. He nodded. He said, Snap.

An obsequious bastard Nye when it came to it. And an effort keeping his end up as the DCI rabbited on. Ever since he'd gone to his old pal in Records personally, got a Car Hire firm off the registration number he'd noted in Clerkenwell, and then a Colombian name with the International brief off of the Car Hire itself, it had been a struggle to concentrate on anything else. Now he'd got pictures to go with it, close on impossible. One was a cracker, Bob himself and behind him the big feller who was doing the biz with the Colombians. A Thursday again, just like the last time. It was hard to credit, an old shrewdie like Bob coming on like it was a regular date for Poker.

Was he taking the piss or what? He owed him one already. When it came to it, it was him, Graham Curtis, who'd come up with the evidence that would make the Mickey White business into a certain conviction, the nicking of the decade. And what had Bob done but come on leery when he'd asked him straight out for a guaranteed witness spot come the trial. The bullshit the tight bastard had come out with.

He unlocked the lower desk drawer and took out the handful of pics. The camera never lied and Bob looked shifty, no two ways about it. What to do with it?

For the hundredth fucking time, what to do with it? Get into the cunt for a slice of what he was taking was the obvious move. Bob wasn't so dumb he couldn't see the writing on the wall.

Why, because the slippery bastard was minting it and would do so till he retired, a retirement he could coast to on the strength of Mickey White.

The phone rang.

"Graham, fancy a drink?"

You thought about someone, they rang you up. How about that!

"I'm a bit snowed under, you know how it is."

DCS Lumley sighed, chuckled, said how about Five thirty, and how being snowed under could lead to not seeing the wood for the trees.

"Yeah OK Bob but not that shithole in Victoria." Lumley laughed loud in his ear. Graham felt pissed off, bold.

"How about Clerkenwell Bob?"

"That's a bit out of the way Graham."

DCS Curtis looked at the Venetian blinds covering his office window. Interesting tricks they played with the light. Amazing. You sat in your office week in week out and noticed nothing. Shadows dancing on the wall. Amazing.

"There's another place, Victoria direction but you'll like it Graham, very quiet. Good for a chat." DCS Curtis said he'd take his word for it, OK, 5:30.

He put down the phone and picked up the report at the top of his in-tray. DS Arthur Sims had heard a strong whisper about some characters who might well be involved with a regular run of red-cellophane wrapped black hash from Rotterdam. Organised from Birmingham but with a London end. There was a note attached: "An eclectic hashish from various resources believed to be re-mixed with who knows what and packaged in a Dutch factory, location of which as yet unknown."

Eclectic!

DS Sims had been to college but then had the good sense to get himself a good informant.

He initialled the report. Said he could have three men on it, and to keep it from the West Midlands squad as far as possible.

The thing was Bob had been sloppy. Bob was sloppy. Amazing but true. And that being so, other officers might see the same thing. All good things could come to an end.

There was another option. Go flat out for the Colombians and he'd have a nicking would put even Mickey White in the shade.

The phone rang. DCI Edwards.

"The Ali case guv. Notebooks look all right, want a look yourself?"

What was this, hadn't he made a real effort to delegate responsibility?

"Take your word for it Nye."

* * *

"They're a fact of life Bob, neighbours. At least they are unless you live right out in the sticks or you're very, very rich," Graham said.

Full marks to the bar for effort: greenery all over the shop; fresh pink and white decor; chairs with criss-cross raffia stuff on the seats.

"But you ain't the one with middle-management next door. He's in canning and has got it into his head that my job is very exciting."

"What's his line? Carrots? Mackerel?"

"What, I've never asked. You must be kidding. I'd be in for hours of it over the garden fence."

"Seen one can and you've seen them all. He probably reckons you like a car chase."

"The TV's got a lot to answer for."

It was right. Graham said so. Lumley asked him if he fancied another, it was his treat. When he came back with the drinks Curtis had his pipe out with his tobacco pouch.

"Bit of a to-do on the stock exchange the other day Graham."

"On the cards wasn't it. These things can't go on for ever and ever, up and up in value, stands to reason. Me, I've got my pension scheme and a few unspectacular gilts and that's fine. You want to make a quick buck, you've got to keep your eyes open full time."

"Coming right on top of that hurricane makes you think don't it. Played havoc with my garden and I kept thinking of Sunday School, hurricanes and plagues. All we need now is a plague of locusts."

OK Bob, if that's the way you want to play it.

"They've got that in Africa Bob, they say it's spreading fast. Still that's a good way off Essex. Or Surrey come to that. Mind you I haven't been down to see the old boat since the storm," Graham said, teasing out a final shred of tobacco. He pressed it down into the bowl and lit up.

"Christ, your boat. I'd forgotten about that. Hope for the best I suppose, you can't argue with the elements.

"Gives you a sense of perspective. Take that rumpus on the stock exchange, so now we've got the politics of greed. I've got nothing against it, it's human nature, but it does mean you've got to be extra careful with the rules don't it." Graham said giving his colleague a look straight in the eyes through the pipe smoke. He waited.

"Funny you should have mentioned Clerkenwell on the phone Graham, I was up there just the other day. Changed a lot since you and I started on the Force. These days it's all studios, whole food shops and Health Clubs."

DCS Curtis was not happy with the way his pipe was burning. He re-lit.

"Yes I know you were up there Bob," he said.

"Blimey, I know liason's the name of the game these days and I'm all for it but I didn't think it stretched to my Desk Diary doing the rounds. I'll tell you who's got one of those health clubs up there, Gordon Murray. Now there's a very interesting character."

Curtis felt tired. He sipped at his scotch. "What's that supposed to mean, An Interesting Character? Care to translate?"

DCS Lumley was smiling. "Interesting, a person I've always taken an interest in. Obviously got a good head for business."

"I reckon you don't do so badly yourself Bob."

"Now it's me who needs a translator."

Graham took a photograph out of his pocket and laid it out on the black japlac'd table.

DCS Lumley's smile didn't falter. It grew broader.

"Unless you're a professional on the side Graham I'd say that's a very good quality picture. A very interesting person there."

"Is that right?"

"Could be one of the most interesting sources of information I've come across in years."

"Could be? That's a bit different from what's tried and tested which is what I'd call Mr Murray."

"Lucky you Graham."

DCS Curtis smiled. "But I'd say you're luckier Bob. You know what, I think we could usefully put our heads together on this one."

"My thought exactly. Here you fancy another one?"

"My round Bob."

CHAPTER FORTY-ONE

No good kidding yourself Gordon, never did anyone any good. But you did do it right when it happened, you went by the book. You checked. You phoned him again and he's tied up, William's away on business, she said.

OK, fair enough, the geezer's got plenty on his plate I said to myself, the cunt, the slippery no good whore's son. On your plate? You ever thought about it William, a fucking scorpion in your beef stroganoff. I don't figure you have because your problem, William, is you don't realise, you just don't fucking know who you're tangling with. This isn't like Tina because that was peanuts and where's she now anyway, a dripper in Toronto at the very best. And I mean, the very best. Forty-seven next birthday and they've heard of AIDS in Canada, they're not stupid the Canadians. They're not but William is. Yes you are because even if you've bought an island in the Caribbean I'll have you. I will have you.

Mr Appleby's away on business, she said. The fourth time I said, that's a lot of business ain't it, when no one's trading too much.

Oh he's working very hard, my worry is that he's overdoing it, she says. The fifth time there was no reply. The phone hadn't been cut off, no it rang and there was an Answerphone message, please leave your name and number, all the bollocks.It all cost me, one Phone Card unit after another just for the privilege of listening to her snooty fucking voice. Oh yeah, what did they take me for, lunch at five at night, lunch at ten in the morning.

And then, just when it's really important and I need

maximum concentration, what happens, Derek comes by the office. Just a passing call he says, but what does he do, this fucking brother of mine, he only succeeds in making lose my rag for the first time in a very long time. Well done Del. There he was putting a good face on the fact that the Iranian's biz is close to being a thing of the past. Yes, because he knows all of us will get our dues out of that down to what I've come up with.

But now I can see that all the while this fucking dinosaur of a brother I've been landed with has been seething underneath. Seething. Because you know what he says to me the cunt, If you're so keen to flog off the business what's going to happen to that bird of your and her needs.

A few weeks back a pal of a pal of his did a little favour for me when me and Sarah went to Spain. I can see now that's a favour I'm supposed to pay for. "Your bird and her needs," that's what he said. I got up from my desk slowly like I was thinking about what he's said, and grabbed him by the throat. I was that mad I was half a mind to tell him about Mickey White and all the trouble he put me to.

I didn't need to he was that shocked, his windsor jammed hard into his adam's apple. See he'd made the same mistake as this fucking clown William. Thinks just because I've developed a lot of self-control that he can take liberties. Must be a level fifteen stone Derek but I had his feet off the deck. Are you by any chance talking about Sarah, I said. Number one she's not My Bird, she's Sarah to you. Number two my own personal concerns will never, and I repeat never influence any business decisions that have to be taken. And lastly if Sarah's got her problems and I happen to be a pal of hers then they're my own, not yours, and not any other cunts.

I eased off his tie knot a little. You got anything else to say then fucking say it, I said. He started mumbling so I opened the door and told him to fuck off. I got a grip of myself and rang the Isle of Man. I kept ringing and all the while I'm saying to myself, William I'm giving you the benefit of the doubt because I don't believe you could be so stupid., I've talked to you, I know you, and I really don't believe it. Later I phoned through a flight reservation to some shithole called Douglas which is the capital of the place. He's got an office there. It's still there, William Appleby Financial Consultant on a brass plate. The office is there all right, but he ain't and it's all locked up. Of course I didn't want to be plastering my face all over the gaff but I got talking to this feller, a local. He hadn't seen anyone for days and no, he didn't think the secretary was local. A blonde, he said.

I'll find the cunt all right no question, but how am I supposed to concentrate when I've got Derek insulting me and Keith on the blower every other hour. There he is, my very bright brother with his research and his dossiers but when it comes to it it's always, Gordon shall I do this, Gordon shall I do that, have I got the go-ahead. Like it's down to me to decide everything. But what's the point in going on about it, Keith's Keith and that's all there is to it. It's no good kidding yourself Gordon, the reality is William.

That'll give him a shock won't it, he'll just be out of the surf and looking for his towel. Maybe he'll have that toffee-nosed slag of a secretary he's got in tow. That'd be about his style, "Financier Absconds With Gold Digger." Maybe the both of them, maybe him on his tod. Same difference. He'll have a tan of tans, his bath towel monogrammed and well laundered, and there's a daquiri waiting up on the terrace. That's where he's headed for, a big smile on his chops, when he'll hear from the whispering palms, William. Only he'll carry on, rubbing himself down, strolling. Tell himself it was just the breeze in the trees only just as he's finishing off, the last drops on his shoulder blades, he'll hear it again and he'll know it's no wind. It'll be me, standing in the palm grove with a shooter.

Fucking hell, sounds dramatic don't it, not my style at all. But that's the way it's going to be. The jock could do it, deliver it to the island, bury it in greased plastic. He'll be pricey though, the jock. Maybe Derek's Mo. Or Billy. Or the other face up north. If it comes to it I'll do it myself. And you know why, because there's some very stupid people out in the world, of whom William is a prime example, who force sensible people to get dramatic.

What Keith again?

"Tell him I'm tied up for the moment Chloe, I'll ring him back."

If I don't get out of this office I'm going to be pestered non-stop.

Fucking hell not again.

"Who?"

It's a Mr Curtis.

Now that's all I need isn't it, Graham rambling on at me in some fucking park the back of beyond. What'll it be next, a recreation ground in Enfield?

"Tell him I'm tied up at the moment."

What, Urgent? He don't know what it means. I've got to have that next quarterly dividend paid to the penny. To the penny, bang on the day it's due. That's one thing is sure and quite frankly, in that context, Graham is not a priority.

"Tell him I'll ring him back as soon as possible."

No, whatever happens that dividend's going to be paid on the dot. Maybe I could make it a little bit less. I mean that's the way it was due to be, Keith heard the scum say it himself. And even Derek can surely understand that every investor the globe over has taken a knock. What I still can't understand is how that piece of shit calls itself William can have been so weak. I was thinking about it on the return flight. Suppose he was in difficulties, and the timing makes it look that way; supposing he had been a bit reckless with our money and that shambles on the stock exchange caught him out. If only he'd just said it straight out, Gordon I've made a bit of a cock-up and as things stand it looks like this. If he'd said that I'd have told him, well you have dropped a bollock but I respect you for telling me William. Just get right back in there and straighten it out. Don't panic and if there's an investment you really fancy, stay with it.

But no, the thieving bastard ups and runs. He won't have lost all of it, he'll have a cosy hideout somewhere. I'll admit I wasn't thinking too straight for a while but fucking hell, we're talking about a very large chunk of dough, the rewards of a lifetime's hard work that's just vanished overnight. Of course I was emotional, I can't just run away from my responsibilities like he's done. That was all I could think of till we're coming in to land when I realize it's not just my money he's had it away with. Which makes me think of the feller who put me on to the thieving bastard in the first place. Where's he at this particular moment.

He's a man I've known for a long while and in all my dealings with him, never a problem. A tough negotiator but dead straight once we'd fixed a price. I rang him straight from Heathrow, never let on anything, just suggested a drink. That was the first thing wasn't it, He hadn't done a runner. Nor even changed his phone number. Second, he don't try to put me off: pleased to hear from me he says, how's it going and all that. I invited him over to Bubbles and he came.

Half four already. I've been here just thinking it out for hours. Chloe might as well go home.

"I may not be in tomorrow love but I think Keith may have a pile of stuff."

See, still polite, still the self-control, everything as normal. Curtis can wait. Probably thinks he's due for another body. Well he's not. He can start learning. Keith, I should ring him; to him especially nothing to look out of the ordinary. Maybe he's found someone serious for the Iranian's biz.

I'll bell him. Tomorrow night I've got that meet with Arthur. That's down to me. Another flash bastard. Younger than our shithouse of a William but the same kind of fanny. Options the cunt was talking about. He pays me a bit over the odds, a very small percentage in advance for the privilege of me holding a large lump of dollop for him on the off-chance he might want to buy it in three or six months time. What's he take me for. The trouble with people like Arthur is they've never had to be out there, on the street, fighting for it. Result? They live in a dream world, cut off from reality.

The phone's ringing again. What do they take me for, one of those outfits you ring up and pay through the nose for the privilege of you pouring out your problems. Problems? They don't know what the fucking word means, some slimy git's just walked off with all my money.

I know it's happened. Until I realized there were some heads turning I gave that door with the brass plate a battering. Yes, I know it's happened, but it's still hard to credit.

So this business acquaintance who put me on to shitbag in the first place comes down to my bar and I pull out one of our Chateau-bottled and we chat about this and that. Long time no see and what a shock, that hurricane. A terrible thing, he said, and how it was the trees really made London.

"Take Kew Gardens," he says. "Why when we was kids that was a real treat for us and in just one night they've lost the half of it. Unrecognizable they say."

I nodded at that while I'm itching to ask him about William. The old self-control see. Then he was off about how trees can't just be replaced overnight. Not like a TV or a motor, he says, you can't just go out and buy a new one.

I said it was a terrible thing and asked him if he'd seen William lately. Always gives a little rub of his left eyebrow he does when he's putting up some moody proposition or giving you a load of fanny. He don't know it but I do because I look at people when I'm doing business and after the first couple of times I clocked it with him. He said, "Well of course I rang him after that stock market shindig. Like he said, fortunately he's got all the funds he's managing diversified. A steady foundation in government bonds and the blue chip stuff will bounce back."

He had his hands round his wine glass while he spoke and you never know, he's a shrewd enough feller, he might have tumbled his little tic I told him William had told me the same thing and left it a moment.

"And now he's done a runner," I said.

I've never had this feller down as an actor, he's never pulled any of that bollox during negotiations, not like Mario. He turned white and I had to catch his glass that was on its way to smithereens. I jumped up for a damp cloth from behind the bar but kept clocking him in the mirror. Looked like a halfwit clutching the table. Don't even notice me rubbing the claret off his strides. It's different ain't it, when you can see it's knocked the bollocks out of someone else, it's not just you.

In the death he asks me where the phone is. I decided for

the moment I was going to take his reaction as genuine and if
he is on the level, I've a good idea his cash-flow don't look too
rosy either. But what I could do, what I have to do, is ask who
propped up William to him and on that he's got to come across.
That's the rules. So the feller comes back from the phone and I
said, still out to lunch are they, that's the longest fucking lunch
in history. Then I tried to get him thinking constructively, no
blaming him see, just We're in the shit what are we going to do
about it. A struggle that was, he kept going off into one, and one
thing I could well do without was him throwing a wobbler in
my bar, in my company. So I suggest his motor or mine and he
goes for mine which is telling me if the guy isn't kosher he's got
plenty of front. More than.

The upshot of it is that the man who's put him on to William
is called Richard Parkinson, pukha up front in some set-up in
the City and almost semi-legal, my acquaintance said. For one
thing he's definitely had a taste of unpaid bullion VAT. My inclination's to go and grab him by the balls till the pips squeak or
he can tell me where the thieving bastard can be found these
days, but then the old self-control takes over and reminds me
of other rules.

When I think about William I'm inclined to forget them. I
just get so mad picturing the git with his risk-spreading flannel.
I just want to be there on that beach or in that hotel room and I
want to hurt him. I want to cripple the cunt and I want my money.
The reason I control myself is because experience tells me that's
the way I'm going to get what I want. For a start I've called in a
couple of people I can rely on to do a job for me without blabbing.
That Kevin and a feller used to work for me full time. I don't have
a minder, a load of nonsense that is, but in the past when I was
more out there in the fray Johnny was around me most of the
time. Came a time when he branched out on his own free-lance,
and fair play to him. I've called him in. Kevin's looking at my
business acquaintance just in case, while me and him have got a
man each on Parkinson, and Johnny's my man there.

I've seen Parkinson from a distance, and heard him on tape.
That was the first thing we fixed up when I'd got my acquaintance

actually thinking. He makes a meet with Parkinson in Green Park, and goes wired up. Right out of the same mould as William and Arthur. I saw him from across the pond and listened to the tape later. He comes on all shocked, not all his dough but a good chunk of it gone if William Really Has Done A Bunk. Really. Oh, really. What's he want, an expenses paid trip to the Isle of Man to find out. I'll give it to my acquaintance, experienced when it comes to negotiations, he cuts through all that crap. Parkinson says he knows William from when they were both starting out in an Investment Trust; that William was the live wire on the firm so that later when he hears the thieving git has set up solo and no question asked, that's where he turns for a home for his money.

Terrific. But what does that tell us, fuck all. My acquaintance got heavy and our Mr Parkinson gets upset but he doesn't shift. He's wild with William. Can't understand it, his old pal must have got carried away with the froth on the bull market. That's what he said, the Froth On The Bull Market. And just wait till he gets his hands on our runaway.

Johnny and Kevin will be phoning in tonight. To Sarah's place over in Acton, I'm basing myself there for a few days. We've got some listening gear rigged up on Parkinson's drum but half the time I'm wondering if we've got enough people on the job. The trouble is they cost money those two. Johnny don't come cheap these days and right now that's the fucking joker. Can hardly credit it myself, having to count the pound notes when all the while I know I've got to come up with a dividend on the specified day.

William. William. When I get my hands round your fucking neck. You made a mistake? Fucking right, the biggest one in your life.

You know what, maybe I've got to a point where I'm not listening to my instincts anymore. All this time and expense just to know if Mr Parkinson is giving me the bollox or not. Really I should just cop hold of the flash cunt and squeeze out what he knows and what he don't.

The neck?

The testicles?

Whatever comes to hand. Grab hold of the cunt and take him to a cellar. No, tell you what, the gym. Get the cunt doing circuits at gunpoint till he's spewing his ring. And if that's not enough, a dig or two.

That's right isn't it? People like him and that Arthur, that's what they're not going to like at all, a bit of pain, not knowing where it's going to end. They've never known it. The shock, that some fellow citizen could possibly do something like that, be nasty.

Maybe I've just been behind a desk too long. But then that would be pricey too, lifting the guy, holding him. For that even Johnny's going to cost. More up the jock's street but that'll be an arm and a leg. It's a fucking joke. Money, it's like the law, never there when you want it like Stevie Burke said one time some little hooligan's done his passenger window and had the stereo away. Of course I've got my own assets, course I have, the house alone's a million plus, but start selling anything, even raise a loan on the strength and Keith'll have his nose in. Shit I've got to give him a bell. One call I've got to make.

What a mess. Six fifteen already and Johnny's due on the blower at eight and that's fucking Acton. All this aggravation just because an arsehole who's supposed to know a thing or two can't face up to the fact he's made a rick. If it is a shooter that's only stage one. I can cover him one-handed which leaves the other to throw that Daquiri, ice-cubes and all, right in his face. Hold on Gordon, get a grip. You're not there yet, a few steps in between and they're going to cost. And there's phone calls to be made, Arthur to meet.

Now there's a thing.

Could be.

Possible. Only problem would be if it got back to Derek. But what did he say there in the Hilton apart from all that flash about spreads and natural resources, something about a bird. We're sitting there over a g and t and it's come out. The feller's been pissing about way down the ladder, he don't even know Terry, just that one time in the Hilton.

I'm right. Got to be. Terry don't know him. Some pusher of his has bottled out and he's a bit leery as well. Not surprising after that caper in the Ripened Hop.

Yes. That's the first dividend with a bit to spare. Not much but enough for wages and wages right now are basic. Because if I don't find that thieving git I'm going to be running like a good un. On a treadmill. For ever.

CHAPTER FORTY-TWO

Rain slopped down out of its grey everywhere. The window was open the width of a floppy disk, a compromise: Vicky seeing GALOSHES on her VDU, Phil aglow with adrenalin. Slip slap plop, the drops on the glass another input to a lit-up day. And Vicky luscious in a pink V-necked sweater. Today was invariably not the beginning of the rest of one's life: this one had that possibility. No reason why not. No reason.

"You see our sandwich-board man this morning?" he said.

"Love of money's the root of all evil, him?"

"First day since the Crash he hasn't looked smug."

"Didn't he? Well he did have to hold up his brolly. Or he was soaked. Maybe he didn't have gloves. Anyway the world hasn't ended has it?"

"Vicky, Vicky, your feet always so surely on the ground." She swung her legs up off the swivel-chair. Phil made a thing of shielding his eyes.

"I'm not just a plodder," she said.

"Oh I know, I know. It's just been postponed I said to him, hoping he'd ask for how long."

"Who?" Vicky asked. Her high-heels were back on the carpeting. She was frowning.

"The woe to all sinners man."

He was loud, he could hear it, the adrenalin sloshing about inside. He moved away from the window, made an effort to keep his voice down. "And then when he didn't reply I wanted to tell him it wasn't just impersonal forces, we're not gardarene swine. Just look at how Greenspan's taken over the tiller at the Fed and the tiller my friend, is a manmade device, gives us control over the elements.

"But you didn't."

"It was pissing down, couldn't stop."

Weird, if anything he felt even sharper in his work since Tom Arthur had cashed in on new trends in management structure and he'd begun to take the other business seriously. A novel sense of detachment is what it was. The crash in the Equities market he had predicted simply added piquancy. A couple of equity-analysts had put their problems down to Treasury Secretary Baker speaking out of turn as if that were Phil's responsibility just because he happened to be a dab hand with the dollar. He'd been tart; when people were borrowing at 15 percent to buy shares with a dividend yield of 3 percent the thing was bound to end in tears. To that they'd had nothing to say. There was nothing to say. Amazing too just how quickly he'd got face to face with Mr Scott once he'd shown himself to be serious with the other business. He'd always known that's the way it would be since the moment he'd caught a glimpse of the real Simone, indecisive on a zebra with a raggle-taggle of kids, just it had been very quick. Of course she'd tried to keep up her image but he'd watched it coming apart in the face of the cash involved and hadn't been surprised to get her call suggesting they'd both be better off carrying on with their present level of work. As if the thing were a hobby. A pity for Simone the hippy but by then he'd had a taste of the future, with Tom Arthur coming on like Prosecuting Counsel. He'd put his foot down, told her if that's what was on offer he'd rather not bother at all. And had to tell her again, nothing at all.

It had been just after that call, just when the dam was about to burst after a day's hurricane-caused non-activity on a chastened stock exchange that he'd been whisked through an intro from her to a guy looking like a '70s rock star. And within another twenty-four hours on to the Mr Scott he could do business with. In a perfectly cut suit. Not off the peg either, not with his size. A bit of a rogue no doubt but wham bang when it came to business. Quite a character in fact, a dour cove but with some apposite turns of phrase.

"Phil! What's nemesis mean, a nasty end?"

"The inevitable result of bad behaviour. Not in one of my reports surely."

"It's Mr Childs," Vicky said. "I have to do for him now, surely you knew." No he bloody didn't. More of Sir Geoge's economy drive? If so he had lost all sense of proportion.

"Of course I know," he said. "And I should have warned you about our Mr Childs. Went to Cambridge."

"I'm prepared mate, chainmail under here," she said pushing her finger through the soft pink stuff into her midriff. Phil gasped. Surely after what Mr Scott called their little bit of business, surely she'd be game for more than just a bite of lunch.

In the meanwhile lunch at its conventionally defined time was out for the day. Things to be done, Jack to be picked up at three thirty. His best of pals carrying the final tranche of the flat sale money. Good old Jack who'd got a deal whereby only 2 percent of the total had stayed in the hands of his friend in the less than kosher bank. Who'd worked so hard once he himself had got such a good deal on the Wapping flat. An American recently posted for a long stint in the Square Mile paying the asking price and giving him another six weeks in which to sort something in the rented line. Jack's contact had then pulled off the disappearance of the flat sale money like it was surplus rainwater down City drains. And re-appearance in accounts at Finchley and Herne Hill with the final amount in a flexi-account at the wrong end of the City. To which cocky Jack had said, Wrong End? That's Dinosaur talk. And to be fair, entitled to be cocky what with Mr Tall Person enthusiastic for a kilo with a reasonable discount.

And still the rain fell. Transparent worms full of colons played jokes on the window pane. He could happily watch them all morning. Only there was work to be done and the pleasure of lunch foregone. As Mr Barley had said one winter's afternoon while Phil's schoolboy self was absorbed in other dotted worms contracting and expanding on the window. Jack would have been there next to him also staring out at the rugger field sodden and empty in the grey light as old Barley droned on. "Profit and hence capital is the reward of consumption foregone." And their arms had been up as one, their question in unison, just how long did a person have to give up present gratification for such a reward. "Ah Sharp and Stone, always worrying about the time factor," the old fart had said, his leather elbow patches shining in the November gloom and making a business out of looking at his watch. "In fact we have just five minutes to go which may set their minds at rest."

Good old Jack. Rallied round when it came to it. Always had. With a bit of chivvying. Like this time, he'd been having kittens at first. What if this Mr Scott was carrying a gun, what about a rip-off. And then suddenly, no qualms at all. A gung-ho Jack who'd rambled on about bloody mathematicians and computer programs thinking they knew everything, and then, Fuck Them, Let's Go For It. It was just the way he was, a bit of a worrier but when it came to it, right by your side.

He looked at his watch. Lunch was definitely out of the question. He said it again an hour later when Vicky said nothing was getting in the way of her lunch hour.

"You know how it is," he said.

"I'm not sure I do Phil, not since you had that afternoon with Sir George and Mr Arthur." He was all primed to put her straight but she was gone, the door closed behind her. From the window he looked down at shunting black umbrellas. Give it a minute and Vicky's would be one more in the fray. She might at least have asked if he could handle a sandwich or at the very least allowed a front to front, his Turbull & Asser against her soft pink. And what was that supposed to mean, him since his afternoon with the boss and his lackey. Give it twenty hours and she'd be seeing something very different. As for Tom Arthur, this time tomorrow and it would need just one word out of turn and the smarmy creep would learn what a hurricane really was.

* * *

By the Woburn Place lights after twenty minutes of the Euston Road Gordon knew he should have tube'd and taxi'd it. Should have done but had to go on, there was a day's work to be done. True he hadn't phoned Graham Curtis but he had phoned Keith at Clerkenwell and taken calls from Johnny and scouse Kevin. The right turn filter lights went green for an instant. Sneeze and he'd have missed it. Maybe next time they'd do him a favour and let him across. In the death if Mr Richard Parkinson or even his business acquaintance, if they were in it with William then they could afford to lie low for a very long time. No way around that.

The light flashed to green. The Rover in front was tentative. Gordon gave him the horn, revved the gas pedal and moved up bumper to bumper. Terrific, what a fucking achievment, finally across the westbound traffic and on his way.

So what then was he expecting off his two pricey employees. What they had come up with had gone back and forth all evening and got him precisely nowhere. Even Sarah in the tightest outfit had noticed, given him the come-on for a while but into the bathroom as soon as was decent and then not interested except in some of her weird sleep.

He gave the windscreen a blast with the washers. The time had come to stop poncing about and listen to his instincts. Give them another forty-eight hours on Parkinson and that was it. Definitely. At the very least they'd have his timetable and contacts so he could grab him. Just grab the cunt and he'd be shitting himself. Pinstripe, pyjamas, or pullover, the stain would show and the smell would stink regardless.

He'd missed the turn-off. Get a grip Gordon!

He threw a U-turn.

The place was like a warehouse from a bygone era. The feller he'd known from years back recognised him, was all over him before giving him the bollox about how dodgy the gear was, what with its associations now. Gordon slipped him a pony. The assistant nodded. "I know clients like you are bona fide," he said, "but you'd be surprised at some of the characters asking for this particular line and it is a considerable quantity." Gordon saw pimples all over the guy's face and palmed him another score. Then turned his back to the counter. These days it was like every arsehole under the sun wanted his cut. The stuff was legit wasn't it. Good for you if you had problems shitting or trouble with your eyes, one of the two. Proper stuff. If there was ever a next time he'd stop by every fucking retail chemist in London. Would buy it gram by fucking gram if it came to it.

He heard a cough and pimple face saying something. A drum of the stuff was on the counter. He paid in cash and signed some paperwork. S. Scott and Partners Medical Services, he wrote. With an address in Edmonton. Next on the agenda, the dollop itself warehoused in a secure bedsit near Archway, part of Derek's set-up.

The rain hadn't changed. He ran to the motor and locked the drum of gear in the boot. He could handle it himself, Parkinson smartarse. Wouldn't need anyone else to scare him shitless. This Can't Be Happening To Me, Mr Almost-Semi-Legal Richard would be saying. Only it would be. First slap and he'd know so. Second dig and he'd remember it wasn't happening to his thieving pal William who was far, far away. Grip his bollocks and the other hand a flat edge to his adam's apple. It was a lot of fucking money. Money that would make friend Richard's VAT scams look small. Money that might tempt him to hope for the best and hold out. Until the flat hand went in deeper and it crossed the tosser's mind that maybe the gym was the last place he was ever going to fucking see in all his natural.

No fucking about. Junction Road was a greasy-surfaced shitheap. He caught the street sign late, pulled a U-turn and made the right into a terraced street. The door numbers were hard to make out. Half of them hadn't bothered at all. He walked back in the rain, keys in his hand.

Ground floor bedsit, Derek had called it. A shithole is what it was, one room that ran to a gasfire, mini-stove, half a jar of Nescafe, an aluminium saucepan and a tin of milk powder. What was it with the brother, an electric kettle was going to put him out of pocket? Never heard of fridges? Ten minutes in the gaff and you'd have the flu. He switched on the stove, put on half a saucepan of water, lit the fire and sat down in a fold-up chair. And if it came to it and Mr fucking Parkinson knew nothing even with death on the cards there'd be nothing lost except the time and effort. Drop him off the far end of East India Dock Road and tell him to clean himself up. No way he'd go running to old bill.

Only he *would* know something.

Gordon's shins were hot, his shoulders were cold.

Give Derek his due, the claw hammer was under the sink like he'd said, eager to please after their little run in. He grabbed at the foam-backed carpeting and pulled it back. He counted out the floorboards and started in with the hammer.

Give Derek his due, triple-wrapped polythene. He eased the parcel out then tapped the boards back down with the side of the hammer, let the carpeting fall back in place and grabbed the saucepan off the stove.

Hard to credit but there wasn't a spoonful of sugar in the place. A piss-up in a brewery? As organised by Derek? You wouldn't chance it. He tipped some coffee granules into the blue and white ringed mug on the sink. The boiling water brought brown spirals up to the surface. He sat down in front of the fire. There was a job in hand. Stage One completed. Arthur's dosh plus the ten kees in his hand to be sold off. Put together say 550, 600 thousand. Minus the two hundred already paid to Mario, say four hundred G. It was a start and if he couldn't have over a cunt like Arthur he might as well jack it in. The feller was a mug, had swallowed thirty-two a gram without a murmur, thirty-two a gram for ten kees.

He swallowed a mouthful of the bitter hot stuff and stared at the fire. It's dirty cream twirls had reddened. This was bollox, running around in the wet, sitting in a dump drinking evil shit. Time to go.

* * *

"It's ten minutes your meeting with Mr Arthur," Vicky said. What?

Extraordinary, he'd been seriously sleeping. Mr Scott had been appealing for a bit of advice on the markets. Something An Ordinary Chap Can Understand, he'd said. Yes, rather large Mr Scott appealing for information. Something An Ordinary Chap Can Understand. Bloody dreams, picking up any old bit of reality and tossing it in the blender. Mr Scott with a note of appeal in his voice and saying Diversification Of Assets like it was a mantra. Like he was a heavyweight parrot. A dour parrot.

"Ten Min-utes. Tom Ar-thur. Mess-age re-ceived?"

"Sorry Vicki, must have turned off the hearing aid, Mr Tom. Very soon. Check. That'll be a bundle of laughs."

She laughed. She sighed. Oh to put his head in the dizzy coming together of that woolly-pink Vee. Oh oh oh how happy he would be.

"You're not going to be with us much longer are you Phil."

"Don't say that Vicki, latest medicals look good," he said and dug in his pocket to finger the gizmo.

"Yes, yes, yes. With the company I meant. I'd give a bit to know what really happened when Sir George had you down for tea. Mr Arthur was there too, I know because Ingrid told me."

"The blonde? Talkative is she?"

"Brunette Mr Stone, and she's a friend of mine."

"So supposing, just supposing that I did feel my future lay elsewhere, would you be a bad girl and follow me through the Highways and Byways of the Square Mile?"

"You must be joking."

Phil sat back from the desk wide-awake. He laughed. "No, just speculating," he said.

"Your pension may be transferable but I'm happy with the one I've got. And now it's five minutes."

He stood up from his desk, shoved the window wide open and breathed deeply for half a minute.

He re-closed it.

"See you," he said on the way out.

Downstairs in the simply furnished room that had been allocated for what Sir George called their sessions, sessions he was Likely to Drop In On, Phil held his own.

"What can I say Tom, U.S. interest rates are down, check."

"Yes, I'd say we can take that as a fact."

"Who wants a recession Tom? Tax takings down; every Tom, Dick, and Orvil with a welfare story; and the result, a budget deficit into the stratosphere. Who wants that? Greenspan's made a good move, a nice interest rate cut now, a commitment to money available."

Tom Arthur was hunched like a gnome the other side of the table.

"So," he said.

"So a slightly weakening dollar with a bit of action each side of the balance of trade statistics announcements, that's what I say."

"But steady?"

"Till the New Year given my proviso of statistics announcements. But then since I see J-curves and very slow price elasticity and thus a trade deficit with us for some time, down Ten to Fifteen yen come the New Year."

Finally Tom Arthur nodded.

In the company car park Sir George popped up like a bony question mark.

"Philip, how good to see that you leave early once in a while. It helps one feel less guilty when one has seen our senior dollar analyst working later than anyone could expect."

Phil had the driver's door open. Surely even Sir George could see that he wanted to get in, that he had somewhere to go. Anyone could see it.

"So your Mr Volcker is off to a well-deserved retirement. Is there life after Paul? Is Western civilization still intact?"

"Pleasingly decisive his successor. Very welcome. Yes I do have a rendezvous."

"Laconic as ever Philip. Ah, rendezvous. Wonderful, the Left Bank in Paris. What memories. The fifties of course, when existentialism was still a bit of a stink. Always the rendezvous."

Phil had got himself in the driver's seat, ignition key in his hand going for the slot. He said Yes, ready to go. But Sir George hung on, long fingers inside the rim of a door waiting to slam

"It's working well the new system? You and the dealing department. Of course it us. I rather think that after that stock exchange shindig a weekly background summary for Equities staff would be useful. So much interdependence these days, it's the the name of the game as you'd put it."

No he wouldn't and this was impossible. Jack could well be stuck there, cursing him on the pavement.

Yet still the bony fingers defied him.

"As an ex-modern I'd say yes, that is a reality yes," he said

"Ah toujours drole Philip, toujous drole as Mehitabel might have said if she'd been more than just a cat."

Phil was properly bewildered. He gave a gentle tug to the door.

"Au revoir Philip."

Yes, he said, slammed the door and charged into the road behind a double-decker. He went for the gap when it reacted late to waving arms at a Request Stop. Down the road a mile he saw his partner coming down steps. Behind him was smart signboard with a script of curls and dots. Jack got in. Everything was OK. He was carrying one hundred and ten thou. Plus Two Ten O in the office. Three three altogether.

"So let me be your chauffeur," Phil said. "The office Mr Sharp?"

"I rather think so Stone, yes. Do you know business took me out to Finchley the other day."

"Oh wild sir, wild," Phil said and accelerated into moving traffic. A taxi driver shook his fist, his mouth opening and closing behind the glass of his window.

"I wouldn't go that far Stone, Gracechurch Street if you please." They pulled up at lights where the cab got in next to them. He lowered his window. The lights changed. Phil smiled, gave the finger and left the cab for dead.

"So on my journey there, you I believe were engaged on other duties, I stopped off in a rather quaint quartier, Hornsey or Crouch End. Happened to look in a shop window and you'll never guess what I saw there."

"Something outlandish obviously but give us a clue, what kind of shop?"

"An all-sorts shop. How can I describe it, off-beat items for upmarket shopaholics. Take a right here."

Phil indicated, slowed and pulled towards the centre of the road. There was no way through. He stopped and got a volley of horns from behind. Phil made thoughtful sounds and moved fast through a gap in the oncoming profit.

"Left just past this building, the company car park. So what did I see?"

"A nasal hair-clipper," Phil said bringing the car to a halt in the Stammer, Case and Mangledorf parking area.

"You devious po-faced fucker Stone."

"What, was I right? Really? A nasal hair-clipper?"

"Don't give me that innocent bullshit Phil, you've been there."

"No honestly, an inspired guess. An association of ideas." Jack held his case tight over the silver-grey of the bonnet. "Wouldn't have thought they had much place in the eighties," he said.

Phil came round and checked the passenger door. "Bananas and penises, that kind of thing, no, but I was thinking of complementary goods."

"If the demand for Tea rises so will that for sugar as a consequence. In this case we call sugar a Complentary Good."

Phil laughed, he said Jack had got old Barley to a Tee.

"Pity we didn't know a bit then. How about cocaine and nasal accessories Mr Barley. What boy, what? For more efficient snorting sir."

They laughed loud on the pavement but as they approached the glass frontage of Stammer, Case and Mangledorff Jack insisted on best behaviour. In the marble and houseplant lobby Jack and the Security Man nodded at each other. Phil made an appropriate remark about interest rates bearing the brunt these days.

They had the elevator to themselves.

"Right, I'm the good boy tonight, working late." Jack said "Which I will till you've checked the goods at your leisure. If they're up to scratch you phone me and I'm straight across with the cash. Allow me ten minutes"

Console lights flashed past. Phil said right, and not to worry about the If.

"If anything I expect it to be rather better given that it will have been through a smaller number of sweaty hands but previous quality is the absolute minimum acceptable."

"And your nose is fresh and clean."

"Wouldn't mind one of your clippers. Maybe Father

Christmas will oblige." The doors slid open and they were out on to thick corridor carpeting.

"Ever felt a floor fabric try to suck the shoes off your feet?"

Jack frowned.

"That's paranoia Phil. OK, lower volume and best behaviour, Alice may still be here." Phil didn't like it but swallowed, took it in his stride.

The office was empty. Jack strode to his desk to sit behind it and wave the finger.

"Your nose is clean I take it."

"Never more so," Phil said. He was sincere, put his hand in his pocket and felt the untouched gizmo smooth, hard and spherical. "A line or two after the formalities have been completed' the way I see it. Only when they're completed." Jack nodded, said he was pleased to hear it but was Mr Scott 100 percent for sure all right. Was Phil definitively sure. Mightn't he be carrying a gun.

"Not that again Jack, we've been through it before. He's a rogue all right, my Mr Scott, not a man to call a wanker to his face, but not a gun. Too many rhetorical questions is his problem."

"It's a lot of money."

"Certainly is but the white British crim of a certain age doesn't like guns. That kind of caper these days and the police shoot to kill. The fact is he's coming to me, doing the deal on my ground. More to the point is your tall man definitely ready."

"Lapped it up. Very pleased. Just don't be rash in your quality judgement. Yes, and make sure it's a sample out of the middle of the package."

"Jack. Jack, it's me OK. I've got the Milton fluid as a make-sure and only when I'm perfectly happy will I call you. No call by ten and it's your bedtime." It took a while then Jack said, OK. Phil sighed. "Don't worry," he said. "If he does try and pull anything it'll be over my dead body and a corpse is something your local crim has an absolute dread of. Hey, did you see what the Weather boys are saying now?"

"What are they still alive, found their voices again?"

"Certainly took some flak. Well what do you expect, citizens being blown off their feet without warning, it's just not on. Anyway now they've pulled themselves together, say they did predict strong winds just that they never expected it to be quite so bad." Jack was incredulous. He was scornful. Said if a forecaster in their business had come out with such a post-mortem they'd be out on their ear a bit sharpish.

"Exactly so, and where does that leave certain colleagues in Equities. Now they're all saying it was bound to happen one day but that's not quite the same as saying, Down 25 percent on October 19th and saying it before it happened. I've got to go. I'll ring you and you're hotfoot over with the readies OK."

* * *

Gordon opted for the Peugeot. Acton was wet but no rain fell when he stepped out. He carried a fat shoulder bag weighing a bit over 20 kilograms. It held two similar triple wrapped polythene parcels; one in a Sainsbury's large size carrier bag, the other in a black canvas affair with ties that tightened at its neck. Sarah stood green in the flat doorway, he could see her as he swung the bag on to the back seat. Do it right, check the car lights. Get a pull from some zealous rozzer just for that, he'd never live it down, a fucking car chase with the gear in the back and the shooter in his pocket. Arsehole of the century.

He got out to check the dip. Sarah was still there. On edge? Not like her. Could be she'd clocked him at the loose tile in the bathroom, clocked the gun. Too bad. He reached in his window, flipped the indicator stick left and walked round the Peugeot. He gave her a wave. She waved back. He nudged the stick down and walked round the back. The right side orange winked at him. She was waving again.

"See you later," he said.

She was still there as he turned the ignition, gave the gas a touch, and waited.

"You'll catch your death," he shouted. The green in the doorway moved. Not indoors, he could see her in the mirror as he pulled away. Maybe it was because he'd just asked her to make up a cocktail with some of her tackle, a mix that does the biz but keeping in mind, he'd said, it's for virgins. Course he had, didn't want to go around killing people did he. And what was she worried about, there was plenty left if her tipple. If in the future it had run dry and he'd failed to persuade her off the habit he'd put a private little clause in any deal with the Iranian and Keith's pals. No asking for favours off Derek again. Anyway he would persuade her, get the present problems out the way and he'd be on it full time. For her own sake.

Coming to the Shepherds Bush roundabout he thought about the Embankment but went for the Westway. A maroon Sierra ahead was too close. Wanker, It was fucking motorway wasn't it. He beeped it till it gave way and had a clear run in the fast lane down into the Marylebone Road. Not a red light till Baker Street. Derek would be at home likely as not, tucked up with a video. Or a woman. Or both. Not a care in the world because what was William to him but a big fat cow pumping out the dosh once a quarter. Taken for granted because big brother was looking after it. Leave it all to Gordon.

Get a grip. The job in hand. He went for the Pentonville Road.

Keep a grip. Arthur had to be a prize mug, swallowing thirty-two, waving his address about. A mug, only people like Arthur had proved to be slippery. A person like Arthur had proved to be a slippery no-good cunt.

Give her her due, Sarah had tried to be helpful. It was only natural, everyone wanted to feel useful some times. She'd sat curled up on the sofa and tried to remember. A snort, she'd said at first. Not a big help. That bit was fucking obvious, he wasn't going to be stalking round the gaff with a shooter in one hand and a needle in the other. But to give her credit she'd gone on, made a little pile of powder by eye which was a start. He'd insisted on scales but between them they'd got somewhere. Her gear, a dose of charlie, and a dollop of barbie.

City Road was gone in a flash and he was on to the Old Street roundabout and into the nowhere before Shoreditch proper. Only when it got serious and he'd made up the envelope she'd got all moody. Or maybe it had been the bathroom tile.

Even in the heavy Peugeot he felt the judder and slowed down on some Spitalifields cobbles. He'd wound up saying something about Paying Your Way Girl which he wouldn't have done only she'd never give him the chance to tell her just what an arsehole this Arthur was. Just gone into one of her moods, not hearing anything.

He ploughed on down Cannon Street Road full of amber lights, Indian sweet shops and mini-cab offices.

Across The Highway ahead of two oncoming heavy lorries the barbed wire of the new newspaper place glinted in the neon and William's face popped up. William's face on William's neck. In his hands. On a beach. It had to be a beach or the guy was a 100 percent dildo. He would caress that neck, nothing more.

He pulled across the road and cut the engine. Arthur's place was just around the corner, he'd checked it just a day after the wollie had come across with his address like they were Fine Art dealers. He checked the dashboard clock. A few minutes late. Give it a few more, never did any harm. Yes, he'd caress William's neck while he spoke softly in his ear and the arsehole would shit himself there and then, a stinky parcel in his trunks seeping down a leg and on to the sand. And he, Gordon Murray, a man William had fatally misunderstood would find this deeply distasteful and give him a slap.

* * *

"Of course Mr Scott."

"Steve, Arthur. Nice place, I can see now why there's been so much excitement about the area."

Gordon was looking down over the empty black river and clocked Arthur looking greedy at the polythene parcel on the table.

"Not for much longer," Phil said.

"Is that right."

"Once exclusive, now up for grabs."

"Is that right. Shall we get down to business. Before pleasure and all that," Gordon said. At the table he undid the two outer layers of polythene and left the inner bag on top. "I'm sure you have but just in case you've never done this kind of bulk, I'd suggest a taste out of the middle. Anywhere you like, a couple of spots if you fancy, it is a lot of money. Ah good, you've got a blade. A neat cut though Arthur, don't want the goods spilling all over the shop do we. Phil frowned. He laughed, made a tiny cut in the polythene and pulled out enough for a few lines.

"You have done this before," Gordon said, "very neat." Phil had made a neat pyramid on a hand mirror, pushed half to one side and started chopping out two lines. He offered Steve a fifty note.

"Customer's first Arthur."

The toot was sweet in Phil's nose. Whoosh. Oh yes. And no brain-frazzle, no nose-burn. If there was anything dodgy it wasn't nasty amphetamine.

"Or women and children first as the captain-in-drag said," Phil said and offered the note again to dour Mr Scott. Yeah yeah yeah, flash cunt. Gordon took his toot and was keyed up on the instant. Which was only right. Anything else and he'd have had words with Mario.

"Shouldn't make me laugh Arthur, might do myself an injury not blowing the dollop all over the carpet." Phil said, Not to worry he'd do a hoover job on the carpet with his nose, if necessary.

Yeah yeah yeah.

Only now he'd like to do a more objective test though it had been superb up the nose. The old Milton's no doubt. It would look good, Terry and his bird bound to have stepped on it whereas this was as pure as it was ever likely to be.

Arthur had stuck some kind of jewelers glass in his eye and had it close up to the mirror. Gordon went to the window to watch. Not a moment for Arthur to feel pressured. Let him take his time. Not a bad place at all. Personally he believed a flat could never match a house but it had its points. The feller put down his eye-glass, said it looked good but would he excuse him for a minute. It was fine by Gordon, Arthur might be a flash bastard but no way was he any kind of law. Gordon checked the two little envelopes in his top pocket. They must not get sweaty. He transferred them to a larger side pocket.

It was the Milton's. Arthur had a bottle in his hand plus a glass container and a box that might be scales. Gordon moved a little closer and watched the feller take a smidgin on his knife from what was left on the mirror. Silly boy, he'd got it arse to front. He put the knife back on the mirror and poured the Milton's into the container. Now they were getting somewhere. Crystals from the blade hit the liquid surface. Pure white spirals corkscrewed down from soft explosions. They both looked closely for any cut that might show up in red or orange spots on the surface.

"On the quality Mr Scott, no complaints at all. Very nice. How about we weigh it together." Gordon said Sure and held open one of the bags for Phil to drop the main package in.

Phil tied the second bag at the top and got out the scales. Mr Scott congratulated him on the quality of his tools. One of Jack's finds in fact. From some little place in Clerkenwell he'd said, accurate to half a gram up to twenty kilos. He was placing the bag square on the weighing tray when Mr Scott said, Hang on a minute. Phil frowned, saw a tolerant grin on Scott's face

"Weigh the spare polythene first eh, Arthur. Then subtract two times its weight when you come to the parcel. Heavy stuff polythene, wouldn't want you to go short." Phil stopped short of blushing and finger tapped his temple.

"Who's a dunce Arthur," he said.

The empty bag weighed in at twenty grams, the main parcel at 10,039 and a half. Phil was impressed. He said so. Couldn't get to Scott's level and be a cowboy, this was professionalism. If it was OK he would now make a phone call and the cash would be there in ten minutes.

While they waited Gordon suggested they finished off what was on the mirror. Then he accepted a small Remy Martin and asked what an ordinary feller like himself should make of stocks and shares In These Perplexing Times.

"Not really my field Steve. Of course there's bound to be some bargains amongst blue-chip stock that simply got caught up in the wash but I'll tell you there's not that many punters leaping in feet first even there. Tell you what did surprise me, though not my partner, and that's gold. The dog that didn't bark in the night."

"It should have gone up?"

"That's what I'd have thought, a safe port in the storm. Shot up for a couple of days but then right back down again."

"Is that right. But who do you reckon lost out, someone must have."

"Bloody right Steve, every punter who lost sight of the fundamentals." The entry phone buzzed.

"My partner himself."

Gordon watched him walk to the door. He was saying greed had got the better of people who should have known better. Was that right? The feller looked through the door spyhole, opened it and another pinstripe came in with a large attaché case. They whispered at the door and then he was introduced, My partner Mr Kruger. Mr Scott.

"Steve," Gordon said to an Arthur lookalike. Bigger maybe, softer in the face and worried-looking. The money man.

Tom, Jack said, and Arthur asked if he would excuse them for a moment.

"Suit yourself," Gordon said.

They went to the same door Arthur had been for the scales, the money-man clutching the case like his life depended on it.

Gordon waited till they were just a murmur, then took Sarah's envelope out of his pocket and poured it on to the white, dusty mirror. The .22 in the other pocket bumped his hip. So? Couldn't see it could they.

He shoveled powder to the left of the mirror and chopped it into four lines. They were too short, too fat. He shoved and scraped till they looked passable and pulled out the envelope with his left hand. The stuff fell as a weight to the right side of the mirror. The powder drifted towards the centre.

Still they were talking.

He fashioned a line out of his gear, shoved the rest to the mirror's border and picked up the rolled Twenty. The four lines of Sarah's blend looked the part, a glint or two: a couple of crystals gave it sparkle.

He could hear the voices louder. Arthur came first, a bottle of champagne in his hand. Gordon ducked down and snorted his own line. They were looking at him as he came back up.

"All right? Just a bit of personal this, pleasure after business," he said pointing to the bottle.

Arthur laughed.

Kruger laughed.

"Decided ten minutes ago Steve. A line first Tom?"

The other feller said, Rather.

Arthur put the bubbly down, took the case off Kruger and handed it to him. He took it and offered back the rolled-up note.

"Your twenty," Gordon said.

"What's twenty among friends Steve, I rather think the three and a bit big ones will prove of more interest."

Gordon laughed. He opened the case and watched the pin-stripes take a line each from the four on the mirror. He made space for himself at the far end of the table and started on a first bundle of Fifties. Arthur said it was smooth, offered a glass of the champagne while wondering if he might not prefer to wait till he'd finished counting.

"Never did any harm. Go on," Gordon said.

Jack's rush felt different. Nice though. Cool. Probably the purest stuff ever. The closer the source, the purer the product. A brain-picture popped up, a spring they'd found with the Danish ladies on a walk near Rethymnon. It had gushed, the water. Good to relax, just what the doctor ordered after a long day, all that money and fretting in his office, wondering if Phil's judgment would be cool and objective.

Cheers, the big man said. He was big. And the way he was counting money Christ, talk about nervous energy.

"To a fruitful business relationship," the big man said. Fruitful? By all means. Had a line or two himself, hadn't he. Now he was holding up a random fifty, looking at it closely under the light closely over the table.

"Don't have printing presses in your bank do they Tom? Thought it was only the brothers in government got up to that kind of caper," Phil said.

The big man was frowning. A Labour man? Surely not.

"Funny money '70s style," Phil said quickly.

The big man laughed. Didn't stop him giving the next note a close look.

No surely not, a bank with a certain reputation yes, but forgery, surely not.

"Or the South Americans 1980s," Jack said.

His voice sounded far off. Far off. He drank a glass straight off. Bubbles surfed his brain with the softness of photogenic detergent. In his stomach they went frisky.

Christ they were. And the big man was really fast. A bank teller in an earlier life? No, surely not. A villain, used to this kind of thing. Routine.

What was it with his stomach. Christ. What had he had for lunch? Left it to Alice, one of those exotic sandwiches she was so keen on. Walnut and cream cheese. Ghastly.

And there was big Mr Scott looking at another note.

"Not that I don't trust you gents but I tell you there's all sorts of villains out there. Shifts about cash does, that's it nature, and the trouble is a lot of people don't even bother giving it a look."

Yes, it was possible. He had a point.

"Like AIDS."

Phil. Laughing. Restrained. Give him his due, not in one of his loud moods. Serious when it was required. Which was them. Exactly.

The big man, he wasn't laughing at all. No sense of humour.

Ah, now he was. A bit slow on the uptake but laughing.

Waving towards the mirror.

"Have another line gents, I'll have another when I've finished my work. Nearly there."

Phil was hovering over him with the bottle.

"Why not," he was saying.

Why not. He could do with another line. Might even do his stomach a bit of good. Just hadn't eaten enough. A walnut and cream cheese sandwich whereas the Bolivian peasant, give him a nibble on a coca leaf and he'd run and run. Bit up the nose, same difference. Lead me to it.

He'd said that out loud? He'd not said it out loud? The hard edge of a banknote in his nostril, that was real enough.

Oh yes.

Plosh it went and he felt soft all over.

Warm too.

Central heating mate, can't beat it.

He touched sweat on his forehead. Bloody was too, wet stuff, Phil with a heavy hand on the thermostat.

The big man had finished his counting. That was a fact.

Phil had finished his line, that was another fact.

"Wholly satisfactory gents, Arthur, Tom. A pleasure to do business. So now if you don't mind, my turn for a last bit of pleasure."

The big man chivvied the last of the powder on the mirror in to a small line. Not just a trader but a consumer himself. Couldn't argue with a consumer. Quite a lad, the way he drained his glass.

"So like we were saying Arthur," the big man said, "the market. See to a feller like me it looks like roulette."

Jack rallied.

"I wouldn't go that far Steve. Market confidence can be irrational now and then but underneath you'll always find the fundamentals."

"Them again, I always thought they were your cranky Christians."

Jack started laughing. His stomach went helter-skelter. It was upside down. But the bulky white bag glinting crystal was in front of him. Within his grasp, a fundamental fact. He started to speak, the fundamental nature of fundamentals. He had things to say on the topic.

One suet pudding too many Sharp.

"Excuse me," Jack said, on his feet and rushing across the room.

"You OK?" Phil said.

Jack nodded from the doorway.

"All right is he Arthur, your pal?"

"Just had a very long day," Phil said.

So he had. All day adrenalin. Unnecessary as it turned out. He might have shrugged off Jack's paranoia on the subject of guns but it had burrowed away in his brain all the same. As it turned out Mr Scott was just another trader worried about where to invest his money. An experienced trader but unable to make that necessary leap in self-confidence.

Smooth gear this, a nice kick and definitely no amphetamine cut.

"A long day yes, me too," Mr Scott said. "Got to be on my way but just before I go, what are these fundamentals you keep mentioning?"

Christ, what a question. Massive. Where to start with a layman?

"Depends what commodity you're talking about there Steve."

As it did. It really did. The parcel sparkled at him despite the dull thickness of its polythene wrapping. Great stuff. Lop off the tall man's needs as soon as convenient and the rest straight into the Safe Deposit. All private, all relaxed, except this Steve looked like he was really interested, really wanted an answer.

"Take currency for example, one of the first things you'd want to know is the state of the issuing country's balance of payments. That's a long term fundamental. In the shorter term there's its internal rate of inflation though that's less important these days, all much of a muchness."

And how was Jack in the short term. Looked a bit pasty and off in a hurry. Good old Jack. Odds were he'd crashed out in the back bedroom. Fair enough, a man who'd done his job, and done it well. Might have been sick. He'd sort it out himself, who wanted to be seen by one's best friends while spewing up.

"So, I've got my dough, my percentage on parcels like this, what's it going to be, the Deutschmark, the dollar, the yen?"

An intense man Steve, but he could do without more interrogation a la Tom Arthur, certainly without putting his feet up. He lifted them on to the cushioned bench at one side of the table and put a cushion behind his neck. He'd give him a bit of time and then assume the guy could take a hint.

A burp came hurrying up his insides. Then another. He let

them go. Mr Scott appeared not to notice, riding high himself even if he'd done this kind of thing many times before.

"Don't want to be stingy Steve but normally it's pricey advice." As it fucking was when every Ben, Sen, Len, and Chen in the world wanted it. There was a rumbling sound. Steve's dour face had broken up. He was laughing.

"Just for a pal Arthur. I mean I just read the papers and it looks like the dollar's Mickey Mouse money but who really knows."

Mickey Mouse money? He laughed himself. It wasn't state secrets, not the general picture if that's what the guy wanted. Burp. Burp. What the hell was it with these things? Too much charlie after no lunch is what it was. A long day and no lunch.

"Interest rates Steve, take a look at them and if they're high ask yourself if that shows panic and they'll go higher still. Or if they're doing their job."

Hypothetical stuff but still the bugger looked keen. A deprived childhood educationally speaking was his guess, finds he's over forty, got plenty of money and there's a thirst for knowledge. What would it have been in his day, Secondary Mod, teachers thinking they'd done well just controlling the class. Probably got kids himself, sent to minor public schools, the chances he'd never had himself, and so on.

"Supposing you take the view that it's panic, currency drops despite high interest rates, vicious circle."

Bloody tired he was. Teachers keeping control. Confidence factor. If not old Barley who'd just lasted out the class when they'd torn him apart. Got to the end, four o'clock. Not till the next day. The next week. Assembly, stank of wood polish. The head, a deadhead, looking serious, Poor Mr Barley etc etc.

Burp. Burp.

Nasty mouth taste. Time to go Steve.

"There's your interest rate differentials per se but another time OK, been a long bloody day."

Up on his feet. Big character. Shithouse door. Even a shithouse door could take a hint.

"Sorry mate, I do get carried away but it's not often you

get to meet someone in the know. Another time. Keep in touch. Dinner maybe. So the case is mine and the parcel is yours. Right. A pleasure. Must have a leak before I go, through there is it."

Through the door Gordon caught the whiff of sick. Money man had spewed his ring up. Give him credit, Kruger had tried to clean up but there was a red and yellow mess round the toilet. He stood and counted fifty then pulled the chain. Out in the corridor he heard snoring. Furthest room. He glanced in. In the half light the guy was diagonal on a bed in his suit.

He walked back to the main room. Lovely smile Arthur had.

Out like a light and staying that way his dreams that sweet. Gordon tiptoed to the window to take five. Opposite, southside, the river was lit up, the water shiny. Below it was matt black, barely a glimmer but when he'd been a nipper, fucking ships, couldn't move for them. Choc-a. All finished now. And no point crying over split milk. That had been Mickey White's department, his spiel: what a great place, the docks, salt of the earth, all that bollox. Got something else to cry over these days, Mickey had. As had he himself, only he wasn't crying; oh no, he was fighting back. Stage One close to completion.

He turned away from the window. Nice one Sarah, nice one girl. Out for the count the both of them. Mr Fundamentals fast asleep without a worry in the world. A feller who could afford it. He picked up the parcel and put it in the tie-up bag. Then the attaché case. A fucking doddle. Just walk away, close the door and bob's your uncle. Thanks a lot mate. A pleasure.

He hesitated at the door. It was tempting, just walk away. Back on the job for the first time in a long while and he'd done it lovely. Just lovely.

But.

Walk away and Arthur one way or another would cop hold of Terry and he'd whinge. He would fucking whinge. Not a problem in itself but then Terry would cop hold of Del.

So?

Terry would be telling him one thing but big brother Gordon would tell him another and Del wouldn't know what to believe.

It was tempting. Derek might give him a look or two but

that would be about the strength of it when the quarterly dividend was there, his share.

But.

A straight rip-off was always likely to end in tears. Come to that why had he laid out good money to the tosser for the substitute.

He wedged a hairy door mat under Arthur's front door leaving it slightly ajar, walked to the lift and pressed the green button. Hard to believe a lift could be so quiet. The door opened and he stepped inside. It was grey and lit-up. There was a mirror. He could see himself with parcel and case. He was smiling..

It was tempting but no. If Arthur wound up with a parcel, different story. It was the right weight, he'd tested it, a trade had been made in good faith. If he complained about that everyone would soon get pissed off with his whingeing. It wouldn't even get past Terry because Terry, if not Terry's bird, would explain the rules of the game and tell him to fuck off.

There were rules and there were reasons for them. One said, Never mug a man off 100 percent. Always give him something to hold his pride with. It was fundamental. Give him a parcel and then it was all down to analysis and they could argue the toss for years. Wouldn't even get that far because Terry would have told him where to get off.

Gordon walked across the lobby to the main door. The doormat said riverside mansions. He opened the door and stuck the mat between it and the doorjamb.

Outside the wind was blowing. He hunched up and made a run for the Peugeot.

CHAPTER FORTY-THREE

I don't believe it. I just don't fucking believe it. What's the law like round here? What's the time. Close on half ten. Fucks sake. Hard to credit, must have been three hours in that gaff all told and all because that Arthur turns out to be a raving fucking nutcase. Screaming he was, clawing at me. I had no choice. He gave me no choice and the joke is, the fucking joke is, I'm only trying to help the geezer. That's right, giving him something so as he can show the money-man, so if Kruger does get stroppy he can at least say here it is, you saw it, you tasted it.

Fucks sake. Come on, let's go Gordon. Rev up and on your way. You're legal my old son, perfectly legal.

Engine starts first time. That's a Peugeot for you. Derek tells me to sell it, even with them there's depreciation he says, like suddenly he's North London's number one motor trader. No point in telling him it's not flash and therefore not pulla-ble. He don't understand, and the point is, see, it's started first time when it mattered even if it is fucking damp and turned November.

Easy does it Gordon. They ain't got nothing on you. Fuck knows what the suit's going to look like come the light of day but we'll come to that my old son. One step at a time.

The Highway. Left indicator. All lit up like a Christmas tree. That's not far off, Christmas. What is this, one lorry, another lorry. And another. A convoy is it? I only want to turn left. Oh, thanks a lot, still a bit of space for a private citizen's saloon on the roads.

I must be the world's number one fucking mug. All I'm doing is giving Arthur a leg to stand on when it comes to a barney with Kruger. I go by the rules. Step out of that block of flats, walk to the Peugeot, put the tie-bag in the boot and the case as far as I can get it under the passenger seat. Yes, which was a risk on its own, just leaving it there so any cunt can walk by, clock it, stave the window in and have it away. Yes all right, all right, you're a red light. I've got the message. Satisfied. I'm not some fucking maniac and I know what's coming next. All that one-way up to Shoreditch. When I'll be rich said the bells. When it happens, when I do catch up with William I'll give you a bell. A lot more than five farthings. Long gone, the old farthing.

So there's an orange winking at me. Great. What am I supposed to do, wait here all night. Green, thanks a lot pal. Proceed forward can I? It was just a dig I gave him and that was only because the geezer was screaming. I'm a thief, I'm a doubledealer, he's shouting. No sooner am I back in the gaff and closing the door, at the top of his voice, screaming and scratching, and the cunt's only got neighbours. He was waiting. He jumped me. No sooner had I closed the door when Arthur who comes across like he's the smoothest thing since Stork margarine, is a wildcat. Aldgate roundabout coming up. Then on to Old Street. Another red light. OK, don't panic, I'm slowing up. I'm coming to a stop. What? Jesus, one of them, an ice-cream Rover. Right next to me but I'm not going to give them as much as a glance. Never look at a rozzer, he don't like it. Learned that years ago. Tried to tell Keith but there was no telling him anything, always had to give them lip. So I've got a scratch or two. You know how it is guv, this bird of mine, latin she is, gets a bit carried away. And they ain't got anything on me. Nothing wrong with this motor, checked for a bleep this morning, checked the lights tonight.

We're off. Take it easy Gordon, nice and easy. Could be some likely lads out of Leman Street just waiting to nick someone, anyone to make the quota. That's it son you just pull ahead, be off your manor in no time.

So I go back with the ten kees of the other stuff. I even rip off the Sainsbury's bag and the third lot of polythene in the lift and the door to his place is just open, just like I left it. All I've got to do is walk in, drop it on the table and walk away. I'm right over the table and the cunt leaps up, grabs me, scratching and screaming like a wildcat.

We're on our way to Old Street

We will not be beat

We're on our way to Old Street

No one's going to pull you my old mate. Got a gang of spades for passengers? Not on your nelly.

The cunt was scratching me, ripping at my face and all I'm trying to do is calm him down. I'm asking him what it's all about and what happens, he gives me a whack. So of course I give him a dig or two. That's all it was, self-defence. What do you expect when he's leapt at me, trying to hit me. And even after I've given him a dig he's coming on like a lunatic so I've had to give him a good one and the cunt's only gone Bam, straight down and cracked his skull on his poncey marble fireplace. Fucking claret everywhere and what's he doing with a fireplace when he's got central heating. Who wants a fucking corpse on their hands so I felt his pulse and I'd have given mouth to mouth if there'd been any fucking point. But there wasn't and I had to face up to facts.

That's it Gordon, not too slow. Nice and even. Highbury Corner next. It wasn't even my idea, I never asked for Arthur if that's who he is. I mean I noticed that right from the off that bell Seven like he's told me hasn't got a name tag. The only one with no name tag. So he's a wiseguy, financial expert but really he's got to be at it himself, the kind of person Curtis ought to be interested in if he could ever be arsed to be interested in the kind of people he should be interested in. I mean what kind of people are walking around with three hundred G odd in cash. The trouble with Curtis is he's interested in all the wrong people. Keith said that once, and some times he's close to the mark Keith is. He'll be at home now, family man. I just hope for his kid's sake he don't show that bitter streak he's got. The scrapes I got that man out of when we were kids. And now I've got one of my own, I can't go to him with it, that's the fucking joke. The last person in the world.

I handled it on my own just like I always have when it's come to it. That's it, thirty-five miles an hour, steady as a rock my foot on the gas pedal and here's the roundabout. Fucking Sarah. Unbelievable. The one thing I've ever asked of her, the one thing and she can't even get that right. I wouldn't even have asked her that only for Christ's sake, it's the one thing she ought to know about but what happens, the cunt's only woken up and gone hysterical. When I saw him there 100 percent brown bread and there's blood all over the shop I had quite a turn. But I handled it. That's the thing. The facts were in front of me.

What's happened to the Holloway Road? Our road that was before Keith fell in with the wrong crowd and made a cock-up. The Murrays Are Coming and there'd be the patter of feet, all trying to get out of the road. Still got the cinema. The video hasn't won hands down but that don't change the fact that the lights are fucking red again. My turn is it? All the traffic lights in London ganging up because it's Gordon Murray's first night out, the first time in years he's carrying at night. Let's fuck him over, is that it. Don't bother because I'll wait. When I saw that hole in the back of his head I felt like spewing up. Close to, as it happens, what with that and the smell of the mess the other face had left behind him in the khasi. But I choked it back and pulled myself together. I said to myself Gordon, you're in this situation, now you've got to get out of it. I could have just run. There's plenty of people would have done just that. Me, I went and sat by the window to take stock. My hands were shaking, I don't mind admitting it. But I was thinking, that was the point. Discipline. Not getting paralyzed. First thing's the door. Course I'd closed it when I came in, even Arthur blowing his top's had the sense to let me do that before going into one. But I remembered he's got a Chubb too, that and my dabs are all over the shop. I hadn't thought of those before, there'd been no need. No one Arthur could go screaming to, not people who take fingerprints.

What's this, some fucking great lorry right up my arse. Not the A1 yet pal. He is, right up behind. Yeah, so some old dear's out the pub, a bit slow on her pins in the road and where's that leave me, braking and Whap, who knows how many tons and even a Peugeot can't take that. SO WHY DON'T YOU JUST FUCK OFF OR KEEP YOUR DISTANCE.

The last thing in the world I wanted, Arthur dead. I wouldn't even have bothered asking Sarah if it weren't for not wanting that risk. But then what about Kruger if she's made the dose so weak. That was my next move, back down that stinky passage. That's what they call keeping your nerve and I can hear the cunt before I see him, snoring away like a good'un. And his feet are still off the bed just like they was. WHY DON'T YOU FUCK OFF. Still right up behind me and here's a boozer. I know it.

Some right staggering pissheads. DON'T YOU UNDERSTAND NOTHING. I don't want it, not a bump or a scratch tonight. What, standing out on the pavement exchanging addresses and Insurance Policy numbers. When I don't know what I look like. With what I've got in the motor. I CAN FUCKING DO WITHOUT IT.

So I've got a bit of a breather with Kruger out of the game and I walk past him, Arthur, into the kitchen. First thing I can see is he's only left his keyring on the table. So I go out again and lock the Chubb and then I'm back for some kitchen gloves. Fucking aggravation that was with a tea towel in my hands ripping at every drawer in sight till I find some. Pink ones. Then I really got my skates on, a whirlwind, rubbed down every surface in sight, chairs, tables, the door, the wrapping round the Borax. And then I forced myself to stop for a moment and think of every place I've been in the flat and some, and what do I see, he's got candlesticks on that mantlepiece that's caused so much grief. What's he want candlesticks for when he's got the electric.

YOU CUNT. It's the Archway one-way and that jack-the-lad in the juggernaut's only cut me up. Outside lane I am, that's reasonable ain't it, in a decent saloon and I want to move inside for the turn-off but oh no. Jesus Christ, I'm on my way to Highgate. This is fucking madness.

Come on Gordon, it's a steep hill. Into third.

This can't be happening. I mean just what is it? Left turn Gordon, just take it. Indicate. YOU CUNT. He's only given me the horn as he's shot past, what can you do with bastards like that. I done him though, that Kruger, done him like a kipper. I saw those candlesticks and I knew what I had to do. Took more bottle than anything in my entire life. Just seeing him was making me sick never mind anything else, but they're shit hot these days, the forensics. I only gave his nut a couple of taps right in the hole, just a couple of taps. Made it the right shape see and there was plenty of blood on it so I'm off down that passage again to shove the candlestick into moneyman's hands and what does he do, Kruger, only pulls it to him like it's his mammy's tit. Can you beat it. What's this say? HAMPSTEAD? Come on Gordon fucks sake, concentrate. His mammy. Or maybe his girlfriend. Or his boyfriend. Embraced it. Pull in. Yes it's a car park now just pull in. Get yourself straightened out. Do you know what you're doing. You're driving around at closing time with a shooter, a ridiculous amount of money and enough dollop for them to throw the key away. All that and you've got lost.

Right. Right, just go through what happened step by step. See if you left out anything, anything you didn't do and then if there's anything else you need to do tonight. Check the A to Z, do whatever you've got to do, then get to the Archway gaff and sleep.

Right.

It took a lot of nerve. There I was and I didn't have all night. Gordon! What did you do?

Kruger had the candlestick in his hands but there had to be more claret, smears and drops of it on his clothes. So I went to the bathroom. There was a sponge there. I went to the lounge and soaked up some blood, not off him, off the floor. I went back to Kruger and squeezed it so some drops fell then gave him a smear. He never budged and I went to the bathroom to wash it out.

Fucking hell I was standing there cleaning that sponge, and the basin, and I'm thinking I'm doing all this for Terry because he's the only one can make the tie-up. I don't want him even thinking, so I know Kruger's got to be bang to rights then all Terry knows is Arthur's been done in by his partner. Shame that, could have been a nice bit of biz and his Intro money's down the drain. And I know, the fucking time I took cleaning that sponge, I know I've done my best for the forensics but there's got to be a motive to give the Pros. a hand. Just a hint, that's all that's needed. As it happens, no way I come into it at all. Kruger's going to start screaming about a Steve Scott who's bound to be alibi'd and the law's going to say, Oh yes. It's obvious he's done it himself. They've been dabbling in drugs, minds have got warped and there's been some skullduggery over money. That's how it is and I know I've got to make it that way. I walk out of that fucking flat with his keys. I close the entrance door and walk to the car. Shivering I was but then with the cold and what I was going through . . .

GORDON. What happened next?

All right then, I skim off a thin layer of the money, two grand, maybe three and grab the bag with the charlie in it. Christ, the fucking performance that was, had to use a spoon out of the kitchen and a cellophane bag I find there, and dole out a couple of oz in it and leave it on the table next to the Borax, then scatter the dough like there's been a rumble.

Still have the gloves on?

Of course, they were never off.

Made a final clean down, sure you cleaned everything?

Not a dab, not a fucking one. I even left the flat with the gloves on. Took them off in the lift, shoved its door when we was down to earth and pushed the main door using the bag. I wasn't going to be in that lobby nor out in the street wearing pink rubber gloves with my suit was I? No fucking way.

So where's the gloves now?

Fucks sake Gordon they're still in the bag, and those wrappers off the parcels.

Right then, what the fuck are you waiting for? There, you see, a litter bin. Specially for you. And the road sign, go on have a look at that. Now the *A to Z*.

Fuck me I was going into one there. But I've sorted myself. Back on an even keel and there it is, back of the old Whittington Hospital. No problem. Just a phone call to Terry. Better do that, he's expecting his dosh and then Arthur's mugshot might hit the papers. I'll tell him I went for the meet and the geezer never showed. If I know him he'll start apologizing and I'll just tell him not to worry: these things happen son, and Arthur seems a sensible bloke, he'll be back in touch.

What a fucking day. Would be more or less finished if Derek wasn't such a cheapskate, a handy little bolthole but the fucking thing hasn't got a phone. Unbelievable. He just don't plan ahead Derek doesn't, doesn't think about the details and he knows I don't trust mobiles. A landline for emergencies only. You'd have thought was basic. Yes, so now I've got to find a fucking phone box, one that works. Better give Sarah a bell too, the way she was performing when I left. That's a fucking joke that is, she's performing but she can't get a simple thing right. All this grief because the one thing I've ever asked her to do she cocks up. But that won't stop her throwing a wobbler if I don't get in touch and then where am I? She's got Keith's number for one thing. That was me being responsible, in case anything happened to me.

Christ my head is fucking pounding. Probably not even a drink in Del's gaff. Here we go, a phone box. Go on work you bastard, give us a break. Takes me a hundred yards for somewhere to park. Now just park, nice and easy. Check the mirror. There's some layabouts around the box, I can see them. Out of the pubs are they? I'll bet they learned plenty there, pissing it away. Christ it's cold. Case? Bag? They'll have to stay in the motor. No fucking choice. Lock the door. The motor will be in line of sight.

It can't go on like this. I'm calling Kevin off. Me and Johnny'll take Parkinson and I'll do the rest. Piece of piss after what I've been through. After tonight's little lot he'll be a doddle. You don't know it yet William but you've just signed your death warrant. At least this shithole runs to street lights. One of the yobs in the box, longhaired, skinny. Can only be sixteen. Making an early start in the boozers? Brilliant kid, that'll get you a long way in life.

At least the phone's working. Three pals of his sitting on the bonnet of a motor, got to be pals, that's logic, they ain't in the queue. I bet it's not their motor either. An Escort. Cheeky bastards, think they own the place. You want your own motor son you've got to get out there and earn it. I can see mine, nice and safe. Make these calls and it'll be all right. One of them's a spade and there's a half-caste. All right cunt I'm not looking at you so just don't start it on me.

A night to freeze your bollocks off, should have had gloves, my leathers. Yes but how was I to know, should have been back in Acton hours ago. I still can't credit it, that Arthur, like he was a nutter. Clawing me.

Come on you cunt. Get a move on. This is all down to Derek this is, just couldn't be bothered to get a phone put in. Like it was some big effort. I'll sort it out myself, I'm not having this again and I'm Not having a mobile whatever Keith says. Yes, I'll put the gear back under the boards for now, I've just had a sample out. Keep the keys, and stash the wedge in mine till the next move. There's plenty for the dividend and by that time Mr Parkinson will be all to pleased to tell me William's whereabouts.. What's this cunt doing, still at it? And I can hear the spade giving it the So I Tell The Man bollox. Oh did you big boy so who was that man? A right wollie, got to be. His pals are laughing. That didn't take much.

This is fucking ridiculous.

The kid in the box, he's laughing too. He's turning and giving his pals the wink. Scored have you son? Some weed? A bird? A bit of dollop? Congratulations. Finished have you. Yes he's coming out and I'm straight forward.

Here what's this, the half caste trying to get ahead of me. I've got him by the shoulder. OY CUNT THERE'S A QUEUE HERE, KNOW WHAT THAT IS. I'VE GOT CALLS TO MAKE.

What? Ouf. In my back. It's only the skinny bastard. You what, cop a bit of this. Smack. Right in his gob, instant claret. And you, know who I am. Smack. Get your back to the wall Gordon, cover your back. Ouf. That's it. ALL RIGHT WHO'S NEXT FOR A BIT OF TRUNCH. YOU, YOU CUNT, COME ON THEN. That's another one on the deck. Ouf. You bastard. A blade. Faces. I'M GORDON MURRAY YOU CUNTS. Smack. Ouf. Was a blade. Get the shooter. Hold on Gordon. Pavement's wet. Bloody blood. The shooter. Boots coming. Got one, I'll have you down. I will. My wrist. My fucking wrist. Cunt. Curl up Gordon. Not the head fucks sake cunt

cunt

CHAPTER FORTY-FOUR

I am sitting down to something called goulash, a three inch square of something. Of what thing or things I ask myself. I remember once eating a piquant beef stew in a Hungarian place where I'd been taken by a junior Investment Manager on a junior expense account. There is no beef involved here. Fetid bacon and pallid spuds is my guess, all mixed up and fried in diesel. With my pale green plastic fork I have consumed about a third of it and that will be all. Hard to believe but I seem to have avoided that ulcer that was on the cards. Now however, is not the time to take liberties with it as Bill would put it.

And who am I to complain? I'm just one of the most wrongly maligned men in history, that's all. Phil was my very best friend. He could be a bit wild, a bit ferocious, Phil could, helped old Barley at school crack up but he was my friend. As for Sir Nick, the bastard, I've been dropped like a ton of the proverbial. Not a word.

There's a sound of footsteps. In all probability it will be Officer Bean or one of his closest colleagues Mr Hay. I'd plump for Bean walking along the heavy lino of the ground floor which is called the Ones. I myself am on the twos, Jebb Avenue SW2. I can picture it, just off Brixton Hill, the main A23. Christ the number of times I had to struggle up it just to get home. Must be the rush hour now and you'd have thought one was bound to hear all the braking and gear changes those misplaced traffic lights demand half way up the hill.

More footsteps only now it's a sequence, locks turning, doors opening, footsteps, locks turning. A finite sequence however. There are rules, set ratios of guardians and clients at any given time. Of course as with all rules there is a certain flexibility, even the Bretton Woods do-gooders understood that, so it's at least possible my door may be opened in this batch. No, my analysis predicts Not This Time though I really don't care, not anymore.

Bill will be out and about on the Ones. He became a cleaner and then additionally, a tea boy. Urged me to do the same, he says it gets you out and about a bit. A bit cheeky I thought. I am an innocent man and have no intention of making this convict business into a career. I am just waiting for my commital proceedings so that this whole thing can be seen for what it is, a ghastly and unforgivable mistake. I didn't say anything to Bill but for a man who introduced himself as a serious investor wanting to know what he should do with his money the manoeuvres just to get his hands on a mop seemed to indicate a drastic narrowing of his horizons. This after I'd written him a set of notes setting out the fundamentals of market analysis. Besides I am a Category A prisoner and could not be considered for such a job.

CRASH CRASH CRASH. The reverse sequence which is in effect a follow up to the previous one, the doors that had been opened now slammed shut. And now the old sequence again. I predict that my door Will open in this batch. I'll go further and say it will be Mr Bean or Mr Oates who opens it. I don't have access to the duty rota but experience tells me . . .

CRASH. "Slop out Sharp" I can't see the face but I know Mr Bean's voice.

I haven't had a piss since teatime so I go out on to the landing with just my eating plastics: mug, plate, knife, and fork. I see that Mr Bean is listening to a colleague on the landing outside the recess.

"Mickey White's been performing again."

Mr Bean grunts.

I step into the recess.

"The old cunt, the quicker he gets weighed off the better."

The recess contains areas for pissing, shitting, and washing. It has a permanent plumbing problem and a dustbin into which the remaining goulash drops with a thud. Only a very sick bastard could have come up with this word Recess, with its suggestion of cosy alcove and yet which touches on the grim reality via its suggestion of the darkest corners of heart and mind.

While I wash my plate thoroughly my neighbour who was a very dangerous man but is now in enormous underpants nods at me, says All right. I'm glad I've got my shoes on, the red-tiled floor is a puddle of water and black smears. I take my plastics back to my room and gear myself up to go back to the recess for a shit. On the landing I say All right to Winston, a black man who is surpringly cheerful given that there is a considerable weight of evidence to say that He was the man who robbed the bank; who hijacked the car; who made for the Motorway; who shot at the cop car.

"In the end Mickey White is just a mouthy old cunt," Mr Bean's colleague is saying. Mr Bean grunts.

It's like shitting in public. There's a sort of half door from knee to shoulder height, shoulder height when sitting, in situ. I can just imagine Sir Nick dropping his drawers under the potentially eagle eye of Mr Bean. I only hope that whatever arsehole he's got in my place is easily given to misplaced optimism and drops a bundle. That's assuming the old fucker has any kind of analyst looking at the fundamentals these days. Of course the Futures and Options markets carry a lot of weight, of course my Quotron software was a useful tool, I'm not some kind of Luddite. But the way trendy Sir Nick is going it will all end up in the hands of mathematicians and their formula-driven trading programs. That came easily enough: shit; wipe. What's falling, my inhibitions or my standards?

"A fairer distribution, that's what's needed, that's what I said to the Branch Secretary," Mr Bean is saying.

"The Bailey, that's where the overtime is, so how's it shared out, that's what I want to know," Mr Bean's colleague says, just before they stir themselves to bang me up again.

Back at my blue formica table I wonder how the famous Mickey White is feeling tonight. Our local celebrity. He's on a special wing but one hears things, that he dowsed an officer with his Christmas dinner for example. He was the main topic of conversation on the exercise yard again today. It seems that another prisoner called Simpson gave evidence against him and is now on Rule 43 for his own protection. He claims that White said to him on the exercise yard of the special Security Wing that he'd had to do it because the victim, one Christian "had been taking him for an absolute c---." There were rumours about it weeks ago and Brian was especially savage about the man. In retrospect I rather wish I'd met Brian before I met Bill, I think he might have made better use of my breakdown of the fundamentals. Too late now though I must say I am delighted he was acquitted. Long firms were his speciality. I'd never heard of them before but the idea is beautifully simple. You create a company using false names, obtain a large number of goods on credit, sell them as quickly as possible at a discount, and then disappear. It was video recorders and CD tackle this time around. Our friendship was cemented when I said, "You were just part of the credit boom Brian." He laughed and laughed and then, when he could speak, said, "You know what Jack, if it goes against me and it's down to mitigation I'll have my brief say that." Brief in this instance meaning barrister rather than driving licence. Or quick.

The thing I admired about Brian was his discipline, his professionalism. One of the main problems in his game, as he put it, is handwriting: there's a fair amount of paperwork involved, signatures at the very least. So he spent six months of a previous sentence learning to write with his left hand when he is naturally righthanded. And it's paid off hasn't it. Not guilty which is good news for me, I rather think Brian is going to be crucial in sorting out the ghastly mistake that has been made in my case.

Yes, I feel he would have benefitted more from my notes than Bill but I do hate to leave a job unfinished. I've already disabused him of the notion that Demand and Supply work in some A to B fashion, giving as example the fact that demand for gold jewellery in the wealthier portions of the Middle East tends to rise as the price of gold rises and vice versa. Conspicuous consumption they call it these days which means, who wants a gold necklace if every shit-shoveler's wife has one strung around her neck. I've explained that a rise in International insecurity will only benefit the gold price at certain times and in certain places: that gold mining shares are a bit of a roller-coaster and so on. However I feel there is one more example I must give.

I sit down at my nasty light blue formica table and take out some sheets of lined paper, close my eyes to the width of its margins, as gross as flared trousers, and pick up my nasty transparent ball point.

Dear Bill, I begin; and tell him how it was, step by step and prepared to think the unthinkable. That price rise in Hong Kong, why had it really happened? Future absorption by mainland China? OK, an anxiety that prompts residents towards gold. But that anxiety had been there a long while, so diligent Jack looked some more. At those enterprise zones on the mainland for one thing.

There's footsteps, voices and a fast rhythm of CLICKCRASH CLICKCRASH. Evening tea. It's getting louder and in this case the straight line A to B explanation Is adequate, the whole process is getting closer to me. I predict mine will arrive in seven minutes from now. Seven Twentytwo. The rhythm is accompanied by an off beat clanking of the tea buckets, nevertheless it is a crescendo that will peak at my door. It is like fucking with Julia; it is like fucking with Alice, the only time I dabbled in-house.

Oh! The whole process has ground to a halt. Coitus interruptus. Tea supplies have been exhausted. In this case fresh production is not required, stocks are available but must be fetched. A question of distribution which is not an entirely effortless business as if space, capacity of container and the finite strength of the carrier did not exist. It's a major problem in the USSR so I'm told.

CLICKCRASH. Here we go again. At the ready with my white plastic mug. Cocked for action. They're three doors away. I hear the scrape of my neighbour's chair. Two away. On my feet, some muffled chat and CRASH. A muscular man in the blue pinstriped shirt lifts the shiny bucket. I proffer my mug and catch half a pint of slosh. Who's that behind him? I do believe it's Mr Rice, now that is a turn up for the books. I won't be asking *him* for my light to stay on after ten. He will make some wiseguy remark about it being bad for my eyes and then I'd be tempted to say something about wanking in the dark, hasn't he heard what that does to the eyes.

Masturbation is probably against the Rules, you know, in complete defiance of the reality of the situation, like Fixed Exchange Rates.

Twentyfour minutes past seven. Allow a minute since my door opened and closed and that little hiccough in the process and I was pretty close. A lot better than the mathematical model fanatics who now run the roost at Stammer, Case and Mangledorf I'll wager. As I tried to tell Sir Nick before this nightmare began. Hedge ratios, deltas, they're not unimportant, I'm not a dinosaur; but to modish Sir Nick they've become more important than the fundamentals.

Nothing, and I repeat, nothing, is more important than the fundamentals.

At least this tea stuff is hot and wet, makes smoking a cigarette into feasible proposition for the throat.

"Yes Bill . . . and immediately saw that neither the enterprise zones nor Shanghai were doing too well: that too much of the wealth produced there was being looted in the form of taxes that found their way as subsidies to various no-no provinces where Li Chu Ploughman is full of honest endeavour and low productivity.

But, and this was the niggling doubt that drove me on, it was just at the moment of the gold price rise I'd predicted, that Deng and his young blood were at last ready to take the plunge and make those absolutely necessary reforms needed to make enterprise in the Zones prosper. Further, if it was the old hardliners regaining control from Deng that the Hong Kong punters were worried about, why hadn't those worries surfaced three months earlier when those damned students had been stirring up trouble. Why no rise in the price of gold then?

Maybe you'll be saying to yourself Bill, that the penny was a bit slow to drop but remember I had been right about the price rise when it did happen."

The hot pipe that runs through my room is clicking away as it does now and then. Poor things, I wonder whether they're up to it. And on top of that there's a Scrape, Scrape, Scrape, the final event of the night before Lights Out. It's what they call the body-count, you know, the kind of thing Mr McNamara was keen on in Vietnam until he saw the light and became that nice old man at the World Bank wanting to do good in the world. Not as dramatic here of course though it can be an ordeal if Mr Oates is on duty. There've been times when he's needed four goes at counting the Twos. Mr Rice is an unknown quantity in this department, he may be a wizard at arithmetic. I wonder if he knows we've got a new arrival on the landing, Kevin his name is, obviously well known in this milieu the way he was being offered packs of cigarettes and toothpaste on the yard. Can't say I like the look of him, a sort of heavy sullenness he has. In fact he reminded me of Mr Scott. Yes, I remember your face you fucker. Don't think you've been forgotten, that you're going to get away with it. Brian is making inquiries about you at this very moment and I've great faith in Brian.

Christ I don't even like to think of the bastard. I see Phil as he was that morning, I see him and start shaking. No point in that, I've got to stay cool.

"SEVENTY SIX ON THE TWOS . . . ON THE TWOS . . . ON THE TWOS"

It sounds like an echo but I suspect it's the message getting passed on down to the Centre. A vital message to Mission Control which will be very impressed with Officer Rice, right first time and decisive with it. Let me tell you Mr Rice that it is also appreciated in other quarters, by 517318 Sharp for one.

"What I did in fact Bill was to try and put myself in the shoes of a Hong Kong manufacturer of internationally competitive sun-glasses. It struck me that such a person might well be alarmed not at the failure of enterprise on the mainland but at its success, Hong Kong goods might then start to look pricey. Having taken this taken on board I then looked at his attitude towards the position being taken by HMG. Did my man really want democratic elections of any sort? Despite strenuous efforts to rectify the situation in recent years democracy costs, bits and pieces of redistributive taxation and welfare state. I decided to keep a close watch on the situation, what with the possibility of rising labour costs and the opportunity to stash away a bit of wealth from the taxman, it could only encourage my man to increase the gold stake in his investment portfolio."

And do those mathematical model bolsheviks understand that? Those screen addicts with their bar, point, and figure charts? Do they fuck. Probably never seen a decent bit of bullion in their lives. Would they understand the feelings of a Turkish peasant sitting on his little hoard? I can well see a Turkish government of the future offering big incentives to mobilize that untapped wealth and if they do, those charts'll go haywire. When's Sir Nick going to wise up? Even the after-the-event-wiseguys are saying computerized trading models turned October's stock market kerfuffle into a near disaster.

What the hell's that row? Someone screaming and pounding on a cell door. Hammering, I can almost feel it shaking though it's somewhere below. There's a few wife-killers on the Ones and they're quite liable to do this kind of thing, so Bill's told me. An awful noise, runs right through you. Now there's a thudding of feet, any second now and that door'll be crashing open.

I don't think there's much more I can do for Bill, I've given him the rudiments of analysis but I think he's a man looking for a specific tip. Why not?

"One last thought Bill, I've a very positive feel for gold in the early to mid-'90s. If Comrade Deng and his friends keep their nerve we're likely to see growth rates the like of which we haven't seen for years. And if I'm right it will at last give the Chinese peasant the wherewithal to do something about his innate desire for the stuff. Look at it this way Bill, there's an awful lot of peasants in China."

There you are, a job finished. Meanwhile, except for some mild clicks from my heating pipe, all quiet on the penal front. I wonder what's happened to that poor sod on the Ones. The dungeons? A nice cup of largactyl? Such a routine day it's been otherwise.

CHAPTER FORTY-FIVE

Walking back from the school Carol smelled the possibility of a good, late autumn day, damp but the sun showing itself in touches from behind racing clouds. Inside she said, Sunny Intervals. Inside her flat door she said, So What. So What. The new washing machine looked at her complacent and luxurious, her last mad fling with Arthur's wonderfully safe and regular six which was no longer on. He'd told her that as if the whole thing, all the business they'd done before, had been just a joke. She lit the gas under the kettle. A nice cup of tea? A nice cup of tea dearie.

When the kettle boiled she made one anyway, took it into Sheila's room and sat down on the sofa. The joke was she still didn't know and would never know. Maybe Arthur was up to something or maybe he was exactly what he'd always seemed, some kind of city gent who liked his coke and who for some reason of his own thought he could make money out of it. And even if it was those awful looking guys who were behind Terry, well it was business wasn't it, surely they made enough without needing rip-offs. Or maybe they didn't. Round and round the garden like a Teddy Bear. The tea was too milky and too sweet. She couldn't even get that right and why, because she hadn't cared enough to pay attention. All round-and-round-the-garden and she wasn't in the here and now.

There was supposed to be fifteen hundred coming from Terry, her introduction fee he'd said, though it might take time, yes and how it wasn't for him to comment but maybe she'd done the right thing. It had been a month now he hadn't phoned but she wasn't going to mug herself off by ringing him. Not yet. At least the tea was hot, enough to do good things to the back of her throat.

She would give it another week, ring Terry if he hadn't rung her, otherwise the future would slip away, her saying she couldn't decide anything till she knew if the fifteen was coming her way. If she would carry on with her bits and pieces clients. It was ridiculous to be at her age, what Marie was now calling the prime of a woman's life, and see the future as a nothing with nothing to go on. She took another sip of tea. It was flannel in her mouth. With the edge of its hotness gone it was just sweet and milky. She could surely at least make a cup of tea.

There was still hot water in the kettle. It boiled quickly. She let the teabag sit in the water for half a minute before prodding it with the teaspoon. It tasted good. There, see, she could still do it and the future *was* there, her and Sheila and Sheila was doing all right. Number One when it came to Geography. So what was this self-pitying bullshit, except her shins were scorched and her shoulders shuddery. Not the flu, she could do without that. Must be weak to even imagine it, it was just the nature of bloody gas fires.

She got her cardigan. Sometimes she thought she was a right dumb mum but then she'd drawn a map of China off the top of her head and put some names in the right places, Beijing, Shanghai; Mongolia where it was; and drawn the course of the Yangtse River. Sheila had checked it in her own Atlas and been impressed. Amazed, and then out of the blue asked where Jimmy was these days. She was finished with lying and said right out they'd had an argument. Sheila said Oh. Supercool. She missed him? She didn't miss him? Leastways she thought about him.

They'd rowed in this very room. Sometimes a person needed a bit of space. That wasn't just her, a freak because sometimes she had a mood on. Everyone needed their own bit of space, not crowded even if it was love. Love.

Anyway there was work to be done. A pile of Sheila's clothes for a start. She crammed them into the washing machine and set the programme. Easy-peasy. The thing was he'd gone on and on about how much he cared but when it came to it, he hadn't rung. He didn't know she hadn't gone through with it so what did this caring amount to. And what did it amount to, her just standing around in the kitchen when the machine switched itself off, when she'd smelled walking weather; when Marie might fancy it too.

Her friend's phone rang and rang. She pictured it, light green, somewhere in the front room; or parked up on top of the TV; or precarious on a sofa arm. No, it would be on the carpet near the door but still there was no Marie to pick it up. What was the matter with her, she could go out for a walk on her own couldn't she. She could go down to the market, never mind if she didn't buy anything, just the swirl of people, the coloured stripes of the canvas awnings, fruit colours. She might even meet someone she knew. A five week old picture hit her straight in the guts. Her, Jimmy and Sheila in the market, him so happy and like they were a family. Him spoiling Sheila, then stopping by a butcher's shop in the row of proper shops that ran down one side of the stalls, telling her daughter that these days chicken had plastic bones. He'd had her going for a moment, the bugger, and poor Sheila trying to puzzle it out: wasn't that very difficult: how did they do it, with injections: and then giving him a smack when he started laughing and she tumbled it. The picture wouldn't stop. It ran on to him in bed with her and she knew she was smiling. Friendly and exciting no matter whether his caring was pure or not. Was any bloody emotion pure?

Ach, the picture was running too fast. She would make a cup of tea and decide something one way or another. The washing machine was going through a gear change. She put a teabag and a flat spoon of sugar into her mug and opened the fridge door. The milk carton was soft, her grip too strong, the white stuff jumped out on to the floor and dribbled out fingers. Carol cursed and reached for the green and yellow sponge 'n scourer. It was soft in her hand and she laughed, it was a message, had to be. She went straight to the phone. It only rang twice.

"This is Jimmy Cochrane. Sorry I'm not here. Please leave your name and number and I'll be back to you. Special message for Carol Curbishley, fancy a walk. I'll be here from Twelve . . . dib dib dib dib."

He sounded like he was underwater, in a tank, and she'd been going to slam the phone down but then heard her own name. Incredible. He'd squeezed it in, perhaps he'd taped different messages every day or perhaps it had been the same for however long it was since the night of the hurricane. He must have other callers, what would they have thought. She ran back to the kitchen, mopped up the milk from the floor while the kettle whistled feeling the laughter tumble out of her stomach.

At Ten past Twelve she rang back and said yes, a walk, and was ready outside the front door with her jacket on and a conscious decision against the umbrella. She ran down the steps and surprised him walking round from the driver's door to the pavement. They stood apart and looked at each other. He looked older.

"Aren't you working?" she said.

"Oh fuck the job Carol. How about Hampstead Heath."

She was decisive.

"No Jim, too far. I want to be walking soon. If it's not too boring let's just drive to the park," she said getting into the passenger door. She didn't want picking up Sheila to be a pressure either, rushing through traffic and getting tense with red lights.

She stayed quiet just looking ahead and felt him looking at her just the once when they caught red lights at the main road. He parked close by the Park gates and was straight out of his door without locking it. Carol pointed it out. He laughed and said he'd probably do better with the insurance money.

"Yes but I'd have to walk home."

He frowned for a moment then laughed, said she'd got a point and walked back to his door.

Inside the gates she took the lead along the path that lead away from the flower garden.

"It was really good getting your call, hearing your voice," he said catching up.

She said it was a nice feeling, hearing a special message for her. "I'm starting to need messages."

They walked on in silence then started speaking at the same time. Carol stopped first and waved him forward. "I was only going to say I reckon I need them too. With a Hearing Aid thrown in," he said.

"Did you really leave that message for three weeks or whatever it is, very flattering."

"Flattering, now that's just what you accused me of the first time we met, you know, on the street."

"So now who's got a good memory?"

He smiled at that and said yes, for some things he had, with his solemn look. She wanted it to stay light, it felt too fragile and important to be plunging into him and her, relationships, wrongs and rights, or what he meant by Some Things, what those things were.

"Like measurements," she said. "You know, windows, shelves, doors."

Good. Now he was really laughing and looked younger again. "Sorry, not so hot there. Stubby old pencils, scraps of paper and then search parties for same scraps."

"Don't they have Calculators with memories now? Should be a tool of the trade, as important as the chisel or saw."

"Hey that's hi-tech you're talking."

An elderly couple were coming towards them. The man had a hairy dog on a lead that was sniffing and dragging along a verge. Carol and Jimmy stepped aside. The woman in a tweed coat and green beret smiled at them. Further on, somewhere off the path in front of plane trees a stalk of smoke rose above neck-high bushes. As they got closer they saw the trunk of a tree stretched out across the grass. A man in a donkey jacket with a plastic orange strip across the shoulders was feeding cut-up, sawn-off branches into a small fire in the middle of a flat circle of ashes. Jimmy made a sad snort. Carol smelled the pleasure of wood smoke.

She stepped off the path towards it. The grass was clipped and damp. She turned to look at Jim. His hair was too long to be so clearly divided left and right. She pictured the flowing hair of a shampoo advert, thought of a haircut for him, shoved the picture out of her mind and stopped some few feet away from the fire. The man in the donkey jacket turned and looked at them. Back, further from the fire was a hole in the ground with thick roots stuck out. The tree trunk she'd seen from the path was laid out by it, piebald and thick.

The fire was modest, low and quiet flames. The man pushed in the end of a longer many-ended branch and the fire flared up. She felt the heat strong but would not step back. She heard Jim from over her shoulder.

"Lose a lot did you?"

"Just the two. This one and another over there," the man said pointing to an empty space at the bottom end of the park. "Something funny about trees when they're together, they look after each other. A solitary banjaxed here and another there."

Carol looked at him properly, had she not noticed him before. She was in the park often enough, did she go around with her eyes shut.

"You really think that?" Jimmy's voice was close by.

The flare of the fire sprung up high. Carol stepped back keeping her eyes open for the leaping spiral of more flames and listening for the spurting round the edges.

"Sounds mystical doesn't it, it's just what I've seen," the man said.

"I just wish I had a potato or two to put in your ashes," Carol said.

Jimmy made a show of looking in his pockets. The man turned away towards a tangle of branches on the grass. Jimmy asked if she didn't fancy waiting for the next flare-up. She said no, she didn't, would he walk some more and how had it been driving home in the hurricane.

CHAPTER FORTY-SIX

What is happening? Just what is happening? Has the world turned upside down? My hands have been shaking. They were shaking just now when I stuck my cup out for some hot slosh. Some of it fell on my wincklepicker slippers. The teaboy didn't notice but the evidence was there, irrefutable. I put my half-full mug on the table and one of my socks is still sodden. Since when I've been sitting here just staring at this filthy hot water, this filthy warm water. Because that's what it is, dishslops straight out of the sink and I've been drinking the fucking stuff for weeks.

They're trying to drive me mad but they won't succeed. In fact I can see things clearer now than at any time since this nightmare began. I can see what this so-called tea is and I won't have it. I simply won't have it. I'm going to stand up and I'm going to throw it at the door.

There! See! Dishwater clinging and sliding down the metal plate of the door and making a puddle on the floor where it belongs. They're not going to succeed. I have endured one of the most terrible days that any man has had to endure but I'm not going to freak out. Oh no. No, I'm going to sit down and analyze what's happened step by step and then I'll know exactly what to do. I'm an analyst. I'm a professional, not some wanker of a wife-killer. Or grandad-basher. This afternoon I had a legal visit and my inclination is to sack my so-called legal representatives and start afresh with a more competent and dynamic firm.

But the ghastliness of the day started long before that scene over there in the legal visits room. That I was to have a legal visit was conveyed to me by one of the assistant governors just before morning exercise. It was the young pudgy slob. I'd have preferred the other one who dresses circa 1956, looks as though he experienced something of existential importance while serving in a colonial police force, and who spoke to me of the Rule Book—it was my first day here—as if it had been handed down to Moses. At least one knows he is completely mad but this arsehole, younger than me and as thick as porridge, after telling me of this visit says, "All right Sharp?" It was a question, not a curt dismissal, one can tell by the way the voice raises. And what am I supposed to reply? "No I'm fucking not all right," obviously. I'm the best gold analyst of my generation and I'm in this shithole on the monstrous charge of killing my best friend in the world.

"Oh yes, I feel great," is what I said. Perhaps I will be put on report, sarcasm is sure to be against the rules.

The spyhole flap is clicking as it rises and falls. Yes I'm here Mr Bean, Mr Oates or whoever you are. You can bank on me, I won't let you down and in case you've lost count you're at 34, forty odd to go.

So I came out of this heart-to-heart with the AG and not far off, standing over his broom, was Bill. He was talking to one of his pals On The Mop. "That Jack Sharp? On the twos?" he was saying. "A fucking nutter. I asked him, you know he's supposed to have been shit hot in his time . . ." I skirted the sides of the Wing Office listening to him just as the un-lock for Exercise had begun and other cons were swarming down on to the Ones. He still couldn't see me but I heard him. "So what do I get off him but him rambling on about wars and China, nothing useful, not till 1993, can you credit it?"

I stood still amongst the throng headed for the main Wing gate. Hours I've spent trying to drum some fundamentals into this arsehole.

"Bumped off his pal over fuck all, a few grand in a dodgy drugs deal."

I felt betrayed, as though my soul had been scratched.

Melodramatic I know but I felt this moment of misery and shock when suddenly someone tapped me on the shoulder. I turned, all ready to snarl. It was a big guy in prison denims who I'd never seen before.

"You Jack, Jack Sharp?" he said. Given the circumstances I was wary. How naïve I'd been trying to help someone whose horizons stretched as far as pushing a mop.

"Message from Brian," he said. My heart leaped, my faith in human nature restored on the instant. Good old Brian. I'd simply made an error of judgement, or rather, I knew all along, from the moment I first talked with Brian, that Bill had just been a makeshift acquaintance until I found someone I could respect a bit and talk to seriously.

"You know he got off. Anyway first thing he sends you all the best." Wonderful. I was genuinely pleased for him and as soon as I'm out I'll look him up and make sure he's got the best available data.

"Then he said to tell you, this Stevie Scott you're interested in, ex–bank robber it turns out, sound feller they say. Mid thirties, blonde hair, about five foot eight."

It was not what I wanted to hear, not at all.

Rather disappointing though of course I'd never hung too much on this line of inquiry. No resemblance at all between this Scott and that face I'll never forget. How long was it, half an hour, before I passed out from the knock-out filth he induced us to take but I'll never forget the fucker's face.

Maybe my disappointment showed because my new acquaintance, Colin he's called, repeated that Brian sent all his best and here was a little something for me. A little paper-made envelope. It's just a gram, he said, but nice for a taste, a bit of charlie.

I don't go around with my eyes closed. There's a thriving contraband trade here but I've never got involved. I've had no wads of cash money smuggled in and thought I ought to say this, that I had no dosh. Fuck off Jack, this is a little prezzie, he said. I was touched. I said so. He laughed and said it was nothing. Then he said it wasn't his business but Brian had said it was a ten kilo deal involved. What had I paid for it he wanted to know. I wasn't shocked because Brian was the only person

I'd described my situation to. "Three hundred and twenty thousand," I said.

"Thirty-two? Fucks sake Jack, a bit over the top on ten. Thirty's close the going rate." I felt like a complete idiot and rather fear it's what he felt because he then said he had one or two people to talk to but would see me later. As things turned out it may well be very much later. I wonder what he's doing now?

What's this? A clicking and the pace of heavy feet close by. Again? It's got to be Mr Oates. Job description? Cretin. One could say he gets his nickers in a twist at around number thirty because his primary school didn't see the point of going on into the forties. One could say that. But it would be pure bleedingheart liberalism, Oates is just an incompetent. Thirty-two a gram was too much, that's what Colin said. Phil was so sure. Confidence become overconfidence. Tom Arthur always earned a lot more than him, even before the re-organization.

Maybe there is something in the tea. I'm up at the door and can see it close up, the dribbles of it still clinging to the surface. It's more than liquid.

Time for a look at the big world outside. Eye over the spyglass. I know he's coming. One, the click is getting louder. Two, there is a military rhythm to the footsteps. Not my fault I never did National Service, that was decided by your superiors Oates. Before I was even in school. Click. Click. Scrape, my spyglass outer flap being lifted.

"Sharp." The voice is muffled but it's definitely Oates. I step back saluting.

"Let's see you Sharp." I step back another pace and salute again. "517318 Sharp. Sir." Why bother. The flap goes down. I've not yet been in a cell in the Punishment block. A similar design but the regime presumably very different. It probably means Colin is not enjoying the option of reading a book or newspaper. A regime of looking at the wall. Or it maybe a real dungeon, that scene on the yard was pretty ghastly. My barrister of the moment—that really was too much—would no doubt call it a romantic gesture to get myself there but perhaps intolerable levels of sarcasm constitutes and offence and Oates will nick me and get me to this ultimate of punishments. Ultimate given that hanging is a bit over the top whatever the general populace might think.

I was walking on my own on the figure-of-eight path and my heart was heavy even if it is now obvious that Bill is an arse-hole, and my setback as regards the name Scott was only related to one line of inquiry. I found myself behind a group of men, some in denims, some in their own clothes. There were one or two from the Twos including the sullen Kevin. Colin was with them and I imagine he was giving them milieu news from the outside world. I got close behind them but overtaking was out of the question. One of them said, a propos of nothing from what I could make out, "I see they've turned off his life-support machine." Someone called Murray or McMurray I think, Christian name Gordon. To which Colin said, "Oh yes, from a king to a fucking cabbage, good fucking riddance."

Without saying anything except You c---, something like that, Kevin jumped at Colin. It was awful. I've never seen anything like it. Vicious kicking, jabbing, really trying to hurt each other while the other men formed a kind of circle around them as if it were some kind of entertainment. Awful. And the turn-keys were slow and reluctant to get involved until a squad of them appeared at full speed and poor Colin was dragged off by several of them, then nasty Kevin soon after. In the circumstances it was not really something I could ask about, why this Gordon character should provoke such emotions. Besides, I was upset for Colin and to be honest rather sickened by the viciousness of it all.

At lunchtime I couldn't face anything more than custard. I kept hearing Bill's horrible sneering voice, the rat, and the scene on the yard kept doing action replays across my mind when I should have been concentrating on what I was going to say to my legal team. And there were a lot of things I had to say, like my Application for Bail. I'm sick of my solicitor's attitude: the old stick just shakes his head as if I'm some kind of idiot to even think of it, as if such an application will inevitably piss off the magistrate. Well so fucking what! Who is this magistrate anyway!

As it turned out I don't think it would have made any difference however well prepared I'd been. I was half an hour in that Legal Visits waiting room and who do I see behind the wired glass of one of the consulting rooms when I'm eventually called? Who? Fucking Geraldine, that spokesperson of blunt, honest, northern bullshit. I couldn't believe it. In fact I think I nearly screamed there and then, a spasm crossed my face. I mean of all the barristers in the world who do I wind up with. I've refused every single social visit on offer. I'm still in denims for one thing and they are not even Heavy Metal but street-sweeper cut. So do I want to see Lady Caroline or Liam Yeats in my present situation? No I do not!

In fact the denims were one of the first things I raised with her, why shouldn't I have my own clothes like most of them? And what does the smug cow say? "Given your situation Mr Sharp I do think that's rather a minor detail. However if you insist I'll make a note to raise it with Instructing Solicitor." An unimportant detail! I noticed she wasn't exactly decked out in sackcloth though no doubt she's all for it in principle.

The gram! I've still got that gram. Don't want to get captured with it. Cell searches are few and far between but you never can tell. Christ, that would be the final straw. I'd never live it down. Still it was kind of Colin and if ever a man deserved a pick-me-up, I am that man.

Very thoughtful of them, my issue mirror the perfect size and with a very solid surround. No powder will escape the nose of Jack Sharp. And a razor I forgot to return upon completion of shaving formalities. Nasty plastic things but if I stamp on it thus. We're away. The old chopping technique still smooth.

Wonderful. Shove the bendy bit out of my transparent bic pen and hey presto.

Nice. Not as pure as I've known but mustn't grumble.

You know what, I think Oates has lost count again and that the dollar still has quite a way to fall before it rebounds. OopsClick OopsClick down the landing. It is, it's him again.

Mission Control's been on the blower. Seventy? Really? You've got two missing. Is there an escape underway? Recount Officer Oates, recount.

Are we to have no peace. A Minor Detail no doubt, this discrepancy and its consequences. Spy-glass up and down. If I was not out of sorts from my legal visit, I'd be laughing now. CLICK CLICK. Oh no, Oates may still be out there, trying to get it right but this is the other click, too loud, too echoey for spyhole flaps.

I bend down close to the hot water pipe. CLICK. The bastards. That's what it is. When it comes down to it this place is a Nineteenth century tangle of incompetent plumbing. CLICK CLICK. You know it's coming but you don't know when. The Japanese or the Chinese, sadistic bastards either way, they refined . . . CLICK CLICK . . . you know it's going to come and you know when it ought to come . . . SEVENTYONE ON THE TWOS . . . CLICK CLICK . . . SEVENTYONE ON THE TWOS. Go on Mission Control, be inmate friendly, accept 71 right or wrong. So some poor sod is trying to escape . . . CLICK CLICK . . . no doubt you've got it all taped, why bother with the dogs and cameras otherwise. CLICK CLICK. Fuck off. You know this torture is what we have to pay just for the privilege of not freezing to death. And if I should happen to mention it to Geraldine . . . CLICK CLICK . . . Like hiccoughs when they're long past a joke. Eleven, twelve. The dogged pipes. Fifteen . . . CLICK . . . see they should have reached sixteen. That's how they work, they get you counting and just when you think you've got it taped . . . CLICK

I know that conspiracy theorists are looked on as mad paranoids, but why Geraldine? Co-incidence? A bit far-fetched. More like it she heard about my case and demanded to be on the team just so as to humiliate me. CLICKCLICK. Back again are you. Why don't you just fuck off. And if I tell the bitch about the plumbing she'll say A Minor Detail. CLICK GURGLE CLICK. Farting shamelessly this pipe of mine. CLICK. Go on then, do your worst.

She also tells me, this minx who's clawed her way out of Bolton or Burnley . . . CLICK CLICK CLICK . . . Go on bastard, do your worst. I'm Jack Sharp and I've faced pressure you couldn't even dream of . . . click . . . is that all you can manage? Bravo!

Well well, sounds as though Mission Control is now content with Officer Oates's tally. The only torture he has left in him, the only one that's in his power is to come and turn off the lights. Well go on, do it . . . CLICK CLICK . . . see if I care. It so happens Oates that I am not in the mood for writing . . . click . . . fucker, that's your last gasp. Oh yes I did once write. I used to write to Bill. A mistake on my part, so you want to rub my nose in it? Don't bother, I know, the rat with his broom . . . CLICK CLICK . . . Ah making a comeback are you, wonderful. I've never thought about the question of privatising the penal system, you could have put me down as a Don't Know but I'm beginning to think that in private hands at least the plumbing problems might be resolved.

Anyway, to keep a sense of perspective Geraldine told me this afternoon . . . CLICK CLICK . . . that I don't understand the seriousness of my situation. It was then that I lent across the table . . . CLICK . . . FART . . . CLICK. Right, let's hope that was the intestinal crisis of the system, the catharsis.

You see Geraldine I am not a paranoid. I know that this is not some conspiracy against me as an individual but merely a general plumbing problem. Nineteenth century infrastructure . . . CLICK CLICK.

Leave me alone please, just leave me alone. Yes Geraldine, you told me the score from your point of view. Fair enough. You told me that objectively I was in the shit, pages and pages of Forensic backed up . . . CLICK CLICK . . . your viewpoint. And then there was the question of motivation . . . click . . . that has got to be you finished. You have shot your final bolt and I, Jack Sharp, have survived. How are you Colin? Wherever you are, BEST WISHES.

But you loved it didn't you Geraldine, telling me just what an arsehole I was when, for better or worse I told you the truth. I woke up one morning with a very dry throat, a whiff of sick, and ready for a cup of very black coffee. I was in Phil's flat and as soon as I got up I realized there was a candlestick in my bed and I was covered in blood . . . CLICK . . . awful. For a moment I clung on to the idea that it was a practical joke because the truth is that

Phil's sense of humour could be a bit exuberant. It couldn't have been worse telling her how it happened than it was, finding my very, very best friend Phil Stone dead and bloody on the dining nook couch. God Almighty it was awful.

"Bumped off his pal over fuck all that Jack Sharp." Bill's voice, the treacherous bastard. Bill the rat.

I was crazy, seeing Phil like that. I told her all of it.

She then piles on the forensic, the blood matches, the fingerprints. "It does look rather conclusive Mr Sharp so I want to look seriously at your . . ." CLICK CLICK . . . back again are you? Wonderful. I asked her, but where's the so-called motive and she's telling me that with that amount of forensic evidence motive is a bit secondary. But even when it's all bullshit there's got to be something of a motive, which is when she tells me what a few grand of cash money, a tiny bit of coke and Ten kilos of borax looks like from that viewpoint. I kill my best friend because he's swindled me. Or vice versa, either will do. It's absurd, I was earning a good six figure salary, does anyone seriously . . . CLICK CLICK FARTCLICK. Bravo, the encore. And what does the minx say to me? "Scorn is an option for defending counsel Mr Sharp, but in my experience it is not enough and may backfire if pushed too far. CLICK CLICK. Oh nice one, just on cue.

And then she tells me about all this other evidence that will show I was a regular cocaine crim and add Significant Weight to this motivation they are wickedly ascribing to me. Mr Kruger. That was a shock, no getting away from it. A real kick in the balls. A voice recording, photo, and signature which all say that I was that man Kruger. Using a false name to purchase weighing scales and talking to the phone service of a known dealer.

That's when I told her the whole story which was eating humble pie, double helpings. You know what humble pie tastes like? It's like eating tiny cubes of foam rubber without a glass of water . . . CLICK CLICK . . . And what do I get for telling her the truth. Exactly what I should have known I'd get, the patronising cow . . . CLICK CLICK.

"It's a bit Boys Own Mr Sharp," that's what she said. CLICK move around my cell slowly feeling the whitewashed walls as I go like a blind man. Mr Oates or his stand-in is somewhere close by. Soon it'll be Lights Out. Who ever it is, he's wearing boots. I could always hang myself. I might even do it if it gets any worse. I can just picture it, Oates and Bean they just won't know where to look. Mr Bean will say, but Sharp wasn't considered suicidal Sir. But the evidence Bean, the facts prove otherwise. Which is what matters so it appears. So who was it left me with the tough sheets? Cashiered the both of them. Won't make Geraldine look too good either, Client Hangs Himself After Barrister's Visit. Yes well, I'm not giving up that easily. Besides the electric piping in the ceiling would no doubt give way under my weight . . . CLICK CLICK . . . And they'd take it as an admission of guilt wouldn't they. Here is fact A; there is only one interpretation, B; as if the real world . . . CLICK CLICK THUD . . . Darkness. Now I will be a blind man till my eyes are used to it. Boys Own, the Girl Guide said. The fact is yes, I'm not trying to deny it, the idea was mine in the first place but it was Phil, Phil Stone, a great guy, who made it real, Your problem Geraldine is that you never knew Phil and the fact is that once he'd got an idea in his head . . . CLICK CLICK . . . Jesus Christ, won't you shut the fuck up. So it's a Minor Detail is it Geraldine, that in these circumstances I can't even think . . . CLICK CLICK. So I try and explain it and it's all Boys Own. Christ's sake were you sitting there that afternoon when old Barley was going on about National Income? There was GNP and there was National Income and it so happened they always matched . . . CLICK CLICK . . . Go on then, click all night and see if I care. Phil Stone was one of the greatest guys you could ever hope to meet even if, looked at objectively, he was a bit wild. I mean I could see that this always perfect National Income sum was a bit dodgy . . . CLICK . . . but the way Phil tore into it you'd have thought he was a fanatic. Poor old Barley just couldn't take it, it was one time too many, pushed him over the edge . . . CLICK CLICK . . . Please pipe, please, just leave it for a while. Barley was a bit second rate it's true but he didn't try and disguise the fact, wouldn't have been a schoolmaster otherwise on a schoolmaster's salary . . . CLICK . . . Phil's problem was he just couldn't see that and there was something of the terrier about him . . . CLICK . . . I mean one day I just happened to mention some fantasy I'd had about cocaine but the trouble was that Phil, genius though he was in his own field . . . CLICK . . . well he started to take it seriously and it's not that I'm trying to evade responsibility . . . CLICK but I didn't kill him, HAVE YOU GOT THAT, I DIDN'T KILL HIM . . . CLICK CLICK . . . Take it easy Jack, all I'm trying to say is that even though old Barley was a bit of an arsehole he didn't deserve a nervous breakdown. And when it came to it there was Phil pleased as punch at 32 the gram and we were both being ripped off even then. Colin told me. CLICK

CLICK CLICK CLICK CLICK.

OK, I know you're there you don't have to prove it.

I've got to face up to my responsibilities, I know that, but the fact is I was dubious about this Big Deal all along. Wouldn't have countenanced it if it hadn't been for Sir Nick and his little chat, the Challenge Of The Future. All my experience and intuition for the fundamentals to service, to SERVICE, those bean-counters with their Elliot Wave Theory and automatic trading programs. What a future! Sir Nick's obsession with being modern. Mumbo-jumbo. CLICK. All right. All right. I admit it, I lost my head. I was pissed off I admit it because I know where it'll end, Computerized Trading, it'll end in tears. I lost my head and didn't stand up to Phil as I should have done. CLICK . . . CLICKCLICK. Yes yes, I heard you. I told her about Mr Scott and she said, But there's not much to go on Mr Sharp . . . CLICK . . . If only Brian had come up with something I could have said but the bastard wasn't . . . CLICKCLICK . . . It was awful Colin and that monster Kevin, scraping the flesh off each other, trying to smash each other's skulls . . . CLICK . . . CLICKCLICK . . . Please please I will be a good boy I promise just SHUT UP . . . CLICK. CLICKCLICK.

AFTERWORD

There's a long story to how and why this novel which is set in 1987, a first draft of which was written much closer to the time, should be appearing now in 2014. What matters though is that what happened back then in London has had consequences that reach into the present. On one side there has been much analysis of whether, or to what degree, the changes initiated by the Thatcher government into the structure of financial markets at that time, and which took place later in the USA, were responsible for the financial crash of 2008 whose consequences have been unleashed on ordinary folk all over the world. On the other the role of cocaine—then subject to stories about its use in London's finance sector—in the composition of financial capital has come under scrutiny. Many heavyweight Latin American politicians have called for an end to the "War on Drugs" which centres on cocaine and which as the novel shows was well underway in 1987.

One of the myths successfully created by Mrs Thatcher, as she then was, was that as "the grocer's daughter" and especially the grocer who never gave credit, she was all financial rectitude and all that "balancing the books" rhetoric now being used in the War against the Poor. In fact it was under her that an explosion in personal debt began as the grip on income going to workers had to be reconciled with the needs of "consumer" capitalism. Something similar was happening in the United States. Phil, the dollar analyst complains of Americans refusing to save at the very time they were to be cast in the role of the world's "consumers of last resort." Similarly, this time with a rhetoric of smashing the London financial world's "old boy network," barriers that separated parts of it structurally were broken in what was called the Big Bang of 1986, a bonfire of regulations. It's immediate rationale was to make London "internationally competitive" as a financial centre; its immediate result, the buying up of City "institutions" like brokers by more heavily financed American banks, as happens to Phil's firm in the novel.

The argument runs that these investment banks, ironically still constrained by the Glass-Steagall Act in the United States itself (a post–Great Depression Act which separated retail from investment banking and for which there is now a similar demand) until its repeal under Bill Clinton, saw London as a great unregulated opportunity and brought with them a "transaction" rather than "client-based" model of banking, and that this brought with it a shift to "short-termism." Condemnation of such short-termism has been a constant of political rhetoric for many years while actual legislation in favour of the financial capital made it the way things were going to be done. At the same time, investment banks, hedge funds and the like carried their own promise that they would, by means of such transactions, make "productive" capital leaner and meaner. It meant especially having fewer workers doing the same work. On the other side, in London, the money that started to flow to individual bankers had, as one consequence, the further development of East London's docklands which is frequently touched on in the novel. The colonization of the "prime sites" of East London which took a "great leap forward" at this time is now a fact on the ground.

This shift did not take place in isolation. The surplus of capital that had been increasing since the 1973 oil-price shock and the advent of petrodollars required and politically demanded the removal of capital controls in the Anglo-Saxon world. This allowed for its free movement to wherever a short-term gain might be made. It could be moved in an out of "emerging" countries at will, and in the process created the debt crisis of that period, the "Third World" starting in Mexico, and which was later repeated later in East Asia. At the same time developments in Information Technology were accelerating and in many instances, pioneered in the finance/banking world. It's in the background of Jack and Phil's world. The "transaction" model was given a huge boost by the very speed at which transactions could be made.

In the present crisis blaming the development of IT has been one way in which its structural cause can be denied, that is the over-valuation of capital, of financial assets, in the world and the refusal of the High and Mighty in the world to countenance their devaluation. The argument about IT are threefold:

- That it did away with face-to-face dealing based on personal trust which has resulted in dodgy assets being bundled up in good sounding packages and passed around with the result that financial institutions no longer trusted each other.

- That with the development of computerized trading programs, a herd mentality was created that made the size of swings in valuations of assets irrational. They included portfolio insurance programs which meant that when prices initially started to fall, it would automatically induce more sales. This in fact was the most popular explanation for the "Black Monday" crash in October of 1987 which is so pivotal to the plot of the novel. The usual wiseguys described it as "an accident waiting to happen." Something of this sort might have caught out Gordon's financial adviser in the Isle of Man one of the many "offshore" financial spaces that sprang up at the time.

- That the mathematicians took over from the bankers in the transaction model and created ever more abstract financial derivatives—futures having been the basic "derivative"—which pumped up asset values with speculative "virtual" money.

These developments, touched on in the novel, facilitated some of the forms that the still continuing financial crisis from 2007 to 2008 took, though they do not explain it. This crisis was, and remains one of a surplus of *claims* to surplus value in relation what is being produced.

The other important context of that time with its well-known consequences, is the radical change in policy being brought about in China. This is brought to light in the coke-fuelled letter that Jack writes to Deng Hsiao-Ping before ripping it up. It is from this time that the holding down of worker incomes in the West begins. Jobs had already been outsourced, but "the Chinese are coming" becomes the subliminal message to workers in the West for years to come. Since then that its trade surplus, and especially that with the USA has been identified as part of the 2007–8 causal chain. At the time of the novel, it was the Japanese whose holdings of U.S. Treasury Bills were propping up the U.S. dollar; now it is the Chinese.

What hasn't changed from then is the confined antagonism between the American and German view of money which Phil comments on; the German "anti-inflationary" view of money as pure and independent and the American, the dollar still the predominant global currency, that one can create it. The pressure by the USA on Germany to loosen its tight money policy is another explanation given for the Black Monday crash of 1987, though at the same time Phil's hero, Paul Volcker of the U.S. Federal Reserve, was about to use German-type deflationary policy which was seen as yet another cause of the crash of the time, on the grounds that stock markets depended too heavily on "easy money." In fact, the real impact of Volcker's policy was to create more downward pressure on wages, and made the American "consumer of last resort" more dependent on credit, and more indebted. It was also a period similar to the present in that gold as a safe haven for money created a self-fulfilling speculative increase in its price in the fetishistic belief that here was "pure" money that could be trusted.

Back in 1987 and for the next twenty years or so, stories of cocaine use in the City would pop up in the Press now and then. Overenthusiastic risk-taking a possible consequence. But when the crash did come and excessive, overconfident risk-taking part of the mainstream explanation for what had happened, there were no references made to cocaine-taking. It was the dog that did not bark in the night. That is until in 2013 Professor David Nott, who had been the British government's independent drug adviser until he told them things they didn't want to hear, claimed that cocaine use was indeed *the* reason for the 2008 crash. It's not *the* reason, but the professor had a point in that cocaine and its capacity for indiscriminate enthusiasm is he perfect drug for the creation of financial bubbles. In the present situation it is precisely the creation of new bubbles as well as the War against the Poor that is the response of a global elite who will not devalue overvalued assets.

The novel is realistic about the economics of cocaine which I learned during two prison sentences, but I also carried on being interested after I had finished the novel. This led to an essay, "From Coca to Capital," which I wrote for the *Potosí Principle* exhibition in Madrid, Berlin, and La Paz, and now follows here. In the novel, Phil and Jack treat cocaine as if it were any other commodity. For them it's not a matter of it being, as is well documented, far less harmful than alcohol; rather they are the real free marketers. The rhetorical free market however is no such thing being stuffed with subsidies and highly selective about what is free. Phil's original mistake was however to rule out the laundering of cocaine money as too risky. "From Coca to Capital" suggests it has been no such thing.

FROM COCA TO CAPITAL: FREE TRADE COCAINE

This essay appeared as part of the *Potosí Principle* exhibition in Madrid, Berlin, and La Paz. It was also published by *Mute* magazine (www.metamute.org).

In December 2009, the British *Observer* newspaper reported the assertion made by the United Nations illegal drugs "czar," Antonio Maria Costa that he had seen evidence that the proceeds of crime were the "only liquid investment capital" available to some banks on the edge of "Credit Crunch" collapse, and that a majority of the estimated $315 billion drugs profit had been absorbed into the legitimate financial system.[1] He was, needless to say, coy about which banks had benefited, revealing only that the evidence came from intelligence sources and state prosecutors. But what he did do is to blow away the myth that drugs profits are laundered only through dodgy offshore concerns.[2] Ben Ehrenreich reminds us that such coyness is unnecessary: writing of the Mexican drugs business he notes that "Investigations in the USA and Mexico have implicated Wells Fargo, Bank of America, Citigroup, HSBC and Santander (among others) in cartel-related money-laundering. Sr. Costa's observations as to the significance of criminal money to the global economy however does not prevent him from being a hard-line exponent of the 'War on Drugs,' a 'war' without which those profits would not be realised and ready for use as that 'liquid investment capital.'"

1   Rajeev Sayal, "Drug Money Saved Banks in Global Crisis, Claims UN Advisor," *The Observer*, October 13, 2009.
2   Ben Ehrenreich, "A Lucrative War," *London Review of Books*, October 21, 2010, 16.

Cocaine is now the most financially significant of the illegal drug industry subject to this "war." At the same time the dynamics of the very capitalism which has recently needed that injection of liquid capital, regardless of its origins, create the conditions that make coca growing the most rational economic choice for many small-scale Andean farmers, while it is also these farmers who are most penalized by this "war-without end." Cocaine is not just functional to the creation of private capital, but the war against it is useful ideologically, and for the selective repression it requires and entails both internationally and internally. This involves notions of "backwardness" in the case of small-scale farming, and of racial character defects of particular consumers. In the United States specifically it has played a large part in creating a self-perpetuating, and racist, "prison-industrial complex."[3]

The drug is also functional to capital as an aid to the "productivity" of certain kinds of labour in what are called creative and financial industries. The capacity of cocaine for both a promiscuous enthusiasm *and* controlled perseverance being especially suited to such project-defined work. In recent years the demand has increased still further as other areas of work demand worker *performance*.[4] This reality however, cannot be given any official or academic recognition.

The 16th-century pragmatism of the Spanish King Philip on the matter of the legality of coca when he overturned the Catholic Church's ban on it in the name of labour productivity, is ideologically impossible now, except for the indigenous peasant movement in Bolivia that has fought to make it legal.[5] The Bolivians,

---

3 Drug Policy Education Group, *Drug Policy News*, vol. 2, no. 1, Spring/Summer 2001.

4 John Barker, "Intensities of Labour: from Amphetamine to Cocaine," *Mute* magazine, March 7, 2006, http://www.metamute.org/editorial/articles/intensities-labour-amphetamine-to-cocaine.

5 The shift of attitude during the Potosí silver boom in Bolivia—which was an important kick-start to European capitalist dynamics—began with the Ecclesiastical Council in Lima condemning coca as the Devil Amulet in 1551, and the Holy Inquisition was charged with enforcing it in 1567. But by 1573 silver mine production was so badly affected that King Philip of Spain abolished the prohibition. Just as in the present capitalist crisis, the cost of the reproduction of labour-power was pushed on to the labourers themselves: Coca was taxed. Anthony Henman in *Mama Coca* estimated the coca market in 17th-century Potosí had twice the turnover of food and clothing.

unlike the king, are fighting for the recognition of its cultural significance and a properly scientific appreciation of its qualities.

BRING FORTH THE BACKWARD

It is hardly coincidental that the major producers of the war-targeted cocaine, heroin, and cannabis are countries designated as "underdeveloped," or what have also been called "backward" areas of the world. In most periods of colonialism words like "savages" depicted ideologies of racial superiority. After the Second World War, a new language emerged, articulated in the Inauguration Speech of U.S. President Harry Truman in 1949, and reasserted in John F. Kennedy's Alliance for Progress. The institutional context of Truman's speech was the birth of the United Nations and the Bretton Woods institutions. In it the "moral" and "civilisational" superiority of the United States which previous presidents had proclaimed was now manifested as its science and technology.[6] Referring to peoples of the world whose "economic life is primitive and stagnant," he said: "We must embark on a bold new program for making the benefits of our scientific advances and industrial progress available for the improvement and growth of underdeveloped areas."

It is from here on that "underdeveloped" becomes part of the language of political economy and, at this time, it is uniquely American technology that will "develop" these others. Truman again: "The United States is preeminent among nations in the development of industrial and scientific techniques. The material resources which we can afford to use for the assistance of other peoples are limited. But our imponderable resources in technical knowledge are constantly growing and are inexhaustible."

Just a year later, in 1950, one Howard Fonda, a banker and president of the U.S. Pharmaceutical Association, led a UN commission to study coca. His study of Aymara and Quechua people (with one translator) concluded that coca chewing was the cause of poverty in the Andean countries because it lowered

---

6   For example, U.S. President Taft at the beginning of the 20th century, claimed: "The whole hemisphere will be ours in fact as, by the superiority of our race, it is already ours morally." Sentiments later echoed by Theodore Roosevelt.

the capacity to work, which was in flat contradiction to the seriously concerned opinions of the conquistador exploiters of silver mines. Apart from its denigration of two "backward cultures," Fonda's report was clearly self-interested and unscientific, "plagued by prejudices, unfounded speculation and third-hand sources."[7] This did not prevent it being ratified by the World Health Authority in 1952, and the power of this self-interested prejudice became ever clearer with a refreshed version of the Truman rhetoric, namely President Kennedy's Alliance for Progress. Its existence was proclaimed in 1961, and in the same year the UN Single Convention on Narcotic Drugs outlawed coca except as a flavouring agent. In the Alliance's charter, "peace-loving peoples" were specifically those who promoted "the conditions that will encourage the flow of foreign investments" to the region. In Latin America, in the interval between Truman and Kennedy, such conditions had to be enforced by the Eisenhower Administration with a coup in Guatemala to the benefit of the United Fruit Company.[8] Since then, a whole array of enforcement measures have been devoted to highly selective versions of free trade and the free flow of capital.

Despite its powers of enforcement, *capitalism, cannot tolerate other socioeconomic modes of living*, not and Andean culture where coca is sacred and life-enabling. In the War on Drugs narrative we don't hear that cocaine was actually synthesized by a European using those "industrial and scientific techniques" Harry Truman boasted of. The affront is that its production still depends on the coca leaf. Equally the 1961 UN Convention on Narcotic Drugs which proclaimed the total prohibition (and therefore eradication) of chewing coca to be completed in twenty-five years, and made cocaine Public Enemy Number One,[9] had a get-out clause, Article 27, by which "It is allowed to plant, transport, market and

---

7   Silvia Rivera Cusicanqui, "An Indigenous Commodity and Its Paradoxes: Coca Leaf in a Globalised World," *Indigenous Affairs* 1–2/2007, 62.

8   Main players in the Truman and Eisenhower administrations included John Moore Cabot, Henry Cabot Lodge, and Bedell Smith, who all had interests in the company.

9   Even heroin was the scare at the time. The relationship between this trend and the Vietnam War was exhaustively described by Alfred W. McCoy at the time.

possess coca leaf in the quantity necessary for the production of *flavouring agents.*" This, as Jorge Hurtado describes, was solely in the interests of the Coca-Cola Company.[10]

At this time "wars" were monopolized by the Cold War, but 1961 marks the beginning of what in our age has become one of many thematically-defined wars: on drugs, subsequently on terrorism, and now—grotesquely—on poverty and cancer. It is ironic that when realpolitik intellectuals routinely talk of a "new Middle Ages" in the context of "underdeveloped" countries, their masters talk not just of wars, but pitch drug *czars* against drug *barons.*[11] A minority of academics and various people who have worked in drug enforcement agencies have talked of the ineffectiveness of this "war," and the many ways in which it is counterproductive.[12] Why then its continuation which depends on the continued illegal status of cocaine, and which has not altered the demand for the drug in a *performance*-oriented world of capitalist work?

THE PRISON-INDUSTRIAL COMPLEX

The "war" against drugs is then partly ideological, of the type that used to be called "cultural imperialism," that is, a racist association of drugs deemed to be illegal, with peoples considered to be inferior and in a state of "backwardness." Built on this there has developed a War on Drugs industry which is a perfect representation of Marx's mordantly witty riff on the productivity of the criminal, "Apologist Conception of the Productivity of All Professions."[13]

---

10 Jorge Hurtado Gumucio, *Cocaine, the Legend,* 55–58. He goes on to describe how cocaine is misnamed as a narcotic, to give it place in the "lazy native" discourse.

11 The "drug czar" title was first coined by the present U.S. vice president, Joe Biden, in October 1982.

12 Academics like Ransalaaer Lee, Eve Bertram, and Jeffrey A. Miron; ex–law enforcement officers like Leigh Maddox and Jack Cole; politicians like ex–Baltimore mayor Kurt Schmoke, ex–culture minister of Brazil Gilberto Gil, and now former president of Mexico Vicente Fox.

13 See Karl Marx, *Economic Manuscripts of 1861–63,* Part 3, "Relative Surplus Value": "The criminal produces not only crimes but also criminal law and with this the professor who gives lectures on criminal law. . . . The criminal moreover produces the whole of the police and of criminal justice, constables, hangmen, juries etc."

This edifice of jobs and "technical" developments has been built up around the world but, as in many other instances, the United States has been the pioneer. The Drug Enforcement Agency, established in 1973 is the neocolonial arm of the War on Drugs, and yet it is but part of one of twelve government counter-drugs policies agencies, agencies now estimated to have a budget of $30 billion a year.[14] Such an edifice of interests requires first of all an overestimation of "the problem" in the interests of all the bureaucracies involved. At the height of the Vietnam War when heroin was perceived to be the main problem, President Nixon told Congress that drug abuse was "America's Public Enemy Number One" and in the process kicked off the language of war.[15] It also requires ideological input from those Armchair Spartans of the U.S. "Power Elite" who see decadence in their own citizens, or rather certain groups of citizens.[16] Decadence in this case is both a mirror of "backwardness" but also a perceived threat to "morality" and "authority." Back then, in 1975, and despite the heroin "scare," the U.S. prison population stood at 380,000, but this was set to change.[17] In 1973 Governor Rockefeller of New York, who had ordered the massacre at Attica prison two years earlier, proposed life sentences without parole for all hard drug dealers and set the tone for what would happen when Ronald Reagan took power in 1980.

It is the unprecedented increase in the numbers of people in U.S. prisons which really tells the War on Drugs story. It has involved far greater levels of public expenditure, but at the same is a considerable source of corporate profit. Between 1975 and 1985 it had more or less doubled to 740,000 prisoners. This was five years into the life of the Reagan Administration during which U.S. interest in Latin America involved stepping up its

14 Tom Feiling, *The Candy Machine: How Cocaine Took Over the World*, (Penguin, 2009).

15 Max Singer described how the numbers bump worked (or "duking the stats" as it is now) in the case of New York City heroin statistics in his article "The Vitality of Mythical Numbers," The Public Interest, 1971.

16 See John Barker "Armchair Spartans and the 'D' Word," *Variant* no. 24, Winter 2005.

17 Loic Wacquant: "From Welfare State to Prison State: Imprisoning the American Poor," *Le Monde Diplomatique*, July 1998.

training of local military and police torturers.[18] The Cold War was still the context, but it is one in which neoliberal political-economic policies also demanded an increase in internal repression, one portrayed as a "culture war."[19]

In this period it was not just Reagan upping the ante, the Congressional Democrats were also competing over who could be the toughest. The Anti-Drug Abuse Act of 1986 is ascribed to their Senate leader Tip O'Neil wanting the party to take control of the Senate in upcoming elections with the support of Senator Joe Biden. Twenty-six new drug crimes with mandatory minimum sentences were included and prosecutors given the right to appeal against sentences considered to be lenient. It coincided—fifteen years into the War on Drugs—with an increase in drug-related violence and the rapid growth of crack cocaine, a form of freebasing for the poor; and with the first stage in American deindustrialisation and attacks on the welfare system. It is at this time that the War becomes what the celebrated novelist Toni Morrison called an attack on and extreme marginalisation of black men; and what Jerome Miller called the *American Gulag*. More specifically, this was an attack on black men and, as it transpires, black women blinkered by a "culture of poverty." All this when to be poor for psychologising neoliberalism is characterised as a character defect.

This was made clear when, at the change-over from Reagan to George Bush Sr., a prototype Armchair Spartan with a nicotine addiction, William Bennett, moved from being Education Secretary to head the Office of the National Drug Policy Control as czar. The agenda he and his team brought with them meant, as Dan Baum points out, that the notion of drugs as a health-

---

18 When the United States was engaged in a not-so-secret destabilisation war against the Nicaraguan government and in the process helped the Contra rebels smuggle cocaine into the United States.

19 Bill Piper of the Drug Policy Alliance misunderstands neoliberal capitalism when he says "Drug policy was one of the few areas where Reagan strayed from his conservative philosophy by expanding the power of the government and undermining the Constitution."

problem was ditched.[20] This was in part because this approach raised the problem of why and how corporate controlled tobacco and alcohol could be legal. Instead, the real issue was "character," a notion of selectively defined decadence combined with the trademark psychologising of neoliberalism. Its flipside was the assertion of authority. The "Stern White Man" must be seen to be in control and morally entitled to be so. Baum describes how cocaine, heroin, and marijuana were subject to circular reasoning: they were immoral because they were illegal, and illegal because immoral. He goes on to cite Bennett himself saying that "the drug crisis is a crisis of authority, in every sense of the word 'authority.'" This could mean only one thing: "a massive wave of arrests is a top priority for the War on Drugs."

In 1995, after a further ten years, the prison population had more than doubled again to 1.6 million. It now stands at around 2.2 million with 5 million either on probation or parole with the state corrections budget standing at $50 billion annually.[21] The racial divide figures also show that Toni Morrison was not being rhetorical. In 2005 there were 4,789 black males per 100,000 in prison compared to 786 white males. For black men between twenty-five and twenty-nine it's 11,695. In parts of Detroit, that icon of U.S. deindustrialisation, one in sixteen males is under correctional control. In addition to the racial disparity, 40 percent of imprisonment had been for drug offences.[22]

An A to B connection between deindustrialisation and an increase in drug convictions, is impossible to make, but this increase has accompanied the imposition of insecure and underpaid jobs, and "restructuring" of the social welfare system to make it more punitive. What is much clearer is how this huge arrest-and-conviction pool has a symbiotic relation with the prison business. As Eric Schlosser explains: "What was

20 Dan Baum, Smoke and Mirrors: The War on Drugs and the Politics of Failure (Little Brown, 1997).
21 Pew Center on the States, Prison Count 2010, http://www.pewstates.org/research/reports/prison-count-2010-85899372907.
22 New York Civil Liberties Union, "The Rockefeller Drug Laws: Unjust, Irrational, Ineffective," http://www.nyclu.org/files/Rock.pdf.

once a niche business for a handful of companies has become a multibillion-dollar industry with its own trade shows and conventions, its own web sites, mail order catalogues, and direct marketing companies. . . . The prison industry now includes some of the nation's largest architecture and construction firms, Wall Street investment banks that handle prison bond issues and invest in private prisons, plumbing supply companies, food service companies, health-care companies, companies that sell everything from bullet-resistant security cameras to padded cells available in a 'vast colour selection'" and now has its own trade paper, *Correctional Building News.*[23]

In the case of state prisons the construction boom has involved a process of geo-social engineering, bringing jobs and income to highly selective locations. Malone, North Country New York is the example spotlighted by Lynne Duke.[24] It was a town in decline, with factories shut or downsized, and dairy farming had collapsed. Now it boasts three prisons, which has brought in 1,600 well-paid jobs and the employment that will service those incomes. "Military Keynsianism" has been rightly identified as the dirty secret of free-market capitalism. "Prison Keynsianism" is a lesser version, but its expansion in an era of tighter social budgets is no less real. And to a considerable degree this whole edifice is built on having made the products of plants, grown by small-scale farmers in "backward" countries, illegal.

"AN UNFORTUNATE STYLE OF CROP DIVERSIFICATION"

It's not hard to see that there are powerful interests at work in the maintenance of this particular war without end. More than that, globalized capitalism creates and re-creates the conditions which make the growing of coca and transportation of cocaine become the only rational options for people in the poorest parts of the world. Rational in the neoliberal sense:

---

23 Eric Schlosser, "The Prison-Industrial Complex," *The Atlantic*, December 1998, http://www.theatlantic.com/past/docs/issues/98dec/pris2.htm. The Wall Street outfits with an interest included Merrill Lynch, Sheason Lehman, and American Express.

24 Lynne Duke: "Building a Boom Behind Bars," *Washington Post*, September 8, 2000.

individualized and calculating; how "human nature" is, and ought to be. The emphasis on the virtues of international "free trade" has increased both the necessity and opportunity for different peoples to become involved in the cocaine business. The opportunity factor is obvious, exponential growth in international trade, proclaimed as an absolute virtue has with its millions of containers, air flights, penetration of new markets, and so on created far more possibilities for the transportation of cocaine across borders. At the same time other distinctive characteristics of "global capitalism" have provided motivation both for growers and transporters.

- The constant push to liberalize capital markets and capital flows has made the laundering of money that much easier.
- Its intolerance of anything but itself, and of particular indigenous, noncapitalist cultures means, materially, an intolerance of noncapitalist agriculture, whether it involves communal land or peasant (*campesino*) farming.[25]
- International trade is not free. The assumption of equal power amongst market participants is an obvious lie, and especially so in agriculture. The West while preaching it has consistently used subsidies, export credits, and import quotas to serve its own interests. Combined with an imposition of its version of free trade and its version of development as monoculture crops for export, it has destroyed a whole class of small farmers producing food for their own markets. This has been most spectacular in the case of Mexico since the imposition of NAFTA, something clearly foreseen and opposed by the Zapatista movement.
- Risk-taking by capital, as creating the optimum allocation of resources, has been its self-proclaimed virtue. The banking crisis of the present period has made a mockery of this claim, and the risk has been passed on to the people

---

25 This can be seen in several phenomena, such as the leasing and buying of large tracts of land in Africa by the capitalist corporations either on their own or with sovereign wealth funds; the concentration of capital in the biotechnology sector; and the development of "terminator" seeds. There is push by large capital to control all the basic necessities of life.

of the world at large. This has been the experience in agriculture for far longer. The power of wholesale oligopolies and increasingly of supermarkets has shifted the risks of small-scale farming for export still further onto the farmer. Already faced with the vagaries of climate, and the possibilities of interest rate and fertiliser price increases, there are now systems of Supply Chain Management made possible by IT developments, which give all power to the buyer.

• Where quotas favourable to small-scale producers did exist like for Caribbean banana growers, corporate lobbying—in this case by Chiquita—has undermined them so that they can boast of its levels of exploitation in the plantations of Ecuador. This follows a pattern started in the Reagan-Bush era of undermining commodity price agreements which offered some security to farmers. At the same time, in the case of sugar for example—produced in Bolivia, Peru, and Colombia as well as the Caribbean—the United States imposed import quotas. It prompted U.S. Congressman Thomas J. Downey to write an amazingly frank letter to the *New York Times* on September 20, 1989, which addressed this matter. Just as President George H.W. Bush was announcing an $8 billion solution to the "drug problem," the congressman pointed out that in the period 1983–89 imports of 200,000 tons of sugar from these countries fell to less than 85,000.[26] The trend was already apparent in 1987 when he notes that State Department officials writing in the *Washington Monthly* warned that this would lead to "an unfortunate style of crop diversification."

TRADE ROUTES

Links then between coca production and the politico-economic realities of the capitalist world are not paranoid fantasy. On the other hand I do not intend to make anything of the well-known U.S. green light to cocaine smuggling in its support for

---

26 Import quotas in favour of domestic production saw sugar imports in general fell by 80 percent between 1975 and the early 1990s.

the Contra War of destabilisation in Nicaragua, nor to claim that there are always A-to-B causal links. Mexico as a major cocaine trade route and the extraordinary levels of violence associated with it, has to do with its location, history, and experience of politically controlled smuggling. But the business has seen an exponential increase since the imposition of NAFTA (North American Free Trade Agreement). This "free trade" agreement meant, in practice, that smuggling was easier with the increase in cross-border trade transport, and the deregulation of the Mexican financial system made money laundering that much easier. As subsidized American corn flooded the market, over a million smack farmers and another 1.4 million dependent on the agricultural sector lost their livelihoods. Monthly incomes for self-employed farmers fell by 90 percent between 1991 and 2003.[27] Ehrenreich notes that in Bandiraguarto, people "have little choice but to become narcos" because there is so little other work, "and with a government that largely doesn't care and a formal economy that takes pity on no one."[28]

Mexico's history made it an ever more important trading route following increased drug police activity in the Caribbean, which had previously been such an important entrepôt with links to marketing in the U.S. itself. In the Caribbean too, its location and a history of political gang violence preceded the cocaine business, but it was also preceded by shifts in the political economy of both sugar and bananas. In their case, effective lobbying from Chiquita via the Americans at the WTO forced the EU to cap its preferential trade terms for Jamaican bananas. Its markets are now full of subsidised American produce that local farmers cannot compete with. It leaves Jamaica and other islands with the choice of tourism or cocaine. To repeat, these are not A-to-B explanations as to why it became such an important place in the transnational drugs business, but it is impor-

---

27 Marceline White, Carlos Salas, and Sarah Gammage, "NAFTA and the FTAA: A Gender Analysis of Employment and Poverty Impacts in Agriculture," Trade Impact Review: Mexico Case Study, Women's Edge Coalition, Washington DC, 2003, iii.

28 Ehrenreich, "A Lucrative War," 18.

tant to make the link when the capitalist ideological appara-
tus is focused on its own forms of "de-linkage" by which it is
able to selectively moralise or produce psycho-social explanations of its own as with the "failed state" label. The Nicaraguan
Miskito coast has also emerged as a perfect entrepôt between
the Northern Colombian coast and Mexico. Here too specific
government neglect and the experience that must have been
gained in the period when Miskito communities supported the
Contras in the 1980s destabilisation war made it a natural place
to make drug business connections. But it is also a place of deep
poverty and high unemployment, and this in a country where
banana pickers are the lowest-paid of all in Latin America.

West Africa has now emerged as a main entrepôt for the
transportation of cocaine into Europe. Guinea-Bissau, a favourite in the circles of "failed state" discourse and voyeuristic-mor-
alizing journalism, has been replaced as a favourite for cocaine
transporters by Senegal with its advantage of better roads and
telecoms which is now saddled with the same discourse. Cocaine
shipments totalling 3,120 kg were seized off its seaboard on
2009. Again there is the geography, and a smuggling history
described by Christopher Thompson: a use of satellite-equipped
canoes (*pirogues*) which had been used to smuggle human beings
into Europe, until that business moved further south. But there
is also an element of "failed state" in his account: "unmoni-
tored coasts, poorly paid officials, porous borders and booming
informal markets."[29] No reference is made to the destruction of
local fishing by bottom trawl net fishing—in which around 75
percent of the catch is discarded dead—by unregulated factory
ships which, flying "flags of convenience" enforce slave-like
crew conditions.[30] The real historical context is that Senegal's
most prosperous year was thirty years ago.

---

29 Christopher Thompson, "Fears for Stability in West Africa as Cartels Move In,"
    Guardian, March 10, 2009.
30 For descriptions of this dirty business see publications of the Environmental
    Justice Network.

COCA, THE SAFEST BET

"Coca just grows. It's a weed. Farmers don't have to worry about markets and diseases. It always gets a good price."
—Liliana Ayalde, USAID, 2003

The very first mission from the post-war Western world, following Truman's development of the backward speech, was Colombia. Headed by Lauchlin Currie, it was the first World Bank "comprehensive economic survey mission" and began on June 30, 1949. On August 19 the country received the first World Bank funding, which was an agricultural machinery project loan. This perfectly reflected Truman's promise to bring technological skills to the backward. Further World Bank credits followed in 1954 and then again in 1966, this time to foster large-scale cattle ranching. Nowhere was attention given to the chronic shortage of land for small farmers in a country where 60 percent of agricultural land is owned by 0.5 percent of the population. Then, as Héctor Mondragón describes at the time of the Clinton Presidency, and after years of FARC activity, "the World Bank granted an induction credit of $1.82 million to fund pilot projects and a Technical Unit, with the goal of 'preparing' a complete support project for 'market-based agrarian reform.'"[31] This "reform" is an object lesson in the dangers of becoming indebted. Mondragón describes it as such: "Here's the paradox: the beneficiary of the subsidy program for land purchases (in the original scheme) becomes a real 'loser' who receives an unpayable credit that leads him to lose the land and to be registered in the data bases listing people who are in arrears. In addition to no longer having land, he can no longer receive any kind of credit."

In the hands of the Pastraña government as of 1998, "It didn't seek to strengthen the *campesino* economy but rather sought the subordination of *campesinos* and the handing over of their property to large farms." With a sleight of hand characteristic of contemporary capitalism, those whose "development"

---

31 Héctor Mondragón, "Colombia: Agrarian Reform, Fake and Genuine," in Peter Rosset, Raj Patel, and Micahel Courville, eds., *Promised Land: Competing Visions of Agrarian Reform* (Food First Books, 2006), 192–207.

policy entails the "maintenance and consolidation of large rural properties," dismiss real land redistribution as "obsolete" or "antiquated." And this, Mondragón argues, has pushed *campesinos* beyond the "agricultural frontier" and into the jungle to grow illicit crops. These circumstances have been further augmented by the dynamics of 'neoliberal' capitalist globalisation.[32]

In 1990 Colombia's food imports accounted for just 6 percent of GDP. By 2004 it had amounted to 46 percent with an emphasis instead on large-scale production of African palm, pineapples and cocoa. Given the history of coffee production, and in indeed of many instances of export monocultures in the "backward" world, this is likely to end in tears. In 1997 the price of organic coffee was $1.34 a kilo.[33] By April 2004 it was down to $0.89. It was a process that started with the July 1989 dissolution of the International Coffee Agreement (ICA) negotiated in 1975, a period when the articulated possibility of a New International Economic Order on the back of OPEC's success, was sidelined by the politico-economic bulldozer of neoliberal policy for which such commodity price agreements, which had given producers some security of income, were denounced as "ideological."

President George H.W. Bush talked awareness-talk on the coffee-coca nexus at the very time Congressman Downey was explicitly linking coca growing to U.S. sugar policy. On September 28, 1989, with a team including drug czar William Bennett, he met with Colombia's President Barca to praise him for his "heroic fight" against the drug trade and said he was prepared to resolve problems with the now hobbled coffee

---

32 Colombia does have its own specific historical characteristics, though it is hard to know the weight of their significance. Francisco Thoumi points to the delegitimisation of the state which precedes the more general trend in this direction in other underdeveloped countries. In "Violence as Market Strategy in Drug Trafficking: The Andean Experience" (in Koonings and Kruijt, eds., *Armed Actors: Organised Violence and State Failure in Latin America*). Menno Vellinga talks of a "'production-speculation' mentality with little investment in long-term capital equipment, a focus on commerce and quick turnover and high short-term profits" as conducive to the illegal drug industry. Since this sounds rather like the UK it's hard to know how distinctive this makes Colombia.

33 In an instance described by Gary Marx, *campesino* coffee bean selling entailed a five-hour mule journey to the point of sale, *Chicago Tribune*, April 19, 2003.

agreement. In fact he did not resolve it, so that by 2003 Gabriel Silva the president of the National Federation of Coffee Growers of Colombia was saying, "We have seen in some marginal areas in the Colombian coffee region farmers switching to illegal crops."[34] By this time the breaking of the Agreement had been cemented by the power of the coffee-buyer oligopoly (consisting of Sara Lee, Kraft, Procter & Gamble, and Nestle). This is part of a trend whereby risk is imposed still further on the farmer. In this instance the ICA being replaced by the supplier-managed inventory (SMI) system whereby the *supplier* is responsible for maintaining the stocks used by the purchasing firm *even if* the stocks are held at a port in that firm's country or its own storage.[35]

In the case of sugar, U.S. import quotas were what might be called the final straw in the matter of risk being thrust down the agricultural ladder. The Peruvian coup of 1968 and subsequent agrarian reform, which involved the nationalisation of the largest sugar plantations on the coast, was blamed by the defenders of U.S. quotas as the real cause of the industry's decline there. But it did not benefit Peru's small farmers either. The APRA corporatist union continued to influence the sugar unions and the leadership of the cooperatives in such a way that casual labourers, nearby smallholders and tenants as well as landless migrants from the highlands working seasonally were excluded from the "cooperatives." Their lives became less secure.

The history of sugar production in the Santa Cruz area of Bolivia followed a similar pattern. It was kick-started by an American mission, the State Department's Bohan Plan of 1942, which did not challenge the local oligarchy's right to control the sugar mills but involved the importing of Altiplano *campesinos* to

---

34 Toby Muse, "Grounds War: International Coffee Prices Stay Low, Forcing Colombian Growers Large and Small to Rethink," *Latin Trade* vol. 12, no. 4, April 2004, http://www.thefreelibrary.com/Grounds+war%3A+international+coffee +prices+stay+low,+forcing+Colombian...-a0116223715.

35 Thomas Lines cites Oxfam on the loose arrangement in export horticulture for example, "Agreements are often verbal, so there is no written contract to break. . . . Such informality gives buyers flexibility to delay payments, break programmes, or cancel orders, forcing suppliers to find last-minute alternatives." See *Making Poverty* (Zed Books, 2008), 105.

the underpopulated Santa Cruz territory in the 1950s. It was they who had all the risk-taking thrust upon them: of over-production and a fall in price while faced with a discriminatory quota system, and a need for fertiliser and the debts that this involved. It meant that they—including former miners from Potosí—gave up and became labourers on sugar farms or became more of those pioneers into virgin forest.

In all these circumstances the obvious irony is that the crop with least income risk is the illegal one, coca, and this despite long periods of murderous repression in all three producing countries. "It has a secure market that guarantees a steady flow of income to the individual peasant households. This is coca's basic advantage."[36] In Bolivia too, the collapse of the coffee price, had a crippling effect on the farmer, and put paid to one element of the UN's Fund for Drug Abuse Control's AGRO YUNGAS programme that began in 1986. Described by Noam Lupu it tells an exemplary security/insecurity-of-income story augmented by the arrogant wishful thinking of UN officers bringing with them what Harry Truman had called "the benefits of our scientific advances."[37] In the case of the Yungas area of Bolivia—the traditional coca growing and chewing, and coffee growing valley in La Paz province—the deal was to introduce four high-yield coffee plant varieties from Brazil and Colombia. These required a "technical package" of fertiliser and insecticides. Several years later only half the plants were in good condition and then a massive infestation of Broca disease destroyed 90 percent of coffee crops including the local Creole variety. It's like a morality tale of arrogant "development," added to by wishful thinking. There was no alternative plan when the coffee price fell (60 percent in the period 1986–90).[38]

---

36 Menno Vellinga, *The Political Economy of the Drug Industry: Latin America and the International System* (University of Florida Press, 2004), 4.

37 *Development Policy Review* vol. 22, no. 4 (2004): 405–21.

38 Lupu's scathing account talks of a counterproductive conditionality on credits, a narrow vision and emphasis on short-term success, blind adherence to pure economic competition model, inadequate market appraisal of viable alternative crops, and paternalistic attitudes. Dominic Streatfield also mentions how the one instance of an Agro Yungas success, a soya project, brought down the wrath of U.S. soya farmers.

Herbert Klein notes that what was special is that coca was overwhelmingly produced on small farms which were grouped into colonies or large peasant unions that were an effective voice for them.[39] Adding insult to injury, "Grown in combination with food crops it requires less investment and attention than other crops once it has been planted and will only require manual labor and no special skills. . . . Also the production of cocaine is not a very elaborate or difficult process . . . the manufacturing process is not capital intensive, does not have large economies of scale, does not require large amounts of skilled labor, and uses production processes that are relatively easy to organize."[40]

In short, there is no place for the inputs of corporate capital. No capitalist boasts about efficiency. No small farmer indebtedness. And finally, as Klein puts it, "Thus for the first time in modern Bolivian history, a primary export product was dominated by small peasant producers."

BIO-TOOL

This crucial *security of income* for the coca farmer depends a on steady demand for cocaine, though this is less true in Bolivia. The evidence that there is such a steady demand in the richer world is well-known, and has sometimes prompted under-fire politicians of coca-producing countries telling the richer world that that it is their problem. But "problem" is the most overused word in the vocabulary, and it is rather the case that cocaine is a means of production, or more specifically a component of the reproduction of certain kinds of labour in this richer world, paid for by the person doing the labour. With the growth of the "white-collar" economy in the late 19th century a new kind of intensity of labour was required and cocaine came into its own. Familiar names like Merck, Parke Davies, and Burrough Wellcome advertised it as both a performance and happy drug. Marek Kohn's comprehensive *Dope Girls* goes on to describe how a mixture of sexual, racial, and military discipline paranoias

39 Herbert S. Klein, *A Concise History of Bolivia* (Cambridge University Press, 2003), 246–48.
40 Vellinga, *The Political Economy of the Drug Industry*, 5.

lead to its outlawing, but that in the meantime, "The [drug-using] individuals believed to be particularly at risk from the pressures of modern life were those with the most refined and sensitive nervous systems, those who worked by brain rather than hand; professional men, businessmen and 'new women'... trying to make their own way in the world."[41]

In the present period there has been a revolution of "brain work" prompted especially by the IT revolution, and a whole section of the population (a group, but still class-differenti-ated) engaged in different forms of the "digital economy." This includes both the till-now burgeoning financial sector and a whole range of the "creative economy." It is no longer an "elite" drug though one imagines that degrees of quality of the cocaine are still class-income based, *and there are horror stories*. When freebasing was simplified to crack the evidence of its effect on U.S. city ghettoes is well documented, though less so that it is a younger ghetto generation who have fought back. In the streets of London it is truly depressing to see a crack "head" early in the morning making speeches to the street minus socks and in a puffa jacket whose zip has broken long ago.

But this is a small section of the market. Even when it is a dance club drug, it is, when there is so much sociological evi-dence of the blurring of work and not-work time, quite likely to be from the IT/media/finance world. Cocaine is especially suited to this work because, as I've said, it can create indiscrimi-nate but focused enthusiasm, by which I mean that the most banal piece of advertising or TV trailer can be felt as truly impor-tant. Unlike amphetamine whose sense of excitement tends to have a serially digressive effect, cocaine will allow you to stay single-mindedly on the task in hand for long hours.[42] This is especially given how much of such work is overtime, and is on short-term contracts. You are only as good as your last perform-

---

41 Marek Kohn, *Dope Girls: The Birth of the British Drug Underground* (Lawrence and Wishart, 1992), 106.

42 There is a perverse mirror here where crack users spoke of the pleasure they got from "running about" and "being on a mission." Described in Alex Harocopos et al., "On the Rocks: A Follow-Up Study of Crack Users in London," Criminal Policy Research Unit, South Bank University, 2003.

ance, while at the same time you may find your next work while having a line or two socially.

Yet its productive use cannot be admitted. There is for example not a single reference to it in Richard Florida's once-iconic *Rise of the Creative Class*. Similarly there has been no reference made to its use in the "financial sector" in this period when unrestrained, overconfident risk-taking caused an unprecedented financial crisis which we, the non-bankers of the world, are now paying for. It has not been even mentioned as a possible causative factor, though in the 1990s there were frequent newspaper articles on City of London cocaine use. In coded language they warned that its confidence-boosting quality might become dysfunctional when combined with a "masters of the universe" view of the world.

A post-crash report by Penny and Baker also concentrates on city traders who are now "clean," or trying to be, with reference to how "professionals in the detox business say bankers have swamped them with calls since the financial crisis widened a year ago [and] some bankers are questioning whether the diminished rewards of the City are worth sacrificing their health for."[43]

Given that the "sacrifice of health" refers to cocaine use, it's clear that it is functional to banking "labour" but only if the rewards are astronomical as they have been, and are becoming again, more than enough to buy as much of the best flake as wanted at any given time. No mention in Baker and Penny's article of any possible link to the crash, but rather a highlighting of that macho fourteen- and sixteen-hour working days with which bankers used to justify their fabulous incomes.

"FAIR TRADE COCAINE," THE POLITICS OF LEGALIZATION

It seems then all too fitting that $315 billion worth of illegal drug profits should have been used, as claimed by the UN's drug czar, as "the only liquid capital" available to some banks on the brink of collapse in 2008. To get some idea of the significance of this

---

43 Stephanie Baker and Thomas Penny, "Cocaine Survivors Losing London Bonus, See End to Bubble's Binge," Bloomberg.com, October 8, 2009.

amount, the IMF estimated that U.S. and European banks losses between June 2007 and September 2009 amounted to $1 trillion. Señor Costa has no need to big-up this phenomenon; the very existence of the War on Drugs and its media support means his organisation will continue to be well-financed. What Costa's assertion suggests is the significance of drug money as capital— that is, of realized profit to the mainstream banking world—and as Ehrenreich says of the Mexican case, "The cartels are not revolutionary cells so much as organizations of global capital."[44]

Figures extrapolated by Feiting suggest that just 1 percent of the retail price of cocaine in the United States goes to the Colombian coca farmer, 4 percent to its processors, and 20 percent to its smugglers.[45] The remaining 75 percent therefore is realized. In this way it can honestly be said that a large portion will be realized as capital. Other estimates reckon that people working in jungle labs are paid 75 cents a kilo.

The mayhem and waste of resources caused by the War on Drugs demands, however, that we open a debate on the political economy of legalization. This might start with a comparison with cocoa bean farmers in Ghana who get around 7 percent of the price of a chocolate bar. The government of Ghana take a larger share in the form of tax. This is at the very least nominally accountable; some at least will go into public health and education facilities. As the position of such farmers in Côte d'Ivoire shows there is no guarantee of such a redistribution, but at least decisions over how cocoa income is distributed are nominally open to public input.[46]

There are no guarantees that coca legalization wouldn't simply mean the development of corporate cocaine oligopolies and high levels of tax in the consuming countries. It should also be remembered that though coca is also consumed by its producers, it is a cash crop. So far it has been grown along-side farmer-consumed food crops. Might this change, and the

---

44 Ehrenreich, "A Lucrative War," 18.

45 Feiting, *The Candy Machine*, 177.

46 For details see Orla Ryan, *Chocolate Nations: Living and Dying for Cocoa in West Africa* (Zed Books, 2011).

dangers associated with monoculture develop? Might it also become a substitute for the redistribution of land in favour of the *campesinos,* which is what really matters in Colombia? Bolivia, since the election of Evo Morales is, by its legalization of coca and the removal of the DEA from its territory, is a "test case." I have heard worries from some Bolivian indigenous people that although cocaine is still illegal, some people have got more involved in it as a business and that this will destroy local communities.

As things stand, there is no public space to even ask these questions. Worldwide consumption of cocaine has not been dented, and eradication campaigns produce only what is called the "balloon" effect, an increase of production in other areas and improved coca crop varieties. Peru has recently taken up the slack. All the evidence points to the failure of the War on Drugs, but it is too useful to the dynamics of global capital accumulation and its need for social and neocolonial discipline to be abandoned. These disciplines involve imprisonment for potentially subversive populations, and interventions, both military and financial, in countries on the geopolitical map. U.S. policy in Colombia and Mexico are visible examples. At the same time the importance of "laundered money" as capital—money that the official banking system has the power to use—has hovered close to the surface of official recognition. However, there are only ever hints at the real use of this laundered money, and legal proceedings that never quite make such recognition. What *is* clear is that the imposition of free trade and structural adjustment policies have contributed to the people in the cocaine business—growers, processors, and smugglers—taking to it as the most rational form of economic activity. At the same time financial liberalisation has made money laundering that much easier. These consequences are so easy to see, but when it comes to cause and effect, capitalism is always highly selective.

ABOUT THE AUTHOR

John Barker was born in London in 1948. In 1969, along with six others, he ripped up his Cambridge University finals papers as part of a campaign against education as a system of exclusion. In 1972 he was convicted with three others of conspiring to cause explosions in what was called the Angry Brigade trial. He served a ten-year prison sentence. A memoir of this time, *Bending the Bars*, was published many years later. He worked as a dustman and welder before being implicated in a conspiracy to import cannabis in 1986. In 1990 he was finally arrested and served a five-year sentence. Since then he has worked constantly as writer and book indexer. From the 1970s onwards he has published a number of texts on political economy, writers and writing, the capitalist psyche, and ideological opportunism. More recently he has been collaborating with the Austrian artist Ines Doujak as writer and performer in the ongoing work on cloth and colonialism Loomshuttles/Warpaths, parts of which have been shown in Vienna, Malmö, Stuttgart, and London.

ACKNOWLEDGMENTS

Futures was made possible with the support of many people, some of whom deserve a special thank you: Oliver Ressler, Roland Gift, Richard Parry, Jim and Penny Ashe, Mark Pith-Daddy Sargent, Eva Dranaz, Jochen Fill, Mike Jenkins, Sarah Wilson, Jane Grant, Mark, and Sandhya.

ABOUT PM PRESS

PM Press was founded at the end of 2007 by a small collection of folks with decades of publishing, media, and organizing experience. PM Press co-conspirators have published and distributed hundreds of books, pamphlets, CDs, and DVDs. Members of PM have founded enduring book fairs, spearheaded victorious tenant organizing campaigns, and worked closely with bookstores, academic conferences, and even rock bands to deliver political and challenging ideas to all walks of life. We're old enough to know what we're doing and young enough to know what's at stake.

We seek to create radical and stimulating fiction and non-fiction books, pamphlets, T-shirts, visual and audio materials to entertain, educate and inspire you. We aim to distribute these through every available channel with every available technology — whether that means you are seeing anarchist classics at our bookfair stalls; reading our latest vegan cookbook at the café; downloading geeky fiction e-books; or digging new music and timely videos from our website.

PM Press is always on the lookout for talented and skilled volunteers, artists, activists and writers to work with. If you have a great idea for a project or can contribute in some way, please get in touch.

PM Press
PO Box 23912
Oakland, CA 94623
www.pmpress.org

FRIENDS OF PM PRESS

These are indisputably momentous times—the financial system is melting down globally and the Empire is stumbling. Now more than ever there is a vital need for radical ideas.

In the six years since its founding—and on a mere shoestring—PM Press has risen to the formidable challenge of publishing and distributing knowledge and entertainment for the struggles ahead. With over 250 releases to date, we have published an impressive and stimulating array of literature, art, music, politics, and culture. Using every available medium, we've succeeded in connecting those hungry for ideas and information to those putting them into practice.

Friends of PM allows you to directly help impact, amplify, and revitalize the discourse and actions of radical writers, filmmakers, and artists. It provides us with a stable foundation from which we can build upon our early successes and provides a much-needed subsidy for the materials that can't necessarily pay their own way. You can help make that happen—and receive every new title automatically delivered to your door once a month—by joining as a Friend of PM Press. And, we'll throw in a free T-shirt when you sign up.

Here are your options:

- **$30 a month** Get all books and pamphlets plus 50% discount on all webstore purchases

- **$40 a month** Get all PM Press releases (including CDs and DVDs) plus 50% discount on all webstore purchases

- **$100 a month** Superstar—Everything plus PM merchandise, free downloads, and 50% discount on all webstore purchases

For those who can't afford $30 or more a month, we're introducing **Sustainer Rates** at $15, $10 and $5. Sustainers get a free PM Press T-shirt and a 50% discount on all purchases from our website.

Your Visa or Mastercard will be billed once a month, until you tell us to stop. Or until our efforts succeed in bringing the revolution around. Or the financial meltdown of Capital makes plastic redundant. Whichever comes first.